The Final Chapter of
Chance McCall

THE Austin·Stoner FILES

Book Two

The Final Chapter

of Chance McCall

Stephen Bly

CROSSWAY BOOKS • WHEATON, ILLINOIS
A DIVISION OF GOOD NEWS PUBLISHERS

The Final Chapter of Chance McCall

Copyright © 1996 by Stephen Bly

Published by Crossway Books
          a division of Good News Publishers
          1300 Crescent Street
          Wheaton, Illinois 60187

Cover illustration: Ed Tadiello

Cover design : Cindy Kiple

First printing 1996

Printed in the United States of America

Library of Congress Cataloging-in-Publication Data
Bly, Stephen A., 1944-
    The final chapter of Chance McCall / Stephen Bly.
       p.   cm. — (The Austin-Stoner files ; bk. 2.)
    ISBN 0-89107-903-3
    1. Treasure-trove—Montana—Fiction. I. Title. II. Series: Bly,
    Stephen A., 1944- Austin-Stoner files ; bk. 2.
    PS3552.L93F55   1996
813'.54—dc20   96-11176

04	03	02	01	00	99	98	97	96
15	14	13	12	11	10	9	8	7	6	5	4	3	2	1

For
George,
who dove for
Jesse's gold

ONE

The short white line blinked incessantly on the deep blue screen. Lynda Austin wrinkled her forehead as she bit her tongue.

Joaquin, you can't have Benton "nod and smile" every time he talks. When will you ever find another way to set off your dialog. "He nods," "she nods," "he smiles," "she smiles" . . . agh!

Lynda twirled her fingers through her dark brown shoulder-length hair and glanced out the window at the fading New York autumn skyline. She reached for the phone almost before it rang.

"Yes?"

"What are you still doing here?"

"Hi, Kell. What's up?"

"Do you have a phone number for Chance McCall?"

"Only his home phone, but he's not there. He's out in the Bahamas diving for some sunken Spanish ship or something."

"I know that, but his sister in Florida called. She said he hasn't reported in for two weeks, and she was wondering if he had called us."

"I haven't talked to McCall for a month. He told me then that he couldn't be reached for about ten weeks."

"I'll call his sister back and tell her we don't know where he is either. Now go home and get ready, girl. It's your big night."

"Yeah, I was just about to leave. As soon as I get Benton Goodnight shot."

"You still working on the latest Joaquin Estaban novel?"

"Yes, behind schedule, of course. Some things never change."

"Listen," Kelly added, "production called, and they're screaming for the last chapter of the McCall book."

"The one with the charts and maps?" Austin reached down and slipped on her black heels.

"Yeah, I guess. Julie Quick said they had to have it today."

"I sent it over yesterday." Lynda stared at a half-empty cup of cold coffee, wishing it were steaming hot. "What's she huffing about?"

"She's going on vacation, like most everyone else, and she needs to get it to the printers before she takes off. So you sent it over already?"

"Yes. Nina hand-carried it for me. You can check with her. Look, don't let them fool around and foul up that chapter. I had to personally guarantee Chance McCall that he could trust us with those charts and maps."

"I'll grab Nina, and we'll go get it straightened out," Kelly assured her. "Now go home and get ready. You need to soak in a tub full of bubbles, manicure your nails, curl your eyelashes— whatever you do to become fabulously beautiful."

"Dream on. All I need to do is change my clothes and smear on some lipstick and dab on a little perfume. Anyway, I've just got a little more and I'll have it—"

"Lynda, you listen to me. Reach down there and hit the exit button. I don't want you to look stringy-haired and ill-prepared tonight! You're standing up there for all of us, and I want you to be stunning. You've got to knock their socks off!"

"Yes, Mother." Lynda sighed.

Maybe I should have gotten my hair done . . . and some of those acrylic nails and . . .

"Now go on. We'll find that chapter and see you tonight."

"Thanks for caring, Kell."

"That's what us lowly associate editors are for. Get out there and accept that award for all of us 'little people.'"

"Princeton, I'm sticking my tongue out at you!"

"I know."

Lynda Austin sat staring at the *Pro Rodeo Sports News* clipping on her bulletin board next to the monitor. The picture showed a bareback rider at the Caldwell, Idaho, Night Rodeo. His hat was mashed in the dirt, his right hand flung in the air, his spurs set high on the bucking horse's neck. His back slapped against the horse's flank strap. The little-boy-having-fun smile on the cowboy was very, very familiar. She pulled a small mirror out of her desk drawer.

I've looked worse.

Her eyes flitted back to the computer screen. "Well, Benton, you've just been given a reprieve. You won't get shot until tomorrow."

◆ ◆ ◆

The moment Lynda Austin spied the network television cameras, she knew that Brady Stoner would be watching. It might be 3:00 A.M. at a truck stop north of El Paso . . . or in a motel in Billings . . . or a cafe in Spokane . . . but sometime, somewhere he would snag a glimpse of her accepting the award.

Then there would be a phone call to the office of Atlantic-Hampton Publishing Company, and he'd ask for his "Sweet Lynda Dawn." Or he'd drawl a message on her machine that he had looked for her in the stands at Redding, Reno, or Red Bluff.

Or maybe, just maybe, she'd be home when he called, and she'd feel that tickle in her throat and the tingle in her heart

when she heard that "Lynda-darlin'." That is, provided David
didn't get to the phone first and hang up on Brady again.

As Lynda approached the etched glass podium at the
Central Park South ballroom, nearly a thousand men dressed
in tuxedos and women in designer silks and satins stood and
applauded. Lynda glanced down at the 3-x-5 card she held in
her hand. The top line read: "Don't adjust the mike. Don't apologize for any mistakes you haven't yet made. Smile & relax.
Have fun!"

*Have fun? You've got to be kidding. I can't believe I wrote this
note. Lord, help me not to blurt out something really dumb. Help me
not to faint.*

Lynda knew that she would relive this moment the rest of
her life. She knew she would rewrite the script a million times
in retrospect.

Her Autumn Rose Blush lipstick was in place.

She caught the aroma of her Prairie Queen perfume.

She resisted the urge to tug down her long black suede
Santa Fe skirt. She felt the weight of the silver-and-turquoise
squash blossom necklace and hoped desperately that nothing
had stuck to her teeth during the banquet.

She accepted the award from B. J. O'Sullivan and then
turned to the now-seated and expectant crowd of editors, publishers, authors, and agents.

The next few minutes blurred as she gave her little speech.
. . . They clapped. . . . There were some handshakes and hugs
. . . and she scooted back to the table and sat down between
Kelly Princeton and Nina DeJong. Her mind didn't clear until
midway through the reception that followed.

"You did it, girl, you did it!" Kelly giggled, holding crystal
glasses of lime green punch in each hand.

"Tell me the truth," Lynda whispered. "Did this outfit look
out of place?"

"Western chic? It's in, Lynda-girl," Kelly encouraged her.

"Of course, I kept expecting you to grab the mike and belt out a Reba McEntire tune."

"It was a little much, wasn't it? I knew it was too much."

"It was perfect!" Kelly proclaimed. "Relax. It's all over now."

"Wow, I've never met anyone who won an L.M.P. before," Nina admitted. "You're a real inspiration. I called my parents in Wisconsin and told them to be watching the news tonight. Imagine, the youngest editor ever to receive the *Literary Marketplace* Award!"

"Well, thirty-one doesn't seem all that young. Besides, it was Martin Taylor Harrison who wrote the book. I was just fortunate enough to get to edit it."

"But you found it. You risked your life," Nina bubbled on. "You faced down the villainous Joe Trent and the reluctant hierarchy at Atlantic-Hampton."

"Not to mention having to suffer the utter humiliation and degradation of becoming a cowboy's love-slave."

"Kelly!" Lynda's green eyes displayed annoyance.

"Now just why is it you told the cowboy not to come to New York for this awards banquet?"

The six-foot, five-inch tuxedoed and lanky frame of T. M. Hampton, IV, blustered into their circle. "Ms. Austin, we've not always seen eye to eye on this Harrison thing, but I sincerely want to congratulate you. This is a grand day for Atlantic-Hampton Publishing Company, and you deserve the credit."

She nodded thanks and took a deep breath. "Thanks, Mr. Hampton. I appreciate the company hosting this reception. It really means a lot to me."

"And you mean a lot to us. We hope you know that. That's why this reception. That's why the corner office. That's why the new Austin Imprint."

Kelly sipped out of the glass in her right hand and then placed the frosty glass to her cheek. "I thought the imprint had to do with Lynda's brother's negotiating skills and the threat of a possible lawsuit." She then swigged from the glass in her left hand.

"Yes . . . that, too." Hampton's eyes searched the crowded room. "Have any of you seen Ms. Sasser?"

"I noticed a crowd of men on the balcony. I presume she's standing in the middle of them," Nina suggested.

"Oh, yes—isn't that dress ravishing? I picked it up for her in Paris." He scooted away from the trio and wormed his way through the crowd toward the balcony.

"I'd be embarrassed to wear that dress to bed on my honeymoon," Kelly whispered.

"I thought you and Andrew broke up last week," Nina teased. "Are you planning on getting married soon?"

"Not soon. And certainly not to Andrew. But I am planning to get married. That's more than I can say about some in this room." She raised her eyebrows at Lynda. "Tell us again, why is it your cowboy isn't here tonight?"

"Lynda!" A short Oriental woman in a tight navy blue wool-blend business suit and cropped jet-black hair scooted into the group. "I'm Rebecca Soto with the *Times*. May I ask you a couple questions?"

"Sure."

"Is *With the Wind in My Face* going to be the last of the Harrison books? Or do you plan to 'discover' another such novel every year or so?"

Lynda glanced at Kelly and Nina and raised her eyebrows.

"Are you questioning the authenticity of this work?" Kelly challenged.

"Oh, my, not me. There seem to be a number of others, eminently more qualified than I, who want to make that point."

"It's all right, Kell," Lynda calmed her. "As far as I know, this is the last novel Mr. Harrison wrote. But next summer we'll be bringing out the autobiographical *Message of the Winds* based on his journal written down in the canyon. I think it will help a lot of people understand the changes that took place in Harrison's life over the last fifty years."

"Which other authors will fall under the new Austin Imprint?"

Lynda stared at Rebecca Soto's long false eyelashes. *She doesn't give a squat about my answer.*

"Terrance O'Brian and Joaquin Estaban, among others. And I look forward to bringing out a great novel by a new author."

Scanning the room, Soto nodded. "Oh, that's nice. Who is this new novelist? . . . Say, is that O'Brian in the black turtleneck?"

"None other than Mr. Hesitant Spy himself," Nina confirmed.

"Yes . . . well, I think . . ." Soto began to pull away from the trio. "Eh, what was the name of that new novelist?"

Lynda looked straight at the departing reporter. "His name is Ernest Hemingway. You might enjoy reading his book."

"Sure. Yeah. Send me a copy," Soto droned as she turned her back. "Think I'll try to catch O'Brian."

"Catching O'Brian is easy. Getting away from him is the hard part," Nina called out.

Kelly laughed and handed Lynda one of the punch glasses.

"You don't really have a new Hemingway, do you?" Nina pressed. "I mean, that last one they dug up and slapped together wasn't much."

"Well, ladies, my fifteen minutes in the limelight has worn off, I suppose. I'd say Ms. Soto wasn't too thrilled to get this assignment."

"What did you think of those lashes?" Nina faked a gag. "They were a little too much even for Manhattan."

"It wasn't the only phony thing she was packing," Kelly put

in. "Speaking of your new author, Nina and I couldn't find that last chapter of McCall's *Confederate Gold* anywhere."

"I know I laid that Fed. Ex. package right on Julie's desk," Nina explained. "She was out of the office, and no one seems to know where it got shuffled."

Kelly shrugged. "With so many hurrying up to go on vacation, it's a wonder that more things don't get lost."

"Well, chapters don't just disappear. I'll go down tomorrow and sort through the files. It's got to—"

"You are supposed to have tomorrow off," Kelly insisted. "You, me, and Nina are all working next week, so we can tackle that chapter on Monday. I don't want to talk work tonight. I want to talk men! Nina, is it just me, or is Lynda ignoring telling us about the cowboy?"

"It seems to me that she's trying to distract us," Nina snickered. "Kind of like when you keep a guy talking about sports so he won't get around to asking you out for another date. You know what I mean?"

"Look, I don't know why you want to make it a big deal. Brady called last Tuesday and said he 'drawed good' in Winslow and Phoenix and figured he should keep going hard until the Finals. There's an outside chance that if things fall his way, he could still make it. I told him all along that he should stay out there and rodeo."

"I think she's afraid to have him come back to New York again. Too much competition," Kelly teased. "I thought Spunky would melt when Brady walked into the office last spring. And Nina-girl here clutched his arm all afternoon."

"I did not! . . . Did I?"

"Brady did tell me to give you and Nina a big hug for him."

Nina scrunched her nose and grinned. "He did?"

"A hug from you, Austin, is about as gratifying as a hamburger without meat," Kelly heckled. "Think I'll go flirt with the square-jawed guy with bulging biceps and cowboy boots. Undoubtedly he's from the West . . . west Jersey."

"Kelly!"

"Are you girls coming with me?"

"You need help?" Lynda baited.

"Nope."

They watched Kelly bob her way between conversations until she reached a small circle of men. She stumbled, and suddenly a tall, strong man reached out and caught her.

Nina groaned. "Not the old 'trip-and-catch' ploy. I tried that once and fell right on my backside. How does she always pull that off?"

"Years of practice. He does have nice boots. Full-quill ostrich."

Nina sorted through a small glass plate of slimy-looking hors d'oeuvres. She bit into a light green one, made a face, and tossed it back.

"That was cute what you said to your cowboy."

"When?"

"You know," Nina prodded, "in your little speech."

"What are you talking about?"

"You didn't mention Brady's name, but . . . Don't you remember?"

"Nina, this entire evening has been unreal. You know how I like being behind the scenes. When I get up front like that, I can't remember a word I said. I'll have to go home and catch it on the late news. What did I say?"

"The whole speech?"

"No, about Brady."

"Well, I think you said, 'Special thanks to the cowboy who gave me what I needed most.'"

"What I needed most? I didn't say that!"

"Yes, you did. That's when everyone laughed. Remember?"

"No." Austin could feel her teeth grinding.

"What exactly did you mean—gave you what you needed most?" Nina questioned.

"I didn't say it that way. What I said was, thanks for being there when I needed him—to help me find the lost manuscript and take care of me when I got hurt . . . and everything."

"Well, that's not how it came across. The expression on your face was so funny. But cute. Really," Nina tried to assure her. "Anyway, I hope you're not too disappointed that he wasn't here. You know, it's not good to keep your disappointment inside."

"Nina, I've told you we're just good friends . . . eh, very good friends, and we had agreed that if he needed to . . . It's his job. He's got to make a living. You know how it is when you're going down the road."

"I know nothing whatsoever about rodeo, but I do know the two of you have the weirdest relationship in the world. My mother thinks so, too."

"There is nothing strange about it. We just live and work in different worlds. So, naturally, there's a distance. I mean, just because we're 2,500 miles apart and—"

"How often have you seen him since last fall?" Nina pressed.

"Well . . . just twice. But—"

"I've dated creeps more often than that. But you think about him all the time. I mean, you wear those Western outfits almost every day, and all the rodeo pictures in your new office, and all you ever talk about is last fall. It's sort of like when I was in the seventh grade and had a crush on this guy who was a senior, but I never told him."

"It is nothing at all like that," Austin snapped. "Brady and I have a very meaningful and—"

"Gosh, you don't have to explain it to me. It's your heart, not mine."

"And it's my reception." She took a deep breath and sighed.

"Let's go hang around L. George Gossman and make him look short or something."

"Is this the end of the conversation about your cowboy?"

"Yes."

◆ ◆ ◆

David was sprawled across the couch when Lynda finally made it back to her sixth-floor condo. He opened one eye to acknowledge her presence and then rolled over and ignored her.

"Boy, you're in a pouty mood. I had a lovely evening—not that you're in the least interested."

She stopped and stared at a very dark, very neat guest room. A seldom-used milk glass hurricane lamp stood sentinel next to a star-quilt-covered bed.

"Did I ever tell you this place is too big?" she called out back toward the living room. "Ever since Janie moved to Atlanta, it feels like a museum or something. We really ought to get a smaller place, but with the raise and all, I only break even now. . . ."

Lynda flipped the light on in her bedroom and jammed her heel into the bootjack. The turquoise cowboy boots slipped off one at a time, remaining like southwestern sentinels in the corner of the light peach wallpapered room. After carefully hanging the suede skirt and jacket on a padded hanger exactly one and a half inches from the blue Western yoked dress with the white fringe, she pulled the black slip over her head.

Wearing a well-worn deep purple silky nightshirt, she padded into the bathroom and stared at the mirror.

Well, girl, you're thirty-one. Single. Tired eyes and fast-fading smile. You pulled out two gray hairs this morning, and at that rate you'll be bald by the time you're forty. You just won the highest award in your field and had a reception thrown in your honor. Lynda Dawn Austin, where are you going to go now?

"There's a big lodge just north of Jackson, Wyoming," she mumbled aloud, "that comes to mind . . . and a rock fireplace six feet tall . . . and a morning sun that reflects pink off the Tetons . . . and a cowboy who . . ."

Lynda pulled out her perfume chart and looked at the schedule for Friday, October 20.

Blossom Amor? Am I back to that already?

" . . . a cowboy who right now is probably sleeping in his truck out behind some dirty-smelling arena . . . or sitting in some crummy restaurant with some silly waitress throwing herself all over him . . . or slapping himself in the face to keep awake as he drives another six hundred miles."

She turned and was startled to see David standing in the doorway of the bathroom. "Oh! I didn't hear you get up. Well, what do you want? As if I didn't know." She scooted by him back into the bedroom.

"Come on, let's get it over with. I'm tired."

David traipsed behind her all the way out to the tiny kitchen. She reached the top pantry shelf and pulled down the small, round tin.

"You know, David, this might come as a shock to you, but many cats eat dry cat food. Really. Their owners just put out a bowl of that stuff, and it lasts for a couple of days."

She jammed the can into the electric opener and listened to the familiar grind. The room reeked with the smell of fish.

"'Chunk light tuna in spring water' with liberal amounts of hydrolyzed soy protein, vegetable broth, and salt. If I could sneak your little furry head past Howard, I'd take you to the lower east side and sell you at a market!"

David rubbed up against her leg and purred.

"Oh, sure, now you like me." She placed the cat's bowl on the floor.

Lynda nuked a mug of water in the microwave and then shuffled out to the living room and flipped on the television.

Tucking her feet beneath her on the green overstuffed sofa, she leaned back and sipped on the water.

I did not say, "Special thanks to the cowboy who gave me what I needed most." I didn't giggle, clear my throat, fool with the mike, or have shrimp sauce on my chin.

Please, Lord, please.

It was 12:27 when the late news flashed the smiling face of Lynda Austin across the screen, accompanied by a thirty-two-second sound bite. At that moment both she and David the cat were asleep on the couch.

◆ ◆ ◆

The phone gave one incessantly loud ring, and then came a crash. Lynda leaped from the sofa and dove toward the telephone by the light of the black-and-white movie that flitted away unwatched on the television.

"David, no! Not again!" she cried. The gray cat with black-striped legs and three white paws had already pounced on the phone. Crawling on her hands and knees, she grabbed the swinging receiver and banged it into her ear.

"Ouch!" she cried, then muttered, "Yes? Hello?"

A young woman's stern voice came on the line. "Lady, you don't have to put up with that jerk. Would you like me to call a Domestic Abuse Hot Line or even the police? If so, just say yes and stay on the line. I'll slip to another phone, and we can get the creep in custody before he hits you again."

"What creep?"

"David."

"David's a tomcat."

"Aren't they all?"

"Who is this? What do you want?"

"Are you all right? I'm a registered nurse. I work Emergency. You can talk to me."

"David is my cat—a feline—you know, meow, meow, purr, purr. He has a bad habit of pouncing on the telephone to make it stop ringing."

"Sure, whatever you say. I suppose the cat gave you a black eye."

"What black eye?"

"Really, I know what it's like to be in an abusive situation."

"What are you talking about? Who is this? What do you want?"

"Are you Lynda Dawn Austin?"

"Yes."

"I'm a nurse at Phoenix General Hospital. A Mr. Brady Stoner was brought in tonight—"

"Oh, no!" The bottom dropped out of Lynda's stomach, and she gasped for breath. "What happened to him?" *Oh, Lord, is he all right?* "What is it?"

"He had a little accident at the rodeo tonight, and he asked me to call you."

"What happened?"

"I'll let him tell you."

"He can talk?"

"He can do a lot more than talk, but he won't be riding broncs for a while. He couldn't reach the phone and asked me to dial the number for him."

"Does he still have his awesome smile?" Lynda quizzed.

The phone fell quiet for a moment. Then the nurse spoke in a relaxed, almost laughing voice. "He sure does! Here's Brady."

"Hello, Lynda Dawn. You still lettin' that cat answer the phone?"

"Brady, what's wrong? What happened?"

"Oh, darlin', it's nothin', really."

"Don't give me any garbage about having been hurt worse, Stoner. I want to know what happened, and I want to know right now! Tell me everything."

"Ever'thing?"

"Everything."

"Well, I told you how I drew Kadafy Skoal, and he was a money horse if I could cover eight."

"Yes."

"So I'm in the chute just settling down when he blows up and decides to go home."

"What?"

"He tries to jump out of the chute before I even get seated. Well, I'm holdin' on with my left hand as always, but Kadafy is startin' to panic, so they turn him outside."

"They what?"

"They open the gate. He kicks the gate against the chute boss, bustin' a nose and scattering teeth."

"Whose nose?"

"The chute boss's. Then the gate swings back, and I ram into it like a yo-yo on a string slammin' into the blacktop."

"What happened?"

"My arm fell off."

"What?" Lynda shouted.

"No, no, not really. It just felt like it."

"What did you do then?"

"I figured I wouldn't get a score, so I turned loose."

"You mean you were still holding on?"

"I don't like gettin' bucked off. A man could get hurt."

"Listen, Stoner, what's the bottom line on the damage? Besides losing your marbles, what other injury did you end up with?"

"Oh, just some bruised ribs, a chipped bone in my right wrist, some pulled tendons, and a severely sprained shoulder."

"Your shoulder?"

"Doc says I've got to rest it up for two months. But I figure a couple weeks, and I'll crack out again."

"Is there a lot of pain?"

"They've got me out in la-la land, so Terri Beth volunteered to look after me tonight. On her own time, too."

"Who's Terri Beth?"

"The emergency room nurse who called you. Sure was nice of her to help ease me through the night. She's a—"

"Yeah, yeah. She's a real sweetheart."

"You got it, darlin'. How'd you get along at that dress-up banquet? Did you wow 'em like I told you to?"

"I think it went pretty well. You didn't catch a blurb on television? CNN was there."

"I've sort of been out of it. But me and Terri Beth will see if we can find it, even if we're awake all night."

"Yeah, I bet you will," Lynda murmured. "So, cowboy, what are you planning on doing now?"

"I've been laying here kickin' myself for not coming back to that banquet of yours. I'd like to have been there when you touched your old North Star."

"Touched my what?"

"I always figured personal dreams and goals were sort of like the North Star. Not many people actually get to touch it, but if you always keep it in view, you will eventually reach your destination."

"Like you chasing that world champion gold buckle?"

"And you with your LMP. You reached out and grabbed that sucker. I should have been there."

"You would've had to wear a tux and smile and visit with a bunch of phony, self-centered people."

"Yeah, well . . . you're right. I would have hated that part."

"What are you going to do now?"

"Figure me and Capt. Patch will mosey up home and visit the folks."

"Do you feel like driving?"

"I think so. 'Course, Terri Beth said she wouldn't mind takin' off a few days and drivin' me."

"All the way to Idaho? Forget it, Stoner."

"I'll get along fine." He laughed. "My left arm's kind of like a limp noodle, but I'm not nearly as disappointed as I thought I'd be. Maybe I'm gettin' used to just missin' the Finals. The hospital wants to observe me until mornin'."

"What are they observing?"

"It was sort of like a mild concussion."

"A concussion? You didn't tell me that."

"Well, it didn't seem all that important. It happens all the time."

"Brady, are all rodeo riders totally crazy to begin with, or is it that the rough stock beat the brains out of them? You shouldn't take your health and life so lightly. It might not be very important to you, but there are others who are counting on you being around for a while."

"*Qui bene amat bene castigat.*"

"Eh . . . the one who loves well . . ."

"Chastises well." He laughed. "Did I ever tell you about my Latin teacher up in the San Juans? Oh, hey, listen—Terri Beth says I better hang up and get some rest. So I'll call you from Reynolds Creek next week."

"Take good care of yourself, cowboy."

"You done good, girl. I surely am proud of you getting that award. Bye, Lynda-darlin'."

"Brady," she blurted out, "let me talk to Terri Beth."

"You got it."

Lynda rapped her fingers on the end table as she waited for a voice on the other end.

"Yes?"

"Terri Beth, there's something you need to know about Brady."

"Oh?"

"Sometimes when he gets a concussion, he has a tendency to bite people."

"He bites?"

"Yes, but he doesn't even remember doing it. He's sort of out of his mind—you know. But usually the symptoms will give a warning."

"What symptoms?"

"Well, his speech slurs, and he starts dropping the *g*'s off his words. You know—singin', yellin', dancin'."

"Oh . . . yeah."

"Then he'll probably start using the word *darlin'* a lot."

"Really?"

"And when he really gets totally out of it, he starts quoting Latin. If that happens, make sure you're across the room. He can do some damage when he bites. But you're a nurse. You know all about this sort of thing."

"Oh, my!"

"I presume you've had some precautionary shots. Have you ever had hepatitis?"

"My word, no."

"Nothing to worry about. Just keep your distance, and don't turn your back on him."

"Thanks for the warning."

"Don't mention it."

◆ ◆ ◆

Wearing a gray wool-blend skirt, white blouse, gold choker chain, matching earrings, and a scent called Slightly Sensuous, Lynda stood in the twelfth-floor lobby of Atlantic-Hampton Publishing Company and stared at an empty receptionist's desk.

Nina DeJong stepped out of the mahogany-paneled elevator and stood beside her. "It's like coming to work on a weekend, isn't it? Most everyone's on vacation."

Lynda nodded as she punched in a security code to enter

the editorial department. "I don't know if we'll get a lot done—or nothing done."

Several inches shorter than Lynda's five feet, ten inches, Nina trailed her into the corner office. "Do you want me to check with production to see if they found that final chapter of McCall's book?"

"No, I'll run it down. I shudder to think about it being shuffled off in a stack of manuscripts somewhere. You know how paranoid Chance was about sending it to us."

"I never could figure that. It's a novel, right?"

"In theory, sure. But McCall claims the maps and charts were exactly the ones they used in 1972 when they dove for the gold."

"But he's going to publish them in a book. So he obviously doesn't care who knows about them."

"Yes, but he feels the need for some security so that the information will be released to everyone at once. He claims the gold is still down there in the reservoir. How many pages were in that stack?"

"I didn't count them. The last two weeks have been so hectic. I just flipped through it since it was already edited. I shoved them all back into the shipping package."

"You didn't make copies, did you?"

"No. I got your note saying absolutely no copies were to be made, and the originals must be returned to him."

Lynda sorted through two towering stacks of paper on her desk. "Well, I still don't have them. Go on, get some work done. I'll figure this out. Manuscripts get misplaced around here, but they don't disappear."

◆ ◆ ◆

The concrete and glass canyon called Madison Avenue dropped off in front of her as Austin stood at the window of her corner office and gazed at broken sunlight reflecting off the tops of shorter buildings across the street. She laid her computer glasses on the edge of her desk and rubbed the bridge of her nose.

I don't believe this. A whole day. I just wasted a whole day looking for a chapter that lay on my desk two days ago.

She glanced at her bookshelf and admired the LMP award.

Sure, you're a hot-shot editor who loses chapters. Lord, are You sure I needed to be humbled so soon?

"Are you going to phone McCall?" Nina DeJong peered in at the doorway.

"I suppose I have to—if I can ever find out how to reach him."

"Surely he has some copies of everything."

"I suppose. But how am I going to explain this? He kept telling me to guard these with my life—that someone might steal them."

"Maybe someone did."

"This is a professional publishing house. We don't go around pirating our own manuscripts."

Nina ran her fingers through the back of her curly brown shoulder-length hair. Her lipstick was dark red—too dark— but Lynda didn't know how to tell her. "Yeah, I know, but it's so frustrating. I really did place that tube on Julie's desk."

"This is such a needless waste of time! It's ridiculous. I set aside Fridays to edit the Harrison journals, and I haven't worked on them in a month."

"Maybe Mr. Gossman can call him."

"It's my imprint. I have to handle it. Besides, Georgie took off on vacation an hour ago."

Kelly popped through the doorway in her stocking feet, a notebook in her hand. "Lynda, NBC called. They want a dozen comp. copies of Joaquin Estaban's latest novel sent over to the studio right away."

"Tell them to call his agent."

"They said he fired his agent."

"Again?" Nina exclaimed.

"What do they think this is—a bookstore? Scout around and see what we have here in the office. I think I have a few over in that pile by the closet. Send them whatever we have."

"What did you decide about McCall's missing chapter?"

"I'm going to try to reach Chance and face the music. He's not going to be a happy camper."

"Maybe he can fax some duplicates."

"If I can find him. He's self-exiled in the Bahamas."

Nina waved her finger at Lynda. "I think someone stole the maps and right now is meeting some shadowy underworld character in Battery Park, exchanging them for a briefcase full of hundred-dollar bills."

"Guess who's working on O'Brian's latest." Lynda laughed.

"I figure someone piled something else on top of those pages, then later grabbed the whole stack, and filed it under some other heading," Kelly suggested.

"In which case we would have to search every individual file folder on the twelfth floor to find it."

Lynda scooted back to her desk and slumped down.

"I'm going to call his sister in Flamingo, Florida, and see if she had any luck in reaching Chance."

Kelly and Nina hovered about her oak desk as she finished the conversation.

"Well?" Nina demanded.

"She said she can't reach him at his last-known hotel, and none of his friends in the islands have seen him. Chance and a friend named Leo went out to the Bahamas somewhere to dive for a sunken ship, and they purposely would not tell anyone where they were going."

"I thought you said McCall was an old man."

"He's about seventy, I suppose."

"Seventy-two, according to his bio. He likes scuba diving, fishing, and collecting old coins," Nina informed them.

"And he goes treasure hunting?" Kelly asked.

"Still looking for the big one probably. She said she'd have him call Atlantic-Hampton as soon as she heard from him. But he might not call back until Thanksgiving."

"Thanksgiving?"

Austin paced the floor. "I can't believe this is happening to me."

"I don't understand these buried-treasure seekers. Do they just wander off for months?" Kelly mused.

"You've read McCall's book. That's about the way they operate."

Nina slammed her hands on her hips. "Did I ever tell you about my one and only date with Drew Hessler?"

"Our Drew? Like in shipping and receiving?"

"Yeah. Right after I came to work here, I dated him once. It was a disaster. I ruined a pair of hose and permanently stained my skirt."

"What did he do?" Kelly gasped. "And why have you been keeping this a secret?"

"We've really got to find that chapter. Does this have anything to do with Chance McCall?" Lynda pressed.

"Maybe. See . . . Drew said he had this really exciting place to show me. So early one Saturday morning we drove to a park upstate and spent the next fourteen hours following his metal detector all over looking for lost coins and rings and things. Here's the thing—I was the one who had to get on my hands and knees with a long screwdriver and dig in the dirt every time that thing beeped."

"Did you find anything?"

"Besides scraps of metal trash? Well, we did find an old axe head. Drew thought it was about a hundred years old. But he tripped over that going back to the car. The crazy beeper didn't locate it. That's all he thinks about. He subscribes to all sorts of treasure-hunter magazines. Didn't you ever see any in that storage closet behind the mail room?"

"Why would anyone go in the storage closet behind the mail room?" Kelly inquired.

Nina wrinkled her nose. "Wouldn't you like to know?"

"Is Drew the type who would, eh, borrow the maps for the weekend and make some copies for himself?"

"No . . . eh, yeah . . . probably," Nina admitted. "He does have a rather inflated idea of himself. He told me his life goal is to make a million dollars before he's thirty."

"If he wanted copies, he could have sneaked to the copy machine and made them here in the office," Lynda reminded her.

"But that chapter was still in the Fed. Ex. package I laid on Julie's desk. I suppose he could have mistakenly picked it up and shipped it."

"At least it gives us an excuse for asking him," Kelly suggested.

Austin whipped around and pointed at Nina. "Go over to shipping and ask Drew if he's seen that misplaced chapter."

"I'll go with her. I wouldn't want young Miss DeJong from Wisconsin to get sweet-talked into the back room," Kelly teased.

"Oh, good. Like going to the store with my mother."

"That's it, girl. I'm ripping your lips out!"

"Go on, you two. I want to know whether we have to stay here all night searching the files."

Within moments Kelly returned out of breath from the sprint. "Drew's not here today. He called in sick."

"Where's Nina?"

"She's trying to reach him at home."

"Just how chummy are they?"

"I never heard a word about it until today."

Nina burst through the door with a pink phone slip in her hand. "Listen to this—I talked with Drew's roommate who said that Drew and some girl named Billie left at 5:00 A.M. this morning on a hunt for some buried treasure in Vermont."

"With his metal detector, no doubt," Kelly jibed.

"Are you sure he didn't head toward Montana?"

"You think Drew might have taken the maps and headed out to try to find Chance McCall's buried gold?"

"Maybe," Lynda responded.

"Are you sure that reservoir's in Montana?"

Lynda punched on her computer and brought up the synopsis of *Confederate Gold*. "I know it's on the Missouri River somewhere in Montana. But all the names of towns in the novel are fictionalized. It was only the maps and charts at the end that gave real directions."

"I can't believe Drew would just walk out of here with the final chapter. That's stealing, isn't it? If you're caught, you could end up in jail."

"Yes, but we don't know for sure that Drew had anything to do with it."

"You're right. Kelly, go check the Fed. Ex. records for yesterday's late mail. Maybe it got picked up and sent back to McCall by mistake."

"What am I looking for?"

"Either something shipped to Chance McCall or something shipped by Drew Hessler himself."

"He doesn't ship anything on his own."

"Exactly."

◆ ◆ ◆

Lynda and Nina could hear Kelly's whoop all the way down the hall. "This is it! This is it!"

"Did you find the chapter?" Lynda called.

"No . . . no. Look at this. A shipping tube was Fed. Exed. to a C. Mendoza in U-Bet, Montana, last Thursday at 4:42 P.M., and it was shipped by D. Hessler."

"U-Bet? That's a town?" Lynda asked.

"That's what it says here."

"Is U-Bet by the Missouri River?"

"I'll check it on the atlas program on my computer." Nina hurried out of the office.

"What do we do, call the police?" Kelly asked.

"Considering that we don't know if the chapter is really stolen, and if it is, we don't know for sure who took it, and we have no way of establishing its value, I don't think we should. Kelly, go check around with whoever's left and see if you can discover any other reason Atlantic-Hampton would be sending anything to U-Bet, Montana."

"It's not here!" Nina announced as she scooted in from her nearby office, passing Kelly at the door. "There isn't any U-Bet in Montana. At least, it's not on the map. Maybe it's too small to be on the map."

"Then Brady would know where it is. I'll call Brady."

"Where is he?"

"Eh . . . he's driving to Idaho after leaving the hospital in Phoenix. Maybe he's at Heather's. I'll call her in St. George."

"Who's Heather?"

"You know, she's Richard's wife, the one who died in the blizzard."

"She's dead?"

"No, Richard's dead."

"So what can your cowboy tell you—about Montana?"

"If Brady says this U-Bet place is near a lake on the Missouri River, that would be a hint that there's some connection."

"Maybe Drew figured to fly out there and check this out and then return the maps before anyone knew they were missing," Nina offered.

"It's about time he brought them back. What bothers me about the whole thing is that those pages could have just been tossed in the trash, and we're dreaming all of this up."

"But no one tosses a Fed. Ex. package into the trash."

"Where do we put them when they're empty?"

"In Drew's storeroom," Nina blurted out. "So they can be recycled."

"Since you're familiar with the place, go see if that Fed. Ex. pak from McCall is there."

Kelly and Nina scooted past each other at the door.

"Well," Kelly began, "no one left in the office knows anything about U-Bet, Montana. Estaban's in Idaho, but as far as I can tell, we aren't working with any Montana writers or artists. Frank Alvarez locks his office, so I couldn't check out his box."

Nina hurried back into the room. "We're all out of shipping paks, so I guess that's a dead-end."

"Let me see that Fed. Ex. receipt." Kelly stepped over to Austin's desk. "Look . . . sender supplied shipping container."

"So?" Nina questioned.

"Maybe Drew shipped it in the same container."

"This is all really far-fetched," Lynda sighed. "If that chapter turns up on someone's desk tomorrow, we're going to feel like fools."

"Well, it better turn up by November 3. If we don't deliver by then, we'll have to renegotiate the whole project with the printer."

"What's the name on the shipment?"

"C. Mendoza."

"Mr.? Mrs.?"

"It just says C. Mendoza."

"Is there a phone number?"

"Nope."

"There has to be a phone number. You can't ship without a phone number," Lynda objected.

"Apparently, Drew did."

"Let me call Montana phone information. I'll see if they have a Mendoza in U-Bet."

Austin was on the phone less than a minute. She looked up and stared at Kelly and Nina.

"Well?" they asked in unison.

"I don't know if there are any Mendozas, because there isn't a U-Bet!"

"There's no town by that name?"

Austin grabbed up the shipping receipt. "But it does have a zip code—59453. Do we have any way of tracing down that number?"

Nina took the slip and headed out the door. "Let me see what I can find out."

Lynda grabbed up the phone. "I'll check with Brady." She unbuttoned the top button on her blouse and rubbed her neck. Waiting for someone to answer, she sniffed her wrists. *It never lasts. Slightly Sensuous is too slightly.*

A girl's voice greeted her.

"May I please speak to Heather Martin?"

"Mom's still at work."

"Is this Heidi?"

"This is Wendy."

"Wendy, this is Lynda Austin from New York City. I'm a friend of Brady Stoner's, and I met you last year, remember?"

"Yeah . . . what do you want?"

"I need to talk to Brady. He doesn't happen to be there, does he?"

"Nope."

"Have you seen him recently?"

"Yep."

"When?"

"This morning."

"Where was he?"

"In the kitchen."

"You mean, he stopped by for breakfast?"

"He stopped by for a couple of days."

"How can I reach him?"

"You can't."

"Where is he now?"

"On the road. They're going to Idaho."

"They?" Lynda's stomach began to churn.

"Brady and Capt. Patch."

"Oh, yes. Did he happen to mention where he would be staying this evening? Maybe I could reach him there."

"Maybe Uncle Brady doesn't want to talk to you."

"Why don't we let him decide that?"

"He said he was going to stay at L. J.'s ranch in Ely."

"L. J. who?"

"L. J. Minor."

"In Ely? Is that E-l-y?"

"Yep."

"You don't happen to have a phone number for L. J., do you?"

"Nope."

"I didn't think so. Well, thanks, Wendy. And tell your mom hello for me."

"Why?"

"Well, because . . . eh, we're good friends."

"Are you going to marry Uncle Brady?"

"What? Who told you that?"

"Mom said if you two ever stopped arguing long enough, you'd probably get married."

"You'll just have to ask your Uncle Brady that question."

"I did."

"What did he say?"

"He changed the subject. Listen, I'll tell Mom you called."

"Thanks, Wendy. Bye."

Lynda looked up to see Nina staring down at her. "Whoa, what was that all about?"

"Oh, it's just that the girls are sort of possessive of their 'Uncle' Brady. What did you find out about that zip code?"

"The good news is I found out that 59453 is for Judith Gap, Montana. The bad news is there are no Mendozas in Judith Gap. In fact, I can't find Judith Gap on my map either."

"See if you can get a phone number for an L. J. Minor ranch in Ely, Utah."

"Does it seem to you that this is all getting more and more complicated, and we still don't know if we're on the right track?" Kelly mused.

Lynda laughed. "What else did you have to do with your afternoon? Look at the time. We've just officially wasted the whole day."

"It gets worse," Nina added, looking up from the phone. "There is no Ely, Utah."

"Try Arizona . . . no, that's south. Try Nevada."

"Okay," Nina complied. "Ely, Nevada . . ."

Lynda dug through her purse and splashed on a little more Slightly Sensuous.

"Look, he's 2,500 miles away. I don't think the perfume matters," Kelly teased.

"Do you want the headquarters, the bunkhouse, the shop, or the Miller place?" Nina asked with her hand over the phone receiver.

"Eh . . . the headquarters, I guess."

"Give me the bunkhouse number," Kelly wisecracked.

Nina punched in a number and handed the phone to Lynda. A woman with a surprisingly soft voice answered the phone. "M Bar J."

"Yes, I'd like to speak to L. J. Minor, please."

"Speakin'."

"Oh . . . well . . . I'm Lynda Austin from New York. I'm a friend of Brady Stoner's and—"

"Brady! How's he doin' anyway? I haven't seen him in a year."

"Oh, he's fine. Well, actually he got banged up at a rodeo in Phoenix last weekend, and he's heading to Idaho to rest. I need to talk to him, Mrs. Minor, and—"

"I'm not married yet, honey."

"I understood that Brady might be headed to your ranch tonight, and I need to talk to him."

"Brady's comin' in tonight? Isn't that nice! Thanks for callin'. It'll give me a chance to wash my hair and slip into a dancin' dress. What did you say your name was?"

"If Brady shows up, have him call Lynda Austin in New York."

"Let me grab a pencil, and I'll jot down your number."

"He knows my number."

"Yeah, I suppose he does. I'll be sure and give him the message. Brady Stoner comin' for supper! That cheers up a girl's day. You know what I mean?"

"I know what you mean," Lynda sighed as she hung up the phone.

"Look, we found out next to nothing today—except that the last chapter of McCall's book is lost."

"And that Drew Hessler sent a Fed. Ex. package to Montana and then took off to hunt for buried treasure," Kelly added.

"I don't know. Let's go home. Maybe it will make better sense Monday."

◆ ◆ ◆

Both Kelly and Nina gawked when Lynda Austin stepped into the nearly empty editorial offices of Atlantic-Hampton Publishing Company on Monday morning.

"Whoa, the casual Ms. Austin." Kelly laughed. "When all the big shots are gone, you wear jeans, boots, Western blouse, and Prairie Rose perfume."

"It's called Enrapture."

"You trying to compete with Sassy? Where's your cowboy hat?"

"With my suitcase in the lobby."

"What?" Kelly exploded. "Are you taking off, too?"

"A business trip." Lynda tried to hold back a smile.

"You talked to Brady this weekend, didn't you?" Nina quizzed.

"Yes, I did. He said that U-Bet, Montana, is near Judith Gap, but he couldn't remember any Mendozas around there."

"Does he know everyone in the West?"

"Almost. Anyway, until we get everyone off vacation or hear from McCall, this thing is at a standstill. So . . ."

"So why not go to Montana and trace down that shipping package?" Kelly asked.

"Right. Brady can't rodeo for a couple of weeks, so he volunteered to help me and—"

"Meet me in Montana!" Kelly squealed. "This is not fair! Lynda Dawn Austin, this is not a business trip. You do not get to deduct it from your taxes. You may not pass Go, and you may not collect two hundred dollars."

"Sure, it's a business trip. I'm taking my laptop and the rest of Joaquin's novel. I can modem in the changes to you and still do a little exploring."

Kelly and Nina followed Lynda out into the lobby.

"Are you leaving right now?"

"Yes. Is this crazy or what?"

"I should be so crazy," Nina sighed. "Are you going to go out there and have another great adventure and make us feel left out again?"

"I hope it will be a very quiet time."

"You want me to take care of David?"

"No, Howard and Millie are watching him."

"What shall we tell Gossman or Hampton if they call in asking for you?"

"Tell them the truth."

"That you ran off to the mountains with some good-looking cowboy, and we haven't seen or heard from you since?" Kelly teased.

"No, tell them I wanted to personally track down a missing chapter as quickly as I could in order to hold production costs to a minimum and," she grinned, "that I ran off to the mountains with a good-looking cowboy."

"Boy, having your own imprint is really tough, dirty work," Kelly bantered, "but somebody has to do it."

"What do you want us to do?"

"If you hear from McCall or Drew Hessler, let me know. And keep an eye out for that missing chapter."

"Where will you be?" Nina asked.

"In some cowboy's pickup." Kelly raised her eyebrows.

"I'll call in every day."

"What if we find the missing chapter someplace?" Nina asked.

Lynda laughed. "I don't want to hear about it for at least three days."

"Really?"

"I'm kidding. Let me know if you discover anything. There's probably an easy explanation for all of this. I just don't want to hear about it until after I go see my cowboy."

"Happy trails!" Kelly called as Lynda jammed her hat on her head and scooped up her suitcase.

TWO

Lynda Austin spent most of the day gazing down on the tops of clouds—round, fluffy, stringy, white, gray, black, billowing, broken, moisture-laden clouds. From her vantage point at 35,000 feet, Pennsylvania stretched out just like Illinois, and Iowa resembled Colorado.

The commuter airlines flight from Denver to Jackson, Wyoming, was no better. The twin engine's ear-numbing whine kept her from concentrating on the manuscript laying in her lap. Instead, her thoughts raced toward the upcoming reunion.

He'll be there wearing Wranglers, boots, long-sleeve shirt, black Resistol, big, shiny buckle, and a wide grin. Only he's hurt. His left arm and shoulder, he said. Maybe he'll have a sling . . . no, not Brady.

Left arm. Don't grab his left arm.

Don't grab him at all!

Good friends. We're just good friends. Just a squeeze of the hand, a peck on the cheek . . . "How have you been? I've missed you. Hope your shoulder is doing better. Sorry about that horse blowing up on you in Phoenix."

Yeah, right. Who are you trying to kid, girl? Just so I don't cry or throw myself all over him or fake a stumble and have him catch me. Don't do anything dumb.

As the plane began its descent through the clouds, she tucked the manuscript back into her briefcase. Then she pulled out her travel bottle of Prairie Rose and dabbed some behind each ear, along her neck, and on her wrists. A glance in her hand mirror revealed rather tired eyes and travel-worn hair.

Maybe I should keep my sunglasses on and push my cowboy hat to the back of my head. I can just say, "Brady, it's so good to see you! Thanks for offering to help me with the missing chapter. I'll fill you in on all the details during dinner . . . eh, supper." Or maybe I should say, "Shut up and kiss me, cowboy!" That's my problem. I can't decide if I'm supposed to be Mary Tyler Moore or Mary-Chapin Carpenter.

Suddenly, the plane dropped straight down. Lynda's stomach raised right up to her throat. A woman behind her gasped. Then the plane lurched to the left, and Lynda slammed against the window.

No, Lord! I won't get to see Brady! I'm not ready.

"Please remain in your seats with your seat belts on. We are experiencing some mild turbulence as we descend toward Jackson." As quickly as it began, the lurching subsided, and the pilot brought the plane swiftly down to a lower elevation.

The copilot stepped back into the aisle. "Hope that little wind shear didn't disturb you too much. Does anyone need any help?"

No one said anything, and Austin refused to turn around, fearing she had been the only one who had panicked.

Austin, you wimp. It was just a little bounce. Get it together, girl. You're Lynda Austin—award-winning New York editor, newly discovered granddaughter of Martin Taylor Harrison, traveling west to trace down a missing chapter. Western chic, but sophisticated—a hard-driving, thick-skinned editor who knows just how much she should soften.

She took a deep breath and sat up in the seat. She could

feel perspiration on her forehead and the back of her neck. Her ears plugged up as the plane continued its descent and the whine of the turboprops seemed more distant. She stared out the window at the Wyoming countryside as they dropped below the clouds.

They swooped lower toward the Bridger-Teton National Forest, then followed Hoback Canyon, banked north, and traced the Snake River. The highway below was close enough to distinguish the cars and pickups, but she couldn't tell what color they were. Snow King Mountain lived up to its name, looming in the northeast, blanketed in white. This time the plane banked to the left, and she heard the landing gear begin to drop into position.

The countryside whizzed by. The plane leveled out at the edge of the runway and bounced twice before hurling itself at almost uncontrollable speed along the blacktop. Slowing quickly, the plane taxied toward the terminal. Lynda strained to look through the glass to catch a glimpse of Brady Stoner.

The aisle filled, and she waited, rapping her fingers on her burgundy briefcase. A cool autumn breeze hit her face as she descended the narrow stairs to the tarmac. Lynda set her briefcase down, zipped up her black satin jacket, and pulled her hat down tight. Well, so much for the chic, casual look.

She searched the crowd at the Gate 4 doorway and finally stepped inside, still not spotting Brady.

There certainly are plenty of reasons he could be late. Road construction. His truck might have broken down. Maybe he took a wrong road and got lost. . . . Brady's never lost. . . . He could have been in an accident! It's hard to drive with one arm for eight straight hours.

Her eyes searched the crowd, flitting from one cowboy hat to the next. She spotted black beaver felt Resistols, white straw Baileys, gray Stetsons with a rancher's crease, and an Australian outback Akubra. But not her Brady.

It was a room crammed full of people looking for somebody.

But no one was looking for her.

She walked slowly toward the baggage claim area. Her heart sank as the crowd dispersed in clumps of twos, threes, and fours. One boy wearing a black cowboy hat scooted by her in such a hurry she had to jump back out of his way.

She retrieved her small, soft-sided suitcase and glanced out the front of the terminal. Yellow leaves flew off in the wind, exposing the limbs of the small aspens. Dust swirled in front of impatient cars. People greeted each other by turning up their collars and nodding. They didn't look happy or sad, just hurried and cold. Lynda plopped down in a chair near the front entrance.

He said it was about four hundred miles from Ely to Jackson. He could make it easily in eight hours. He'd be in Jackson before I was. Brady, don't make me worry so. I'm sure he's all right. It's just that I wanted him here . . . with some flowers . . . looking lost and lonesome. Lynda Dawn, you spend too much time editing fiction. Dear Lord, he's just got to be all right.

Lord, sometimes it's like I'm playing a game. I don't want to be in a game. This is real life, girl.

Real people.

Real relationships.

A little girl in a red corduroy jumper leaped into her daddy's arms. Age seemed to slip away from around his eyes as he lifted her high for a kiss on the cheek. A smiling mother wearing a blue sweater with the manufacturer's label tab stuck up in the back slipped her arm around his waist. The trio floated out of the terminal on a sea of laughs and hugs.

The reunions went on until the terminal was empty except for the car rental employees, one skycap, and the young man in the black Resistol who had scurried back to the baggage claim three times empty-handed.

I could probably get a taxi to take me to the lodge—I think they have taxis. On the other hand, Brady will be along any minute. It feels pretty empty showing up with no one waiting for you. Sometimes I think he just lives for the minute. Doesn't he know how lonely this feels?

Good grief, girl, cut him some slack. Maybe he got tired and took a nap alongside the road. Maybe he stopped to help a motorist in distress, who, no doubt, was a real sweetheart. Maybe he was late getting out of Ely. Maybe that ranch lady kept him out late, with her newly washed hair and her dancing dress. I'll rip her lips out.

For a few minutes she glanced through the front entrance of a small gift shop and contemplated peeking in to see if they carried any perfume. Lynda finally opened the top of her briefcase and clutched the four-hundred-page manuscript she had been editing. She pulled it halfway out of the case and stared down at it.

I really don't want to do this! What I want . . . I want Brady to be here.

Shoving the manuscript back down, she was slowly snapping the locks on the briefcase when she heard her name called over the loudspeaker. She started.

"Paging Lynda Dawn Austin. Would you please pick up a blue courtesy phone? Lynda Dawn Austin, please pick up a blue courtesy phone."

Lynda Dawn? It's Brady. Something's happened to him!

There were two blue phones on the painted concrete block wall, one of which was being used by the young man in the black Resistol. She scooted her bags over to the other phone, but before she could reach for the receiver, the young man turned toward her. "Are you Miss Lynda Dawn?"

"Yes, I'm Lynda Austin. Who are you?"

He put his phone back on the hook and stepped closer. "Eh . . . well . . ." He looked down at his boots. "I'm Robert Lofton, but ever'one calls me Bronc."

"Are you the one who paged me?" She tried to bend down

so she could see his eyes, which seemed to be locked to the floor. *I've seen shy, young men, but, Bronc, you might win the prize.*

"Yes, ma'am," he replied softly.

"Why?"

"Eh . . . Brady sent me out to give you a lift into town."

"Brady Stoner sent you?"

"Yes, ma'am."

"You can look up at me, can't you?"

The boy slowly raised his head. "I'm just a little embarrassed I didn't spot you before."

Bronc looked about fourteen with smooth face and shaggy, thick black hair. He stood almost six feet tall. He was thin, yet muscular. His Wranglers and his boots were well broken in. His blue-striped flannel shirt was faded by wash or by wear, or both.

"Brady couldn't make it?" she asked.

Finally Bronc looked up with his round blue eyes and a trace of acne on his chin and cheek. "He got to town early, but I guess Peggy Gregg had a job or two for him, so he sent me and Capt. Patch out to pick you up." He reached down and retrieved her suitcase and briefcase.

"Capt. Patch is here?"

"He's out in Brady's truck waitin' for us." Bronc smiled revealing straight teeth and a cut on his lip that still sported a couple of stitches.

"Brady's truck? Who drove it out here—you or Capt. Patch?"

"Eh . . . I did."

"Do you have a driver's license?"

"Yes, ma'am, I'm almost seventeen."

You're getting old, Austin. "But where is Brady?"

"He's in town, like I said, helping out Miss Peggy Gregg."

Lynda followed the young man out the door, across the roadway, and into the parking lot. The cool breeze bathed her face.

"Bronc, just who is this Miss Peggy?"

"She runs the Bird Cage. She's somethin' else. You've probably heard him talk about her."

"Eh . . . well . . ." Austin spotted the black-and-silver Dodge pickup. The familiar black-and-white dog with a black patch over his right eye stood on top of the cab.

"Capt. Patch! Come on, boy!" she called.

The dog bounded off the truck and ran to her. His tail end hung low, and his head waited an approving pat. After she scuffed his ears and scratched his head, he sniffed her boots and then bounded back into the pickup. Loading the bags into the back, Bronc slid in behind the steering wheel. He gunned out of the parking lot and was heading north toward Jackson when Lynda glanced over at him.

"Bronc, why did you say you were embarrassed back there?"

"Well, ma'am, I'm really sorry I didn't spot you sooner. I mean, I saw you sittin' there and ever'thing. I guess I'm kind of embarrassed by what I was thinkin'."

"What were you thinking?"

She watched Bronc take a deep breath. "Well . . . I figured if I hadn't promised Brady I'd give a ride to some New York City editor, I'd surely like to . . . you know, come over and visit with that cowgirl sitting alone by the door 'cause you sure are purdy, you know, for a city gal. I felt pretty dumb not recognizing you. I surely am sorry I kept you waitin'."

"It's quite understandable since we've never met."

"Yeah, but . . . well, Brady said to look for some classy, dark-haired lady who looks like she belongs in New York City."

"Just what does such a person look like?"

"You know, sort of up-tight and out of place. But, to tell you the truth, Miss Lynda Dawn, you look more like a barrel racer from Rock Springs or Miss Rodeo Wyoming wearing that cowboy hat and that black NFR jacket."

"Brady gave me the jacket."

"Yes, ma'am, and I reckon he surely was right about you bein' the prettiest one at the airport. I ain't never been to New York City. Never did want to . . . until now."

"Thanks, Bronc. That's the nicest thing anyone has said to me today."

"Really?"

"Well, so far anyway."

Austin, you always could charm the young men. It's when they grow older that they get more discriminating. Bronc, you've been hiding in the barn too long.

Motels and gift shops lined the side streets. Retail buildings sported rough, unpainted wood storefronts. Art galleries shared quarters with ice cream shops. Custom clothing stores jammed alongside outlets stacked high with "genuine Western artifacts" imported from the Orient. It was only six blocks from the city limits to downtown Jackson. Even on a cool, cloudy autumn day, traffic was thick and slow as they approached the center of town.

"Brady said to park over here and take Capt. Patch with me. He said he'd meet you downtown over by the southeast antler gate at the city park."

"Aren't you coming with me?"

"Nah, I've got to get back to work. I'll just slip your suitcases up in the cab so they won't walk away."

"What kind of work do you do, Bronc?"

"When I ain't learnin' to ride broncs, I help Miss Peggy fix up the Bird Cage."

"How did you bust your lip?"

"I fell forward when that sunfishin' black bucker jerked his head back. Sort of kissed him in the back of his head."

"Does it still hurt?"

"No, ma'am. Shoot, Miss Lynda Dawn, I've been hurt a lot worse than this."

Where do they teach them to say that? Is it required memoriza-tion in rodeo school?

"So I'm to meet Brady down at the park."

"Yes, ma'am."

Lynda shoved her cowboy hat tight on her head so it wouldn't catch the stiff wind and then started walking toward the center of town. Most of the bundled tourists that lined the covered boardwalk were senior citizens following tour guides and still sporting their "Hello: My Name Is____" tags. One guide spoke German, another Japanese. Lynda's previous trip to Jackson had been in late November, and everything had been covered with snow. This time it was just cold.

A tall, middle-aged man in a beat-up gray hat leaned against the paint-chipped brick wall of an eating place named "Cowboy Calf-A." He wore buckaroo boots with fifteen-inch shafts pulled up outside his Wranglers. Lynda watched him slip a small, round can from his back pocket and shove a pinch of tobacco between his cheek and gum. She had almost passed him when she heard him clear his throat.

"Darlin', you lookin' for some company?"

She whipped around and glared at the unshaven man with narrow, tired eyes and a wrinkled long-sleeve shirt.

"I'm looking for Brady Stoner—that's who I'm looking for."

"Brady? Well, you better hurry, darlin'. I hear he's about to get into some trouble over at the park." He pointed to the city park across the street.

"Trouble?"

"Somethin's brewin' up. Look at that crowd over there."

Several hundred people crowded around the southeast cor-ner of the park. She scooted out into the street, holding her hat secure with her right hand.

"If ol' Brady don't come through, you can always come dance with me, darlin'!" the man yelled at her above the traffic noise. "You look mighty fine in them tight britches!"

She waited in the middle of the street for a blue-and-silver tour bus to diesel-smoke its way past. Then she scooted through the antler gate on the northwest corner of the park. Jogging diagonally on uneven concrete, she could hear every clomp of her boots on the hard walk. Her heels slipped and rubbed sore inside the stiff leather.

They are not tight britches.

Out of breath by the time she reached the crowd, she scooted in between several Oriental men with cameras and in front of an extremely heavy-set woman wearing a green sweatshirt that read, "If Mama Ain't Happy, Nobody's Happy."

A woman in an old-fashioned dance-hall dress of purple satin with black lace sleeves and deep scooped neck was waving a gun at a short man in a top hat and bow tie. At least two bodies sprawled across the asphalt next to a stagecoach hitched to six horses. Three to four hundred people crowded around the sidewalk gawking.

What's going on here?

"You're next, Mayor," the woman with the gun shouted, pointing the pistol at the man in the top hat. Suddenly, the big woman behind her with the "Mama" sweatshirt stepped out into the clearing and hollered, "Someone's got to stop this!"

A blast of fire and smoke from the dance-hall girl's pistol toppled the big woman straight to the asphalt right by Lynda's feet. The crowd gasped and moved back several feet.

Good grief! She shot the tourist? What kind of skit . . . Something's going wrong here!

Lynda looked up, and suddenly a man ran out into the clearing at the other end of the crowd and started tugging a revolver out of the hand of one of the dead men.

"Brady?" she choked.

"You can't just go around shootin' innocent people in the crowd!" he yelled.

Before he could raise the revolver, the dance-hall girl

pointed her long-barreled pistol at him. Two quick shots exploded, filling the air with thick acidic-smelling smoke. With a cry, Brady crumpled to the ground.

"No!" Lynda screamed. "Brady! What's going on here?"

She ran to Brady's side as the woman with the gun just stared at her and laughed.

"You can't shoot him! You can't . . ."

"Oh, no?" the woman yelled. "I can shoot you, too." She raised the pistol and pointed it at Lynda. The crowd grew quiet. Austin grabbed the revolver out of Brady's hand and spun around. Using both her thumbs, she tried to cock the hammer of the single-action Colt .44.

The dance-hall girl's gun roared with an ear-rumbling explosion, and Lynda flinched, expecting the bullet to tear into her. But when there was no pain, she pointed the heavy weapon toward the woman and pulled the trigger. This time the explosion hurt her ears and kicked the gun straight above her head. The dance-hall girl staggered back with a cry and a groan and collapsed in the arms of one of the Oriental men in the crowd.

Oh, Lord, what have I done? I didn't . . . I . . . she . . . Brady! She felt tears well up in her eyes. *I didn't kill her, did I? I don't even know who she is! I didn't want to pull the trigger. I don't even know what's going on. I thought . . . oh, man.*

Her head felt light, and the crowd started to spin around her.

Suddenly they broke into thunderous applause.

"But what . . . what am I going to do now?" She began to cry, tossing the gun to the street.

"Take a bow, darlin'. It was a great performance," came a whispered response from somewhere on the blacktop.

"Brady?" She scooted down on her hands and knees next to him.

He rose to his feet, obviously unhurt, and brushed off his jeans. "Come on, Lynda Dawn, the whole cast is bowing."

Half a dozen people, including those who had looked wounded or dead, the large woman in the sweatshirt, and the dance-hall girl, stood in the middle of the crowd bowing. Brady tipped his hat to the crowd.

"The whole cast?"

"You ought to curtsey or somethin'," he instructed under his breath.

"All of this is just a play?"

Still grinning at the crowd, Brady mumbled, "Ain't it a kick? 'Course, it had a different endin' today."

She couldn't keep the tears from streaming down her cheeks. "Brady Stoner, you jerk. I thought you were dead," she hollered and slugged him in the arm.

The left arm.

Brady let out a pained cry and grabbed his sagging left shoulder as the crowd laughed and cheered.

"Your bad arm! Oh . . . I'm sorry. I . . ." Finally she threw her arms around his neck and kissed him on the lips.

The crowd roared approval.

"Tonight at 8:00 P.M. at the Bird Cage," the dance-hall girl yelled, "we'll present the melodrama, 'Daring Dan's Diabolical Deeds!' See you all there!"

The laughing crowd dispersed, and the actors, including the dance-hall girl, encircled Brady and Lynda.

"Whoa, girl, that was quite a performance. Brady, why didn't you let us know you wanted to change the script?"

"Oh . . . eh, listen, Miss Peggy . . . and everyone, this is my—my good friend from New York City, Miss Lynda Dawn Austin."

"A New York actress? I've done a little Off-Broadway myself. You looking for work, honey?" Peggy asked. "I think we can find a part for you in the melodrama. The pay won't hardly buy peanuts, but it gives you an acting credit for your resume."

"Wait a minute. W-wait," Lynda stammered. "Brady, can I talk to you—alone?"

"Peggy, I told you I could only give you this one performance," Brady reminded her. "Me and Lynda Dawn have to get on down the road."

"Well . . ." Peggy leaned over and kissed Brady on the cheek. "When she runs back to New York, you be sure and come back to see us."

Tugging Brady by his right arm, Lynda pulled him toward the big arched gate made of stacked antlers.

"Stoner, what's going on here? I expected you to be at the airport."

"Didn't Bronc come pick you up?"

"Yes, but what's all this acting about? Brady, I can't believe I thought this thing was real. I just knew I'd killed that woman. I can't stand it when I'm so naive."

"Peggy's a real sweetheart. She saw me in town this afternoon and begged me to help her out. Normally they don't run the evenin' street melodrama except in the summer. But this big tour group came in today and offered her some extra money to see the daily hanging."

"Daily hanging?"

"Yeah. Last time you were here it was too close to winter for it. In the summer they have a skit every day where someone ends up gettin' hung. Anyway, she was short a few actors 'cause some had to go back to college. Well, I agreed to help her out—after all she did for me that time."

"What time? Do I want to hear this story?"

Brady groaned. "Probably not. Boy, I was impressed at how you jumped in there and gunned down Miss Peggy. Sort of reminded me of you beatin' back the deputies out in the desert."

"Brady, I lost total control of myself because I was worried about you needlessly. I don't appreciate that. I can't believe I pulled the trigger on that gun. I pointed it at a human being and pulled the trigger. I was trying to kill her!"

She sat down on a bench, pulled off her hat, and put her head between her knees, taking big, gasping breaths.

"She had just shot me and was trying to kill you. Of course you pulled the trigger."

"But she hadn't shot you, and she wasn't trying to kill me. It was all a charade, and I got sucked in so much I was willing to kill. Don't you see? I can't believe I did that. I can't believe I've been with you ten minutes, and I've already tossed out every civilizing force in my life." Her throat started to constrict, and she gasped for breath.

"Now don't be so hard on yourself, darlin'. It was just a little skit."

"Hard on myself? You're the one who gets me into these things. I don't act this way in New York. It's like I lose all self-control when I come west."

"All self-control?" Brady raised his eyebrows.

"Yes . . . and right now I'm either going to cry or wet my pants or barf!"

"I take it this is not the way you planned our meeting?"

"You got that right, buster."

"Well, I might as well tell you the other bad news."

She sat up and looked straight at him. "What?"

"I, eh, couldn't get us rooms at the lodge. What with these tour busses and all, you need reservations way in advance. In fact, there aren't any rooms available in town."

"Oh, joy. What do you intend on us doing?"

"I figured we might just drive north until we find a place to stop."

"Whatever." *No quiet supper at the lodge, no walk in the moonlight, no soft, tender good-night kiss at the door, no Tetons in the morning, no big rock fireplace, no walking hand in hand at day-*

break, no soft, warm kiss on the lips. How come my dreams are so much better than my reality?

"That's mighty pretty perfume," Brady offered.

"Yeah, sure, change the subject."

"Darlin', what is the subject? Are you mad at me?"

"Am I mad at you? You act like there's nothing to be mad about. I can't believe your insensitivity."

"Well," Brady murmured, "nothin' like gettin' off to a good start."

Without speaking, they walked side by side, hands shoved in pockets, up the tourist-clogged boardwalk toward the lot where Bronc had parked the pickup. Lynda was just about to break the ice when Brady let out a shout. "Oh, no, not again! Look at this! Look at this!" He sprinted toward the pickup. "Man, I can't believe this happened!"

"How can you have four flat tires all at once?" she asked, surveying the pickup that now rested on steel rims, the tires limp and squashed around them.

Brady slammed his hand on the hood and kicked one of the flats. "I can't believe this. Who did this? I'll get 'em. Whoever did this, I'll get you!" he shouted at the top of his voice.

"Brady, calm down. It's only four flats. Are the tires ruined?"

"No," he shouted, surveying the people who had stopped on the sidewalk to gawk at the commotion. "They just pulled out the valve stems again."

"What do you mean, again?"

"The same thing happened to me Friday night in Phoenix."

"It's just probably some kids or something."

"Kids? Didn't you hear me? They did it in Phoenix . . . and now in Jackson. Someone thinks this is real cute. If you can hear me," he hollered, "I will get you!" The watching crowd began to disperse.

"Do you mean you think the same person did it both times?"

"Of course they did. It's the same method of operation."

"But it could just be a coincidence."

"That's the stupidest thing I ever heard."

"And you think a grand conspiracy to let the air out of Brady Stoner's tires is a rational conclusion?"

Brady pulled off his hat and scratched his head. Then he sighed deeply and leaned against the truck. Looking toward his boots, he shook his head. "I think *ira furor brevis est.*"

"Okay, what's it mean?"

"Anger is brief madness . . . or something like that. Okay, you're right. I overreacted. This whole thing makes me edgy, I guess."

"Me, too," Lynda concurred. "What are you going to do now?"

"Call the auto club to come inflate these tires. Let's go grab something to eat in the meantime."

"Good. We've got a lot to talk about, Stoner. Where are we eating?"

"How about a place called the Cowboy Calf-A?"

"They have food? I thought maybe it was just a bar."

"Best food in town for the price."

"Nothing personal, but I don't enjoy the clientele there. How about some other place?"

"Sure, but I don't aim to do all the talkin'. You've got to tell me all about life in New York."

"That's a deal."

"Come on, darlin'." He reached out and slipped his fingers into hers. They felt rough, strong, cold—and tender. "This isn't exactly the way I figured our meetin' would go either."

They had walked several blocks when he tugged her across the street to a cafe called Little Venice.

"Brady, do you think we'll ever get along as well in person as we do on the telephone?"

"Why, sure. Maybe, you know, when we're fifty."

She started to slug him in the left arm, but his wince made her hold up.

"Well, Lynda Dawn," he said with a grin, "welcome back to Wyomin'."

◆ ◆ ◆

They finished a supper of green salad, lasagna, and garlic bread right after dark. When they returned to the parking lot, they found the truck tires inflated and a pink invoice stuck under the windshield wiper. Brady whistled between his teeth. Capt. Patch bounded up from deep in the shadows.

"You feel up to drivin'?" Brady asked. "This old left arm is beginnin' to ache."

"You know how poorly I drive your rig, but I'll give it a try."

Lynda slid into the driver's seat.

"Why does Capt. Patch always sit in the middle?" she asked.

"He's a cowboy dog."

"What does that mean?"

"It means if he sits in the middle, he don't have to drive, and he don't have to get out and open the gate."

◆ ◆ ◆

The thick cloud cover insured a dark and starless night sky as they drove north out of Jackson. Other than the glare of an occasional oncoming car, there was no light at all.

No houses could be seen.

No business establishments.

No street lights.

Nothing.

Brady stretched his right arm and then looked over at her. "You finally get all those contract details worked out with the publishing company on that Harrison manuscript?"

"Most of the details are worked out. The attorneys are still battling over some of it."

"You aren't aimin' on retirin' and movin' to Florida, are you?"

"There won't be that much money, especially since it will be split with my brother and sister. But I have thought about moving up to Connecticut and even buying a car."

"Are things startin' to calm down around the office?"

"A little, I guess. That is, until this week."

"Have you completed your God-given task?" he quizzed.

"My what?"

"Last year you were sayin' that publishin' Harrison's lost manuscript might be your task in life."

"Well, I'm hoping there are still some other things I ought to be doing."

"Yeah, I always figured if we finished off one task, the Lord would give us another."

For almost an hour they talked about rodeo, the lawsuits to settle royalties on the lost Harrison manuscript, perfumes, Heather Martin and the girls, Atlantic-Hampton Publishing Company, pulled shoulder muscles, dogs with one eye, and how many miles it is between the Rocky Mountains and New York City.

Brady rubbed his sore left shoulder with his right hand, unsnapped the top button of his blue-and-white-striped Western shirt, and then scrunched down in the seat with his hat pulled almost over his eyes. "You promised to fill me in on the story of why we're goin' to Montana to look for some book chapter. The road is long and straight for a while. You want to tell me how this all came about?"

It's pitch-dark. I can't even see him. I don't think I've put on any fresh perfume since midafternoon. I might as well be in New York talking to him over the phone.

"The lost final chapter? Sure . . . well, here goes. While I was in Boca Raton last February teaching at a writer's conference—remember, I called you at the rodeo in Houston? Anyway, I ran across a man who had written a manuscript that he called *Confederate Gold*! Well, it's not normally a place where I actually find any material I can use, but this man's story was fascinating."

"Is it a Civil War story?"

"Nope. It all takes place just a little over twenty years ago. Chance McCall is a retired fishing boat captain down in south Florida. He specialized in fishing trips into the backwater."

"Where?"

"The shallow waters on the west side of the keys, back up into the Everglades. He is also quite some scuba diver. He worked off and on for Mel Fisher and others."

"The sunken-ship-full-of-Spanish-gold guy?"

"Yes. Well, back in 1972 Chance got a call from an old navy friend who asked him if he could round up a couple more divers and meet him in Denver by the next evening. He had a diving job for them that would pay three hundred dollars a day."

"Whoa. That's short notice."

"What is this we're passing?"

"The entrance to Yellowstone Park."

"Yellowstone? You mean my first trip to Yellowstone, and it's going to be pitch-black?"

"Don't worry, I'll describe everything."

"But it's dark, Stoner!"

"We'll buy some postcards."

"I can hear it now. 'How was Yellowstone?' they ask me back at the office. 'Why, it's lovely at night. It looks just like southern New Jersey!'"

"I think all the lodges are closed this time of the year. We'll have to drive a little farther north to find a place."

"How far?"

"Montana."

She stared out into the darkness. "What am I missing here?"

"It's kind of boring—spectacular mountains, beautiful forests, scenic Lewis Creek . . . it's part of the headwaters of the famed Snake River . . . and occasional deer, elk, and bear. You know, the same old stuff."

"Thanks a lot, Stoner. You sure know how to give a girl a great time."

"Come on, get back to your story. This guy in Florida just got a call about scuba diving in the Rockies—or something."

Lynda yanked off her cowboy hat and tossed it into the tiny backseat of the extended cab. "Well . . . always looking for a new adventure, Chance corrals a couple of cronies and flies out to Denver. He meets up with the buddy, and the whole group charter a private jet and fly to Great Falls, Montana. When they arrive, a couple more men join them, and the whole gang went downtown and purchased a new travel home and a new Jeep—for cash. When Chance questions the operation, he is told, 'Don't worry. Number 1 has approved this.' Of course, they don't say who Number 1 is."

"Cash? We're talkin' big bucks." Brady rolled up the sleeves of his shirt. Even in the dark shadows of the pickup cab, she caught sight of his soft, easy smile.

"It gets crazier. They also buy a lot of equipment and fishing and hunting licenses because they tell all the locals they are hunters from the East. Then they leave Great Falls and travel out to a reservoir or lake."

"What direction?"

"That's what I don't know."

"Isn't it in the book?"

"In the book McCall fictionalized all the towns and locations. Anyway, they drive out to the lake, and while they are taking the boat—which they also purchased for cash—across the lake, this buddy of McCall's tells him about the gold."

"Gold?"

Hanging onto the leather-wrapped steering wheel with her left hand, Lynda scratched her nose with the back of her right hand. "Yes. It seems that some group of investors had run across maps and charts showing where Jesse James and his gang had buried forty tons of Confederate gold. This was going to be cached until the Confederacy re-emerged."

"Forty tons? That's a lot of weight to come upriver with."

She thought she saw a clearing on the left side of the highway. "What's that over there?"

"It's just a lake."

"Just a lake? What lake? Is it something important?"

"It's Lewis Lake. Lewis Falls are just below it. They sure are pretty in June when the snowmelt is really boilin'."

"Great! Yellowstone at night. This is really incredibly dumb." She raised her left wrist and tried to smell her perfume, but all she detected was the aroma of sweat, leather, and dog.

Brady straightened around in the seat. "You'll have to come back."

"Why do you keep looking out the back window?"

"Checking to see if anyone's following us."

"Are they?"

"Not that I can tell."

"Who would follow us?"

"I don't know. But having the air let out of my tires in Phoenix and then in Jackson makes me wonder if someone is."

"That's a cheery thought. It doesn't really happen, does it? People following people. That's only in the movies and books, right?"

"Probably. Go on with your story. Where were we?"

"Looking for gold. Anyway . . . supposedly Jesse James came upriver, buried the gold in a cave, sealed up the mouth of the cave with mortar and brick, and then pulled rocks over its mouth so it couldn't be seen."

"And the gold's just waiting for someone to find it?"

"Right. I guess, so the legend goes, James went back to Missouri and was killed."

"By Robert Ford."

"Who?"

"The 'dirty little coward that shot Mr. Howard and laid poor Jesse in his grave.' You know that old song, don't you?"

"Eh . . . no." She glanced over at his square-jawed shadow and thought she could smell his aftershave.

I need more perfume!

"There's a million lost gold stories in the West. What makes this one credible?"

"Credible? It doesn't have to be credible. We're publishing the whole thing as a novel."

"So why did they need a diver to find a cave?"

"Sometime around the turn of the century, the government dammed off the river and flooded the area, making a lake."

"What river?"

"I think it's the Missouri."

"It's a big river. There are lots and lots of lakes."

"That's what I'm afraid of."

"Now the cave's underwater?"

"Precisely. So McCall goes out and surveys the site. They fly him to Seattle to buy all the diving equipment they would need."

"Let me guess. He paid for it in cash."

"You got it. All the while they keep telling Chance, 'Don't worry. Number 1 has approved this.' Well, when they get back out to the lake, they have to pretend to be fishermen, and they begin to look for Indian pictographs that match the map."

Suddenly, Austin slammed on the brakes. Capt. Patch let out a bark, and all three of them bounced forward in the cab of the pickup. "What's that thing?"

"An American plains bison, better known as a buffalo."

"In the middle of the road?"

"It's his road."

"Is he dead?"

"Looks like he's dozin' off."

"Well, aren't you going to get out there and shoo him off?"

"Nope."

"What are we going to do?"

"Drive around him."

"I can't believe this. How can they let buffalo sleep in the middle of the road?"

"When you're a national treasure, you can do just about anything you please," Brady lectured her. "That's the way, darlin'. Just ease on around."

"Are there more buffalo out here?"

"Oh, yeah, hundreds . . . maybe thousands."

"I thought they were all gone."

"And a year ago you thought cowboys were all gone, too. Now go on. You've got this guy Chance out there diving somewhere." Brady lifted his left arm with his right hand and placed it on the back of the pickup seat behind the curled-up Capt. Patch.

"On the third day they find the exact drawings, and the charts indicate that the cave is below water level."

Dogs should definitely ride in the back of the pickup.

"So they start this secretive diving?"

"Yes, but just as they start, Chance notices several men on the shore sitting there just watching them. When he questions his buddy, he is reassured, 'Don't worry. I hired those men to protect you divers.'"

"Protect them from what?"

"He wouldn't say. All I can remember from the book is that at that time it was illegal for a private citizen to hoard that much gold, so they had given someone in the government $60,000 cash to secure some special permit."

"Well, did they find Jesse's gold?"

"After about a week of diving, they hadn't found the entrance of the cave, so they sent Chance to the Bahamas to rent a huge underwater light that had been developed for a James Bond movie."

"*Thunderball.*"

"What?"

"That was the Bond film with all the underwater scenes. You know, he saves the babe who has her swim fin caught in the coral reef?"

"Well, I'm glad you know your Bond films."

"I watch them for all the special effects and action stuff."

"Anyway, Chance brings back the big light from the Bahamas."

"Does this help?"

"No. Actually it makes everything worse." She slowed down a little to read a road sign. "What's this Grant's Village?"

"It's on the west thumb of Yellowstone Lake."

"Yellowstone Lake—that sounds pretty."

"Oh, it's just your typical crystal-clear high mountain lake perched on the continental divide. It happens to be the largest mountain lake in North America."

"It's so lovely," Lynda mimicked, glaring into the darkness on the left side of the pickup.

"It's over here on this side." Brady pointed.

"I can't believe I'm doing this. Which way? Left or right?"

"Go left. That way you'll be able to drive right past Old Faithful. You're buildin' memories, darlin'. Now finish your story."

"Where was I?"

"The big underwater lamp."

"Okay. Well, the light just reflects off silt suspended in the water and makes the underwater view worse."

"But they keep looking?"

"Oh, yeah, they are just sure they will find all this gold. They even have the means to raise it up."

"How would they do that?"

"Chance said they were going to sink fifty-five-gallon steel drums, then pump them full of air, and float the gold bars to the surface."

"I guess that would work."

"He said that a chartered 727 parked at the airport in Denver waited to fly the cargo to Switzerland."

"This is sounding very James Bondish itself. I mean, without the babes."

"Anyway, after a couple of weeks—"

"Hey, there it is!" Brady hollered, pointing at the darkness.

"What? Where?"

"Old Faithful! It's right over there somewhere."

"Funny, Stoner."

"I thought you might want to know."

He thinks this is funny. Well . . . maybe it is funny, I mean, ten years from now.

"It's cold in here," she complained. "How do I turn on the heater?"

"I'll get the heater goin'. By the way," he said grinning, "that's a nice jacket you're wearin'."

"Oh, this old National Finals Rodeo jacket? A bareback rider gave it to me."

"You get a lot of presents from cowboys?"

"Oh, just about anything I want. But I have to ask for it quick."

"How come?"

"Because a relationship with a rodeo cowboy only lasts about eight seconds," she teased. "You're looking out the back window again."

"It's a habit."

"This would be a lonely road to have someone follow us on."

"Yeah, I was thinkin' the same thing. Go on with the adventures of Chance McCall."

"Like I said, after two weeks of diving, Chance had to get back to Florida or lose his job. They hadn't found even a trace of the cave, so he boxed up his stuff and went home."

"How about the rest of them?"

"They dove four more weeks and finally abandoned the project. I guess the whole crew packed up and went to Texas. They had a map of some hidden gold in a cave covered by an underground lake."

"True fortune hunters. So that's the end of the story? No shots fired, no terrorists or foreign agents, no instant millionaires? Reminds me of *The Maltese Falcon*. No one gets the money in the end."

"Chance estimated the outfit spent around $600,000 looking for Jesse James's buried gold."

"So what's the deal about the last chapter in the book? Take a right up here at Madison."

"This is a town?"

"Just a campground. Pretty country. 'Course, a lot of it was burnt out by that big fire in 1988."

Austin swerved to miss a large animal that darted across the highway.

"That was a big deer!"

"That was an elk."

"Eh . . . right. With all those horns, it was a buck elk, right?"

Brady roared and shoved his hat to the back of his head. "Now here's your nature lesson. A male deer is a buck, and a female is a doe. Same is true for an antelope. But a male elk is a bull, and a female is a cow. Same thing with moose."

"How about cowboys? Are they bucks or bulls?"

"Depends on their age. You've got young bucks and old bulls."

"Sorry I asked. What's up ahead?"

"Sooner or later we'll get to Mammoth Hot Springs. That's a fascinating place."

"I can hardly wait to miss it."

"What I can't figure is, if this whole deal about diving for lost gold turned out to be a dead-end street, what's the punch line in the book?"

"Ah, that's where the fiction part comes in. Chance added a couple of murders to the story and cranked out quite a thriller."

"Okay, you have a good mystery somewhat based on a real experience. But why did you have to fly out here?"

"To find the final chapter."

"You mentioned that a little on the phone, but I didn't understand."

"Even though most of the towns are fictitious in the book, Chance decided to put the real maps and charts at the end of the last chapter." She slowed the pickup a little. "Can we scoot the seat forward a little? This distance is a pain."

After the seat was adjusted, she sat up and stretched her back.

"Are you telling me that good old Chance had the original maps and charts?"

"Years after the whole thing fizzled, he hunted up his friend and bought all the old documents for a hundred dollars."

"Why would he want to publish all of that in a novel?"

"He thought it might make an interesting hook for people to buy the book. Real treasure maps and all."

"Sounds interesting to me."

"But he was almost paranoid about someone wanting to steal the maps. That's why he wouldn't send us the final chapter until we were ready to go to the printers. He figured that if everyone had the same information at the same time, no one could sneak in there and find the gold on their own. It would just be common knowledge."

"If there is any gold."

"Exactly. But Chance certainly thinks there is some gold there. And as long as it hasn't been found, people will want to buy the book."

"Sounds good to me."

"But here's the problem. The last chapter got to our office last week and was sent to production, but it disappeared."

"What do you mean, disappeared?"

"We can't find it anywhere in the office." She waved her hand at him. "You can turn down the heater a little now."

He adjusted the control. "I suppose you spied around to see which employee quit and moved to Montana."

"That's one of the problems. Most of the staff just went on vacation. I don't know where any of them are."

"You said one of the problems."

"I tried to call Chance McCall to see if he could send duplicates, but he's off in the Bahamas diving for a lost ship and won't be coming back until Christmas. I can't even reach him."

"And here I figured the publishin' business was about the most boring in the world."

"Boring?"

"Sure, you know, one of those places where all the women are desperate and the men are wimps."

"What?" She slammed on the brakes and brought the truck to a standstill, jarring Capt. Patch out of his sleep. "Out! Stoner, I don't have to put up with this."

"Did I say something wrong?"

"Out, Stoner! You're walking from here."

"But it's my pickup."

"Oh, yeah. Well, you can ride as long as I never hear

another degrading, malicious remark like that about the men and women in the publishing business again."

"'Oh, beat the drum slowly and play the fife lowly,'" Brady began to sing. "'Play the dead march as you carry me along; take me to the green valley, there lay the sod o'er me, for I'm a young cowboy, and I know I've done wrong.'"

"Are you poking fun at me, Stoner?"

"What I want to know is, which ticked you off most—the part about desperate women or the mention of wimpy men?"

"I refuse to engage in such an insulting conversation."

"Then go on, and tell me again why we're drivin' lickety-split to U-Bet, Montana."

"Well, I found out one of the guys in the office—his name is Drew Hessler—is an amateur fortune hunter. With metal detector, treasure maps, and all that. He had access to McCall's final chapter and may have been the last to see it in the office. He's off somewhere on a treasure hunt and hasn't shown up for work for a few days."

"So he's a suspect?"

"Yes. Even though it's against company policy to ship any personal items on the company account, I know he shipped a Fed. Ex. package to someone named Mendoza in U-Bet, Montana, last Thursday."

"So you think maybe he's out here somewhere with the last chapter?"

"That's what's confusing. Why would he ship it if he's going out there anyway? But he would have known its value and had numerous opportunities to steal it. He waltzes in and out of our offices all the time." The cab of the pickup felt stuffy. She unzipped the black satin jacket and rolled the window down just an inch.

"It's a long shot." Brady pulled off his hat, ran his fingers through his hair, and jammed the hat back down.

"Yeah, I know. It just gave me a good excuse to come see . . ."

"See who?"

"To come see Yellowstone Park!" she exclaimed.

"Did everyone in the office believe that line?"

"Stoner, sometimes you are the most egotistical man I ever met."

"I suppose you're right about that. I know I get to teasing too much. I am really glad you came out."

"You are?"

"Yep. I miss you, Lynda Dawn. I especially miss these long night talks."

"You do? Most of the time all we do is argue."

"I know. But I can't think of anyone on the face of this earth that I'd rather argue with."

"I've got to think about that for a while. I think it's a compliment."

"Turn left."

"Are we leaving the park?"

"Pretty soon. Now make a quick left behind those dumpsters."

"What?"

"Quick."

Austin pulled off behind four large trash bins that paralleled the highway.

"What are we doing? You didn't do this so you could make a pass at me, did you?" she scolded.

Brady laughed and looked out the back window. "Now that sounds like a desperate . . . eh, no, I wanted to see who's following us."

"Following us? Really?"

"There's a rig back there. . . . Wait. . . . Here it comes."

"Who is it? Can you tell?"

"Actually that looked like a forest service truck. I guess I'm just jumpy. Come on, let's get back on the road."

"You sure are suspicious. Is there something going on I don't know about?"

"No. No, I didn't really want to . . . I mean, I didn't think it was anything until . . . It's probably nothing."

"What's nothing?"

"A couple weeks ago, there was some mail waitin' for me in Albuquerque. One letter just said, 'I'll get even with you, Brady Stoner.' It was probably nothing."

"Nothing? Did you take it to the police?"

"What for? It's just a crank letter."

"Could it be Joe Trent or one of his buddies?"

"Nope."

"Are they still in jail?"

"No, they were released after six months. But it's not them."

"How can you be so sure?"

"It was a woman's handwriting."

"A woman?"

"And the letter had perfume on it."

"What kind of perfume?"

"Good-smellin' perfume."

"Where's the letter?"

"In the glove compartment."

"Let me see it."

"You can't read it in the dark."

"No, but I can smell the perfume."

"Here it is."

"It's Abandoned Restraint."

"What?"

"The perfume fragrance is called Abandoned Restraint. It's very popular."

"Does it work?" he teased.

She ignored his remark. "You weren't planning on telling me about this letter?"

"When you travel down the road with mostly the same

people, weird things come up now and again. I figured once I got off the circuit to come help you, she wouldn't know where I went, so that would end the matter."

"That's why your flat tires in Jackson touched you off."

"Yeah. Sort of puts a little excitement into this journey, doesn't it?"

"Somehow, Brady Stoner, I never figured it would be dull. After all, we're out West where all the women are sweethearts named Darlin' and all the men are quick-tempered, handsome cowboys."

"You're razzing me, aren't you?"

"Why on earth would I do that?" Lynda rubbed her eyes and tried to glance down at her watch. "What time is it?"

"About time for breakfast. Are you gettin' hungry?"

"Breakfast? You mean we're just going to drive all night?"

"I know a great place to eat up here. It's open all night . . . I think."

"I'm tired, Stoner. I want a shower and some clean sheets."

"I think they've got some rooms out back."

"Good. How far is it?"

"About an hour."

"An hour?"

"You gettin' tired? You want me to drive?" he offered.

"I'll make it. You just stay awake and keep me company."

They drove a winding, mountain road while the tape player serenaded them with Ian Tyson's "Lights of Laramie" and "When the Rocks Began to Roll." The drone of tires on the asphalt highway, the monotony of the yellow center line, and the stuffiness of the cab kept Austin fighting to stay awake. She had just about decided to either slap herself in the face or pull the rig over when Brady sat up and pointed.

"There it is up there. See . . . LaVerne's Big Sky Cafe."

"LaVerne's? Oh, great. Not another ditsy woman who's in awe of Brady's awesome smile," she grumbled.

"LaVerne's a man."

"What?"

"It's a good Southern man's name—LaVerne."

"So LaVerne's a man? That will be different."

"'Course, if that blonde-headed daughter of his is still waitressin'—"

"I'm tired, Stoner. I don't want to hear about her."

"Yes, ma'am."

THREE

Lynda Austin slept until a little past 11:30 A.M., and she just didn't care. The cabin behind LaVerne's Big Sky Cafe was smoky, small, and cold. The porcelain was flaking off the iron bathtub that served as a shower. On the bottom of the tub were little feet, each surrounding a crystal globe. The water ran hot and cold but never comfortable, and the faded pink shower curtain that completely surrounded the tub showed signs of heavy wear and increasing mold.

She consoled herself by remembering that she had been through worse. *Like those times down in Shotgun Canyon when there were no baths at all.*

With most of her hair in place, with her jeans, boots, and Western shirt tucked in, and with Provocative Proposal splashed liberally on just the right spots, she exited the cabin into the freezing Montana air and hiked toward the cafe toting her suitcase. The gravel of the parking lot was still frozen solid, and each step crunched as if she walked on uneven brown asphalt. She found Brady's pickup unlocked and empty. She shoved her suitcase and briefcase behind the seat. Austin walked over to the cafe and strained to peer through the windows, which reflected her image like the dull, seldom-cleaned mirrors in a service station bathroom.

"Linda Dawn, are you lookin' for me?"

She squinted her eyes and gazed toward the roof of the cafe. Brady and the dog were standing high up near the pitch line of the shake-covered building.

"What are you doing up there?"

"LaVerne had a leak over the kitchen, and I told him I'd patch the roof." He carried a hatchet in his right hand, attached to his wrist by a leather strap.

"Well, what help are you? You can't use that left hand."

"That's why the Captain volunteered to come up and help me. I'll be down in a minute. Order me up a chicken-fried steak, and I'll join you for dinner."

"I guess I missed breakfast."

"Don't worry, darlin', so did I."

Even though it was too cloudy to see the sun, his image was silhouetted distinctly against the gray sky.

Classic cowboy from boots to hat.

"Be careful up there, Mr. Stoner!"

"Yes, ma'am, I will."

I will never in my life get used to him saying, "Yes, ma'am."

The minute she ordered chicken-fried steak for herself, she knew she had made a mistake.

But I didn't have breakfast, and I'm hungry, and I never order anything like this in New York, and it's sort of the house specialty, but I have no idea . . . What if I don't like it? I should have ordered a Reuben. But I always have a Reuben. When in doubt order a chef salad. You can always toss out the cheese. A salad at a place called LaVerne's Big Sky Cafe? They probably don't have fresh vegetables. Where do they go to shop for groceries? It can't be all that bad. Brady ordered it. On the other hand, I've never known him to have discriminating taste—present company excluded, of course.

Brady Stoner strolled into the cafe and flashed a dimpled

smile from under his hat as he scooted into the tattered green Naugahyde booth across the table from her. The cafe smelled of fried food and sweet pipe smoke.

"I guess we're getting a late start," she opened.

"We made up for it last night. We covered a lot of ground. Wasn't Yellowstone lovely?"

She stuck out her tongue at him.

"How'd you sleep?"

"Soundly. I didn't wake up until an hour ago," she replied. "How about you?"

"It was okay." He shrugged. "I'm a little stiff and sore, but that's to be expected."

"Were you in that little green cabin?"

"Well, no, I, eh, . . ."

"Where were you?"

"It's just . . . I thought maybe, you know . . ."

"Stoner?"

"I slept in the rig."

"Where?"

"In my truck."

"Why? Didn't they have another room?"

"It's just . . . the thing about someone following me. I figured I'd protect the truck."

"But you could have frozen out there!"

"Nope. It wasn't much below thirty-two degrees actually. I been out in colder weather than that."

Even when I'm with him, I can't keep track of him.

"Did anything happen?"

"Right before daylight a big old boat of a Cadillac pulled in and cruised through the parking lot. I was pretty sleepy and sat straight up. I guess when they spotted me, they zipped on back to the highway."

"That could have been someone looking for an early breakfast."

"It was probably nothin'. Do you know anyone who drives a big, dark Caddy?"

"In Montana?"

"Yeah."

"I don't know anyone in Montana."

"Aren't you and Harrison Ford buddies? I think he lives somewhere in Montana."

"I've never met him. But I have talked to Tom Clancy several times. He knows him. But I thought Harrison Ford lived in Wyoming."

She glanced up to see a full-figured waitress with long, curly hair bleached almost white stacking dishes on the counter. Lynda pointed to the woman in the soft pink blouse that needed to be buttoned a little higher. "Is that LaVerne's daughter?" she whispered.

"Nah, Shelby got married, moved to Billings, and has twins now."

"Who's that then?"

"I don't have any idea in the world." Brady shrugged. "You don't really think I know every woman in the West, do you?"

"There are times when I begin to wonder."

"Lynda Dawn, don't you know all the employees of that place you're always goin' to for lunch?"

"At Barton's?"

"Yeah."

"Sure, I guess I know everyone. But I've eaten there every day for years."

"When you live on the rodeo road, you tend to eat at the same places over and over, so naturally you strike up a conversation now and again. But I don't know everyone, and I decidedly don't know this gal."

"Can we make it to U-Bet today?"

"We can be there in less than three hours . . . if it doesn't snow. But I still don't think anything's there."

"Someone named Mendoza is around, because he was sent a Fed. Ex. package. We need to find Mendoza."

"What will you say to him when you find him? 'Hello, I'm from New York, and I believe you've stolen a valuable chapter from my publishing company'?"

"No, I'm going to say that we believe some papers were accidently included in a shipping package sent to him, and I'm trying to locate those papers."

The waitress brought slabs of chicken-fried steak the size of dinner plates. The mashed potatoes came family style in a bowl large enough to supply a tour bus, and the white gravy was housed in a one-gallon blue-enameled tin pitcher.

Once the waitress finished piling the food on the table, she turned to Stoner with her generous backside toward Lynda Dawn. "Brady Stoner, you mean to tell me you're goin' to set there in the booth starin' at that tuna fish in designer shades and not even tell me hello?"

Tuna fish in designer shades? Is she talking about me? Am I supposed to be offended? I'm not about to get in a wrestling match with this woman.

"Well . . . actually . . ."

Lynda could see Brady searching for a name tag on the waitress's slightly smudged blouse.

"Eh, Jewel Anne . . . Julie Anne? Julie Anne Raymond?"

"That's better. I didn't think you'd forget so easy."

"But that was . . . five years ago, in Reno. You still throwin' steers?"

This lady throws steers?

"Nah. That WRCA tour don't pay enough to keep a girl in Wranglers. So I went from throwin' steers to slingin' hash."

"Julie Anne, this is Lynda Dawn Austin."

The woman turned around and examined Austin from boots to hat. "Well, I hope you ain't one of them snotty barrel racers."

Brady leaned a little closer to the woman's pleasantly round face. "Actually, Lynda and me are involved in some private investigation, but keep it quiet."

"Brady!" Lynda protested.

"That's all right, darlin'. Julie Anne can keep a secret. We're headin' up to Judith Gap to investigate an extremely serious disappearance—"

The waitress's eyes got as big as silver dollars. "Did someone steal a horse?"

"Even more important than that."

"Brady, honey, you be careful. You remember that time you went after my doggin' horse when he was stole right out of the stall? You almost got your head blowed off."

"Well," drawled Brady with a wink, "there's two of us this time. Lynda Dawn got all her training in New York City."

"I'll be!" Julie Anne looked Lynda over real close once again. "And I thought you were one of them Wrangler-chasin' air-headed buckle bunnies. I do apologize, and you two make sure you don't get hurt, y'hear?"

"Thanks, Julie Anne."

As soon as the waitress left, Brady dug into the steaming food.

"Brady, why did you give her that line?"

"It was all true."

"But you made it sound . . . mysterious."

"It is mysterious."

"But you acted like it might be dangerous."

"It could be dangerous."

"It's just a final chapter of a book."

"Yeah, it's probably no more dangerous than finding the Harrison manuscript last year."

"That kind of thing doesn't happen very often. That was different. We were fighting against principalities and powers then."

"Maybe so. But the point is, we've given Julie Anne something fun to think about all day. Now if you worked at LaVerne's Big Sky Cafe, wouldn't a break in the boredom be appreciated?"

Lynda nodded, took a deep breath, and sliced into the inch-thick chicken-fried steak.

Brady was scraping his plate by the time she had finished less than a fourth of her meal. Her stomach felt bloated, her breath shortened, her teeth and gums sore.

"I can't eat any more," she groaned.

"It just doesn't get any better than this, does it? There's nothing like this meal north of Ft. Worth."

"I hate to waste all this food, but there's no way I could stuff down another bite."

"No waste. I'll get Julie Anne to box it up, and we'll eat it for supper."

"We will? Oh, yeah, you said there might not be a cafe in U-Bet."

"A cafe? Darlin', I said there isn't a building left at U-Bet."

◆ ◆ ◆

Lynda was trying to clean her teeth with her tongue when Brady sauntered back to the truck and pulled himself up on the passenger's side. Capt. Patch opted to stay in the back and bark at a large cat that ignored him with a yawn as Lynda maneuvered out of the gravel parking lot.

"Brady, I told you I'd cover expenses on this trip."

"You got it."

"Then why did you pay for our rooms, I mean, my room and our meals?"

"I didn't."

"But I didn't give you any money."

"LaVerne and me traded off. I patched the roof, and we get the cabin and a meal. There's no reason spendin' your money until we have to."

He could be flat broke for years and never know it. It's like hav-
ing a whole social security system built right into relationships.

The clouds hung low almost at the treetops as they wound
their way down the two lanes of narrow blacktop separated by
an unsteady yellow line and cavernous potholes. They were
slicing through forests of pine, fir, aspen, and cedar. The air was
still, and the trees, most of which leaned south, swayed only
from the wind of a passing vehicle. Each plant, shrub, and tree
seemed to be waiting for a distant command to drop the pre-
tense of autumn and yield to winter.

Lord, sometimes it seems as if I'm like these trees—waiting for
something to happen. But I'm not sure what I'm waiting for. I just
have a real strong feeling I'll know it when I see it.

Wide spots in the road, some not large enough to earn the
title town, with names like Emigrant, Grey Owl, Pray, Mill
Creek, Paradise, Mallard's Rest, and Pine Creek, led them
down the Yellowstone River, past Wineglass Mountain and
into Livingston. Each bleached house and deteriorating store
bore traces of frontier life like faded memories.

They rejoined the twentieth century when they turned east
on Interstate 90, but Brady had her abandon the traffic at
Mission Station. They aimed east on the Old Stage Road. On
portions of it the broken blacktop was the only sign of the
modern era.

Just north of Big Timber, originally named for some of the
state's largest cottonwood trees—now deceased—they turned
north and resumed their journey through ranch land on the eastern slope of the Crazy Mountains, up the grade of the Sweet
Grass Creek drainage, and over into Musselshell River country.
The pickup whined, Capt. Patch slept, and Brady scrunched
down in the seat with his hat pulled almost low enough to keep
Lynda from seeing him constantly checking his rearview mirror.

"Stoner, you're unreasonably suspicious. Quit looking out
that mirror. It's driving me zonkers."

"Just keepin' an eye on our blind side."

"Blind? I can see fifty miles ahead of us and fifty miles behind us, and there isn't another car on the road. There is no blind side. Brady, are you in some kind of trouble you haven't told me about?"

"Darlin', the only trouble I ever have is when you come out to visit me. Let's talk about Jesse James's gold."

She glanced over at him, trying to read his eyes. "Are we changing the subject?"

"We're gettin' down to business. That final chapter is why you came out here, right?"

"It's one of the reasons." She raised her eyebrows but didn't think he noticed. *I really came out here to see if I've been wasting my life yearning for a certain cowboy.*

She glanced toward the rearview mirror, ran her fingers through her hair, and wondered if she should put a little more Autumn Rose Blush on her lips.

"Do you think there could be any such gold buried out here?" she asked.

"Nope."

"Why not?"

"First, forty tons of gold is a lot of weight to transport by steamer under cover. There are thousands of caves in Missouri. Why not use one of them instead? It would be easier to rearm the Confederacy from Missouri than . . . say, Ft. Benton.

"Second, there's nothing I ever read about the James brothers that would convince me they ever stole that much money or were so noble as not to spend it on themselves. It doesn't make sense to hoard it away with a very real possibility of losing it all.

"Frank James lived to be seventy years old and was so hard up he used to sell tours of his Missouri farm for fifty cents a person. That would have been a real good time to slip up to Montana on the train and supplement his income with that gold."

"But McCall's search for the gold in 1972 does make a fascinating story," Lynda declared. "Some folks will believe it even if we call it a novel."

"Someone already believes it."

"You mean, whoever took the final chapter?"

"Yeah. I can't believe someone in your office walked off with it. Did they think no one would notice?"

"Sometimes projects lay around the office for a few weeks. The other chapters have been gathering dust for over a month. They could have assumed they had some time. But this was a hurry-up deal once we had the final chapter."

The cab of the truck felt stuffy to Lynda, and she thought about rolling her window down an inch or two and leaving the heater on. She wiped her forehead with the palm of her hand but left the window alone.

Brady sat up and stretched out his left arm. "What are you going to do when you find someone with the chapter? I mean, what if your guy Drew is up the road with those papers in his hands?"

"I'll tell him to give them back."

"Will you fire him?"

"I don't hire or fire anyone, but stealing company documents seems to be cause for dismissal."

"What if we run across him, and he refuses to surrender the chapter?"

"Then," Lynda said with a grin, "I'll just have you beat him to a pulp."

"One-armed?"

"Oh, well, I'll have Capt. Patch bite him or something. I don't know. I guess I'd just get the county sheriff to do his work."

"What county are we in?"

"How would I know?"

His brown eyes seemed to narrow with each question.

"Then you wouldn't know where the sheriff was, would you?"

"Good grief, Stoner, that's why you're along. You do something for the big bucks I'm paying you as a guide, don't you?"

"You mean I'm gettin' paid?" Brady laughed.

"Sure. The same wages as last year. All expenses paid and one hundred dollars, plus a bonus if we recover the final chapter."

"Wow, big bucks. Maybe I can buy that thousand-acre ranch in Wyomin' this year after all!"

"Dream on." Lynda studied the horizon and was surprised to see buildings pushing their way out of the prairie. "Hey, what's this place up here? This looks like a real town."

"You are approaching Harlowton, Montana, county seat of Wheatland County, located on the banks of the famous Musselshell River. It's the home of one thousand nice folks and six old grouches."

"What?"

"That's what the sign on the east edge of town says."

"Should we try for something to eat?" she asked.

"Are you hungry? We've still got plenty of that chicken-fried steak, or we could just push on."

"Come on, Stoner, there must be some waitress with an awesome smile who's a real sweetheart in this town."

"I really haven't spent much time out here. It's a little too far east."

"I thought you said you knew some folks up this way."

"Maybe up at Judith Gap. Actually I don't think I know a soul in Harlowton."

"I want a Diet Coke. Let's stop at the mini-mart."

"Think I'll pass. You need any help?"

"No. . . . You sure you don't want me to bring you something?"

"Your sweet smile and alluring perfume is all I'll ever need."

You better need more than that someday, Stoner.

He stayed with his head resting on the back of the pickup seat as she parked the rig and entered the store.

Returning with a small brown sack of goodies, Lynda popped back into the truck.

"Well, Capt. Patch, I'm glad someone's happy to see me."

Stoner never lifted his hat or his head. "You weren't gone all that long. You didn't give me time to miss you."

"The guy who runs this mini-mart says he knows you. He recognized the Captain."

"Oh, who's that?" Brady yawned.

"His name tag read Domingo. But I don't know if that's his first or last name."

"He works here?" Brady sat up, adjusted his hat, and squared his chin. "I thought he still lived in Lewistown."

"He moved last summer. Do you want to go in and say hello?"

"Not hardly. Last time I saw Domingo, he was threatenin' to shoot me."

"Oh? Well, he did sound anxious for us to get out of town."

"I bet. It's a long story."

She started the truck and eased it out of the parking lot. "He wanted to know if you were going to stop by and see Buster."

"Buster lives here in town? No wonder Domingo's here."

"Who's Buster?"

"He didn't tell you?"

"No. Domingo didn't seem like a very happy fellow. His tattoos were kind of . . . demonic."

"You should see the one on his back."

"Eh, no thanks. What's with you and him?" she quizzed.

"Take 191 to the east, and then it will swing north. We're crossing Highway 12. You know, you can take that road right into Idaho."

"I want to know about Buster. Who is he, and why are you avoiding Domingo like a swamp?" she pressed.

"There's the turn." He pointed.

A honking horn almost brought Brady right up to the top of the cab. He whipped around to stare out the back window.

"It's a big orange van. They seem to be honking at us."

"Can you still see the mini-mart back there?"

"No."

"Okay, then pull over."

"It's pulling in behind us. I think there's a lady driving it."

"Yeah, I'll go talk to her. You stay here. There's no reason for you to have to get out in the cold."

"Who is it?"

"Buster."

"Her name's Buster?"

"Yeah."

After commanding Capt. Patch to stay put, he crawled out of the pickup and slammed the door.

Lynda rolled down the window and strained to hear the conversation. The air was bitter cold. The initial greeting was fuzzy, but she heard a woman with a slurred accent. "Junior misses you, Brady Stoner!"

"He got the present I sent, didn't he?"

"Yes, but it's not the same."

Junior? What do you mean, junior? A kid? Brady has a kid? Why's he sending this lady a present for her kid? Why is she called Buster?

Austin felt her face flush red and hot even as she opened the door and the cold air flooded around her. The whole scene felt strange, as if she had been watching a movie and suddenly stepped into the scene. Stomping back toward the van, she halted as Brady raised his hand.

"Maybe you should wait in the car!"

Austin continued to approach. "What's going on here?"

"Is that her?" the woman almost shouted. "Don't you fall for his lies! All these rodeo bums are liars and deceivers! Ever' last one of them!"

"Brady?"

"Darlin', I'll be right there and explain it all," Brady called. "Wait in the car. . . . Please."

"I will do nothing of the kind."

The brown-skinned woman implored Brady. "You're going to come by and see little Brady, aren't you?"

"Buster, you know I won't do that. We've gone all through that before."

"He's just a four-year-old boy."

"And this is almost a five-year-old lie. Goodbye, Buster. Don't follow us anymore, and don't send any more letters to my folks. If they get one more note from you, there will be no more presents. Do you understand?"

Buster glared at Lynda. "Well, what are you starin' at? You mess around and start havin' kids, you won't look any better than this either!"

"I . . . eh," Lynda stammered.

"Come on, darlin'. Time to go." He took her by the arm and ushered her back to the pickup.

"We'll come visit you one of these days, Brady Stoner! Me and little Brady will come and visit you!"

"Brady," Lynda began, "what's this woman—"

"She's drunk."

"That's obvious."

"Get in the truck and drive."

"What?"

"If Domingo catches us here, we're in lots of trouble."

"Domingo? What's he got to do with this?"

"Then I'll drive!" Brady jumped into the pickup and pulled out into the highway just as Austin barely closed her door.

"Just when do I get an explanation for all of this?" she demanded.

He rubbed his forehead and shook his head. "I don't suppose you want to let it slide."

"No way."

"It really is a long story."

"I've got lots of time."

The countryside north of Harlowton and the Musselshell River spread in unbroken rangeland. The grass was buckskin brown, and the rolling hills sported crops of rocks and occasional barbed wire fences. About three miles out of town the road turned north, straight as a string.

Just when I think I know everything about him, it seems like I know nothing! Lord, maybe everything is a big game with him. Maybe he's been leading me on for a whole year. He could be married for all I really know, and . . . no, that's not fair. Girl, you panic too easily. Let him explain.

"Well, Stoner, I'm waiting."

"Okay. Here's a little tale about Brady Stoner you might not have heard before."

"Do you have a lot more of these secrets?"

"Not too many. And you?"

"A few. But it's your turn."

"About five years ago, I was competing at a rodeo in Lewistown."

"How far away is that?"

"About an hour on up the road. Anyway, my truck broke down, and I needed to get to Sheridan, Wyoming, for another afternoon rodeo the next day. Billy Atherton said I could hitch a ride with him, but he wasn't leavin' until daylight. Well, that worked for me, so I tagged along with Billy. Only he decided to go visit with a lady friend on the outskirts of town."

"Buster?"

"Exactly. I don't aim to be bargin' in on nothin', so I sleep out in the driveway in his rig while he and Buster spend some time, eh, visitin'. The next day we reach Sheridan, and both of us cover our mounts and win a little money. While I'm hangin' around the rodeo tryin' to find someone who's drivin' back north, Billy goes out and gets soused and runs head-on into a semi."

"An eighteen-wheeler?"

"Yep. I hear about it and rush up to the hospital. He tells me to take what's left of his winnin's up to Buster, that he figures he's fumed. Within an hour he's dead."

"That's horrible."

"Oh, but the complications get worse."

"When I finally reach Buster's place, Domingo's there rantin' and ravin'. I guess he was an ex-boyfriend that she couldn't seem to shake off. He thinks she's been cheatin' on him by bein' with me. He's wavin' a shotgun and threatenin' to shoot me if I don't leave immediately."

"Well, I'm only too glad to leave, but I tell her about Billy and leave the money. She starts bawlin', and Domingo is ready to kill me because he figures she's cryin' over me."

"What happened after that?"

"Well, I make up my mind that I won't rodeo in Lewistown anymore. I figure everything's behind me, until about nine months later when my folks get a letter announcing the birth of their grandson."

"What?"

"Buster had a kid, and I guess it was Billy's. I don't know about that. She's not always thinking clear. So Domingo is hoppin' mad at me for not supporting Buster in her pregnancy."

"What did your parents say?"

"They probably died a thousand times until I could explain to them what really happened."

"Why in the world didn't she name the kid Billy instead of Brady?"

He scratched the back of his neck and took a deep breath. "Well, she told me one time that she didn't want to name the kid after someone who's dead. It would be unlucky. And since she thought I was the luckiest one around, she named him Brady."

"Do you think the kid thinks you're his father?"

"I'm not sure what the little guy thinks. I've never seen him. I was glad he wasn't in the rig with Buster just now. I don't want to hurt the boy, and I don't want to hurt Buster, but I don't want to play this game."

"What about the presents?"

"I made a deal with her a few years back. I would send the boy presents on his birthday and Christmas if she would just let the whole matter drop."

"So Domingo still thinks you're the one who ruined his relationship with Buster."

"I guess. Anyway, she gets to drinkin' and starts believin' the whole story, so once a year I'll get a teary-eyed call about why don't I ever come and see little Brady. If I had known they were in Harlowton, I would have insisted we drive straight through. I should have never gotten involved in the first place. It's just that with Billy dyin' like that, I felt obliged to do somethin'. Anyway . . . that's the way it is."

"Why didn't you ever tell me that story before?"

"Would you tell someone a story like that if you didn't have to?"

"I guess not. So you figure Domingo's the type to chase us down?"

"You saw him. He's about as crazy as she is."

"Could he be the one who let the air out of your tires?"

"I don't think so. He's not smart enough to follow me through six states. Besides, he has a job. He'd be more likely to slash the tires than just deflate them. He once took on the entire sheriff's department of Musselshell County."

"Are they married now?"

"Not that I know of."

"Do they live together?"

"I don't think so. She always says she can't stand him."

"I can't believe we could be out here, a zillion miles from nowhere, and run into someone who hates you so."

Brady glanced in the rearview mirror and then back ahead of them.

"Yeah, isn't life great on the Western frontier?"

She stared out at the narrow paved road. "Brady, how come whenever I'm with you, life seems to whiz by like it's on fast forward?"

"I've been wonderin' the same thing about you."

"Me?"

"Yeah. When you called me last week and said you were comin' out and wanted me to take you to U-bet, Montana, I figured I was in for a wild ride. Kind of like a chemical reaction, isn't it?"

"What do you mean?"

"By themselves the elements are fairly stable, but when mixed together, the whole works boils over. We seem to be just like that."

"Is that bad?"

"If I'm goin' to get in trouble, I can't think of anyone I'd rather be with than some award-winnin' New York editor."

"Yeah, thanks, I think. But if it's all right with you, I'd just as soon avoid trouble. I keep thinking I'm going to call the office, and they'll tell me they found that final chapter stuck in a file box somewhere."

"Don't let 'em find it for a few days. There's some pretty country up here I've been plannin' on showin' you. Have you ever been up to Glacier Park?"

"During the night? Or were you planning on a day trip?"

"You're never going to forgive me for Yellowstone, are you?"

"Nope. Never."

"Good."

"Why?"

"Because never forgivin' sounds like you plan on bein' around for a long time. Has this been a good year for us?"

"Are you getting serious, Stoner?" Austin suddenly realized she was slouching in the seat. She sat up and tried to brush her brown hair behind her ears. *I probably need more perfume.*

"Yep. A year ago we said let's be good friends. Just really good friends. And I was wonderin', has it worked?"

"I didn't think we'd get around to this conversation for a few more days," she admitted.

"You have your little speech ready, don't you?"

"No speech this time, Stoner. But I've got to tell you I certainly enjoyed all the calls, cards, letters, and your visit to New York, and our time at Jackson Hole last fall. Is that what you mean?"

"I think so." Brady turned off the blacktop onto a narrow gravel road stretching west.

"How have you enjoyed the year, cowboy?"

"Well . . ." He cleared his throat and shoved his black cowboy hat to the back of his head. "To tell you the truth . . ."

"Yes?"

"Dad gum it . . . Listen, there were some nights that I surely wished I could give you a hug and smell some of that pretty perfume. And some nights, I must confess, I thought about more than a hug. You know what I mean?"

Suddenly the cab grew quiet. Lynda felt like she wanted to shout, cry, whisper, and sigh all at once.

"Yeah, I know," she finally replied. "I have some nights when I can't decide if we were really smart or really stupid for leaving things this way."

"Lynda Dawn, what choice do we have? I can't give this up, and you can't give up New York."

"Yeah, it always gives me a headache when I think about it

too much. I thought about quitting Atlantic-Hampton and moving to Jackson or Scottsdale or Sun Valley and doing some free lancing back when I thought being a Harrison heir might bring in the big bucks. I must have thought about it night after night for months."

"I know what you mean."

"You do?"

"Yeah, I have to admit I actually thought about quittin' the circuit and movin' to New York City."

"You did?"

"Yep."

"You thought about that every night for months?"

"Not exactly." He cracked a full-toothed smile. "I thought about it for about thirty seconds one time. Lynda Dawn, I just don't know anything else except roaming around the West. New York City is like puttin' a wild animal in a cage. I'd just mope around until I died of lonesomeness. But you belong back there. You tackled the establishment with your high moral values and faith, and you whipped it, girl. I think the Lord needs you in New York."

"You do?"

"Yep. If you weren't there, who would put the moral squeeze on Atlantic-Hampton?"

"Well, Brady Stoner, I guess we just have a hopelessly frustrating relationship."

"Yeah, isn't it fun?"

"Fun? That's not exactly the term . . ." She stared out at the bleak rangeland. They had come to a bouncing stop next to two broken-down log buildings. "What is this? Do you know where we are?"

"U-Bet."

"Is this a joke?"

"Nope. A-Joke is up the road. This is U-Bet."

"What is U-Bet? Stoner, there's nothing here!"

They got out of the truck and walked over to the ruins.

"That's what I've been telling you for a week."

"But when you said nothing, I didn't think you meant absolutely nothing. I thought you meant . . . you know . . . mostly nothing." There was little vegetation to rustle in the wind, but the cold breeze caused her to shiver.

"Look, as far as I know, a pioneer family named Barrows came out here and homesteaded or built a little stage stop, a store and cafe. Anyway, when Mr. Barrows went to apply for post office status, the commissioner asked if he had a name for his town, and he said, "You bet." And the postal service decided that was a good enough name. But when the branch train went through between Harlowton and Lewistown, ever'thing here closed up."

"Then how in the world can Fed. Ex. send something out here?"

"Aren't they wonderful? You've seen those commercials, haven't you?"

"I'm serious, Stoner."

"I reckon they take it to the nearest community or something like that."

"Is that Judith Gap? I think the zip code was for a place called Judith Gap."

"We drove right through Judith Gap! Why didn't you tell me that's where we were headed?"

"We didn't go through any towns, did we?"

"I didn't say towns. Didn't you remember that clump of trees sittin' off by themselves?"

"With the broken-down corral?"

"Behind those trees is the Judith Gap post office."

"Let's go back and ask where Mr. Mendoza lives."

"You want to drive? My arm's hurtin' a little."

"Sure. Where do I turn around?"

"On Main Street."

"Main Street? Stoner, there're no streets here at all. We are parked in the middle of someone's cow pasture!"

"Oh, you noticed? Well, the highway's back in that direction."

When Lynda Austin backed the Dodge pickup between the two shells of broken buildings, the back tires spun in something slick. Suddenly there was a loud backfire, and she felt the steering wheel grab to the left. She stepped on the accelerator, and another backfire made the whole rig lunge even more severely to the left. Brady screamed something.

I can drive this truck without your coaching, Stoner!

Trying to hit the brakes, she instead slammed down the accelerator. The truck spun half a circle, and two more blasts lowered the truck half a foot. Brady jerked open her door and wrenched her to the ground.

"Stay down! Someone's shooting at us! Get away from the truck! If they hit the gas tank, it will explode like a bomb!"

"Shooting? It's just a backfire!"

Brady's right hand clutched the front of her jeans at the belt buckle, and he dragged her along the ground.

"Brady, what are you doing?"

"Savin' your life, darlin'."

"Brady Stoner, turn me loose. You're hurting me! My face is in the dirt. Stoner!" she screamed.

He continued dragging her, kicking and punching, through the dirt and dried tumbleweeds. Then he shoved her into the crumbled decaying logs of one of the buildings.

"Lynda Dawn, someone's shooting at us. We've got to stay in here."

Spitting the dirt out of her mouth, she could tell her voice was halfway between a cry of fear and a scream of anger. "Brady Stoner, you hurt me! And you scared me! You're getting paranoid. No one is—"

He huddled down beside her and took her head in both

hands, forcing her to look at the pickup. "Backfires don't shoot holes in tires."

"Oh . . . oh . . . someone *is* shooting at us," she sobbed.

"It's okay, darlin'. We're safe in here."

"All four tires? How did they hit all four? Are we surrounded?"

"Nope. They're out near the highway. You turned the rig around and gave them a better target."

"Who's shooting at us? Who is it? We haven't done anything!"

"I don't know. I can barely see the road from here. I can't even see a rig out there. They must have a high-powered scope. I've got to get to the truck and grab my carbine."

"A gun? Since when did you start carrying a gun in your truck?"

"I always have a gun in my truck. Just a little 30-30 model '94. Pre-1964, of course."

Stoner sprinted to the truck and returned carrying a lever-action carbine and the carton with the leftover lunch. Capt. Patch followed behind, head down and tail dragging the dirt, as if he had gone through this before.

"Do you think they're trying to kill us?"

"Nope. If they wanted to do that, we'd be dead by now."

"Is it Domingo?"

"Maybe. But he's the type who would try to shoot *us*, not the tires."

"Then who could it be?"

"I don't know, darlin'; I don't know. It could be whoever's been following me for a week or the guy named Mendoza who doesn't want visitors or just the guy who operates this ranch and figures we're trespassing."

"I thought you knew all the ranchers up here."

"Not me, Lynda Dawn. I've rodeod all over Montana, but I haven't cowboyed up here in this ranch country."

"What are we going to do?"

"We'd better wait back here and see if they try something else."

"You mean just squat here in the dirt?"

"I'm thinkin' about eatin' some of your chicken-fried steak and cold mashed potatoes and gravy."

"That sounds disgusting."

"Thank you."

"How can you possibly be hungry when someone's just taken a shot at you?"

"I eat when I'm nervous, don't you?"

"Not that stuff."

Sitting cross-legged under the shelter of the broken wall of the old log building, Stoner laid the carbine across his lap and gazed out at the silent, rolling rangeland and at the black-and-silver pickup hunkered on its rims. Lynda was on her hands and knees behind him, peeking out over his shoulder.

"You treated me roughly when you pulled me out of the truck."

"I'm surely sorry, darlin'. I panicked thinkin' about one of those bullets ricocheting into the gas tank. I didn't think I had time to persuade you with fancy words." He sliced through the chicken-fried steak with his pocket knife. "It truly grieves me to know I inflicted pain on you."

"It's all right, really. I understand now. I just felt helpless and scared."

Still on her hands and knees, she glanced down at the now-lumpy mass of white gravy. "I can't believe you just had someone shoot the tires off your truck, and all you're going to do is sit and eat cold gravy."

"It is kind of pitiful, ain't it? But I just couldn't think of any-way to warm it up in this container."

"I'm not having fun, Stoner. I think I'm ready to go home. Maybe I'm better off just watching this kind of stuff on TV."

Brady wiped some gravy off his mouth with the back of his coat sleeve and gave her a slightly greasy kiss on the neck. "Don't worry. I don't think they're goin' to shoot anymore. We don't have any more tires."

She resisted the strong urge to wipe the gravied kiss off her neck. "What are we going to do now?"

"We sure aren't goin' to drive that truck until it has new tires."

"So we're just going to sit here and freeze to death? You've got to do something besides eat."

"I am doin' somethin' besides eat."

"What?"

"I'm surmisin'."

"What do you mean, surmising?"

"Just tryin' to figure out why we're bein' shot at."

"Is it safe to go back over to the truck?"

"Yep."

"I want to clean up a little. I'm not used to being dragged through the dirt."

"It wears well on you, Lynda Dawn."

"You mean it covers up some of my obvious flaws?"

"Nope. I mean you're such a pretty woman that dirt can't detract from your beauty."

"Why is it I get the distinct feeling that you've used that line before? But no matter how ravishing I look, I don't intend to let the dirt become a permanent feature."

Inside the cab of the truck, Lynda cleaned the smudges off her face with an unused cleansing towelette retrieved from an old fried chicken sack found under the seat. She combed her hair and put on fresh lipstick. While Brady wasn't looking, she dug through her purse for a small orange glass bottle of a fragrance she had ordered from Dodge City called Drover's Delite. She splashed it in appropriate places and studied herself in the mirror.

Lord, why am I not surprised at all of this? It's like I expected it to happen. Sometimes it feels like every ounce of adventure and excitement is squeezed out of my whole year in New York and poured in abundance into the few days I have with Brady. Does he ever have a boring day?

She glanced out where he sat. All six feet of him was scrunched cross-legged under a decaying log building. His eyes were hard to see; the cowboy hat was pulled low. A carbine lay across his folded legs. A dog with a patch over one eye sat loyally beside him waiting for a kind word or a scrap of meat. Cautiously surveying the horizon, Brady ate his cold dinner with the blade of his knife.

It could be 1895—except for the Styrofoam box. He's like a man out of his time. He absolutely loves it. I guess, Lord, I sort of love it too—if people would stop shooting at us.

She hurried back and scooted in next to him.

"Are you finished surmising?"

"For the moment."

"Well? What did you decide we should do next?"

"I figured I'd wait here, and you go out on the highway and flag a ride."

"Me? I'm not going out there!"

"I'm busy eatin' supper. And there you are all prettied up and smellin' sweeter than new-mown hay. You surely don't want me to interrupt my meal, do you?"

"Scoot over, Stoner. If I remember, that's supposed to be *my* supper."

New-mown hay? Is that good? Maybe he's trying to tell me he doesn't like it.

She chewed slowly on a grisly bite of the leftover meat, but she refused to even look at the potatoes and gravy.

Fifteen minutes later, the bones in her fingers ached with pain from the cold, and she could tell that every joint in her body was getting stiff. For the first time since she was twelve years old at a Girl Scout camp in the upper peninsula of Michigan, she thought about freezing to death. "Tell me again why we're still sitting out here?"

"I don't want to go hiking up the road and find someone waiting for us. I wanted to give them plenty of time to get out of the country."

"It's going to get dark soon."

"We better traipse out to the road and get a ride to town."

"What town?"

"Depends on which way folks are drivin'. Are you through eatin'?"

"I think I might be chewing this bite for the next week."

They locked up the truck, which now resembled a ship slowly sinking in a dark brown dirt sea, and started walking toward the road.

"How are we going to get a ride if you're carrying that rifle."

"It's a carbine. Rifle barrels are longer."

"Whatever. I still don't think anyone would pick up someone with a gun."

"I'm not about to hike up there without it after bein' shot at."

"You said they were aiming at the tires, not us."

"But I don't know about next time. I'll keep it out of sight. Cover it with my coat or something."

"And I say we'll never get a ride. You know what's really strange, Brady Stoner? I live in New York City where there's all that crime and violence and mugging and murder. But I never seem to be in danger until I come out here."

"That's because we're still on the frontier."

"I read that the frontier was tamed a hundred years ago."

"You're a book editor. Surely you don't believe everything printed in a book, do you?"

"I think you might romanticize the frontier."

"All right, Miss Award-Winning Editor, you've made

several jaunts into the less populated places in the Western frontier. From your firsthand observation, is the West still wild?"

"Empty . . . and yet wild. Okay, maybe there still is a faint trace of the old frontier left."

"Life out here challenges the mind, the body, and the spirit. Maybe that's why I can't ever give it up."

They reached the roadway and looked both directions. There was not a vehicle in sight. Brady hiked over to a short wooden guardrail over a culvert and sat down.

"Come on, we might as well wait over here." He waved his arm, and she joined him, their backs toward the west and the wind. Capt. Patch scampered down to explore the wash. As they sat side by side, Brady slipped his arm around her waist and pulled her close. The strength of his arm and blockage of the wind made her feel warmer.

"Look at this country, Lynda Dawn. In a way it reminds me of the Arizona Strip."

"But that was desert down there. We're freezing to death up here. Nothing's the same at all."

"Other than that, I mean. They're both so empty. Look down that perfectly straight road to the north, and what do you see?"

"Nothing."

"Yeah, no cars, no houses, no horses, no fences, no telephone poles, no trees. Nothing. Just rolling rangeland, distant mountains, heavy gray clouds, and a ribbon of asphalt."

"And railroad tracks."

"The Burlington Northern. Look to the south, and what do you see? Same thing, right?"

"Yeah. Plus a pair of headlights!"

Brady jerked around. "All right! He's headed north. That means Lewistown. I know a guy there that runs a service station."

"Stay here," she offered. "I'll go thumb us a ride."

"You? Have you done this before?" he asked.

"No. But I saw this movie the other day, and it's always the woman who can get them to stop."

"I don't think it's a good—"

"Wait here, Stoner, and watch me."

"All right, Lynda Dawn, but be careful!"

The oncoming older model green pickup with Oregon license plates whizzed past them.

"It didn't work, Lynda Dawn!" Stoner yelled from the other side of the road.

"Just wait . . . look!"

Austin pointed north and watched the brake lights flash on the pickup. Suddenly the truck began to back toward them.

The truck rumbled up to Lynda, separating her from Brady. The passenger's window rolled down revealing two men in their thirties, both clean-shaven and light-complected.

"You need a lift?" the blond-headed one closest to her asked. His eyes roamed from her hat to her belt.

"Yes. Are you going into Lewistown?"

"We are now!" the driver responded. "Unless you'd like to go with us to Calgary."

"No. Lewistown is just great! We need a ride. Our rig had a little, eh, trouble with the tires."

"That guy and the dog are with you?" the blond asked.

"Yes. Do you have room?"

"Eh . . . sure." The driver rolled down his window and shouted, "Hop in the back, buddy!"

"But there's room for you up here." The blond slipped out of the rig and motioned for Lynda to scoot across into the middle of the seat. She looked back for some assurance from

Brady, but he was busy loading Capt. Patch and trying to climb into the truck without revealing the carbine.

Immediately when she reached the center of the truck seat, the blond man jumped back in and slammed the door. As he did so, he scooted close, his hips and legs touching hers.

Lord, this is not working. I want out of here, and I want out now!

The truck roared back onto the highway and hurled northward.

"Is that your old man back there?" the driver asked.

"No, actually he's a . . . he's my fiancé," she lied.

Lord, forgive me, but this is not good.

"Can't be much, I say, eh, Danny? What without taking better care of such a pretty lady. What kind of guy would strand a proper lady like yourself out here in the wilderness and then force you to flag down a ride for him?"

"Actually it was—"

"You know," the blond leaned closer toward her until his mouth was only an inch from her ear, "if you like to be better taken care of, that could easily be arranged." She could feel his arm start to slip around the back of her shoulders.

"I think you better stop this rig right now!" Her voice cracked with panic.

"We'll do nothing of the sort," the blond one sneered. "Why, I've got charms you haven't even dreamed of. We aren't stopping, eh, Danny?"

"Actually," the driver said, suddenly slamming on the brakes and pulling over, "it's not a bad idea."

"What are you doing?" the blond one yelled. "We ought to have a little fun with her before we stop!"

"It's not a question of morals, Peter. It's much more pragmatic."

"What do you mean?"

"There's a rifle pointed our way, and I believe it's aimed at your head."

Peter and Lynda jerked around to look in the back of the truck where Brady sat, leaning against the tailgate, pointing the Winchester at the blond man's head. The hammer was cocked back, and Brady's finger was tight on the trigger. He smiled and nodded his head at them.

"Actually it's only a carbine, pre-'64, of course," Lynda remarked as the driver crawled out of the rig with his hands in the air. She scooted out behind him. Brady and Capt. Patch jumped out of the truck. The driver jumped back in and spun the rig's wheels in the gravel trying to get back onto the road.

"So much for that ride."

"Lynda Dawn, it was stupid. I should have never let you . . . I mean . . ."

"It was my dumb idea. How come things that look so smart and easy in the movies are so difficult and dumb in real life? I was one happy lady to look back and see that gun pointed at Peter."

"Oh, so it's Peter, is it? You mean you had time to get acquainted?"

"They did offer me a ride to Calgary. I've never been to Calgary."

"Come on, let's walk north. There's got to be someone else out here somewhere."

They hiked north. The cold breeze drifted against their left sides and caused them to turn up their collars and lean into the wind. Capt. Patch scampered in delight ahead of them. Lynda could tell it was about time the sun would be setting, if they could have seen the sun.

"You know what's strange, Lynda Dawn? I don't know what adventure we're a part of. Are we in this mess because of something I've done? Or something you've done? Or is it something someone thinks we might do?"

"If it has to do with me, then maybe we're on the right track searching for McCall's chapter. Only I can't figure who in the world would know where I am. I mean, if I disappeared right now, no one on earth, besides you, knows where I am."

"That's a cheery thought." Brady looked back south. "Here comes someone. This time they have to take us at face value. Man, dog, carbine, and good-lookin' babe."

The trio huddled like passengers at a bus stop as the small white van slowed down in the middle of the road.

"Hey, it's Fed. Ex. They actually do come out here!" she exclaimed.

A young man with a navy blue jacket leaned over and rolled down the window on the passenger side.

"Sorry, folks, I can't give you a ride, or I'd lose my job. Can I take a message or anything?"

"I had a little trouble with my truck and am going to need some tires."

"Where are you parked? Maybe I can send someone back to help."

"The rig's at U-Bet. It's off the road a ways."

"There's nothing back there. I went in the other day lookin' for a customer for a delivery."

"Mendoza?" Austin asked.

The driver whistled in amazement. "I can't discuss any deliveries. Sorry."

"We're looking for a Mr. Mendoza. Do you know where he lives?"

"I have no idea in the world. But all I can say is that if you're serious about it, you might ask the postmaster at Judith Gap. If it weren't for him, I'd still be toting that package myself."

"Thanks."

"Now how can I help?"

"You headed to Lewistown?"

"Yep."

"Does One-Eye Gillette still run the station next to the city park?"

"Yep."

"Tell him that if Brady Stoner hasn't made it in by closin' time, he should bring his truck and four sixteen-inch tires to U-Bet tonight."

"Four tires? You mean all four blew out?"

"Yeah, it was really somethin'."

"I guess so! That must have sounded like gunfire. Well, I'll tell One-Eye."

"Thanks."

The van started forward, then backed up.

"Say, I've got some coffee left in my Thermos. You're welcome to it. You could just leave the jug at One-Eye's."

"I think we'll take you up on that. Thanks, mister."

It was half dark, and Lynda watched the taillights of the delivery van disappear as Brady poured her a lid of steaming coffee.

"So there's no Mendoza around here."

Brady took a sip of coffee and then handed it to Austin. "But the postmaster at Judith Gap knows something. It gives us something to do tomorrow."

"If we make it until tomorrow." The steam warmed her nose and eyes, causing both to water.

"Hey, this is turning into a freeway. Look! Another rig's coming up."

"Are they pulling a trailer?"

"It looks like a four-horse slant."

"A what?"

"They're slowin' down. . . . Come on, darlin'."

A woman with windblown, graying hair, leathery face, and deep wrinkles at the corners of her eyes and wearing a blanket-lined gray coat coasted up to them. In the cab with her were five children ranging from infant seat to about age ten. All seemed to be whining at once.

"You folks are goin' to freeze to death out here!" she called out.

"We had a little trouble with our rig and need a ride into Lewistown."

The baby started to cry, and the two biggest children seemed bent on pounding each other in the head. The lady hollered above the noise, "Climb on in. Scoot over, kids—we've got company! Kids, keep it down!"

"Eh, what do you have in the trailer?"

"Just Hulk and Bandit."

"We could just camp at the back of the trailer," Brady suggested.

"Oh, no need for that." The woman tried to settle the baby. "Well, maybe you're right. I'll come close the tailgate as soon as little Ty settles down."

◆ ◆ ◆

Bandit turned out to be a paint mustang who didn't like being trailered. Hulk was a Palomino who did not like Bandit. But both distrusted anyone with a dog.

"Are we going to have to stand up the whole way?" Lynda asked.

"You wouldn't want to sit down in this trailer—trust me. Think of it as a subway."

"If those horses get loose, will they kick us?"

"Yep."

"Any chance of them getting loose?"

"Let's hope not."

"That's one woman who has her hands full. How'd she ever watch them and load these two horses in the trailer?"

"She probably had to feed the cows, doctor a sick hog, sew missy a dress, and bake a couple pies for supper."

"Women like that make me feel like a wimp," Austin admitted.

"Women like that make me feel like a wimp," Stoner echoed.

Austin grabbed onto the side of the trailer with her right hand and Stoner's coat pocket with her left. The dark trailer smelled of hay, wet horsehair, and manure. She closed her eyes as they jostled along, trying to imagine a log fire and a cozy lodge.

Suddenly she laughed. It was a laugh that started in her head, but her whole body joined in the chorus until she could feel tiny tears swell and burst at the corners of her eyes and roll joyfully down her cheeks.

"You feelin' all right?" Brady asked.

"Wonderful!" she shouted in such a way that both horses at the front of the trailer jumped in unison.

"What's the matter?"

"I just got to figuring. I landed in Jackson about this time yesterday."

"Yeah?"

"Well, in twenty-four hours I've been stranded at an airport, thrust into a mock fight where I tried to kill someone, drove all night through Yellowstone Park, slept in a crummy little cabin, been insulted by a woman named Buster, got shot at by unknown assailants, had to fend off the advances of a couple of good old boys from Oregon, and am riding in the back of a stinking, freezing horse trailer."

"Are you braggin' or complainin'?"

"Visiting you, Stoner, is like falling into one of the novels I edit," she hollered above the noise.

"They always live happily ever after, don't they?" he shouted back.

"They never live happily ever after!"

"Well, it's a good thing this is real life and not a novel."

"Stoner, there is absolutely nothing about this scene that is real life!" She finally gained some control of her laughter. She looked at him with a straight face. "I love it. I might not live through it . . . but I love it!"

This time they both began to laugh.

FOUR

"Someone shot your what?"

Lynda thought the motel room smelled like carpet cleaner. She doodled on a tiny note pad on the wobbly nightstand. "They shot our tires."

"You mean, with bullets?"

"What did you think, Kelly—with arrows?"

"You could have gotten killed, Lynda Austin!"

"Brady said they were shooting at the tires, not us."

"Somehow I don't find that very comforting. So where's your cowboy this morning?"

"He's still in bed."

There was a long pause. "Oh?"

"In another room, Kelly! You know me better than that." Lynda put the telephone receiver in the other hand and began to fiddle with her dangling, silver-feathered earring. "What's new around the office?"

"The wedding."

"The wedding? What wedding?"

"Who just had his divorce finalized last month?"

"Junior? He actually did it? T. H. Hampton, IV, married Spunky Sasser?"

"They flew to the Dominican Republic over the weekend and got married."

"And now we have to start calling her Mrs. Hampton?"

"Yeah, isn't that wild?"

"I never thought they would actually get married."

"Rumor has it that Spunky insisted on it."

"Good for her."

"You want another surprise?"

"I don't know if I can take any more."

"Well, guess where they're going on their honeymoon?"

"Around the world, I suppose."

"Nope. They're in Montana."

"You've got to be kidding!"

"Wild, huh? Be sure and say hello when you see them."

"Where in Montana?" Lynda demanded.

"I don't have any idea. They want it to be a secret so they won't be bothered."

"This whole thing's unbelievable."

"Yeah. Just like us losing that final chapter of McCall's novel is unbelievable."

"You gals haven't found a trace of it?"

"No, and no one can find a trace of Chance McCall either. He seems to have disappeared. Nina's searched for that chapter for three days. It is not in this office. How are you and Brady doing? Or did you tell him about searching for the chapter yet?"

"Of course I did. That's why I'm here, isn't it?"

"Say, what?" Kelly laughed. "Girl, do you remember who you're talking to? I know why you went out there. What I want to know is, has he proposed to you yet?"

"Kelly!"

"Well, have you proposed to him?"

"Of course not!"

"So far it sounds pretty boring—other than being shot at and stuff. What are the police going to do about that?"

"Brady figures there's not much they can do. Whoever did the shooting was a jillion miles away with long-range scope and all."

"So what are you going to do for an encore? You going out to start a stampede or something?"

"Today we have a lead on where to find out about this guy Mendoza that Drew sent the package to. Is Drew back in the office yet?"

"He called in and said there was a family emergency. He won't be back until next Monday."

"This is all starting to sound a little strange. People and manuscripts vanishing at the same time? Maybe we'll learn something if we find this Mendoza guy."

"What if you're chasing a dead-end?"

"I thought maybe we'd just drive to Helena and check the state archives to see if they had any stories or legends about some hidden Confederate gold. Who knows? Maybe everyone in Montana has heard the story."

"Where will that lead you?"

"To a reservoir."

"And what do you think you'll find there?"

"Somebody who is suspiciously looking for an underwater cave, who knows where our chapter is."

"Keep us informed. You're living out our dreams. You know that, don't you?"

"It's really not all that big a deal."

"Compared to copy editing in a cubbyhole, it is. Listen," Kelly continued, "you had a call from Joaquin Estaban."

"What did he want?"

"When he heard you were in Montana, he said he'd just drive over and visit with you personally."

"I'll call him and see what we can arrange."

"He said not to bother—he'll find you."

"But he doesn't know where we are. I don't know where we

are. Montana's a huge state. You just don't drive over and find someone!"

"Whatever. But he said he'd find you. Anyway, I've got to go. All the phone lights are blinking, and we don't have a receptionist. Be good. Give that cowboy a big hug just for me."

"A hug for you? Dream on, Princeton. Dream on."

◆ ◆ ◆

It was 9:30 A.M. when Austin strolled out into the parking lot of the Covered Wagon Motel and checked on the Dodge pickup. Capt. Patch sprawled in the back, his head cocked sideways, his tongue lolling out.

"Look at that. You got the new tires, didn't you? What time did you get in, boy? Pretty late if Brady's not up yet. If you see Brady, tell him I'm going over there to the Well-Come On In Cafe."

Capt. Patch let out one sharp, crisp bark.

Why do I get the feeling that dog understood everything I said?

Lewistown sat down in a coulee with the rolling range and farmland high on the windswept rim. The road was wide, the traffic sparse, yet the constant frigid breeze seemed to keep the air in a continual fog of fine dust. Lynda jogged across the road and could feel her toes already getting very cold in her boots.

The narrow cafe with a floor that slanted somewhat toward the door held five tables and had six stools at the counter. It was about half-filled, with most of the customers drinking coffee. All the patrons were men, and all wore cowboy hats.

When she walked into the cafe, no one stared at her, and very few even bothered to look her direction. She slipped up to the counter, and a cup of coffee was shoved her direction even before she opened her mouth.

The talk was loud.

And rural.

No one tried to flirt with her. No one made suggestive remarks. No one sat down on either side. They all seemed content to let her alone.

"I lost another steer last weekend. That makes four since July. Dad gum it, boys, if I catch who's doin' it, I'll shoot 'em. . . . I swear I'll shoot 'em!"

"Emmitt Earl, you aren't going to shoot nobody!"

"How can you be so sure?"

"'Cause I seen you shoot, and you couldn't hit a rustler if he was ten feet tall and six feet wide."

The room filled with good-natured laughter. Lynda sipped the steaming hot, deep-flavored coffee and glanced forward at the door of the microwave, which acted as a mirror allowing her to see the others in the room.

"You boys laugh at my shootin', but I can knock the tires off a pickup truck from halfway across the valley."

Lynda sat still and strained to see which canvas-jacketed man was speaking. Her neck was taut, her eyes focused.

"Yes, sir, I believe in shootin' first and askin' questions later. We got this whole county posted. It used to be folks respected No Trespassing signs."

Lynda spun around on the stool and faced the other customers.

"Excuse me, gentlemen." She spoke a little louder than she needed to. "May I ask you a question?"

A gray-haired man with sideburns and mustache pushed back his hat and nodded. "Sure enough, ma'am. Go right ahead."

"I overheard you mention shooting. Well, yesterday a friend and I stopped by the ruins of U-Bet and got the tires shot out of our pickup."

"All four of 'em?"

"Yes. Now I was wondering who would do that. I didn't

think we were trespassing, and we certainly didn't harm any cows. I didn't even see a cow anywhere."

A small, older man with a bent back and a tattered black hat peered at her from behind gold-framed glasses. "What's your name, sweetheart?" His voice was soft and gentle.

"Eh . . . Lynda. Lynda Dawn Austin."

"Well, Lynda Dawn from Austin, there ain't no reason for nobody shootin' at you down at U-Bet."

"No, ma'am, Virgil is right. Ain't no cows down there this time of the year. A purdy, young Texas lady like you shouldn't have to put up with that."

Texas? They think I'm from Texas?

"C. Bob, you better check around down there. If some jerk-water is takin' to shootin' at purdy gals, I say we run his hide out of the country."

"Well . . . I don't want to cause anyone bother. It's just that," she stammered, "I wanted to make sure we weren't doing anything wrong."

"No, ma'am," another interjected. "You just look at this country all you want. We'll find out who did this! You figurin' to buy a ranch or just lookin'?"

"Oh, just lookin' right now." Lynda nodded her head and turned back around to her coffee cup that had been refilled.

It's like being at a family reunion. They don't know exactly who you are, but if you're one of them, they plan on taking care of you. I like that. I just don't have the nerve to tell them I'm from New York. I really do need to live somewhere else, somewhere I don't have to apologize about. Denver maybe. Or Spokane. Santa Fe? Wow, Santa Fe sounds great. Of course, I've never been to Santa Fe. A big, sprawling adobe house with red tile floor and flat roof, a shaded patio with a string of red peppers hanging at the door.

Lynda Austin of Santa Fe, New Mexico.

Lynda Dawn Austin.

Lynda Dawn Austin-Stoner.

Lynda Dawn Stoner.

"Mornin', lonesome lady. You look like you could use some company."

She broke out of her daydream. Brady Stoner sat down beside her, a wide grin on his face. Suddenly a voice bellowed from the back of the room, "Lynda Dawn, is that yahoo botherin' you? We can throw him out on his ear if you want us to!"

She watched Brady's mouth drop open. Then Lynda spun around and grinned. "It's all right, Emmitt Earl. This particular yahoo is with me."

There were several nods of approval around the room, and everyone eased right back into their conversations.

"Whoa!" Brady exclaimed under his breath. "The lady has friends."

"One false move, Stoner, and you're history."

"I guess so. What's goin' on here?"

"I told them about getting shot at, and they became very protective. They said there's been a little cattle rustling around lately. Do things like that really still happen?"

"You better believe it."

"They're going to check around. They thought they might be able to find out who did the shooting."

"No kidding? Man, I can't believe I sleep in one morning, and you find out all of that."

"Capt. Patch said you were out late getting your truck fixed."

"The Captain told you that?"

"Sort of. At least he agreed with me."

"Oh, sure, he blabs everything to the ladies," Brady teased. "We had to drive down there, pull off the tires, bring them back to town and mount them, then haul them back, and slap them on the rig. It must have been around 3:30 this mornin' before I got to my room."

"Well, where's the bill? It must have been pretty expensive."

"Only $250."

"For four truck tires?"

"For the deductible. The insurance company picked up the rest. But let's wait and see if it was your friends or mine who did the shootin'."

"Did you tell One-Eye what we're doing here?"

"I just mentioned we wanted to talk to a man named Mendoza, but he didn't know anyone by that name. At least, not in Lewistown. Did you order breakfast?"

"No, but I'm thinking about having a bowl of oatmeal." She pointed to the chalkboard menu.

"Bloatmeal? Why on earth would you do that?"

"I happen to like oatmeal. What are you having?"

"Biscuits and gravy."

"But you ate all that gravy yesterday," she complained.

"Yep. My daddy always said there are two things in life a man can never get enough of."

"Do I want to know the answer to this?"

"Good gravy and the prayers of the righteous."

"Your daddy is as weird as you are, Stoner."

"One of these days I've got to take you home to meet my folks."

"Today?" She winked.

"No, not today. We've got work to do, woman!"

"Now it comes out. For over a year I've been expecting you to call me 'woman' in that gruff macho voice."

"I was teasin' you, darlin'."

"Stoner, why is it you can continually treat me in such sexist, condescending ways, and somehow instead of feeling insulted, I feel important and special?"

"I've spent my whole life out here on the frontier. Women have always been considered up there pretty close to the angels. The men came out here and tamed a wild and wonderful land. The women came and tamed the men. At least, some of them."

"But that was a hundred years ago."

"For some of us it was only yesterday."

"Sometimes, Brady, it's like we don't even live in the same century."

"Are you sayin' that I need to change the way I treat ya?"

"Stoner . . . if you ever change, it will break my heart. Now hush up and eat that disgusting gravy."

The waitress was sixtyish. Her bright red lipstick seemed to miss her lips by a quarter of an inch.

"Sausage gravy and two beautiful women." He grinned. "It jist don't git no better than this!"

The older woman slid a bowl of oatmeal toward Lynda. "Watch out for this one, honey," she cautioned. "They start lyin' like that when they want you to give 'em somethin' you don't plan on givin' 'em."

"Whew!" Brady sighed. "This is one tough cafe!"

"I might look like some young thing," the waitress teased, "but I've been around."

The gravy was wiped clean by biscuits and bread and the oatmeal half-eaten when Brady sauntered toward the cash register and retrieved a toothpick. When he returned to the counter, he slid onto the stool, facing away from the counter.

"Where do we head today, boss? I do think it might snow."

"I want to go back down to Judith Gap. The Fed. Ex. guy said they knew something about Mendoza."

"Excuse me, boys," Brady broadcasted to everyone left in the cafe. "Me and Miss Lynda Dawn here need to head back down the basin toward Buffalo and Garneil today. We're lookin' for a man named Mendoza. Any of you know where that hombre lives?"

"Mendoza? Is that who you're lookin' fer?" Emmitt Earl drawled.

Lynda spun around on her stool. "Yes, do you know him?"

"Her."

"What?"

"Claudia Mendoza."

"Mendoza's a woman?"

"Well, there ain't none of us claimed to have got too close to her, but at fifty feet, lookin' down the barrel of a Winchester .32 special, she surely looked like a woman."

"Dad blast it, E. E., maybe it was Mrs. Mendoza that shot out missy's tires."

"That could be. She's threatened ever'one in the county."

"Where does she live?" Lynda asked.

"Ah, missy, it ain't hard to find. She moved into the old Double Diamond headquarters house early last summer and generally made a nuisance out of herself. I heard she rented the place for a year, but who knows? I do know that a San Francisco bank owns the property."

"She's from New York City," one of the other men called out from his spot behind a long-ashed cigarette and a mug of coffee. "Can you imagine someone from New York City movin' out here by herself?"

"I once chased my old braymer-cross bull down toward the headquarters, and she was sittin' out there on the porch with a four-point blanket over her head howlin' like a coyote," one man reported.

"She bought two tons of hay from me last July, and she don't have one animal out there. Not one. Now what's a woman want with hay if she has no stock?"

"Live and let live, boys," Emmitt Earl cautioned. "There ain't nobody in Montana that's normal."

"Amen and praise the Lord!" another echoed.

"Where does Mrs. Mendoza live?" Austin asked. "How can I find the Double Diamond?"

Emmitt Earl pushed his hat back, revealing a white upper forehead that hadn't seen the light of the sun in fifty years. "Missy, she lives at the base of the Little Belts. Jist go south on

191 'til you get to the railroad siding at Straw. That's right on Ross Fork Crick. Head east until you git to the gravel pits and turn south."

"They can't turn south, E. E. That road got washed out last month."

"Oh, yeah . . . turn south at that Weber Crick road. It's kind of rough. You got a truck with a winch?"

"How about four-wheel drive?"

"That'll help. Then east on that little dirt road where Coyote Crick comes into Buffalo Crick. You'll go a couple miles, and that road will git narrow and start wigglin' all over the hillside."

"How narrow is the road?"

"Don't let E. E. scare you, Lynda Dawn. I took a cattle truck up that road and didn't get stuck more than three or four times."

"That's reassuring."

"After you take a sharp right turn, look for a trail headin' off to the south—the left."

"A trail?"

"Well, it's a road, but it sure ain't as smooth as them others. But don't take the first road—no, ma'am. That leads up Martin Coulee and into the Little Belts. You want the second road. Right there's where the old Basin schoolhouse used to be. 'Course there ain't nothin' there now, exceptin' maybe a cor-ral."

"Turn south?"

"Correct. Now the road gets rough. Just don't bottom out, and you'll do okay. When you git up at the head of Sager Canyon, there'll be a gate and a red No Trespassing sign. Well, look around to make sure no one's pointin' a gun at you, then open the gate, and go on in. About three miles beyond the gate, the road will dead-end at the hitchin' post in front of the Double Diamond headquarters. But I expect she'll spot you and come out long before that."

"Stay in your truck until she waves you in."

"Waves us in?"

"Like I said, she don't cotton up to surprises."

"Only don't miss the Sager Canyon turnoff. You wander on up Coyote Crick, and we won't see you 'til spring."

"Yeah, well, thanks," Lynda murmured.

"Y'all thinkin' about buyin' the Double Diamond?"

"Is it for sale?"

"If you've got a big bag of Texas money, Lynda Dawn, ever' ranch in Montana's for sale."

"We just want to ask her a few questions. Actually, Brady wants to buy a place down in Wyoming."

"Wyomin'? Why in heaven's name would anyone want to move to Wyomin'? Son," he addressed Brady, "Lynda Dawn bein' a ranch-raised Texas girl, she shouldn't have to live out in Wyomin'. You'll just have to do better than that for her."

"Texas?" Brady started to protest but was cut short by a silencing jab of her elbow to his midsection.

"Thanks for the directions. We're goin' to drive down and visit with Mrs. Mendoza. I don't suppose she has a telephone so we can call and let her know we're coming?"

"Nope. No phone, no electricity, and no runnin' water. I never figured she would try to spend the winter back there, but what with that hay . . . Anyway, you two be careful."

"Thanks, boys." She smiled. "If we don't come out in two days, come look for us, will you? Say, if any of you ever git around Austin at sun-up, ride on by the ranch, and I'll whomp up a batch of red-eye gravy that will make this stuff taste like the Powder River, if you git my drift."

Brady's mouth hung open as she paid the check and walked to the door. Every man in the building tipped his hat as she pushed open the squeaking wooden door.

"Wait a minute, wait a minute," Brady called to her as she

tucked her head down and scampered into the wind and across the street.

"What's all of this about Texas?"

"I said my name was Austin, and they thought I was from Austin."

"You from Texas? You've got to be kidding. No sane person on earth would think you were from Texas."

"They did, Brady Stoner, and for a moment, I liked it."

"So you lied to them."

"I wasn't planning on lying. It just sort of popped out unexpected."

"And that makes it acceptable?"

She reached the pickup and flung open the driver's side door. "No, it was wrong. But you've got to admit, they treated me like one of the family."

"That they did."

"It felt good, Brady. It's the first time I've been out here that I didn't feel like an outsider looking in. I guess I got carried away. You want me to drive?"

"Can you find the Double Diamond?"

"I doubt it. Can you?"

"I guess we'll find out, Lynda Dawn from Austin."

"Are you going to keep badgering me about that?"

"Nope, but you do have to tell me where you came up with that line about gravy and the Powder River."

"*Black Night at Lookout Pass.*"

"Joaquin's novel?"

"Yeah. It's the closing line. Did I tell you Joaquin's driving over to Montana to see me?"

"No. When's he comin' by?"

"I don't know. He didn't even say where to meet. I don't suppose we'll run across him. You just can't drive to Montana and find someone."

"Why not?"

"It's so big . . . and empty."

"That makes 'em easier to spot."

"Mr. Hampton and Sassy are out here, too. I hope we don't run into them."

"They're probably at Ted and Jane's place."

"Where's that?"

"South of here."

◆ ◆ ◆

Six miles out of town Lynda noticed tiny flakes of snow blowing in from the west and bouncing off the pickup like specks of dust. The heavy, dark, drooping clouds seemed kept off the ground only by the strong gusts of wind. She fought the current to keep the truck from swerving to the middle line and turned the heat fan up a notch.

"Should we be driving out here on a day like this?" she asked.

"Probably not, but it's an adventure. You didn't come all the way to Montana to sit around a boring motel room, right?"

"Not really."

He looked at her with a sparkle in his eyes and dimples in his smile. "Why did you come out here, Lynda Dawn?"

"To find that final chapter, of course."

"The final chapter of Lynda Dawn's Western adventure?"

"What are you talking about?"

"What are the times in your life when you are really living?"

"Stoner, are you getting philosophical?"

"Maybe. But it seems to me there are certain times in our brief existence when we experience life at a deeper level. More joy, more sorrow, more satisfaction, more . . . well, more thrill in the soul."

"And I suppose you're going to tell me that for you, it's those eight seconds on the back of a bronc."

"No, that's mostly just an adrenalin rush. For me, it was times like when I gave Heather the money for her and the girls, or one time Petey and me pulled two old people out of a burning travel home, or that sunrise when you and me had a little stick fire burning down in the desert next to the deserted church, or ridin' with you on the Staten Island Ferry at night holdin' hands and lookin' at the Manhattan skyline, or seein' that little girl's smile—the one who had leukemia—when I lifted her up on that pony and led her around the arena, or when I walked into that bookstore in San Antonio and saw my first copy of *With the Wind in My Face* by Martin Taylor Harrison, edited by Lynda Dawn Austin. I can't believe you actually put a picture of dawn on the cover of that book."

"I had a cowboy once tell me my name meant a beautiful sunrise."

"Yeah, some guys will try anything. But you know what I mean. There are some moments that catch you up in such a dynamic way that every other moment of life seems flat."

"I know what you're saying." She nodded. "That's what keeps us going, isn't it? They say people play golf because every once in a long while they do it right, and the thrill is so great you plug away waiting for that good shot to come back again."

"So isn't that why you really came out here?"

"Just for thrills? Stoner, are you saying my life in New York is boring, and I have to come out here for a little action?"

"That doesn't sound right, does it?"

"No, but bringing that Harrison manuscript out of the canyon with you and all that happened after that—it was the best time in my entire life."

"So how's Lynda Dawn Austin really been since then?"

"Busy . . . and bored, I guess. I've thought about this before."

"I thought you might have."

"See, I sort of like being young and having a great life goal waiting out there someplace." She slowed down as the blowing snow became thicker. It was still not sticking to the rig or piling up on the road. "I found that I could put up with a whole bunch of boring activities because one day I was going to do something important."

"Find that God-given task?"

"Exactly. But this year I kept thinking—what if that novel is the most important thing I ever do? What about the rest of my life? Do I just coast or what?"

"So you jumped at the chance to trace down a missing final chapter."

"Yeah, I suppose you're right."

"But this project doesn't have any eternal significance, does it? Even if you had McCall's book published, it wouldn't lead others to faith or anything spiritual like that."

"Right. I think my main motivation is anger that someone in the office ran off with a final chapter of an Austin Imprint."

"And here I thought I was your motivation for being here."

"Brady Stoner, I don't need to travel 2,500 miles to be ignored. I can be ignored in mid-Manhattan."

"Ignored? We've been together almost night and day."

"Well, other than that pathetic peck on the cheek at Jackson, you haven't bothered to . . . Oh, man! There it is!"

She slammed on the brakes, and the pickup slid sideways, tossing Capt. Patch against the dash and flinging Brady to the outer reaches of his seat belt. When he slammed into the glove compartment, it popped open, and the entire contents scattered throughout the cab.

"What? What is it?" he hollered.

"Didn't you see that sign? This is the Straw siding turnoff. Didn't they say to turn west at Straw siding?"

"Yep."

"Which way is west?"

"You're headed west. Only I wouldn't leave the rig out here in the middle of the highway."

"Sorry about that sudden stop. I just panicked, I guess."

"About the sign or the way the conversation was going?"

"Both. Why don't you play us some music?"

"What do you want to hear?"

"Something about riding down the trail."

I can't believe I almost begged the guy to kiss me. Austin, you're crazy. This is not me. Someone has taken over my mind. My whole body! This is not me.

"Now that we've found the road, what were you sayin' about bein' neglected?" he asked as he pushed a tape into the truck stereo.

"Nothing. Absolutely nothing. Look, the way the snow is blowing straight at us, you'd better find the turnoffs."

Visibility was no more than fifty feet. The rolling prairie covered with dead grass blended in more and more with the skyline.

"It's almost like being lost at sea," she commented.

"Except that we're on land, and we aren't lost."

"Yeah, other than that. Do I turn left here or right?"

"Are those the gravel pits up there?"

"Where?"

"Up there on the left."

"No, it's just a big hole in the ground and a pile of rocks."

"That's a gravel pit," he maintained.

"It is?"

"Turn south on that road."

"South? I thought he said north."

"He said south, darlin'."

"Are you sure?"

"Trust me."

"I don't think that's a road. It looks like a driveway."

"That would be a pleasant surprise. It's not a driveway."

"How can you be so sure?"

"Because it's too wide."

"Wide? Your truck will barely fit down it. I don't know what we'll do if we meet another car," she stewed.

"Besides that, there's no gate at the fence. Driveways always have gates."

"Why?"

"To keep the cows in the yard."

Austin drove twenty miles per hour up a frozen dirt road. The trail of tire tracks cut through the dead grass and followed the contour of every hillock and wallow. The road dead-ended into a east and west crossroad. She stopped the rig and stared out into the blowing storm.

"Where does all this snow end up? It's not staying on the ground. It's just blowing past."

"Well, if it doesn't snag on the Little Snowy mountains, I guess it will end up in the Dakotas."

"You're kidding me."

"I don't think so. Turn right."

"Why right? That's into the storm."

"Then that's west. The Little Belt Mountains are south and west. Your buddies back at the cafe said the Double Diamond is up against the Little Belts."

"Brady, are we going to get lost out here? This is starting to get scary. If we got stuck, and a blizzard blew in, and we couldn't find any wood to build a fire, and—"

"We could always burn cow chips."

"I think I'd rather freeze to death."

"Lynda Dawn, it's October—not January. This won't last long. The sun could be shining by noon."

"Is that the road up Sager Canyon?"

"It doesn't look much like a canyon," he replied.

"Of course not. It looks like a snowstorm, just like everything else."

"I don't think this is it," Brady maintained.

"They said the first road, didn't they?"

"They said the next to the last road."

"How in the world are we going to know if it's the right one?"

"Well, if we drive up into the mountains and haven't found a ranch headquarters, then it's the wrong road," he suggested.

"What will the Double Diamond headquarters look like?"

"There will be a big barn, corrals, a broken-down beaver slide, a wheelless, rusted John Deere two-banger, several out-buildings, two broken swathers with weeds and bushes growin' up through them, a busted windmill, assorted stock trailers—most of which have flat tires, a 1959 Cadillac that has been converted into a chicken coop, a dog that looks like a cross between a coyote and a jackrabbit, and an old farmhouse in worse condition than the barn."

"You've been there before?" Lynda asked.

"I've been to a lot of ranch headquarters before."

"Are we going to try this road?"

"I think it's the wrong one," he insisted.

"And I think it's the right one."

"You're the boss."

Austin drove five miles up a rocky draw in the blowing, dry snow. The road turned right, and the visibility lessened.

"Just another mile or two," she insisted.

"You havin' a hard time admitting you're wrong? The road's gettin' steep. You want me to drive?"

"Is there something wrong with my driving, Stoner?"

"Nope." He pushed his cowboy hat forward and scrunched down in the seat. "If you run off a cliff or anything and need a little help, just holler."

"I don't know why you think women are so helpless. I've driven you around in this truck for two years. I can assure you, I am quite capable of taking care of myself, Brady Stoner."

"Yeah, but can you take care of me?"

"I am perfectly . . . capable of taking care of you any day, cowboy. If you don't think so, you're . . . missing out on a very . . . good time."

"What are you mumbling about?"

She jammed on the brakes and killed the engine. "What is that?"

"What?" Brady sat straight up and stared out into the storm.

"Right there. In the road. That's not a buffalo, is it?"

"Nope. It's a dead cow."

"What's it doing there?"

"It's not doin' anything. It's dead."

"Did it get run over?"

"Maybe. Looks like the coyotes have been lunchin' on it."

"I think I'm going to be sick," she groaned.

"Not in the truck."

"Well, I'm not going out there."

"Then don't get sick. By the looks of things, that carcass has been there quite a while. So I say this isn't the road to any headquarters. Can we go back now?"

"Yes. I was wrong. I made an error. It is completely my fault. This isn't the road. Is that what you're waiting for?"

"Nope. I'm waitin' for you to turn this rig around."

"Where? It's too narrow."

"You want me to drive?"

"Your arm's useless. You can't turn it—can you?"

"I'll manage. Put it in neutral and step on the emergency. Then scoot over here."

"What?"

"You can get out and walk around if you want to, but with that cow up front and the storm blowing thirty miles an hour, I figure if you crawl over, I'll scoot under, and we won't have to freeze."

Stoner shoved Capt. Patch into the luggage-crammed narrow backseat of the extended cab, and Austin scooted out from behind the wheel. She tried to crawl over the gearshift knob as Brady scooted under her toward the driver's side. Pushing herself toward the dash, she heard the gears grind.

"Whoa! Don't shove it in gear!" Brady hollered, trying to reach the steering wheel with his right hand.

"I got my boot stuck!" she cried out.

"Just don't—," he shouted. "Wait!"

Suddenly the pickup lunged down the hill.

"You put it in gear!"

"I didn't mean to!"

"Get over there!" Brady shouted. "Get!"

"I'm trying!"

"Hang on, darlin', we're going off the road!"

On the first bump she slammed against the roof of the cab, and on the second, she came down on Brady's legs, which he was trying to drag across the seat. Pinned down, all he could do was steer the truck backwards down the hill into the blinding storm.

"Brady, do something!" she cried.

He reached over with his limp left hand and tugged the key out of the ignition. She grabbed the gearshift and jammed it out of reverse into neutral.

"No!" he screamed.

The truck picked up speed. "It needed to be in gear to slow it down!"

"But I thought—"

"Well, don't think! Get off my legs. There's no power steering now!"

"I'm trying the best I can," she sobbed.

The gradually descending mountainside was free of trees and sage, covered mainly with short, dead grass and occasional outcroppings of rock, which Brady tried to avoid as he steered the coasting pickup backwards.

Lord, I don't want to die yet—not when we're screaming and yelling at each other! She tried to catch her breath, but the view of the mountainside and the blowing snowstorm out the rear window locked her throat both to intelligible words or fresh air.

Brady's left foot jerked out from under her, and he slammed it hard on the brakes. "No power brakes either!"

Pulling the other leg from under her, he finally was able to smash both feet on the brake. The truck spun left 180 degrees, and suddenly they found themselves facing the downhill slope and the storm, instead of backing into it. Brady stomped on the emergency brake, put the truck in reverse, and left the motor off. The truck stopped sliding. He took a deep breath and leaned against the steering wheel.

Capt. Patch let out a bark, and Brady slid the back window open. The dog leaped out into the truck bed and into the storm. Austin was still on her knees on the seat facing the rear of the truck. She scooted around and sat down. Tears smeared across her face as she rubbed the cold, slick, satinlike sleeve of her coat across them.

"Are you okay, darlin'?"

"Yeah." Her voice was so quiet she could barely hear it herself.

"I'm sorry I yelled and screamed at you. I had no right to do that. I guess I got a little panicked—a little concerned there for a minute."

"That's all right. I wasn't all that pleasant myself. I thought I had put the emergency on."

"Oh, you have to romp this one all the way down."

"I didn't know I could shove it in gear without using the clutch."

"Neither did I."

"What do you figure we should do now?"

"I think we ought to creep along this hill to the east until we run across the road. I don't remember any coulees or rocky draws. What do you think we should do?"

Austin scooted over to Stoner, threw her arms around his neck, and pulled his face close to hers. Without saying a word, she pulled his head down and pressed her lips into his. At first they felt tight, cold, almost chapped, but within a moment, she felt them relax, warm, and respond with enthusiasm. His right arm surrounded her shoulders and drew her even tighter.

Don't kid yourself, girl. This is the reason you came to Montana.

Finally, she pulled herself slowly back until their lips barely touched each other's. Then she slipped her head down and rested it on his shoulder as his arm continued to encircle her. She could feel his chest heave a big sigh.

"Well, darlin', welcome back. I've been waitin' for two days for that kiss."

"Two days? I've been waiting for six months!"

"Yeah . . . me, too!"

"All the way down this hillside I kept thinking, *We can't crash. I haven't even kissed him yet.*"

"It's not just a friendship thing, is it?"

"You and me?"

"Yeah. We say all year we're just goin' to be really good friends, but it's more than that, isn't it?"

With her head still on his chest, she spoke in a soft, low tone. "I got this thing all figured out in my mind, but the rest of me won't cooperate. Honey, I really, really missed you."

"Why in the world didn't we greet each other like this at the airport?"

"Because you weren't there to meet me, Brady Stoner."

"That's my gift—never there at the right time."

"But you're here now."

"You know what, darlin'? I could get addicted to holding you like this."

"You mean you could get so dependent on it you couldn't live without it?"

"Yep." He reached back and shoved open the sliding glass door on the back window. A blast of hostile, snow-laden air flooded the cab.

"What are you doing?" She sat up and shivered.

"Coolin' off, darlin'—just coolin' off."

"Really? I think I'm nearly frozen, just in case you want to shove that shut and preserve our lives a little longer."

He let out a loud whistle that seemed to echo in the cab but die the minute it fought its way out into the storm. From up on the hillside, Capt. Patch appeared on the run. His first leap brought him to the back of the truck. The second one propelled him through the open back window and into the front seat between Brady and Lynda. He shook the snow and water out of his fur, spreading the two of them even further apart. Then he circled three times and lay down on the front seat.

"If he wasn't a dog, I'd swear he's trying to keep us apart." Lynda laughed.

Brady reached over and patted Capt. Patch. "I don't guess he intends on givin' up that center seat. You might have to wrestle him for it."

"Me? Why on earth do you think I want to sit there?"

"So that blast of air cooled you off, too?"

"Mr. Stoner, I have no idea what you are talking about!" Lynda flipped down the sun visor and looked in the mirror. She dug in her purse and pulled out a brush.

Brady started the engine, jammed the truck into four-wheel drive, and began to creep along through the storm.

"How does that phrase go? *'Amare et sapere vix deo conceditur.'*"

She looked over at him. "It's difficult for God to do what?"

"'Even a god finds it hard to love and be wise at the same time.'"

STEPHEN BLY

She found a little green opaque glass bottle in her purse and splashed its contents on her wrists. "Have you been studying Latin all summer just to impress me?"

"Is it working?"

"Maybe."

"Well, I needed something to counter that perfume. I can tell you one thing," he laughed, "*that's* definitely working."

Austin dabbed some perfume behind her ears and then quickly shoved the bottle back into her purse.

"Did you ever notice how you put on more perfume every time you get excited or nervous?"

"I do not! I just didn't remember if I'd put any on this morning."

"Why is it I don't really believe that? Is that the road over there?"

"It's a road. But I don't know if it's the one we were just on."

"What's the name of it?"

"The road?"

"The perfume."

"Oh, it's . . . well, it's nice, isn't it?"

"The name, Austin. What's on the bottle, just in case I ever want to buy you some myself."

"It's a Swedish name. Janie brought it back for me one time. I can't even pronounce it in Swedish. I don't think they sell it in the States."

"Come on, Lynda Dawn. I'm holdin' you accountable. I'm guessin' that you know what it means in English."

"I don't care to reveal that, Brady Stoner."

"You too embarrassed?"

"I am not. . . . It happens to be called Sensuous Ambition. So there!"

"You're a tease, Lynda Dawn. Did any man ever call you a tease?"

"Sooner or later every man I ever dated called me a tease."

"Why do you think they said that?"

"I guess they figured I didn't deliver on whatever they thought I was promising."

He didn't look over at her, and she didn't look at him. "Well, I think you're about the sweetest tease I've ever known."

"Coming from a man who thinks every woman's a sweetheart, I like that compliment. Is this the road we were on up there?"

"I suppose. They all look pretty much the same in a storm."

"I'm sorry I sent us up the wrong road."

"I'm not. It turned out pretty good, babe." Holding the steering wheel with his weak left hand, he reached over Capt. Patch with his right. Lynda intertwined her fingers in his.

How can a man with such hard, callused hands have such a warm, tender touch? Stoner, you have no idea how many nights I went to sleep wishing I was holding your hand.

Brady kept the speed about fifteen. The pickup bounced down the sloping road that was little more than two frozen ruts in the hillside. Lynda kept her hand in his.

"This isn't the road we came up on," he announced.

"Are you sure?"

"Yep."

"How can you be sure?"

He stopped the rig and pointed into the storm. "There wasn't a gate across the other one."

"A gate? You mean we're driving in someone's field—I mean, ranch?"

"Nope. It just means there's a gate. It's all right. Sit tight. I'll open it."

"We're going to keep driving on this road?"

"We don't have any other choice. Besides, this is shaping up to be a real adventure."

Stoner came back, drove the truck forward fifty feet, then got out, and shut the gate.

"Can they just put a gate across a road like this?"

"Yep."

"Are we lost?"

"I don't know where I am, but I know I'm not lost. It surely is freezing out there."

A few more miles down the coulee, they came to another gate across the road. This time he glanced over at her and waited. When she failed to respond, he got out and opened the gate. Once they had passed it, they came to a crossroad that was wider and looked as if it might have been graded and graveled at one time.

"Okay, Pioneer Stoner, which way now?"

"East."

"Which way is east?"

"Right . . . I think."

"Why east?"

"Because the highway is out there someplace. And if we can't find the Double Diamond, we'll at least be on the blacktop."

The snow was blowing, swirling, flying, rushing along the ground like a stream without borders. But very little was actually staying on the ground. And none was melting. The flakes that bounced off the windshield were no larger than a grain of sand.

Two miles down the road Brady pulled off in front of a closed corral gate and stared at a sign that read: Absolutely No Trespassing.

"Why are we stopping here?"

"I think this is the entrance to the Double Diamond. We probably circled around Sager Canyon when we were up in the hills and slid down to another road."

"This isn't a road; it's a corral, and there's a No Trespassing sign."

"It's a road, darling. This gate doesn't lead into the corrals but through the corrals, and somewhere up that dirt road is a headquarters."

"How do you know that?"

"What's burnt into the wood of that gatepost?"

"Two diamonds? Is that the Double Diamond brand?"

"Yep. And look at that water trough. It's pipe-fed. That is, in the summertime it's pipe-fed. So where does that pipe come from?"

"The water company? I don't know. It's buried in the ground."

"It comes from uphill somewhere, because there's obviously no well around here. So why would you have a well up this lonely road?"

"Because headquarters is up there?"

"Exactly!"

"Do you want me to open the gate for you?" she asked.

"Sure."

"Really?"

Brady glanced over at her. "You were serious in that offer, weren't you?"

"Yes, but I didn't think you'd . . . I mean, it looks very cold out there."

"Here, you might want to wear these gloves."

"Well . . ." She slipped them on. "You did open the other gate."

"That's only because you didn't offer. I figured you didn't understand Western etiquette."

"What's etiquette have to do with this, Stoner?"

"It's common courtesy for the person ridin' shotgun to open and close the gates. But that's all right, I'll—"

"Oh, no. I'll do it."

The blast of frigid air hit her face like a wave at a New Hampshire beach in early June. She sucked in air, trying to keep her teeth from chattering. The second gust sent her cowboy hat over the hood of the truck. She scampered around the front of the rig, expecting to see Brady jump out and retrieve her hat.

He didn't budge, and by the time she pulled her hat off a stack of tumbleweeds that had lodged against the weather-worn corral, she felt frozen to the bone. Lynda didn't bother to put the hat back on her head but clutched it in her right hand and leaned into the storm.

The tiny snowflakes burned and stung her face like a horrible sandstorm. She abandoned any hope of keeping her teeth from chattering and now felt her hands, her arms, her shoulders begin to shake.

Brady Stoner, how dare you make me come out here in this storm! What kind of jerk would sit there in the warm truck and allow a woman to do such a job?

The gate was latched by a piece of barbed wire that had been dropped over the posts, but she found it so tight she couldn't lift it up. Even gloved, she was beginning to feel numb. She wanted to look back at him in disgust, but she refused to admit she couldn't complete the task.

Finally, she climbed up on the bottom rail of the gate to get more leverage at lifting the barbed-wire loop. A frantic yank flipped the loop off, but in the process her fleece-lined suede glove caught on a barb. The sharp point ripped her glove, flung it from her hand, and tore into the flesh of her palm. Feeling the torn skin and seeing the blood, she jammed the hand to her mouth and realized there was no feeling in her lips or her hand.

At the same time the entire gate, with her still on the bottom rail, swung open. Brady drove the pickup through and in doing so ran right over the top of her discarded glove. He parked the truck and waited for her to close the gate.

She swung the gate closed and was delighted that the barbed loop slipped back down easily. Retrieving her glove, she hurried to the pickup, clutching her wounded hand.

"I can't believe you did that, Brady Stoner!" Her cheeks were so stiff she could hardly talk. She held her right hand with her left and bounced up and down in the seat in unison with her shivers.

He handed her a red handkerchief he pulled from his duffel bag. "It's clean. Wrap that around your hand. It's too cold to bleed a lot. If you're going to cut yourself, always do it in the winter."

"Brady Stoner, if I wasn't frozen, I'd punch your lights out!"

"I know, darlin'. That's one of the toughest things I've ever done."

"Come on, Stoner, you were sitting in the cab with the heater on full blast. I didn't even know what I was doing."

"I know, darlin'. It was an experiment."

"Experiment? What were you trying to find out? How long I could live in the cold?"

He started driving up the narrow dirt roadway. There were still no buildings in sight. "Do you want to scoot over here and warm up?" He held out his arm.

"No, I most certainly do not! You tried to kill me back there, Stoner, and I want to know why."

"Well, you did offer to open the gate."

"Of course I did. I was trying to be polite. But you knew how cold it was. Why didn't you insist I stay in the truck?"

"Because it's cold and windy in this country about six months of the year, and, you know . . . I've been wonderin' how a city girl would do in this weather. Supposin' one of 'em decided to move out here."

"You mean this was a test to see if I'm sturdy enough for high-plains winters? Well, I suppose I flunked. Should I just go get on the plane and fly home now?" she snapped.

"No, darlin', it's just—"

"Don't call me darlin'. I'm tired of—"

"Lynda Dawn, can I squeeze a word in edgewise here?"

"Why?"

"My experiment wasn't to test you at all. I know what you're made of. I was testing the Mendoza woman."

"You were what?"

"I cannot figure why or how any woman from New York City would move out here completely on her own."

"Are you saying women aren't strong enough to survive?"

"Nope. I'm saying it's mighty uncomfortable weather if you aren't used to it. So why subject yourself to it?"

"There're some buildings—back in the trees. Maybe you can ask her yourself."

With the corrals empty and the snow blowing, the huge unpainted, well-worn barn stood like a sentinel and relic of an age past. Some of the siding had shrunk so much there were gaps of one-half to two inches between boards. A wall of hay lined its entrance. Next to it stood a three-sided storage shed, even more broken down than the barn, and inside Lynda spotted some rusting, broken farm equipment.

She noticed the two outhouses before she saw the headquarters house. The main building was a single-story, sprawling wood-frame building that looked like it had suffered numerous additions. At one time it had been painted white, but at least half of the paint had flaked off. One end of the front porch sagged several feet and was propped up by an aluminum crutch bolted to a broken beam. An old white car, with hood up and wheels missing, sat on top of log rounds. The yard, which showed a slight sprinkling of snow, was all dirt and tumbleweeds. Brady drove right up to the front door and parked next to a battered hitching post.

"Is anyone home?" she asked.

"Don't know."

"I don't see any light on."

"There's no electricity out here. But I don't see any vehicle that's operable. Maybe she went somewhere. I'll go see."

"You want me to go with you?" she asked.

"It's up to you."

"Is this a test?"

"Nope."

"Then I'll come with you."

Lynda left her hat in the pickup, but she pulled on Brady's heavy gloves, leaving the bandanna wrapped around her palm. She turned up the collar of her coat. The minute she opened the door, Capt. Patch scampered across her legs and jumped to the ground. He was out of sight before they reached the front door.

Turning his back to the howling wind and dry snow, Brady banged on the door and waited. After repeated pounding, he turned the brass knob of the door and slid it open a few inches.

"What are you doing?"

"Seein' if anyone's home." He stuck his face into the opening of the door. "Hello, in the house!" he shouted. "Mrs. Mendoza? Anyone here?"

"No one's here, Brady. Maybe we should go."

"Go? Are you kidding? You traveled all the way from New York to talk to this Mendoza. We can't leave without seeing her."

"But no one's here. Maybe we should come back some other day."

"Mrs. Mendoza?" Brady called again.

"She's not here. Maybe this isn't the right house. How do we even know this is the headquarters where she was staying?"

"You're right. We ought to find that out first." Brady shoved the old door open and entered the house.

"Brady! What are you doing?"

"Come on, let's check it out!" He grabbed her arm and pulled her inside. The room was dark and very musty smelling.

"Are there any kind of lights in here?" she asked. "I really can't see anything."

"Looks like a kerosene lamp on the table."

"Just like Harrison's cabin down in the canyon."

"You feeling a little déjà vu?"

"I don't think so. I know I've never been here before."

The light from the lantern gave the room a dull, mono-chromatic tint of dusty yellow. The floor was protected by faded linoleum covered with worn braided oval rugs. The sofa was brown leather, cracked badly. A pile of magazines and newspapers were tossed by the rock fireplace.

Stoner walked over to the hearth. "There was no fire here last night, but there's surely been one in the last couple of days."

"Brady, we can't just roam around in someone else's house."

"We're just steppin' out of the cold. It's part of Western hospitality."

"In the East we call it breaking and entering."

"We didn't break anything."

She made a face at him. "Let's wait out in the truck."

"How long you figure we should wait?"

"I don't know—an hour maybe?"

"And I figure no one will be home until evenin'—if then."

"Why do you say that?"

"'Cause it takes two or three hours to get anywhere from here. Three hours out, three hours there, three hours back. That's an all-day trek. We can't run the heater in the truck that long. I say we build a fire and sit right here until she comes back. It's the Western way. Trust me."

"I still don't . . . Brady, this is a different culture. I always wind up feeling like I'm in a foreign country out here."

"Oh, it's the same country. Just about fifty years behind schedule, that's all."

"Fifty? More like a hundred out here. No electricity. No indoor plumbing. No telephones."

Stoner looked up from the stack of newspapers he was

gathering for a fire starter. "Well! They do get Fed. Ex. Look at this, Ms. Austin."

He tossed her a blue and white shipping envelope. She jumped back, then reached out, and fumbled to catch it in her gloved hands. Finally she picked it up off the floor.

"This is it! The one sent from our offices. We really did find the right place! I can't believe it!" she shouted.

"You doubted my ability?"

"No, it's just . . . Do you know what this means?"

"Actually, no," Brady admitted. "The package is empty. So we have no idea what was in there."

"But Mrs. Mendoza knows. And sooner or later she'll be back, right?"

"We don't know that for sure. Maybe she's been sittin' here waitin' for the contents of that pak. Maybe she pulled out this morning."

"Going to the lake to look for the hidden gold?"

"Could be." He nodded.

"Then we could be staying here a long time."

"That's what I'm thinkin'."

"So what's your plan, Stoner?"

"Sit here until dark, then leave a note on the door, and head back to Lewistown if she doesn't show, I suppose."

"Are you sure we can't get arrested for being in this house?"

"I know one thing. No one will be drivin' out here in this storm except for Mendoza."

When the fire blazed, Brady yanked on his brown leather gloves and walked toward the front door.

"Where are you going?" Austin asked.

"To check on the other buildings, especially that little one, if you catch my point."

"Oh, yeah. Well, hurry back. I really feel weird about being in someone else's house, especially all alone."

"I'll be back quick enough. There's no way I want to stay out in that blowin' snow any longer than necessary."

The door closed behind him, but she didn't hear anything but the howling wind. She slowly surveyed the room—from dusty table to dusty bookshelf to dusty stuffed chair.

Something's wrong here, Lord. I'm out of my element. I shouldn't be in someone else's home. If Brady wasn't here . . .

Her hands and arms quivered. Her throat constricted. The room seemed to spin in her head. She moved closer to the fire and pushed her hands toward the flames.

I can't turn my back to the door. I just can't. Stoner, get your business done and get back in here. What would I do if this Mendoza woman walked through the door and caught me here in her home? Just die, I guess.

FIVE

Lynda grasped her knees as she hunched on the worn brick hearth, her backside to the crackling fire, eyes boring into the chipped white-painted front door. Just as she began to relax, the door suddenly flew open. She jumped to her feet and faced a rifle-wielding, fur-parka-clad, fair-skinned woman.

"Have you got one good reason why I shouldn't shoot you dead for being in my house?" the woman shouted. The hood of her coat slipped back on her shoulders revealing long, slightly gray-streaked black hair pulled behind her head. Her unyielding eyes raked over Lynda.

"Shoot me?" Lynda could barely force the words out. "But . . . wait! There's a misunderstanding."

Dark eyebrows furrowed above her brown eyes. "You broke into my house!"

"Are you Mrs. Mendoza?"

"Do I know you?" She stepped closer to Austin, with cotton-gloved hands squeezing the gun.

"Eh, no, we've never met." Lynda started to walk toward her, then hesitated, and took a step back. "I needed to talk to you. But you weren't home, and it was freezing outside."

"So I'm supposed to believe you just came in and built a

fire? If I wouldn't have come in when I did, you might have stolen me blind!"

Brady Stoner, get in here. I told you I didn't want to do this.

"I didn't take anything. I was just sitting by the fire when you came in. I thought it was part of Western hospitality to allow people access to your fire."

What is there in this house I would possibly want to steal?

"Well, I'm not from the West." Austin flinched as Mendoza cocked the lever-action rifle.

"Neither am I, so please excuse the intrusion."

The gun swung up to the woman's shoulder, the barrel pointed at Lynda's head.

I don't want to be here, Lord. I want to go home! Brady! I don't . . . oh, no, I am not going to cry.

"Why are you snooping around my place?"

Lynda forced herself to speak slowly, trying to mask her quivering lips. "Look, I don't know what you think is going on. I'm Lynda Austin from Atlantic-Hampton Publishing Company in New York City. All I wanted to talk to you about is the contents of that envelope." She pointed a shaking hand at the Fed. Ex. package laying on the table.

"What about it?" The woman stood about two inches shorter than Lynda and wore jeans and heavy distressed leather hiking boots.

"I'm merely trying to trace down some papers from our office. I had reason to believe they might have gotten shipped in that package by mistake."

"They didn't." It was a husky, determined voice.

"What did we send you anyway, Mrs. Mendoza?"

"It was a . . . personal package—a birthday present. Which is none of your business."

"Hessler sent you a birthday present?"

"So what?"

"What's your connection with Drew?"

"You're asking me questions? Lady, you don't seem to realize the trouble you're in. You've broken into my house, and I caught you red-handed. If I shoot you, no jury in Montana would convict me."

"The men in Lewistown would. See, I told them I was coming out here for a visit with you. No one who's planning a burglary goes around announcing her destination to an entire cafe full of people."

Brady, if you don't come through that door! Maybe . . . maybe she already shot him! But I didn't hear anything.

The rifle drooped from Mendoza's shoulder. "Who knows you're out here?"

"Emmitt Earl, Virgil, C. Bob, and the others. They were afraid I'd get lost, so they said they'd come look for me if I didn't show up in town."

Mendoza waved the gun barrel in Lynda's direction. "Lay down on that rug."

"Do what?"

"I said, put your scrawny carcass on that rug while you still have all your body parts!"

She's going to shoot me! Oh, Lord, she really is going to shoot me. And I don't even know why! Please, Lord, not yet!

Even on top of the braided rug, the floor was hard and smelled like mildew. Fully clothed, in front of a roaring fire, Lynda still felt exposed, cold, and defenseless. Hearing Mendoza rummage through a cupboard, she raised up on one elbow and strained to see what was happening.

"Put your head down!" came the shout.

Lynda immediately mashed her nose back into the grimy braided rug.

"Oh, that's great!" Mendoza stopped her frantic ransacking of the kitchen. "I should have known you weren't smart enough to come out here by yourself."

Lynda looked around again as a half-frozen, yet smiling

Brady Stoner pushed open the front door. "Hey, guess what I found? . . . What are you doing down there?"

"Brady, she's got a gun!"

"Who's got—"

He turned toward Mendoza and caught the full force of the rifle barrel as it crashed into his head just above his left ear. His body crumpled, and his head hit the floor with a loud, sickening smack.

"Brady!" Lynda cried out.

"He won't help you much now, cream puff."

"You killed him!" Lynda raised up to her hands and knees as Mendoza kicked Brady's legs over and closed the front door.

"I doubt it. Lay back down or I'll mess up your prissy hair, too."

Austin slumped to the floor fighting back rage, hatred, and mostly fear.

She hit Brady hard, Lord. And I couldn't do anything about it! I just watched. But I am not a cream puff. And my hair is not prissy. Never in my life has my hair been prissy.

Her arms were roughly jerked behind her back, nearly pulled out of the sockets. She could feel duct tape being wrapped tight around her wrists.

"Why are you doing this?" Lynda fought back the tears. "I just came to find the last chapter of a novel."

"Novel? You think it's just a novel?"

I sure don't think it's worth shooting someone over, especially me!

Mendoza wrapped tape around Austin's ankles.

"This is a crime. You'll be caught!"

"You'll live through it, so just relax. I'm not going to be caught, because it's no crime to tie up someone who broke into your own home. Go back to New York where there's cops on every corner to protect you. That's where your kind belongs."

My kind? My wimpy kind? It's only the one with the gun who gets to call names.

Bound on the rug, Austin could hear Mendoza scurry through the house tossing things in a box.

Brady's got to be all right. I've got to help him. How can I take care of him if I'm tied up like this? He's supposed to help me!

"Is he your husband?" Mendoza asked.

"No, we're not married . . . yet," Lynda replied.

"He's kind of cute. Except for that blood in his hair. Maybe I should just toss him in the backseat and take him with me. That chapter was supposed to be sent to me in July. I've been stuck in this isolated dump for a long time. There are some things a woman begins to really miss. Even a piece of fluff like you ought to know that."

"You can't kidnap Brady. Kidnapping is a capital offense!"

"Who's to protest? I can tell you one thing, when I got through taking care of him, there wouldn't be any complaints. There never are. Now just take a little nap and dream about doing lunch at the club and imported French water. Then when Mr. Awesome comes to, he can cut you loose. Unless he likes his lovers tied up."

Lord, she's lawless, vulgar, and socially unredeemable. If You wanted to strike her dead instantly, I'll not try to stop You. Right now, Lord. Right now!

"You won't get away with this," Austin shouted.

"That has got to be the stupidest line ever uttered. Of course, I'm going to get away with it. You and I both know that. It's a cinch you won't be following me in this gale."

The front door slammed tight. The only light was the stormy daylight coming through the narrow, dirty windows and the flames of a slowly fading fire. The air in the room hung heavy and stale.

Four rifle shots blasted in the yard. Austin flinched each time.

Who's she shooting at? Capt. Patch? No!

She won't get away with this. I'll see that she's in jail for a long,

long time! Lord, that woman made me feel like a flyspeck on the ceiling of life. If I felt better, I'd just cry.

Lynda turned her face to the left and laid her cheek on the soiled braided rug. She tugged on her taped wrists, only to feel the silver bonds dig deeper into her skin.

"Brady?" she called out. "Are you all right?"

He's got to have a concussion or worse. He's tough; he'll do all right. Won't he, Lord?

"Brady, you've got to come to and help! Do you hear me?"

She began to wiggle her feet back and forth, finding a little slack in the tape that pinned her jeans legs to her boots. Breathing hard, she quit struggling and lay her head back on the rug.

It's going to get cold in here. I've got to do something.

After several attempts at raising her shoulders and head off the rug and swinging to the left, she was able to roll over on her back, slightly propped up on her elbows that were pinned behind her. Lynda took a deep breath and flung her body forward in order to sit up. The force of the struggle could be felt in the burning pain of her wrists. Just before she gained her balance, she fell face-first into the wooden arm of the couch. Her face slammed off the worn oak surface and crashed back into the floor.

There was sharp pain in her nose and forehead.

I'm not going to cry. Lord, I'm not going to cry. I might cuss, but I won't cry. Eh . . . I didn't mean it, Lord. I don't like this. I am definitely not having fun. Come on, Austin, you cream puff, do something!

After two more attempts, she sat up, bound feet in front of her, taped arms behind her.

"Come on, Stoner, this is where I need some help."

In the dim shadows of the room, she saw blood drying in his hair. Outside, a vehicle roared out of the yard.

At least she didn't shoot either of us.

"Brady, every time I've come west, I get into this situation. Something happens, and I think I'm going to die. And I start to cry because . . . Are you sure you're not awake, Stoner?"

She waited for a minute.

"I cry because, well, because I want you, Brady Stoner. I want you to be my husband. And I want you all to myself. Heaven might be a whole lot better, but I'd really like to have something to compare it to. So don't you go dyin' on me, and I promise I won't die on you. And I don't care if you heard that part. Did you hear that part?"

Again she waited.

"I didn't think so."

She scooted next to the couch and leaned her back against it. By forcing her weight against the divan and pushing with her feet, she gradually lifted herself off the floor. Her wrists burned with pain from the tape.

Flopping back on the sofa, she kicked her legs back and forth, loosening the tape strapped on her jeans.

"Brady? Come on, honey, I really need you. This is your world, not mine. I'm just a visitor."

Finally, she stopped struggling and leaned back on the couch, her arms pinned behind her.

I can't believe anyone would take a book so seriously. I mean, what if McCall was making most of this up? I just want to find that chapter and go home. They can have the gold—if there is any. I want that book published. I want some peace and quiet. I want to live in a world where no one threatens my life again. I want some new perfume. And . . . and I want my cowboy!

Feeling a little strength return to her legs and finding they now had a tiny bit more movement, she flung herself forward. She was surprised when the effort brought her to her feet, but unable to balance herself, she fell forward toward the rock hearth.

"No!"

Austin frantically started a two-footed hop to regain her balance. She careened off of furniture and walls and finally crashed into the front door with her chest and stood there propped against it. Leaning her cheek against the faded white paint of the wooden door, she gasped for breath and tried to relieve the pressure on her wrists.

Lord, if I were watching this in a movie, I'd be rolling in the aisles. How come it's not funny now?

Her hands continued to be bound tight, but she felt some more slack in the feet and found if she scooted them back and forth, she could take baby steps around the room.

"Okay, Stoner, I'm on my feet—which is a lot more than I can say for you. But how in the world do I get this tape off?"

Let's see, Kathleen Turner would ... She'd burn the tape off! No way! Or she'd find a sharp object and painstakingly rub against it until the ropes are cut, with a bomb ticking in the background and sweat rolling down her soiled but cosmetically beautiful face.

She glanced around the room.

Yeah, right. Austin, you've been editing fiction too long. There just don't happen to be any swords protruding from the walls. The kitchen! There's got to be something sharp in the kitchen.

"Don't bother getting up, Brady, dear. I just have to hop out to the kitchen and get something."

The tiny steps seemed to take forever, but she finally made it. The kitchen had a faded wallpapered ceiling that was a good two feet lower than the one in the living room. The floor sloped suspiciously toward the back door. The room was painted a faded light green and had a wooden counter. Most of the cupboard doors were open, showing only a few scattered dishes.

Backing up to a drawer, she tried to tug it open. It slid about two inches and then stuck.

"Come on. . . . This is the knife drawer. I can see them in there!"

With one fierce tug, she yanked the entire drawer out into her hands. The contents crashed and tinkled all over the floor.

"Great! That's just great!" She dropped the wooden drawer to the floor.

"That black-handled knife would work just fine. Of course, it's down there, and I'm up here."

She stood staring at the knife for several moments.

"I may regret this." She sighed as she dropped down into a clear spot on the floor. She let out a cry of pain as both knees crashed full force into the linoleum.

"Okay, I didn't fall over. That's good."

Austin tried hopping on her knees toward the large carving knife that lay among the spoons and forks of a very old silverware set. She eased backward until she could reach down and pick up the knife.

"All right! Now what, Austin?" She peered back toward the living room. "Brady, honey, could you come in here a minute? I need your help in the kitchen. Men! They never help out around the house!"

Lord, I'm babbling, aren't I? Why do I always sound like a raving idiot when I get real nervous?

She slowly leaned back and began to saw the knife back and forth on the silver duct tape. There was little progress.

"The tape can't be that tough!" She glanced back over the corner of her shoulder. "Of course, it would help if I used the sharp side of the knife."

Carefully trying to avoid dropping the knife, she turned it over in her hand and now sawed quickly through the tape that bound her feet.

She stood up more easily, but her legs wobbled. She staggered back into the living room with the knife, her hands still taped behind her back.

"Stoner, I'm trying the best I can. If you're not dead, this would be a very good time to wake up."

A large knot had formed on his head, but the bleeding had stopped, and the blood now caked in his hair.

"Water. I need to pour some water on your face."

Lynda stepped back and dropped the knife to the floor. She was surprised that it landed point down and stuck tight in a worn spot in the linoleum that exposed the wooden floor. She hurried back to the tiny sink and grabbed a pan of petrified noodles. Backing up to the faucet, she turned the handle.

"Where's the water? Come on, faucet!"

She yanked back and forth on the other handle, but still there was no water.

"There's water down there for the cows; there has to be water up here! Maybe she has bottled water somewhere. How do they run a refrigerator without electricity?"

She tossed the pan in the sink and backed up to the ice-box. Stooping a little, she opened the door. There was no light, but she could feel cold air billow out. *No water. One cola . . . one beer . . . and something that looks like . . . Jell-o? Okay.*

She scrunched around and jammed her back side into the refrigerator. Feeling a cold can, she pulled it out and then turned around.

"Good. I got the Pepsi."

Maneuvering it around in her left hand, she pulled the tab and opened the can. Then she walked back out to where Brady lay on the floor.

"Okay, cowboy, just a little splash of this, and you can wake up and get us out of this mess." She staggered back and shook the can, sprinkling the contents all over Brady and the floor.

"Oh, man." She grimaced. "I missed. I poured it mainly all over your shirt. The very least you could do is wake up and complain!"

Stepping around the erect knife, she returned to the kitchen, backed up to the ice box, and wiggled around until she laid hold of the beer can.

"Okay, Stoner, you know how I feel about men who get drunk, but . . . well, keep your mouth closed."

She backed up to him, opened the can, and began to pour. It immediately slipped out of her hand, hit him on the chin, causing a slight cut, and rolled to his chest where the contents gurgled out onto his jacket and down his neck.

"Eh . . . sorry, honey. Brady, this isn't working, and I'm getting worried. You've got to wake up so we can go find that Mendoza woman and kill her. No . . . no, I didn't mean that. We'll find her and torture her slowly."

She couldn't keep from shaking all over.

Lord, I'm getting real nervous about this. He's not waking up. I don't think I can handle this. You promised that You wouldn't put me in any situation that I couldn't handle. But You overestimated me this time. I really can't do this. I like dull routine. I'm not cut out for life in the West. This is not my idea of a good time. Oh, man, I'm going to cry.

Looking down at Brady, she began to sob.

Lynda Dawn Austin, he needs you. If you were lying down there, and he was standing up here, he'd find some way to help you. Girl, stop shaking! You've got to get that tape off!

Tears streaming down her cheeks, she searched the room again. She walked over to the front door, backed into it, pulled it open, turned around, and stared outside. The storm still blew, but she thought the visibility was a little better.

"She did it, Brady. She shot your tires. I can't believe you lost those new tires!" Austin took several deep breaths of the frigid air and felt her head clear. Then she swung the door almost closed and stepped back over to Stoner.

Dropping hard to her tender knees, she sat on the floor near the table and backed over to the stuck butcher knife. With a look back over her shoulder, she gently rubbed the taped wrists up and down against the sharp edge of the knife blade.

The front door banged open. Lynda jumped and slightly cut her thumb.

She came back!

Capt. Patch pounced through the door instead.

"Close the door!" she shouted.

The dog stopped and cocked his head.

"Close the door. You'll freeze Brady!" she called.

The dog ignored her command and proceeded to investigate Stoner closely. He seemed especially interested in what had been spilled on his master's chest.

Lynda could feel the knife slicing through the tape. She strained to see behind her. Suddenly her left hand broke free of the tape, and both hands swung around in front of her. She carefully pulled the tape off her painful wrists and sucked the drops of blood off her thumb. She rubbed her wrists as she stood up and walked over to close the front door.

Capt. Patch busily licked up the cola and beer that soaked Brady's neck.

"No, Captain! Brady's hurt. Get away from him!"

Brady opened one eye and then the other. He sat up quickly, grabbed his head, and then sank down on one elbow.

"Oh . . . Captain! I thought that was Miss Lynda Dawn licking my neck!"

"This is no time for humor, Stoner."

"Who coldcocked me?"

"Ms. Mendoza."

"Why? Did I do something, or does she just hate men in general?"

"You walked in her door uninvited. She doesn't like company. Don't take it personal."

He lifted up his soaked jacket and sniffed. "This smells horrible!" He rubbed his chin and smeared some blood across it. "Have I been drinking?"

"No. I tried to wake you up."

"By pouring beer all over me?"

"I was aiming for your face and missed."

"Missed? How can you miss?"

"My hands were tied behind my back at the time, Stoner."

"Did you cut your thumb?"

"A little. And there's a cut on your chin."

"Did she hit me twice?"

"Nope. Just once. That chin injury came when I . . . dropped the full can of beer on your face."

He sat up and leaned against the door, patting Capt. Patch with his right hand. Struggling to lift his left hand up to his wounded head, he gingerly traced his wound with his fingers.

"We must be on the right track. Did she have the final chapter?"

"All she said was that Drew mailed her a birthday present in the container."

"Well, that's nice—send birthday presents by Fed. Ex. and charge it to your company."

"That's what I'm thinking. You need to bandage that head."

"I'll tell you what I need. I need some painkiller and a clean shirt. I don't aim to smell this bad all day." He struggled to his feet, staggered over to the sofa, and flopped down.

She stepped to the door, swung it open, and then closed it quickly.

"Eh . . . she shot your new tires, Brady."

"You've got to be kidding. All four of them?"

"It looks like it."

"Man, I can't believe this. For thirty years I have never had my tires tampered with or slashed, let alone shot at. I'm gettin' very, very angry!"

"I don't think she wanted us to follow her."

"Where did she go? What kind of rig did she have?"

"I didn't see it," Lynda admitted.

"I bet it had a trailer hitch. Do you know what I found out there in the barn?"

"What took you so long? I needed you in the house."

"Sorry, babe. I was investigating. I didn't turn out to be much help anyway. Guess what I found behind those one hundred bales of hay in the barn?"

"The final chapter of Chance McCall?"

"No. A large boat."

"But there isn't a lake for miles around here."

"My guess is that it's for locating an underwater cave full of gold. It looked like she was stockpiling diving and food supplies."

"But there's a snowstorm blowing, and we're in the middle of the prairie. Why would she come out here?"

"It's almost exactly dead center in the middle of the state." Brady dragged himself over to the fireplace and stirred up the embers and then sat down on the hearth, holding his head in his hands.

"So?"

"So let's suppose you thought there was some buried gold in a Montana lake, but you didn't know where. Yet you wanted to go out there and get your gear together."

"Then why not a remote, secluded location in the middle of the state that would be about equidistant from every spot?"

"Exactly. You gather supplies unnoticed and wait. But she surely waited a long time. Didn't they say she moved out here early last summer?"

"Something like that. But we thought this chapter would be in the office by the first of July. She must have been working with someone in the office."

"Like good, old Drew?"

"I guess. I didn't know he was that close to our production schedule."

Brady carefully stroked the wound on his head. "I've got a splitting headache."

"Stoner, we've got to get you to a doctor."

"Oh, darlin', I've been horse-kicked in the head worse than this."

Lynda let out a piercing scream. Brady jumped straight to his feet. Capt. Patch began to bark.

"What's the matter?" he hollered. "What is it? What's wrong? What do you see?"

"I told you, Stoner, that if I ever hear you say, 'Oh, shucks, ma'am, I've been hurt worse than this,' one more time, I would scream!"

"Okay. I'll let a doc take a look."

"Good."

"That is, if the swellin' don't go down in a few days!"

"Stoner, you want me to start screaming again?"

"No, but I want you to tell me why you thought that chapter would be turned in by the first of Ju-ly."

"McCall was scheduled to deliver the whole works by the first, but he held back on that last chapter until a couple weeks ago. Remember, I told you how paranoid he was?"

"Paranoid, or justifiably suspicious. So Ms. Mendoza got stuck out here a lot longer than she expected. No wonder she was so ticked."

"And now she's headed off to some lake in the fall instead of in the summer."

Brady stood up, pulled off his coat, and started unbuttoning his shirt. "But who's in this with her? She can't expect to dive for a cave that professional divers couldn't find."

"Maybe Drew and his girlfriend are going to meet her somewhere," Lynda suggested.

"Then why ship the package? Why not just hand-deliver it?"

"You think maybe she hired some locals to help her?"

"Not from the Judith Basin. Can't be many professional divers out on this prairie."

"There must be some divers in Montana somewhere."

"But they wouldn't be better than Chance and his buddies, would they?"

"You're right about that. Several of them are now in the Divers' Hall of Fame." Lynda turned back toward Brady. "What are you doing?"

"Taking off my shirt. Remember, you're going out to get my duffel bag—and some Advil. I'd burn this shirt, but the flare-up would probably catch the house on fire."

"Are you going to be okay?"

"You're just going out to the rig, right?"

"The last time one of us left the house, everything exploded on us."

"Go on, darlin', before I start liking this place. Your friends in Lewistown didn't say how much they were askin' for it, did they?"

"That's a joke, right?"

"No, I'm serious. With a little personal care, this could make a fine ranch."

"Stoner, I don't understand the way your mind works. This place is teetering on the edge of the earth. It is severely inhospitable and truly inaccessible."

"Yeah, ain't it grand? I wonder how many acres go with it? Don't you think this would make a great house to raise kids in?"

"Not my kids," she huffed and headed for the pickup.

Lord, we are totally incompatible. Well, not totally, but for all practical purposes. I can't believe he'd say that about this place. It's horrid. I was scared to death. We could both have been killed. This is so remote I don't know how we'll ever get back to civilization, and he wants to move here?

She pulled her purse and his duffel bag out of the pickup,

slammed the door shut, and charged back through the howling snow.

Maybe it was that blow to the head. He's been hit there before. He's delirious. Or maybe he's got a chemical deficiency. With plenty of rest and proper diet . . . Nah, he'll always be the same.

Brady pulled on a black T-shirt and a P.R.C.A. sweatshirt, but he still smelled like beer. His head was swollen too large for his hat, and not finding any running water, he had to let the blood remain in his hair.

"How are we going to get out to the highway this time?" Lynda prodded.

"We'll drive my truck."

"The tires are gone."

"We'll drive on the rims."

"We can do that?"

"Sure. At least until we get to blacktop."

"But won't that ruin your pickup?"

"Nope, but it will definitely ruin the wheels. It's a cinch neither of us is going to hike out of here."

"Your tires keep getting the worst of it."

"Well, it's different this time."

"How's that?"

"At least I know who did the damage. Maybe I should start carrying four spares with me. Are you ready to run out there?"

"But where are we going after you get more tires?"

Brady nursed his head wound with the back of his hand. "We'll start checking every reservoir on the Missouri from Fort Peck Lake to Three Forks."

"What are we looking for?"

"A white boat with a wide blue stripe."

"Won't there be a lot of boats like that?"

"I'm guessing there aren't many out in weather like this. And fewer still that are called *Montana Princess*. That sort of sounds like one of those weak-willed perfumes you wear."

"You think my wearing perfume shows that I'm weak-willed?"

"Nope. What I meant was, it makes the men around you weak-willed."

"Oh." Lynda instantly raised her right wrist to her nose to see if she could smell any perfume.

She couldn't.

◆ ◆ ◆

The trip out to the highway was tedious to the point of being hilarious. The flopping tires lasted only a couple of miles. After that it was just the grinding of steel rims on the gravel roadway. Setting low on the road, the pickup had the feel of a sports car but the speed of a tricycle. Five miles an hour seemed to be the maximum for making sure they had clearance for the dips and boulders. The heater roared but just broke even with the cold air that seemed to blow into the pickup even though the doors were closed and windows shut tight.

Disgusted with the pace, Capt. Patch chose to run alongside the truck, investigating every rock and post. He returned to the cab from time to time to shake down and warm up.

"You been in many parades?" Brady asked.

"Not really. How about you?"

"A lot of rodeos have parades, so I've had my share of riding along. It's about this slow."

Brady grinned and waved his right hand at a phantom crowd.

"Smile and wave, darlin'. Look! There are the Blankenship Triplets! Talk about sweethearts—I can't believe they're already twenty-one."

"Is that their age or their combined IQ?" Lynda shot back. "I refuse to wave at a crowd made up of the Brady Stoner fan club."

Brady studied a map as Lynda steered the disabled truck.

"What are we going to do if we do happen to find our way to the blacktop?"

"Go buy some bulletproof tires."

"Do they make such a thing?"

"I don't think so. Maybe it would be safer to rent a rig and put mine in a garage."

"Do you want to?"

"I was just teasin'."

"Why are you making a joke out of everything? It's no laughing matter."

"I know, babe. But if I don't laugh, I'll get so mad I'll do something really awful. I've not always had the best self-control. But when I'm around you . . . well, I really do try harder. There's somethin' about you, Lynda girl. I just seem to have to try when you're around."

"How's your head feel? It looks horrible."

"It feels like somewhere between havin' a bronc kick you when you fall off in the chute and divin' off the high dive when the pool is empty. But I can still think straight, and it doesn't make sense."

"What's that?"

"This reservoir that we're lookin' for has to be on the Missouri River."

"Why?"

"Because the Missouri and the Yellowstone were the only two navigable rivers a hundred years ago. And there aren't any reservoirs on the Yellowstone."

"Okay, that makes sense. It's on the Missouri."

Suddenly Austin slammed on the brakes. "Brady, what's that?"

"A pronghorn. An antelope. But don't stop. We aren't givin' him a lift."

"There are dozens of them. What are they doing out here?"

"Trying to find some supper, I suppose."

"But it's cold out there. Don't they have someplace to go—a shelter or something?"

"Well, there's the retirement home for antelopes without any living relatives up at Big Sandy, but that's mainly for the older ones."

"Come on, Stoner," she drawled, "you think I just fell off a taxi? You're talkin' to Lynda Dawn of Austin. I got me friends on this trail, so don't you try pullin' nothin' on me, or that bump on your head will seem like a mosquito bite in comparison. You savvy what I'm sayin'?"

"Yes, ma'am!" Brady grinned. "Man, I love it when you start droppin' those *g*'s."

"You do?"

"Yep. It makes me think there's hope for us yet. You know, when this fruitless search is over, I'm goin' to check on what they want for the Double Diamond."

"Brady, let's get something straight. There is no way possible ever that I could live in a place as remote as that ranch!"

"What if it had running water and indoor plumbing?"

"No."

"And electricity?"

"No way."

"And a nice graveled drive?"

"Not even if it were blacktopped."

"And a telephone?"

"Forget it, Stoner."

"And a fax, modem, and satellite dish receiver?"

"Absolutely not."

"And a huge, brand-new log home with real leather furniture and gingham curtains?"

"Get real!"

"And a freezer full of beef and a pantry with enough supplies to last six months?"

"You're dreaming, Stoner."

"And a great big king-size featherbed with a hunter-green comforter three inches thick?"

"With an electric blanket?"

"Yeah, sure." He laughed.

"No, I don't think so."

"And his-and-her hot tubs in a room with big bay windows that give you a view of the entire ranch."

"Nope."

"Really?" he challenged.

"I said no, Stoner." Then she glanced over at him and winked. "We're only going to have one hot tub."

Brady slapped his leg and laughed. "All right, Linda Dawn. If I had that forty tons of Confederate gold, I could probably do all of that. Maybe we ought to buy some diving gear."

"That blow to the head has obviously made you hallucinate."

"Maybe so, but it was a mighty pretty little dream for a while, wasn't it, Miss Lynda Dawn? And I didn't even get to the part about papered horses and registered cattle and a corral full of Brady juniors."

You might have just shot yourself in the foot, Brady dear.

"You can sure make a girl's head spin, Stoner. Now back to reality—tell me why you called this a fruitless search."

"Whoa! You did hear me. Looks like I lost Lynda Dawn of Austin and am stuck with the New York editor. Well, Ms. Austin, as far as I can tell, the only reservoir on the Missouri before you get to Great Falls is Fort Peck Lake."

"Then let's go there."

"Well, that's what I figured. But on the map it looks like it has about 1,500 miles of shoreline, with dozens of boat ramps and enough nooks and crannies to take a year of searching. Even then I doubt if we could find anything."

"Doesn't sound good."

"But in the other direction, it's not much better. Everything shipped upstream past Ft. Benton had to be hauled out of the water and portaged around the falls."

"What falls?"

"Great Falls. Where do you think they got the name?"

"Oh, yeah."

"In the old days it would have taken weeks to carry all that gold around the falls and load it back into boats upstream. Of course, there are several reservoirs between Great Falls and Three Forks. Are you sure you don't remember any landmarks or directions?"

"None. But I could care less about finding the supposed cave. I just want to find my final chapter. I don't need to go where it really is—just wherever someone else thinks it is. If they think it's on upstream, then that's where we need to go."

"How much time do we have to look? Personally, I'm not signed up to rodeo until the circuit Finals, if my riding arm cooperates."

"My return ticket is on Monday."

He glanced over at her and stared from boots to head. "Ma'am, that surely doesn't give me much time."

"For what, Stoner?"

"For finding that chapter for you. What did you think I meant?"

You know perfectly well what I thought you meant. I thought you meant exactly what you wanted me to think you meant. I think . . . I need some perfume.

Brady stared at the map, then tapped it with his finger. "Wait a minute! You said the government built the reservoir right after the turn of the century, right?"

"As far as I can remember."

"I told you that it didn't make any sense that Frank James didn't sneak up here and retrieve the gold after the hope of the

Confederacy faded. But maybe he was too late. Maybe the place was already covered with water by then."

"So? That's what I've been saying all along."

"But I think the Fort Peck Dam was built in the 1930s—you know, a Works Progress Administration project."

"Are you sure? That would be great if it's true. It would eliminate anything east of Great Falls."

"It should be easy enough to check out. But I once went with Marcia Mack to look at some horses in a place called New Deal, Montana. It was right near Fort Peck Dam. You know—New Deal, Depression. Franklin D. Roosevelt was president."

"It surely wouldn't be called New Deal just after the turn of the century. I think you're right. Who's Marcia Mack?"

"I forget. I think she owned a ranch up near Dubois. But I'm sure she was a real—"

"Sweetheart? Aren't they all? Listen, Stoner, by eliminating Fort Peck Lake, we are making progress."

"Aren't I wonderful?"

She glanced over and examined him from boots to head. "I was thinking of another description."

"What?"

"Rustically handsome and clever." She refused to look over and see his reaction to her remarks. "So this means we're headed to Great Falls and then on upriver to some smaller lakes. That is, if we survive the storm, get more tires, and have a doctor look at your head."

"Darlin', trust me—there's nothin' they can do even if it's a slight concussion. I've had it happen before, and they just say no bronc-ridin' for two weeks, and two days later I'm crawlin' back on board."

"Brady, you are going to get some medical attention," she commanded.

He stared at her without smiling and rubbed his one-day-old beard. "Yeah. Maybe you're right. I think Spring Cooper's still the emergency room nurse at the hospital in Lewistown. Maybe we could go back there. I'll pop in there while you go buy us some tires. Now Spring's a real sweetheart. Did I ever tell you the time me and her were stuck for five hours in an empty—"

"I don't want to hear this, Stoner!"

"Oh . . . okay."

They ground their way through the dry, blowing snow.

"In an empty what?" she finally asked.

"Oh, it was nothin', really."

"Stoner!"

"An empty grain silo."

"And just how in the world did you get stuck in a—no, I don't want to know. Let's change the subject."

"Look up there. Blacktop. I told you we could find the highway."

"Are we going to drive like this all the way back to Lewistown?"

"Nope. We'd ruin the car and the road, plus get plowed into from behind. We've got to flag a ride. Only I'm not too sure how many will want to pull over and give a ride to someone who looks like this." He pointed to his injured head. "On the other hand, I didn't like the way you lined up a ride yesterday."

"It's too cold for either of us to get out there. Maybe we'll just pull over to the side of the highway and wait for someone to stop."

"Sure, we can do that the first couple hours, but when we run out of gas and can't run the heater, we'll have to think of a better plan. No one's coming down this road on a day like today," Brady declared, "and it's a cinch they won't stop for us."

"Hey, there are some headlights. It's a pickup, and they're slowing down!"

"Let me do the talkin', darlin'. I'll see if I can convince him into givin' us a lift," Brady insisted.

"I think it's Emmitt Earl."

"Who?"

"One of the men in the cafe at Lewistown."

"You know them all by name?"

"Well, not all of them. Emmitt's a regular sweetheart," she purred. "Look, he's pulling over."

She rolled down her window as the man in the white tobacco-stained pickup pulled in very close to them, pointed the other direction.

"Howdy, Miss Lynda. Say, does this old boy ever aim to put tires on this rig? Or is this the latest style in Idaho?"

"Ms. Mendoza practiced on it with her Winchester .32 special."

"Well, don't that beat all? Is she still holed up back there? I can call the sheriff."

"There's a phone around here?"

"I got my cellular, darlin'." Emmitt Earl spat tobacco out into the storm with the ease of a lifetime of practice and then wiped his mouth on the back of his hand. "You want me to call someone to bring you out some tires?" He stared down at Brady's truck. "And wheels? Or if you like, I can just give you a ride back to town, and you can leave your yahoo out here."

"Emmitt Earl, this my friend Brady Stoner."

"Howdy, sir." Brady started to tip his hat, then remembered he wasn't wearing it.

"You the one that won third money riding barebacks at Miles City this year?"

"Yes, sir."

"That was a good ride, son. They scored you too low."

"Thank you, sir."

"Well, Lynda Dawn, you already got yourself a good 'un. Texas girls always could pick 'em. The missus is from Lubbock herself. You ain't the one that hit him with a fryin' pan, are ya?"

Brady leaned across Capt. Patch and shouted out Lynda's

window. "Can you get One-Eye Gillette on the line? He'll know what I need."

"I can do you one better. I can get someone to pay for it, too."

"What do you mean?" Lynda asked.

"I found out who shot your tires out over at U-Bet yesterday."

"Who?"

"Percy Hamilton's youngest."

"Who's Percy Hamilton?"

"He's got a big spread across the road there. I guess Billie was out on a four-wheeler huntin' antelope and decided that you were the ones rustling cattle. So your tires got plinked."

"He's a good shot."

"She. Billie's their twelve-year-old daughter. Anyway, by the time she went to get her daddy and they came back, you'd left. They were going to go to town in a day or two and report it. Percy said to pay you whatever the tires cost. He said Billie will pay him back when she sells her calves next month."

"He can buy the tires, but I need to buy the wheels. Do you mind if I come over to your rig and use the cellular? We're going to freeze with the windows down!" Brady called.

"You're right about that. Come on, but it's a little dirty. I ain't washed it in a few . . . years."

◆ ◆ ◆

Brady and Lynda Dawn spent the next two hours in Emmitt Earl's pickup. Gillette reported that it would be that long before he could get new tires mounted and reach them. But they didn't park by the roadway. Instead, Emmitt Earl gave them a whirlwind tour of the Double Diamond's lower range. He drove fifty miles an hour down narrow roads and trails, pointing out geographical features and sites of historical events.

Unfortunately, all Brady and Lynda saw was a narrow strip of dead grass and blowing snow.

They got back to the pickup in time to help One-Eye mount the last two tires. Emmitt Earl left them there and headed back to town. When they were finished, Lynda and Brady piled into the tow truck to settle up accounts.

"Stoner," Gillette said grinning, "if I had one more customer like you, I could retire in a week."

"They just don't make tires like they used to," Brady complained. "Used to be you could get 'em to last three, four days."

"I can get you some of them solid rubber tires like the South American *presidentes* use. 'Course they cost about a thousand apiece. At the rate you're going, you'll have that paid for in a week. Listen, Percy's paying for the tires, and I had the used rims on the rack for twenty-five dollars each. Send me a couple NFR tickets, and we'll call it a push."

"You got it, partner. Thanks. I'm hopin' I won't need any more tires from you. We're leavin' the basin."

"Don't blame you, Stoner. Is it a secret where you're goin'? You know, just in case someone else asks about you."

"What do you mean, someone else?"

"Hey, didn't I tell you? About an hour before you called, this gal drives into the station and asks if Brady Stoner was in town."

Brady glanced over at Lynda. She raised her eyebrows and sulked.

"Who was lookin' for me?"

"Didn't say. She wasn't from around here though. She had Nevada plates."

"Was it an old dark green Cadillac?" Brady quizzed.

"Yeah. Who is she? She looked kind of rough."

"I don't know, but I saw a big green car down at LaVerne's a couple of nights ago. Nevada plates, huh?"

"Could it be that L. G. Minor from Ely?" Lynda asked.

"L. G.? Oh, no, she drives a Dodge truck. And, besides, L. G. definitely does not look rough."

Stoner, the girl who marries you will have to chain you to the gatepost. Or live in the absolute boonies . . . like the Double Diamond.

"What did she look like, One-Eye?"

"Remember that blonde schoolteacher you were sweet on a couple years ago?"

What blonde schoolteacher? I don't remember him mentioning anything about a schoolteacher.

"Sort of looked like an older version though. Maybe forty. If she's lived a hard life, maybe she was actually younger. Her voice was deep and kind of rusty-soundin'. Her hair was pretty yellow, but like I said, she didn't take care of herself too much. Anyway, I told her you came through and were out looking for a ranch in the Judith Basin. For some reason, she headed out east instead of south. No tellin' where she is now. That's all I know."

"I don't know any gal in Nevada who drives a Cadillac. If you see her again, try to get her name and maybe a license plate number."

"Sure. You want me to point her your way?"

"Nope."

"Oh? One of those deals!" He turned toward Lynda. "Miss Austin, I don't know how long you've known Brady, but he's got more—"

"Charm with the ladies?" she interjected.

"Yeah. That's about what I was going to say."

"One-Eye, we're going to head down the road before you get me in big trouble."

At Eddie's Corner, they turned west into the blowing storm and away from Lewistown. By the time they reached the north edge of the Little Belt Mountains, the storm had lifted, and the snow stopped. The heavy clouds hung just above the power poles and brought darkness early, but the wind slacked as they approached the lights of Great Falls.

"What's our plan for tonight, boss?" Brady asked.

"Boss? I have been in control of nothing on this trip," she retorted. "How about cleaning up and a quiet supper in some restaurant that has a big fireplace?"

"Are you hungry?"

"Starved. I haven't had anything since that bowl of oatmeal."

"I know a place with thick steaks and great atmosphere."

"Oh, sure. And waitresses with ear-to-ear grins and silicone implants?"

"Ah, but they can't measure up to you, Lynda Dawn—in the smile category, that is."

"Don't get personal, Stoner! Are you going to get that head wound checked out?"

"If the swellin' isn't goin' down in the mornin', I'll see a doc. Have you got any preference where we stay?"

"How about across the street from a mall? I need to buy a few things." *Like stronger perfume.*

"I've been thinkin' about some supplies myself."

"What kinds of things?"

"Well, if we're poking around a lake or two, how about a little camping gear—you know, just in case we get stranded?"

"There is no way I'm sleeping out in this kind of weather, Brady Stoner."

"It would make us look like campers. That gives us an excuse for exploring all around. You have any hiking shoes?"

"Just boots and tennies."

"I'll pick us up some gear."

"Brady, I really can't afford to spend—"

"Hey, no cost. I've got a friend that owns a pawn shop across town. I can borrow whatever we need and then just bring it back. We'll only have to pay for what we lose. What do you say?"

"As long as you don't come back with two green-broke horses. I'm not in a riding mood."

"Trust me."

I do not think that word means what you think it means, Señor Stoner.

◆ ◆ ◆

Lynda Austin had cleaned up, changed clothes, and was heading out of her motel room when she thought about calling Kelly Princeton. Finding Kelly's home phone busy, she called Nina DeJong instead.

To a continuing chorus of "Oh, wow!" and "I don't believe it!" and "Gosh, really?" she told Nina of the day's activities.

"Lynda, maybe you'd better come back to New York. It's not safe out there."

"If I remember, the city isn't all that innocuous either."

"But I don't understand a mind-set that says you get hit over the head and tires shot, but you don't report it to Wyatt Earp, or whomever."

"We were in the lady's house at the time."

"You were trying to keep from freezing to death."

"We did find the shipping package. That must mean something. Did you have any luck in the office?"

"Sort of," Nina reported.

"What did you find?"

"I just happened to think that the recycling guy doesn't come until tomorrow, so I spent the afternoon digging through a week's worth of shredding."

"Did you find anything?"

"Sort of—maybe. I think it's something."

"Well? What is it?"

"It's shredded, of course, but it could be some maps or charts."

"Good grief, you think someone shredded the final chapter?"

"No, it was copy paper that was shredded. But it was a really dark copy, like maybe the machine wasn't adjusted or something. In fact, it was so dark it could have been a map of Manhattan."

"I signed a notarized document pledging to McCall that we would not photocopy that final chapter. I should have known that wouldn't work. Could you read anything at all?"

"I have it piled on my desk at work, but you know how the shredder is. There's nothing but some disjointed wiggly lines and broken letters. I did find a scrap that had some sort of X marked next to a capital *W* and a capital *C* underneath, I think. But it's worse than one of those little map circles in the *Saturday Evening Post*."

"Search through it one more time. But it doesn't make any sense to have photocopied the maps if you're going to steal them anyway."

"Chance McCall's sister in Florida called Kelly," Nina reported.

"Does she know where Chance is?"

"No, but she heard from a mutual friend that Chance's diving buddy, Leo, called a loan shark in south Florida and had some funds wired to him."

"Where? Did they have an address?"

"She didn't know. Somewhere in the Bahamas."

"A loan shark? That sounds like they're desperate for more operating capital."

"She thought you might want to know."

"Everything about this book project is weird. Do we know if Chance was still with this Leo?"

"Nope. She sounded worried though. She kept saying that maybe the Bermuda Triangle got him."

"Great. How can one project suddenly get so complicated?"

"Lynda, what do we do if Chance does get word that you're trying to phone him and calls the office?"

"Get a number where he can be reached, and I'll call him. Don't tell him anything about the missing chapter. That's my job."

"And how can I reach you?"

"I'll call you or Kelly every evening that I can—provided I'm not camping out in the wilderness with Brady."

"Oh, really? You mean, you and the cowboy sharing a sleeping bag and campfire and all that?"

"Campfire, but not sleeping bags. We're headed out to a couple of lakes tomorrow. Who knows? This whole trip is strange."

"It gets stranger," Nina announced.

"How's that?"

"L. George Gossman phoned Kelly today. He said that he and Mrs. Gossman changed their vacation plans. Instead of going to Mexico, they decided on Yellowstone Park. They're staying in a place called West Yellowstone, Montana. Is that near you?"

"We just drove through Yellowstone the night before last!"

"Is it getting crowded out there yet?"

"Crowded? It was nice to be in Great Falls. It's the first time in four days that I've been around more than six people."

"You didn't run across Mr. Hampton and Spunky yet?"

"It's a big state. They'll be tucked away in some fancy resort somewhere, I'm sure."

"Yeah, well, if you see them, tell them I said hello and hope they're having a wonderful time."

"Kissy, kissy? Well, right now I'm going to the mall. They have a Perfume Emporium."

"Oh, no." Nina laughed. "Poor old Brady doesn't have a chance."

"Yeah, he'll probably take one sniff of my exotic fragrance and beg me to marry him. Nina, I'll check in with you two tomorrow if I can. Call Kelly for me."

"I don't know—it's pretty boring news. So far you were held at gunpoint, tied down, the pickup shot at, but other than that, not even a kiss?"

"I didn't say there were no kisses."

"What? You didn't tell me the best part!"

"I have to go, Nina."

"Tell me about the kissing part."

"It was sweet."

"Sweet? That's it? You think I'm still in junior high? That's all you're going to say?"

"It was real, real, real sweet. Bye."

◆ ◆ ◆

Lynda spent several minutes reviewing her weekly perfume chart as she walked across the street to the mall. *Tomorrow it says, "Fragrant Fountain or new scent." Well, Brady Stoner, you're in for a new scent—whatever it is. I'll know it when I smell it.*

She found the Montana Perfume Emporium appropriately lodged between Victoria's Secret and Bernie's Jewelry Outlet. She started at one end of the counter and had whiffed a dozen fragrances, placing the samples on a little blotter that was provided, when a clerk with glittering turquoise eye shadow came up to her.

"Excuse me, this may sound a little strange," the clerk began, "but do you happen to be Lynda Austin from New York City?"

Lynda looked up at the girl's dramatic swirling blonde hair and bright blue million-dollar eyes.

"Eh . . . yes, I am. Have we met?"

"Oh, wow, really! You're really her? I mean, I didn't think someone from New York City would be wearing cowboy boots and jeans. I've never been east of Plentywood, but I figure you could guess that."

"But how did you know me?"

If she mentions she saw me on tabloid TV as a cowboy's love-slave, I'll—I'll smear her mascara!

"You just made me one hundred dollars, Mrs. Austin."

"Miss."

"Yes?"

"No, I'm *Miss* Austin, not Mrs. Austin."

"Oh, yeah . . . Well, yesterday about noon this big guy—dark-complected, sort of gray wavy hair—came walking into the shop. I knew I had seen him somewhere before, so I'm thinking maybe he's one of those Hollywood types who's buying up ranches around here, you know? Well, he says to Jammi and me, if we see a woman with dark brown shoulder-length hair, five-foot-ten, with green eyes, light skin, slightly freckled, long neck, small . . . eh, chest, wearing Autumn Rose Blush lipstick and Vuarnet Cat-eye sunglasses, smelling like a perfume factory and looking for a different scent, we're supposed to call him. If we found you, he'd give us one hundred dollars."

I feel like a sample patient on the first day of med. school. Only one person on earth gives that kind of detailed description.

"You'll never guess who it is!"

Lynda looked around the room, almost expecting someone to be hiding behind the counter.

"Joaquin Estaban?"

"You did know! He's the one who writes all those great westerns."

"I know. I'm his editor."

"You are? Wow! My boyfriend Charles has read every one

of those novels. He was so totally jealous that I got to meet Mr. Estaban. Maybe Charlie would like to meet you." The girl took an up-and-down look at Austin. "On second thought, I'd better keep him away."

"Oh, does he go for women with . . . long necks?"

"What?"

"Never mind. So Joaquin told you I was coming in here? I didn't know I was coming here until a few minutes ago."

"He said for you to call him. I'll get the number for you. He's staying at the motel across the street from the mall."

"What a coincidence. So am I."

"You know, he's kind of handsome for an older man. He reminds me a lot of my father."

"I'll be sure and tell him that."

"Here's the phone."

Lynda dialed the number.

"*¡Hola! ¿Qué quiere usted?*"

"Cut the Spanish, Joaquin. Where are the proofs to *Ambush on the Nez Perce Trail?*"

"Ms. Austin! You are a slave driver! What do you say we hop a plane and fly to Cabo San Lucas for the weekend?"

"Get real, Joaquin!"

"I have the finished proofs with me."

"That's only four weeks behind schedule."

"Doesn't time fly when you're havin' fun?"

"How in the world did you know I would come to this shop?"

"Deduction, Ms. Austin. It's the only perfumery in the state. Sooner or later you'd sniff it out."

"So why did you really drive clear to Montana to see me?"

"Why, just to see your enchanting smile and reflect in your radiant beauty."

"Save that for perfume counter clerks."

"I just came up with a tremendous idea for a new western

saga set in the Black Hills. So how about letting me take you and Brady—you are still with Brady, aren't you?"

"Yes."

"Are you married yet?"

"No."

"Engaged?"

"What has this to do with anything?"

"I'll take that for a no. Look, Lynda Dawn, don't ever marry a rodeo hand. It will be nothing but a wild ride and plenty of bruises."

"Joaquin, I can't believe I'm standing here listening to your dumb jokes."

"If you'll remember, I'm the one responsible for you two meeting. And I haven't seen either of you in six, eight months. So I'll treat you to the best Chinese food in the state of Montana, and we'll talk about a series that will have the studios beating a path to your door for movie rights."

"Not tonight, Joaquin. But you can treat us to breakfast."

"They don't serve breakfast."

"Who doesn't?"

"The Flaming Dragon Chinese Restaurant."

"Joaquin, it's been a very tiring day. Brady and I are going to have a quiet supper tonight . . . alone. *¿Comprende?* So let's meet for breakfast."

"You're breaking my heart."

"You'll survive. Where's the best place in town for biscuits and gravy?"

"Thelma & Louise's Cafe on 10th."

"You're kidding. Thelma & Louise?"

"Yep. What time shall we meet?"

"How about 9:00 A.M.?"

"Oh, you mean for lunch? I thought you said breakfast."

"Okay, 8:00 A.M."

"You got it. Have a nice evening."

"You too, Joaquin. I really do appreciate your driving clear over here."

"Sure, kiddo. Would you give Steffani a message for me?"

"Who?"

"The blonde who works there. Tell her to meet me at the Flaming Dragon Chinese Restaurant at 9:15 P.M., and I have the money I promised her. In fact, I'll buy her supper."

"Yeah, I bet you will. Are you going to buy her boyfriend Charlie supper, too?"

"Oh, if good old Charlie shows up, all she gets is the money."

"I'll tell her. She might go along with it. She did mention how much you reminded her of her father."

"That's mean, real mean, Lynda Dawn."

"It's a gift we editors have. *Hasta mañana, Señor Estaban.*"

◆ ◆ ◆

Lynda left the mall with one bottle of perfume oil, a mixture of 70 percent Sweet Virtue and 30 percent Rosy Rose. She went back to her room and changed for dinner, wearing the one dress she had brought on the trip.

Tonight it's Western chic and plenty of perfume. Hang on to your riggin', cowboy, because this evening is just for the two of us.

She had barely finished combing her hair and had changed her mind about the black-and-silver earrings when the phone rang.

"Hi, darlin, I just got back. I got us everything we're going to need out at those lakes."

"Great. I'm starved and really looking forward to this place we're going. You'll never guess who I talked to."

"And you'll never guess who I talked to!"

"I'm sure she's a real sweetheart. Listen, Joaquin Estaban's in town, and we're going to have breakfast with him in the morning at a place called Thelma & Louise's Cafe."

"Hey, that's the best biscuit-and-gravy place in the state!"

"That's what I hear."

"You want to hear somethin' wild? I'm coming out of the pawn shop, and who walks in but your boss?"

"L. George Gossman?"

"No, the big boss—Mr. Hampton, IV, himself along with that firecracker receptionist."

"Spunky? She's the former receptionist. I told you they got married, didn't I? What in the world was Mr. Hampton doing at a pawn shop in Great Falls?"

"He was kind of secret-like and changed the subject. I don't think he recognized me at first, but Spunky grabbed me like I was a new twenty-dollar bill."

"She did, did she?"

"And here's the best part. I talked them into havin' supper with us."

"You what?"

"Yeah, don't that beat all? I'll be ready in five minutes. I'll meet you down at the parking lot. Isn't it going to be a great evenin'?"

Lynda slumped down on the motel bed and sighed.

SIX

"Well, Lynda Dawn, wasn't that a delightful evening? An intimate dinner with publishing tycoon T. H. Hampton, Jr., and his lovely new bride."

The face staring back at her in the mirror reminded her of someone she had met before. The navy blue sweat suit that served as pajamas glittered a gold PRO-RODEO above the silhouette of a bareback rider taking a wild ride on a bronc. The whole emblem reflected backwards.

"Get real, Austin. It was one of the most disappointing nights of your life. It was like having to take your little sister with you on a date. No, it was worse." She continued the conversation with her mirrored image.

"Four hours with Spunky gushing over Junior and him looking like the cat who had swallowed the mouse. Never once were Brady and I alone. Never once did we have time to relax. Never once did we have a private conversation. Good grief, they never even told us why they decided to honeymoon in Great Falls, Montana."

Time to clean up, girl. Wash your hair. Wear something feminine. Sure, like a parka with lace trim! Maybe it won't be so cold today. Anyway, you get to be with him all day. Nothing will come between you. Except Capt. Patch. And a search for an unnamed lake. It's my own fault. Why do I only come out to see him when there's some business to take care of? We ought to just go to that resort in Jackson Hole and . . . eh, no, maybe not. Lord, this is the toughest relationship I've ever had to do right.

And I do want to do it right.

Most of the time.

◆ ◆ ◆

Lynda finished her shower and stood, half-dressed, on the charcoal-gray carpet to examine her perfume chart. *Now when I wear rose pink, I usually wear Basically Beautiful, but it doesn't do well in the cold. Maybe I should wear the Sweet Virtue–Rosy Rose. Dream on, girl. You've never worn the same perfume two days in a row in your entire life.*

Is it snowing today?

Austin walked to the window and stuck her head out between the heavy peach flowered curtains.

Wow! It's going to be clear today. Where did that storm go? To the Black Hills, I guess. The parking lot looks wet. It must have rained a little, but at least the sun is coming up. I'll wear the Basically Beautiful.

"Hey!" she found herself hollering. In the parking lot a woman with a gray-and-black knit cap pulled over her ears held a rifle in her hand as she stalked Brady's pickup, now loaded down with what looked like half the contents of an army surplus store, including a green aluminum canoe.

"What's she doing?" Lynda mumbled as the woman approached the front of the rig and suddenly slammed the butt of the rifle into the left headlight, exploding glass across the pavement.

"You can't do that!" Lynda scrambled to open the second-story window, but she couldn't unlatch it. The woman proceeded to shatter the other headlight. Someone in the parking lot shouted at her, and she sprinted across a flower bed to a dark green Cadillac, tossed the rifle into the front seat, then roared out into the street, and turned left.

Lynda pulled on her sweatshirt and ran out of the room barefoot. Taking the carpet-lined stairs two at a time, she ran to the parking lot. The ice-cold sidewalk froze her feet. Stepping gingerly across the wet blacktop, she got to the truck about the time several others approached.

"Watch out for the glass, lady!" one man called.

"Is this your rig?" another asked.

"Yes. Well, it belongs to my, eh, my friend."

"Did you see the woman who did this?" one of the men asked her.

"Only from the room. Did anyone see her close enough to tell who it was?"

"I barely saw her. Besides, I don't know anyone around here. I'm from Vancouver. But I did notice it was a green Cadillac that she drove, if that's of any help."

"Did you get a license number?"

"No. Quite sorry about this."

"I think you better call the police," one man suggested.

"And your insurance company. I mean, your friend's insurance company," added the other man.

Where's Capt. Patch? What kind of watchdog is he?

By the time she reached her room, her toes were curled and blue. It wasn't until she approached the door to her room that she realized she had forgotten to take her key.

"Oh, great!" she moaned as she trotted off to the lobby.

It took several minutes for the clerk to find the time to walk with her to her room and unlock the door, then find a piece of photo I.D. to prove that she was indeed Lynda Dawn Austin. Once the clerk left, she immediately dialed Brady's room.

"Yeah?" a young woman's voice replied.

Austin immediately slammed the phone down.

Did I dial the right room? It's 104, right? I'll try again.

She lifted the receiver, punched in a 1 and an 0, and then hung up.

I can't try again. What if it is the right room? It's 7:30 A.M. What's she doing in Brady's room at 7:30?

Lynda grabbed up her key and dashed out of the room. Once again she scooted down the stairs and up the hall. A house-cleaning cart blocked the open door to Room 104. A maid scurried about inside the room making the bed.

Housekeeping? Of course! Thank You, Lord. Why do I always think the worst?

"Excuse me," Lynda called out to a black-haired girl who looked about eighteen. "Do you know where the man is who was in this room?"

"Brady? Oh, he checked out half an hour ago. Why are so many women looking for him? As if I didn't know." She giggled like a girl even younger than eighteen.

Other women? Checked out? His truck's still in the lot. How is it that every woman in the West knows his first name?

Scampering into the lobby on freezing feet, she almost stumbled into Joaquin Estaban.

"Well, Miss Lynda Dawn, the weather did warm considerably, but you really should wear some shoes."

"Joaquin, have you seen Brady?"

"Did you lose him?"

"This is serious, Joaquin. Someone just trashed his truck, and I can't find Brady."

The woman at the reservation desk looked over at them. "Are you looking for Mr. Stoner?"

"Yes." Lynda scooted over to the counter.

"Brady checked out about forty minutes ago. I believe he went to walk his dog. He said if I saw a really classy lady from

Austin, Texas, with an awesome smile, I should tell her he'll be back at quarter till."

The woman looked at Lynda from head to foot and slowly shook her head. "That wouldn't be you by any chance, would it?"

"From Austin?" Joaquin quizzed.

"Eh, it's a little joke. Anyway, yes, I am the one. He was obviously teasing."

"Obviously," the woman replied.

Thank you for that snotty, little put-down. You obviously will remain single for a long time to come, lady. I didn't mean that. Look who's talking. I'm just upset, Lord, really upset. And I'm not very gracious when I'm upset.

She sighed deeply and tried to smile at the woman behind the desk.

"Joaquin, could you wait for Brady out front and tell him about his truck? I'll go finish getting ready and be down as soon as I can. I can't believe he walked that dog. In all the times I've been with him, he's never walked Capt. Patch anywhere."

"Maybe the dog's walking him. Go on, I'm glad to hear you are going to wear shoes. Maybe there's still a little New York left in you."

◆ ◆ ◆

Brady, in Wranglers, a denim jacket, and black beaver felt cowboy hat, was twirling a screwdriver to remove the remains of the headlights when Lynda finally made it to the parking lot, rolling her suitcase across the uneven asphalt.

He looked up when she got closer. "The lady in the Cadillac?" he asked.

She nodded.

"You look mighty pretty, darlin'."

"Yeah, eh, thanks," she mumbled, feeling awkward with

Joaquin standing there. "Where were you, Brady? I looked all over for you. I was really worried."

"Me and the Captain took a walk. There was this cute, little brown lady dog in a fenced yard that he wanted me to meet," Brady reported. "Can you describe the gal?"

"Medium height, medium size, brown coat, knit hat pulled down over her ears."

"That could be anyone in town."

"I didn't see her face. Brady, did you call the police?"

"I figured I'd just take care of this myself."

"Take care of what? This lady's been harassing you for two weeks, and you don't even know who it is."

"Darlin', I've got a gut feelin' I need to wait on this one." He wiped his jacket sleeve across his mouth.

"What are you talking about? Your truck was vandalized. Someone has to catch this crazy person. You have to turn this in. I can't imagine Brady Stoner sitting on his hands."

"Actually, she just punched out a couple bulbs. Twenty-five bucks and a little work, and everything will be fine. Besides, this wasn't just some crazy person."

"Brady, I insist. I hired you to help me find the final chapter. So I'm leading this expedition. And I say we are going to report this."

"Lynda Dawn," he ordered, "you're going to have to trust me on this one. I am not goin' to file a complaint. And neither are you. It's not your truck."

"Brady Stoner, you have got to be the most stubborn, unreasonable man I've ever met. You go around marching to your own tune and won't tell me why. Sometimes you are totally impossible to get along with. Has anyone ever told you that?"

"Most every gal I've ever known."

Lynda put her hands on her hips and spun around, refusing to face Brady. As she did, she noticed Joaquin Estaban down on his hands and knees examining a plot filled with dead weeds and flowers.

"What are you doing?" she questioned.

"Did the lady in the Caddy run through here?"

"Eh, yes. How could you tell?"

"Brady, come here," Estaban called. "I think there's a couple of good prints here."

Lynda and Brady walked over but not together.

"Look." Estaban pointed to the bent weeds.

"I don't see anything," she responded.

"See the way the grass is interlaced at the toe? Just two steps and she was back on asphalt. One is here." He placed the palm of his right hand on the weeds and mashed them down. "And the other here." He scooted along and again put his right hand down on a print.

"I still can't see anything," Lynda complained.

"It's a flat print, Brady."

"You figure she's wearing moccasins, Joaquin?"

"Yeah, that's what it looks like."

Estaban pulled the weeds back and examined the print left in the mud.

"Good thing it warmed up, or there wouldn't be any print at all. Look at how she rolled her right foot. Seems to have a bum right leg—maybe a pulled muscle or something."

"But I don't see anything. Are you making this up?" Lynda complained.

Brady didn't even bother bending down to look at the print. "Size five or six?" he asked.

Joaquin looked up at him. "Yeah, that's my guess. You know who this is?"

Brady glanced over at Lynda and back at Joaquin. "Maybe."

"Who?" Lynda demanded.

"I, eh . . . I've got to ponder this thing, darlin'. Don't push me on it."

"What's going on here? This whole thing affects me, too! You don't plan on standing there saying you think you know who it is and not tell me, do you?"

"Yep."

"I can't believe this," she shouted.

Joaquin Estaban stood up and studied Austin and then Stoner. "I take it breakfast is off?"

"Oh, there's no reason for that," Brady assured him.

"Yes, it's off. I'll call you next week from New York," Lynda announced.

"There you go. Another happy couple. I'll leave now if you two promise not to inflict bodily harm upon each other."

"I don't promise anything," Lynda muttered.

"See you on down the road, partner," Estaban called to Brady. "I'm headed for some biscuits and gravy at Thelma & Louise's. Now which one is Thelma?"

"The light-haired one."

◆ ◆ ◆

Austin deposited herself in the pickup and waited for Brady to pull off the last broken headlight. They didn't say a word.

It's not fair. I can't go around putting myself in danger from the actions of some crazy woman with him not even telling me what's going on. I wouldn't treat him that way. I wouldn't treat anyone in the world that way.

He drove them to an auto parts store. She waited in the pickup while he spent about thirty minutes replacing the lamps.

If he'd just tell me what's going on, I could help him. I could forgive him. . . . Well, at least I could help him.

Brady drove west out of Great Falls on Interstate 15. Six

miles out of town he exited the freeway at the Missouri Dunes. Pulling the rig between two of the giant sand dunes, he parked by a faded turquoise oil barrel used as a trash container. Surrounded on three sides by sand dunes more than twenty feet tall, Lynda took a deep breath and sank down in the seat.

"Well, Stoner, why did we stop here? Obviously there is no gold buried in the sand. Or is this another of those 'trust-me' places?"

Brady's head leaned forward, his chin on his chest. "You've got every right to be mad at me, darlin'. But I've got to think this through on my own. I have to handle it this way. Give me some time, honey. I could be wrong about this whole thing. It's somethin' personal, and this is the way I've got to deal with it."

"Brady, it's like we get really close, and then something comes along, and I feel like I don't know you at all. I'm not trying to sound melodramatic, but it scares me."

Lord, I can't figure out if I want to punch his lights out or hug and kiss him.

Capt. Patch whined in the backseat. Brady turned to open the sliding window. The dog leaped out of the truck and disappeared behind the dunes. Brady left the window open, but he turned back to face the front of the truck. The air felt cool, yet comfortable.

"I'm tryin' real hard to be the guy you think I am. I'm just not that simple. I spend a whole lot of my time alone on the road. It's a rare thing to spend two nights in the same place. Never talkin' to the same person twice. Even when I am in crowds—well, it's pretty lonely." He finally looked over at her. His smile was sheepish and shallow.

"As you've noticed, I've got friends all over the West. But none of them are real close. I wish they were. At least some of them. I just don't know how to let someone get close. Whenever I've tried it, things kind of fall apart. I'm sort of an expert on one-day relationships. I take it on myself to, eh, you know, make sure everyone's happy and keep them at a distance."

"Is that how you treat me? Just try to keep me happy?"

"Lynda Dawn . . . it's pretty obvious how I feel about you."

What's obvious? Now would be a really good time to tell me, Stoner.

"You scare me to death," Brady continued.

"I scare you?"

"Yeah, darlin', I'm afraid I'm goin' to start needin' you so much I can't live without you."

"Why does that scare you?" Lynda felt extremely warm. She unfastened her jacket.

"I don't know. I figure the more you get to know me, you won't want to put up with my ways."

"You mean that after all we've been through, I really don't know you? It's all been a charade?"

"No, no, that's not what I mean! But you see how I am. I don't think I have the skills you need. I like rodeoin', I like livin' in the boonies, I like keepin' important things inside, I like—"

"Gravy every day."

He turned to her and grinned. "Yeah. Can you make gravy, darlin'?"

"I have never made gravy in my life. You might as well just take me to the airport and send me back to New York."

"Oh, no, it's an acquired skill. Maybe you could take a homemaking course at Columbia this spring: Introduction to Gravy."

Lynda could feel the tension melt in the back of her neck and above her eyes. "I really don't think they have such a course."

"They should. There wouldn't be so many old maids in New York."

"That did it. Step outside, buster! Your breathing days are over!" Lynda faked a growl.

"Whoa, not you, darlin'. I can guarantee you aren't going to be an old maid."

"And just how can you guarantee that?" She glanced back to make sure the little window was still open. Her face felt flushed and sweaty.

"You'll just have to trust me on that one, Lynda Dawn."

"You're asking me to trust you on lots of things today."

"That's how this whole discussion got started, isn't it? You've got to believe I have our best interests in mind. It's just that when I don't know what to do, I've got to think it out. Maybe someday you can teach me how to handle things differently, but that's the only way I know right now. When I blurt things out, I have a tendency to embarrass the Lord—and myself."

Lynda stared ahead for a few minutes. *Why is it I can't ever stay mad at this man? He can explain away everything.*

"I'm glad we stopped," she finally acknowledged. "I think I'm okay now. Brady, I got so upset back there. I want to tell you something not many people know. I'm a really fragile person."

"Ms. Lynda Austin, career woman?"

"Brady, the only way I can survive day by day is to have every element of my life under total control. If one thing falls apart—like in Jackson or at U-Bet or at the Double Diamond or there at the motel this morning—I just fall apart and do and say all sorts of horrid things. It really scares me, Brady, to be so vulnerable."

"It sort of keeps us prayin', doesn't it?"

"Day and night."

He looked up and stared at her green eyes, then glanced at the rest of her.

"What are you looking at, cowboy?" she asked.

"I've never been around someone who's so open with me and so dad gum pretty!" He quickly looked back out at the dunes. "I don't know. Sometimes I feel like a little boy in an old-fashioned candy shop. All those beautiful, delightful temptations, and I can't get close to any of them."

He took a deep breath and flashed her his killer smile. The tanned chiseled features of his face reflected years of hard outdoor work. His shoulders were wide and strong. There was a deep tingling feeling in her throat. She looked down and murmured softly, "You can get close to some of them."

Just then Capt. Patch let out a series of startled barks.

"Wait a minute, darlin'. I think Capt. Patch needs some help. That's his 'grab-the-varmint-gun-and-come-runnin' bark!"

A large balloon of disappointment hovering above her head suddenly burst and drenched her from hat to boot. She slumped in the truck seat and seriously thought about crying.

"Grab the carbine and come on!" he hollered as he hopped out of the truck and jogged toward the sound of barking.

The air was not nearly as cold as it had been the day before, but Lynda felt a chill to the bone as she stepped down out of the truck and pulled the gun out of the scabbard.

I don't know whether to laugh or cry. This is an insane relationship. If I'm not mad at him, I'm throwing myself at him. I want to be curled up with him in the truck, and I'm hiking through the wilderness toting a gun. This is crazy. It wouldn't even make a good novel. It's too disjointed. Stoner, there have to be better transitions. You can't whisper sweet nothings and then jump out of the truck and chase your dog.

She fastened up her jacket and followed Brady's tracks across the sand. Around the corner of a huge dune, she was shocked to see T. H. Hampton, IV, sunk to his shins in a five-foot dune. He wore a cheap camouflage cloth hat and binoculars around his neck. He was trying to keep Capt. Patch at bay.

"Call off your dog, Stoner," Hampton screamed.

"Mr. Hampton?" Lynda gasped.

"Says he just happened to stop here for a little bird-watching." Brady smiled. His hat was pushed back on his head, his hands jammed into his back pockets.

Lynda felt strange holding the carbine in her hand. "But I haven't seen any birds in these dunes," she pointed out.

"Yeah, that's what I told him. You know, darlin', if a person stood right there on that dune, I'll bet with those binoculars you could peek right into the cab of my truck."

Us? In the truck? Oh, wow! Maybe things turned out okay after all.

"Stoner, that is a disgusting remark," Hampton objected.

"Then you won't mind me steppin' up there and taking a peek through your spyglass just to see if I can look into my truck?"

"Yes, I'd mind."

"Were you spyin' on us?"

"Make your dog back off."

Capt. Patch's barking provided background noise that caused everyone to shout.

"I don't tell him who to bark at, and he doesn't tell me who to talk to. It's a little arrangement we have. Now maybe you'd like to tell me what you are doin' followin' us?"

"Ms. Austin, if you'll just hold that animal, I'll get back to the car, and we'll be going."

"We? You mean Spunky's out here with you? Where?"

"Oh, well . . . we're parked over there." Hampton waved in a northerly direction. "Now hold him back while I climb down off here."

"I can't do that, Mr. Hampton. The Captain's not my dog. We're just real good friends. You see, I don't hold him back if he wants to attack, and he doesn't hold me back if I want to attack. Were you spying on us?"

"I was merely exploring for gold."

"This is getting too complicated for me. I think I'll go visit with Spunky."

Austin found a new black Blazer parked behind a wooden windbreak that had been constructed to protect a picnic table. The table was almost completely covered with sand.

As Lynda approached the rig, Spunky Sasser-Hampton climbed out and stepped toward Lynda. Her long black hair flowed back with the breeze. Spunky toted a three-foot rolled document in her hand. Lynda still packed the Winchester '94 carbine.

"Lynda, what's with the gun? Is Tommy all right?"

"You mean Mr. Hampton?"

"I told him this is crazy."

Spunky wore tight black leather pants, black-fringed cowboy boots, a black Western leather jacket with turquoise insets and yoke. Under the jacket was a black suede vest with fringe, beads, and feather trim. As far as Lynda could tell, nothing was under the vest.

"Spunky, what's going on here? Were you guys really following us?"

"Didn't Tommy tell you?"

"I left him and Brady talking, but why don't you tell me?" Austin swung the gun over her shoulder to point it behind her.

"Oh, it's that old Jesse James gold. Tommy thought it would be fun to try and find it. Is that any way to spend a honeymoon?" Spunky rocked back and forth in her boots as she talked.

"Mr. Hampton wants to find the gold?"

"Yeah, like he needed the money, right? Isn't that the way men are, once they get a crazy notion in their heads? But it hasn't been too bad. I'm going over our house plans. Did I tell you we're building a place on Martha's Vineyard?"

"Eh, no. I didn't know. Spunky, are you telling me Mr. Hampton was following us and spying on us?"

"Well, you do know where that gold is supposed to be

buried, don't you? And we don't have the whole chapter, so it's sort of a guess."

"What do you mean you don't have the whole chapter? You actually have some of the chapter?" Lynda let the gun slip down off her shoulder.

"Obviously." Spunky pointed toward the Blazer. "Oh, it's just a photocopy of course. But there're two pages missing. Tommy thought one might have been a map page. But he doesn't know what's on the other one."

"Where did you get that chapter? Why didn't you mention it last night?"

"Well, it's not like it's the original. That's what you asked about. We have no idea where that is. Tommy said he put the whole thing back on Julie's desk."

"Put it back? You mean, he took it and photocopied it?"

"Sure. How else would he have it?"

"But I guaranteed McCall it would not be photocopied."

"Tommy owns the company, remember? He can do what-ever he wants. Frankly, I don't think there's any gold out here, do you? Seriously, Lynda, after all this time, do they really expect to find any gold?"

"I don't know, and I don't care. If I could find my final chap-ter, I'd just go back to New York and forget this whole thing."

"You would?" Spunky's toothy grin stretched between her white-and-black feathered earrings. "You mean you'd leave that cowboy?"

"Eh, well, I didn't mean . . ."

Spunky shoved her left hand into her back pocket. "Look, I know we haven't always seen things exactly the same around the office. And I know that you and some of the others think I was goldbricking to grab onto the boss, but, well, every woman does the best she can with what's available to her. And I really like Tommy. He is absolutely crazy about me, and he's quite wealthy."

Austin studied Spunky's dark brown, fiery eyes. "Why are you telling me this?"

"Because if I would have had a chance at a guy like Brady, I'd have sold Manhattan back to the Indians and moved west. So what I'm telling you is, you are such a take-charge, everything-for-my-career, no-nonsense woman you could fool around and lose this guy. He's a winner, Lynda. I don't think a girl gets too many chances to have a winner."

"A winner?"

"A breadwinner. A family-winner. A career-winner. A relationship-winner. Now take that from a gal who has made a career of studying men."

"Yeah, well, I, eh, this is sort of . . ."

"And here come our two winners!" Spunky wiggled her way over to T. H. Hampton, IV, and slipped her arm in his. "Honey, are you all right?"

"This is incredible," Hampton huffed. "They don't have any of the final chapter at all!"

Brady raised his eyebrows and glanced at Lynda Dawn. "You hear the whole story?"

"Most of it." She nodded.

"Well, old Hampty here agreed to let you have his copy of the final chapter."

"He did?"

"You did?" Spunky echoed.

Hampton pulled off his shoes and dumped out the sand.

"Yep," Brady continued, "he told me havin' you for his wife was worth all the gold on the face of the earth."

"Wow, really?"

"Well . . . words to that effect."

Spunky stood on her tiptoes, pulled Hampton down, and kissed him on the cheek.

"Actually what I said was . . ." Hampton paused and looked

down at Spunky's enthusiastic smile. "I suppose Stoner summed it up well."

"Then we can go look at those places for sale down at Red Lodge!" Spunky jumped up and down, confirming Lynda's earlier suspicions about her clothing.

"Why not? And if we can't find what you like, we'll just build it!"

Spunky turned to Lynda with an ear-to-ear grin. She raised her eyebrow and mouthed, "I really love this man!"

Hampton reached into the rig and pulled out a thick manila envelope.

"You know, Ms. Austin, this whole thing is your fault."

She took the envelope and looked up at the tall and lanky Hampton. "What do you mean?"

"Your triumph last year in finding the lost Harrison manuscript. The whole office became infected with adventurism. It's as contagious as lottery fever."

"I'm not sure I get the blame for that. But thank you, Mr. Hampton, for this much of the chapter. If I can trace down those two missing pages, we can get the book printed. Then everyone in the world can search for the gold."

"Yes, well, we're off to search for a log home down around Red Lodge."

"That's mighty pretty country down there." Brady nodded. "I hope you two find just what you want."

Spunky latched onto Hampton's arm. "Ted and Jane said it's lovely at Red Lodge. And I certainly hope you two find what you want, too!"

"Thanks, Spunky," Lynda replied.

Ted Turner and Jane Fonda? Spunky is really getting into her new status! Who knows? Maybe she's just the right type.

"Listen, Stoner, I have a request for you. Could you take something back to that pawn shop in Great Falls?"

"What?"

"I, eh . . . well, I picked up a metal detector."

"A metal detector?" Lynda asked.

"Does it detect under water?" Brady queried.

"Probably not. Anyway, I don't want to lug it around. I rented it for a week, but I don't suppose there'll be a refund for returning it early."

Brady held the metal detector, Lynda held the carbine, and Capt. Patch stood guard at their side as Spunky and T. H. Hampton drove off.

"Look at us." Brady laughed. "Three of a kind. Adventure-seekers. Maybe Hampton was right. What about it, Ms. Austin? Are you a thrill junkie like me and the Captain?"

"In moderation. Sometimes I think a few days a year with you two is all the excitement I can handle."

"Well, we can toughen you up. Can't we, Captain?"

The short-eared dog barked once, then walked over and sprawled on the toe of Lynda's boot.

"Yeah, right," Brady joked, "now the Captain is taking your side. I should have known he'd take up with the good-lookin' gal. Well, I'm sorry the Hamptons had to leave. I'm beginnin' to like Junior."

"I can't believe he was actually spying on us in the cab of the truck. Makes me feel kind of creepy." Lynda shivered.

"Come on, you two. Spied on or not, this adventure isn't over yet."

◆ ◆ ◆

The old Highway 91, renamed the Missouri River Recreation Road, paralleled Interstate 15 and allowed them to travel at their own speed and check out the river as they went.

Lynda examined the papers delivered to her by T. H. Hampton, IV. "If we had had this much of the final chapter, we could have gone straight to Great Falls."

"But think of all the fun we would have missed."

Lynda turned to Brady and stuck her tongue out. "He could have told us about this last night at supper. He sure didn't make any effort to help us, did he?"

"That's why I wasn't in a hurry to call off the Captain. But I think Junior's come to his senses."

"Here's what I can't figure," she continued. "These two missing pages."

"They seem to be the most important ones."

"Yes, but were they stolen from Mr. Hampton's copied chapter? Or were they taken from the original? He didn't know they were missing until he got to Montana."

"Does it make any difference?"

"Not really. Only someone still has the originals. And maybe someone different has the copies. How many people are searching for this gold anyway?"

"I don't know, darlin', but it's nice to know we've narrowed it down to only one-third of the state of Montana."

She watched him driving. In over a year of knowing him, she had never seen him wear anything except long-sleeved Western shirts. The faded blue-striped shirt he now had on was the same one he had worn a year earlier when she had first met him behind the chutes at the Dixie Roundup in St. George.

I think he only has three pair of Wranglers and five shirts to his name. The portable Brady Stoner. Sounds delightful. Not so many choices.

Maybe I could live that simply.

Except for perfume.

"Hey, that's what I've been looking for!" Brady blurted out.

Lynda glanced over to a clump of cottonwood trees that held about half of their now-yellow leaves. In their midst was an old, unpainted one-story building about the size of a small garage. Neon beer signs clustered in the only window, and a faded gray-and-white sign read Cow Punchers' Bar. The gravel and mud parking lot was filled with half a dozen pickups, most covered bumper to bumper with mud.

"Why in the world are you stopping here?" she complained. "You didn't take up drinking, did you?"

"Nope. I gave up booze years ago."

"Oh. When was that?"

"I was ten."

"Ten?"

"Yeah. A guy named Large Paul worked on the ranch. He always hid a bottle in the barn. I found it one day, snuck up into the loft, and downed a few swallows."

"What happened? Did you get caught?"

"Worse. I threw up and was still sick the next day. I had to miss a junior rodeo. Right then I figured alcohol was just about the nastiest stuff you could put in your mouth. Twenty years later I haven't changed my mind."

"Then why did we stop here?"

"Inside that bar will be half a dozen cowboys that know every hill and draw, every creek and pond, every trail and sage for a hundred miles in every direction. They can also tell me if anyone's been snoopin' around the river anyplace between Great Falls and Helena. You comin'?"

"I think I'll see if that pay phone works and call Kelly at the office. Then I'll just wait out in the rig. That place looks like one of those my mama told me to stay out of."

"Well, you're right. You walk in there, and they'll treat you like you're a queen. I wouldn't want you spoiled like that."

"No good, Stoner. I don't fall for that old line. I'm staying out here."

"Have fun, and don't get into trouble," he teased. "I'll be out as soon as I make the rounds."

Lynda climbed out of the truck and shoved on her cowboy hat. She walked over to the phone and, to her delight, heard a tone when she raised the receiver. She dialed the office number.

An operator's nasal monotone came on. "I'm sorry, all the lines are occupied. Please call later."

All what lines are occupied? At Atlantic-Hampton?

"Excuse me. All the lines are what?"

The operator droned, "All lines leaving Montana are occupied. Please call back."

"What? Wait?"

Lynda listened to the dial tone.

All outgoing lines are tied up? What does this state have—two lines? Maybe they have one line and call-waiting!

She hiked around behind the cottonwoods. A tiny stream coursed through a brown grassy meadow before it sloped off the ridge and into the Missouri River.

The cool air held a deep invigorating taste. Each gulp of it made her feel alert and refreshed. Tucking her hand into the front pockets of her jeans, Lynda hiked up the little creek toward a hill that rose behind the cottonwoods and the Cow Punchers' Bar. She had gone about halfway up the hill when Capt. Patch joined her.

"You figure he'll be in there awhile, Captain?"

The cow dog took one look back at her when she spoke his name and then resumed his journey up the hill about five steps ahead of her. When they reached the top, she found the mountain was bald except for a downed and slightly rotting pine tree.

Sitting on the log, she gazed west. The mountains stretched one row behind the other as far as she could see. Each row looked taller than the previous one, each more covered with the dark green color of forests. The tallest range showed snow still dusted on the trees, even though the sun was fairly high in the east, and there were very few clouds. From where she sat, she figured she could see at least a hundred miles.

A hundred miles without a town. Hardly a road. Very few houses. Probably not a commercial building. Except the Punchers' Bar. If you call that commerce. If you call that a building.

She smiled as she thought of Brady talking rodeo and cattle with the cowboys at the bar.

It's him, Lord. It's where he belongs. Oh, not in a bar, but with these people. He knows them. He understands them. He likes them. He talks their language. He dreams their dreams. He sees the world the way they see it. Crisp. Clear. Right and wrong. Wide-eyed. It's different out here, Lord.

Look at those mountains. They stretch on forever. The sky really is big. Everything from the taste of the air to the smell of the grass is big, expansive—thrilling. And it seems the farther I get from the cities, the more intoxicating this land is.

I don't blame Brady for never wanting to leave it. I love it, too. Every day out here is exhilarating. It's something primal, I guess. Something in my heart tells me, "Girl, don't you leave this country. It's where you belong." But, Lord, it overwhelms me, too. I don't know much about this country. I'm not sure of the rules. And I don't even know if I can handle the rough winters.

This land is kind of like Brady, isn't it, Lord? Ever since I met him, I keep thinking this is where I belong. Being with him is like being home. But . . . he scares me sometimes. There's a lot about him I don't know yet. What if he's, You know, not as perfect for me as I think? He keeps things inside, and that worries me.

Something in me tells me I'll have heartaches if I move out here with Brady. And something inside tells me I'll die a bitter old maid if I don't. Lord, sometimes life isn't easy. I guess You know, don't You?

No shortcuts. No allowing physical attraction to override spiritual common sense. I'm doing this one Your way, Lord. Please, please, please let Brady be Your way!

She brushed back a tear from the corner of each eye and stood up. Slowly she panned the horizon—again to the north, then the east, blocking the glare of the dull late fall sun with the brim of her hat. To the south she spotted a mirrored reflection in the mountains. *It's either a lake or a wide spot in the river. Maybe we're closer than I thought.*

She glanced back at the fallen log.

Lord, I wish I had a place like this at home to come to. Maybe I'd see things more clearly. Maybe I'd see You more clearly.

The journey down the hill seemed steeper than the ascent. Capt. Patch had hopped back into the pickup before she was halfway down. When she reached the cottonwoods, she noticed that Brady had not returned to the truck, so she headed for the telephone.

This time Montana had a free line out.

"Kelly? This is Lynda."

"Our favorite cowgirl! Ride any wild broncs lately?"

"It's been quite a ride. Did Nina fill you in?"

"That doesn't count. I want to hear it all firsthand. Come on, you've got to tell me everything."

And she did.

Almost everything.

◆ ◆ ◆

Turning back to the parking lot, Lynda noticed that only Capt. Patch waited at the heavily laden Dodge pickup.

Maybe I ought to go in there and see how he's doing. Oh, sure . . . a woman waiting impatiently out in the truck for her man to come out of the bar. That wouldn't be too cool. He invited me to go with him. I'll just wait.

Returning to the truck, she was startled to see an older model dark green Cadillac parked at the end of the row of pickups.

She's here? Maybe she's in the bar. That's why he's so late. Oh, no! Nevada plates. It is her! Maybe Brady will need me to help. But who is she?

Lynda looked through the window of the car. The back-seat was stuffed with blankets, pillows, potato chip bags, empty

Coke cans, an ice chest, a cardboard box of groceries, and assorted trash.

Bending down, she peered into the front seat and noticed open maps, a box of bullets, a half-eaten package of peanut butter cookies, binoculars, a carton of Virginia Slim cigarettes, and a camera with a telephoto lens. A *Pro Rodeo Sports News* lay on the dash. Lynda thought about reaching through the half-open window and grabbing it to see the name and mailing address on the front cover.

She glanced back toward the bar and almost bumped into the octagon barrel of a rifle pointed at her head.

"Get in and shut up!" a woman's voice commanded.

Stunned, Lynda blinked her eyes, trying to focus on the woman holding the gun. Half expecting it to be Claudia Mendoza, she was surprised to see a thin-faced, streaky-haired blonde wearing jeans, moccasins, and a hooded green sweatshirt.

This time the barrel jabbed Lynda's ribs.

"I said, get in!"

"But . . . but I don't know who you are."

"Well, I know who you are, honey. Get in and scoot over!"

Lynda opened the door and slid across the seat, sweeping it clean as she went. "What are you doing?"

"It's payback time, sister."

The woman slipped in behind the wheel. She laid her right arm on the back of the seat and propped up the gun to aim at Lynda's neck. Her finger never left the trigger.

"What do you mean, payback time?"

"Oh, I'm not paying you back. It's him. You're just the bait. It wouldn't matter which buckle bunny Brady was shacked up with. It's just your lucky day."

"I'm not a buckle bunny, and we are not shacked up!"

"You've been with him ever since Jackson. Now shut up!" Her face and voice expressed extreme anger and bitterness. "Or I'll part your prissy hair with the barrel of this rifle."

My hair is NOT prissy.

"Why are you doing this?" Lynda demanded. She could hear her voice start to crack.

The barrel rammed into her neck with a painful thrust. "I said, shut up!"

Lynda rubbed her sore neck with her left hand and tried to keep her heart from racing. The Cadillac spun out of the crude parking lot, crossed the blacktop highway, and bounced along a gravel road to the west.

The car smelled of stale smoke and even staler food. The woman obviously hadn't had a bath for a while. Lynda longed to roll down a window.

"I'm not feeling well. I need some air," Lynda finally told her. They were going about fifty on the narrow road, throwing up a tail of gravel behind them.

"Roll down your window and throw your hat out."

"What?"

"Brady hasn't latched onto a complete idiot, has he? Throw your hat out the window before I shoot it off!"

But I like this hat. I really, really . . .

Lynda tossed the hat out into the wind and watched in the side-view mirror as it spun in the dust and crashed into the sage.

"Now pull off your jacket!"

"Do what?"

The rifle barrel struck her ear.

Tears welled up in Austin's eyes. "I'm taking off my jacket. Why are you hurting me?"

"You don't have any idea in the world what pain really is! We're going to turn left up here at the junction. Throw out the jacket as soon as we turn left."

"Why are you doing this?" Lynda cried out as she tossed out her jacket. "I'm cold."

"You're going to get a lot colder before we're through littering the hillside with your clothes!"

The woman's voice was deep and tormented. It didn't seem to match her thin, shallow features.

"Look, I know you hate Brady. I don't know what he did to you, but I'm sorry it's made your life miserable."

"I'm holding the gun," she barked. "Do I look miserable?"

"Yes, you do. You're living out of your car, following a man across the country, harassing him. You haven't had a hot bath in a week and probably can't remember what perfume even smells like. I wouldn't call this happy."

"Brady will follow you up here. Then I'll get a lot happier. Pull that cutesy little belt off and toss it."

Lynda unhitched the buckle and pulled the belt from the loops in her Wranglers.

"Go ahead, throw it out. We want to make sure he doesn't miss the trail."

Austin tossed the brown leather and silver-conchoed belt out the window. It wiggled like a snake until it disappeared from sight in the dust of the roadway.

"I'm Lynda Austin. I'm obviously a friend of Brady's. Who are you?"

"I'm Cynthia, and I'm obviously not a friend of Brady's. Not anymore anyway."

They turned off the gravel onto two dirt tracks that led up the side of a rocky butte.

"Now pull off the blouse and throw it out. . . . Wait. Better yet, rip it in two and throw out half of it."

Lynda looked straight ahead and stared out the front window. She was caught between a scream and a cry.

"You heard me!" the woman yelled and slammed on the brakes. Both women fell forward. "Pull off the blouse!"

"I won't."

"What did you say?"

"I am not taking off my blouse. Not for you. Not for any-one."

"You'll pull it off, or I'll put a bullet through your brain."

"Cynthia, there's one thing I've learned from Brady. There are worse things than dying."

"You can say that again, sister, and I've been through them. I've been through them all!"

Lynda glanced at the woman and could see tears cutting a streak through the dirt on her face. "I'm sorry your life has been tough, Cynthia."

"Tough? My life's been a living hell. Pull off the blouse. I'm not joking."

"Shoot me. I'm not joking either," Lynda replied.

"Yeah, I begged them to kill me, too. They just laughed."

"Who laughed?"

Cynthia stepped on the accelerator and raced the car on up the hill. She rammed it in behind some boulders. "Come on," she commanded, "we'll hike to the top of those rocks."

"I'm cold!"

"Grab a blanket from the backseat."

"Thanks."

"I still might shoot you."

"I don't think so."

"You don't know me."

"Then tell me about yourself."

"Go on up there to the top."

"Couldn't we stop here? It would block the wind."

Cynthia nodded her head and motioned Lynda to a boul-der. She took one several feet behind and kept the rifle pointed at Austin. Cynthia of Nevada was about the same height and size as Lynda of Austin.

"Did Brady start drinking?" Cynthia asked.

"No."

"Then why was he in that bar?"

"He was hoping to find out something about a lake around here. He just went in to talk."

"And you trusted him?"

"Yes. I trust Brady."

"Yeah, well, I trusted him once. And he let me down."

"Tell me about it, Cynthia."

"Cindy. Everyone calls me Cindy."

"Cindy? Cindy LaCoste? From Carson City?" Lynda blurted out.

"You know about me?"

That's why Brady couldn't talk about it! He must have figured out that it was Cindy!

"I know a little about that New Year's party."

"What do you know?"

"I know that you refused to go with Brady and decided to go with Joe Trent, that Brady didn't want to give you a lift home, but offered to call a cab. That you got mad, stuck with Joe, and he drove you out to the desert. Then he ran off when the bikers pulled in, and you were . . ."

"I was what?"

"That you were horribly beaten and raped and left for dead. Did I get the story right?"

"Sure, so far. Only you never said what it's like to live the last five years in such fear that I can't sleep more than an hour or two at night and then never without my gun and never without nightmares."

"But why take it out on Brady? It's Joe Trent who is the absolute jerk. Brady and I sent him to jail last year."

"Yeah, I figured you were the 'cowboy's love-slave.'"

"That interview was a complete hoax. They made it all up."

"I know."

"What do you mean, you know?"

"Brady flirts, but he doesn't mess around. It's his thing. Is that the way he still is?"

Lynda nodded her head without turning around.

Neither spoke for several minutes. Lynda stared down the mountain at the narrow one-lane dirt road leading up to them. Any vehicle could be seen for five miles. But Lynda couldn't see any rig at all.

"Cindy, why didn't you go with Brady to that New Year's party?"

She was silent. Then when she spoke, it was for the first time a soft, almost quiet voice. "I got real . . . well, let me say lonesome one night and drove all the way out to the bunkhouse to visit Brady. It was a Saturday night, and everyone had gone to town. Everyone except Brady. He never went in with the others. Oh, sometimes they would call, and he'd have to go drive them home. Anyway, we were visiting just fine, and then I—like I said, I was real, real lonesome—wanted to spend the night with him. But he refused. Said he wouldn't want to disappoint me or God. That's what he said."

"What did you say?"

"I think I probably cussed him out and challenged his manhood. I was plenty mad and hurt and . . ."

"Lonesome?"

"Yeah. Anyway, I went home, and the next week when Joe Trent asked me out on New Year's, I accepted."

"To get even with Brady?"

"I guess."

"But why Trent?"

"Because I knew it would make Brady mad. But all along my plan was to get Joe drunk and con a ride home with Brady."

"But he didn't give you the ride."

"He probably knew it was all a plan to get at him again. So he had the nerve to call me a cab. Said he'd pay for it."

"Why didn't you take it, Cindy?"

"I guess I had too much to drink, and it sounded too

humiliating. No woman wants to ride home by herself in a taxi on New Year's Eve."

"But why take it out on Brady? Why not go after that scumbag Joe Trent?"

"Why didn't he want me?" The voice was so soft Lynda could hardly hear it. It was a voice full of hurt, disappointment, and questions.

"Brady?"

"I was lonesome. I really wanted him that night at the bunkhouse. Why didn't he want me? I was pretty back then. Lots of cowboys tried to get me in bed. I was real pretty, like you. How old are you, Lynda?"

"Thirty-one. Two days older than Brady."

"I'm only twenty-nine. Turn around and look at me."

Lynda glanced back, then swiveled to the front again.

"I said, look at me!" Cindy cried out.

Lynda turned around again and this time focused on Cindy. The eyes were almost glassy, the color of her face pallid under the tear-streaked dirt. The blonde hair was matted and barely combed. She wore no lipstick or makeup. No earrings or jewelry.

"I look forty, don't I?"

"Cindy, you just need to take care of yourself, that's all."

"Why take care of myself? No man wants a woman who wakes up screaming most every night. No man wants a woman who shakes and cries if a man bumps against her in an elevator. No man wants a woman who has to go around all day on drugs so strong her mind's always in a daze."

"I think you're underestimating yourself."

"You don't even know me."

"I know you're smart enough to follow Brady from Phoenix up to Jackson and to Great Falls. I know you let air out of tires, broke headlights, tracked him down to that little cowboy bar, and kidnapped me because you know he'll try and find me. You've got something working for you."

"Revenge and hatred."

"But don't you see? It takes planning, effort, discipline, and determination to do all this. If you could just focus it on something positive in your life."

"You sound like one of those state-appointed psychologists. They haven't been able to help me in five years. You aren't going to help me in five minutes."

"You're right, Cindy. I can't do much. I've never even been able to help myself very much. Look at me out here. I've been carried off, a gun pointed at me, my life threatened, and I can't do anything about it. But I don't feel hopeless."

"Why not?"

"Because I believe God's in control of my life. He's in charge, and I'm in His hands. That makes all the difference in the world to me."

"God? Oh sure. You can play like there's a God if you want to. I spent four hours out in the desert that night begging God to help me, and then I spent four hours begging Him to let me die. He didn't deliver on either case. So don't give me that God-cares-about-me bull."

"But He does care, Cindy. We live in a world where men and women sin. That's the immoral and violent world we've created. And we do horrible things to each other. But He came along and offered us a way to survive in this world, and He promises us a better world to come."

"You aren't going to start in on that Jesus stuff, are you? That's what Brady used to do."

"He did?"

"We had to go to church every Sunday. He even took me to a crusade over in Vegas."

"What happened?"

"Nothing. I didn't think I needed all of that."

"Maybe your life would have turned out differently if you had taken God seriously."

"You mean to say it's my fault that I was attacked by those bikers."

"No, but each one of them will be accountable to God. So will Joe Trent. And the Lord won't let them off easy. He's a God of justice, and they will get exactly what they deserve."

"Now that's the part of religion I like."

"But you and I are accountable to the Lord, too, Cindy. You've got fifty or more years of life left on this earth. And it's up to you what quality of life you have. God will help you, you know."

"He's never helped me before."

"He brought you and me together."

"What do you mean?"

"Maybe He wanted us to have this talk."

"Now you're sounding real spacey," Cindy chided. "Maybe you ought to be in a home in Carson City."

"Think about it." Lynda felt the words lump in her throat before she even spoke them. "How else could God let you know that He still loves you and cares about you? He'd send someone to talk to you about it, wouldn't He?"

"I'm tired of all this discussion. Turn around and watch out for Stoner," Cindy ordered.

Lynda gazed at the bright autumn day. The slight wind was still cool, but she could feel sweat on her forehead. She allowed the blanket to slip down around her waist.

I hope Brady finds my hat, my belt, and my jacket.

I hope he finds me!

Lord, I don't know why I'm not scared anymore. I know the gun's still pointed at me. Back there in the parking lot, I was so scared I thought I'd have a heart attack and die on the spot. But You sent me here for a reason, didn't You?

I can't believe it. How in the world could You orchestrate this whole final-chapter episode just so I'd get to spend this time with Cindy?

Maybe Brady's right. Maybe there's not just one big purpose in my life, but a whole string of little ones. Like a visit on a Montana mountain with a lady pointing a gun at my back.

Lord, don't let Cindy shoot Brady. Or me. Or herself.

She pulled the smoky-smelling blanket up around her shoulders again. It felt good.

"Here comes that worthless cowboy," Cindy called out. "Stand up! I want him to see you."

Lynda balanced herself on a boulder and stood with the green wool blanket flowing behind her. Below she could see Brady's truck bouncing up the road. "What are you going to do now, Cindy?"

"I'm going to kill him."

"No, you're not. If that's all you wanted, you could have done that in Phoenix or Jackson or Great Falls."

"I'm going to make him pay!"

"For what? For having moral values? For your hurt feelings after being rejected? He's paid his dues. He's had to live with his own conscience. Do you know what that's like for a man with such a high code to live up to? I want to tell you, hardly a week goes by that he doesn't regret not giving you that ride. He told me so. Why do you think he got arrested for beating Joe Trent to a pulp last year?"

"He's got to pay more!"

Lynda turned around and faced Cindy. "What am I supposed to do—just stand here and watch?"

"Maybe."

"Why don't we walk down and meet him at the car?"

"Let him walk. He can walk to me. I'm not going to walk to him," Cindy hissed. Again her face looked tight and tormented.

"Can you put down the gun? You don't really want to shoot anyone, do you?"

"I don't know. Sometimes I want to shoot everyone."

Brady parked his truck next to the green Cadillac.

Don't bring the gun. Please don't bring the gun.

Capt. Patch led the way as Brady hiked up the mountain. Black cowboy hat in place. Denim jacket with corduroy collar. A deliberate, lanky stride.

And the '94 Winchester in his hand.

I've got to do something, Lord. I've got to say something!

"Cindy," Lynda blurted out, "I'm glad I got to meet you."

"You might not be glad very long."

"No, really. I believe the Lord brought me out here all the way from New York City just to visit with you on this mountain."

"Well, if He did, He wasted your time. You didn't convert me."

"But that's not my role. I couldn't convert anyone. That's the Lord's business. My job was to tell you some spiritual truth and to let you know God hasn't given up on you."

"I suppose that makes you feel good. You've done your spiritual good deed for today. You stay between me and Brady. You understand?"

"Yes, I'll stay right here. You know what I think?"

"What do you think?"

"I think that you know in your heart that the Lord sent me to talk with you today."

Just as Brady came into view, Lynda saw out of the corner of her eye that Cindy had raised the gun to her shoulder.

Then she pulled the trigger.

SEVEN

The blast of the small rifle and Austin's scream echoed simultaneously. The pounding of her heart vibrated her entire body. She gasped for breath as her ears rang, sweat popped out on her forehead, and her knees began to buckle. The air filled with the bitter tinge of gun smoke.

The bullet struck a granite outcropping twenty feet in front of Brady. He jumped back and cocked the lever on the carbine, throwing it to his shoulder. Lynda heard Cindy pump another cartridge into the chamber of her rifle, and again all Lynda could do was scream.

"Cindy, no! Please. No!"

At the sound of Austin's voice, Brady lowered his carbine to his side and stared up the mountain at the women who were about one hundred feet away.

Cindy's second bullet shattered granite only a few feet to Brady's left and sprayed him with chips. She followed up with a string of angry obscenities. He tossed his carbine down on the hillside and hiked straight toward them.

"Cindy, put down that gun!" he hollered.

"I'll kill you, Brady Stoner. I'll kill you!" Cindy screamed and pumped another bullet into the chamber.

"Cindy, you aren't going to kill me with that old model 90. You're not a good enough shot. You'll just wound me and get sent to jail for attempted murder. Put it down!"

"You didn't give me a ride home! That's all I wanted. Why didn't you give me a ride home?"

He kept right on walking toward them, and Lynda noticed the rifle begin to droop down from Cindy's shoulder.

"I'll give you a ride home now, Cindy."

Brady was almost even with Lynda Austin.

"What about her?" Cindy pointed the barrel of her rifle toward Lynda.

"We'll both give you a ride home." He walked past Austin and straight at LaCoste.

"I could kill you with this rifle at this range."

"At this distance you could either kill me or hug me. Come on, darlin', put down the gun. Please."

Cindy LaCoste lowered the rifle and began to sob—deep, pain-wracked, body-shaking sobs. When Brady got within two feet of Cindy, she dropped the .22 WRF into the dirt and threw her arms around his neck. He grabbed her around the waist almost lifting her up off the ground and held her tight. Laying her head on his shoulder, she continued to cry, almost like a convulsion. He stroked her matted hair and turned to Lynda.

"Are you all right?" he mouthed.

Lynda nodded her head up and down.

He motioned for her to come down off the rock and over to where they stood. As she neared them, again he glanced at her.

"She needs a bath!" he mouthed.

Lynda nodded her head and sat down on a rock next to Capt. Patch, who kept his distance from Brady and Cindy. The two watched as LaCoste continued to cry, and Stoner continued to hug.

Finally Brady tried to talk to her. "It's all right, darlin'. It's okay. You just cry all you want. We've got all day. We don't have to go anywhere."

Lynda began to feel chilled and pulled the blanket up around her neck. *Lord, I don't know why I'm not jealous. Normally I'd be fighting back the urge to shove them apart. He truly cares about her. She knows it. That's why he just might be the only man on earth she can hold close without losing her lunch. Help me to continue to care about Cindy.*

Within a few minutes, Capt. Patch had disappeared beyond the crest of the hill, and Cindy stood, still in Brady's arms, but unable to shed any more tears.

"Did you mean it about taking me home?" Cindy's voice sounded younger than her looks.

Brady glanced over at Lynda, who nodded her approval.

"Yep. You know I meant it. Now me and Lynda Dawn have some business to take care of here in Montana. But as soon as we've . . ."

Lynda walked toward them. "Brady, we can take Cindy home right now. The other will wait."

"Are you kiddin' me?"

"No."

"But we're gettin' mighty close to those lakes."

"Cindy's more important than any book manuscript. Let's take her home."

"I can't believe you're saying that."

I can't believe I'm saying this. Lord, what are You doing here?

"You're serious?"

"My word's good, Stoner. It's the code of the West, you know."

Brady stepped back from Cindy, who lifted up her sweatshirt to dry her eyes. She wore beige long johns under the sweats.

"Cindy, are you still living in Carson City?"

She tilted her head, then let her chin drop to her chest. "I'm living in that old Fleetwood down there."

"Yes, but—"

"I haven't lived in Carson City in over a year. I was in South Dakota when I saw you two on television last year. That's when I decided to look you up. But it took me some time to save my Social Security checks and buy that car."

"Social Security?" Lynda questioned.

"Psychological disability, they call it."

"So you've just been living out of your car?"

"Yeah."

"Well, I think you can do better than that," Brady encouraged her. "Come on, ladies, let's get off this mountain. If you don't mind, I'll carry both guns."

"Where are we going?" Cindy asked.

"I'm not sure, but I'm workin' on a plan."

The sun was lifting higher in the sky, and Lynda was amazed that the temperature had warmed so much from the previous two days. The ground was hard-packed and showed no trace of the recent storm. The wind had dried out the crust, and already there was a fine dust in the air. Capt. Patch raced ahead and reached the truck first.

"Well, cowboy," Lynda called, "what's the big plan?"

"We're drivin' into Helena."

"What do we do there?" Cindy asked.

"I'll tell you when we get to town. You follow us, all right?"

"Maybe I will, maybe I won't."

"You have to. I promised to get you home, and I will."

"But I don't have a . . ."

"Cindy-girl, you just follow us to town, okay?"

"Yeah, I don't have any other place to go. Are you going to give me my gun back?"

"Not until we get to town."

"I wasn't really going to shoot you, Brady."

"I know that, Cindy. You follow us. We'll take the 11th Street exit."

Brady and Lynda walked over to the truck. She pulled back on her belt, jacket, and hat. "You want me to drive?"

"Yeah. Lifting that gun really hurt my arm. As long as I never lift it much, I think it's gettin' better. But then I use it a little, and it pains up again."

Lynda waited for Capt. Patch to jump in her door, then climbed in, and began the drive back down the mountainside. Brady waved to Cindy who followed close behind.

"You knew it was Cindy back in Great Falls, didn't you?" she asked him.

"Yeah, that's what I began to figure. The Nevada plates, the general description, moccasins, and slight limp."

"I didn't notice a limp."

"Her right leg. One of the legacies from a biker's boot."

"Why didn't you tell me it was her?"

"I wasn't sure. Besides, it's hard to describe how I feel about Cindy," he added.

"How do you feel?"

"Responsible."

"For her misery?"

"Some of it. I didn't want her arrested in Great Falls. I wanted her healed from all of that in her past."

"I understand."

"You do?"

"You know what's funny, Brady? Sitting up on that mountain waiting for you—and, by the way, we both knew you would be there—I had an opportunity to talk to Cindy a little about the Lord."

"You did?"

"Well, I just blurted out a few things actually."

"Was she still bitter and angry with God?"

"She's mad at God and Brady Stoner. But the point is, I

sort of think that conversation might have been one of the reasons I flew out here."

"You feel that strongly about it?"

"Yeah. Is that weird or what?"

"I'm glad you feel that way. And I'm mighty glad Cindy didn't shoot you."

"Or you. I was doing so good. I felt so at peace, and then she took a shot at you, and I totally fell apart."

"I knew she wouldn't kill me."

"She knew that, and you knew that, but I didn't know that. Anyway, I wasn't much help standing there like a petrified log."

"A screaming petrified log."

"Don't remind me. What are we going to do with Cindy?"

"I'm takin' her home."

"But—"

"There must be someplace she can go and find a little peace and rest."

"I hope it has a bathtub."

"Isn't that awful? During the whole time I was hugging her, I thought about how sweet you smell all the time."

"Is that all you were thinking?" Lynda challenged.

"Well . . . I was thinking how this scene would be different if I had taken her home from that New Year's party."

"Or how it would have been if you'd let her sleep over at the bunkhouse?"

"She told you about that?"

"Yes."

"You two must have talked a lot."

"Not really. I'd like to talk to her more."

"Are you serious?"

"Yes. Why?"

"Because I really don't have a plan for Cindy yet. But in the meantime, how about getting her a warm room and a hot bath at a motel?"

"And some fresh clothes."

"And clean out that Cadillac. It's a health hazard."

"And some makeup, jewelry, and—"

"Perfume."

"She can use some of mine."

"Do you actually share your perfume? I thought maybe it was your own secret formula."

"I have some generic stuff. It will make her smell nice but not attract cowboys." Lynda grinned.

"Sounds boring."

"I never use it myself."

Suddenly Brady waved his right arm toward the frontage road. "Look at that! There it is!" he shouted.

"What?"

"That boat behind that van. That's it. That's the boat that was at the Double Diamond. That's Mendoza's boat!"

"Where's it going?"

"Lower Holter Lake."

"On the Missouri."

"Yep."

"That must be our reservoir! What shall we do? Shall I take the next exit and try to follow her?"

"Yeah, but we'll need to keep a safe distance for a while and—"

"What about Cindy back there?" Lynda quizzed.

"Oh, yeah! Listen . . . we'll, eh, maybe we could have her pull over and ride with us. Then we would . . ." Brady looked over at Lynda, and they both shook their heads.

"Forget the boat. You've got to get that lady to a bathtub," Lynda announced.

"But what about Mendoza?"

"Chance said a team of professional divers dove six weeks and didn't find that underwater cave. We'll just have to drive back out here later and see if we can find her."

"Are you serious, Lynda Dawn? This is why you came out here. Remember?"

"Baloney. I came out here to be with Brady Stoner. Everybody but a dumb cowboy could see that. Let's take care of Cindy first."

"I was hopin' you'd say that. Lower Holter Lake—that must be the spot. But I still wonder how they thought anyone would want to carry that gold clear around the falls."

◆ ◆ ◆

Within an hour they could see Helena across the valley, perched on the eastern slope of the Rocky Mountains. The gold capitol dome glistened in the autumn sunlight.

"Shall we get three rooms at the motel?" Brady asked.

"Two."

"Oh?"

"Cindy and I can share one," Lynda offered. "I think she just might wander off if we don't keep her close."

"I can't believe you, darlin'. You only met this lady this morning, and she kidnapped you and shot at me. Now you're ready to take her into your room."

"You keep the guns with you." Lynda laughed. "Cindy is an utterly, completely, thoroughly crushed woman. But the only one she's a real danger to is herself."

Lynda realized Brady was staring at her. Finally she looked back at him. "What are you doing?"

"Every once in a while I see a side of you, darlin', that I've never seen. I'm really impressed."

"Don't get too impressed. I might kick her out before dark."

"Listen," Brady continued, "I'm sure she won't have any money, but I'm going to see if I can talk her into selling this nice little model 90 Winchester. I think I can get around four hundred dollars for it. I'll use the money to buy her some new clothes while you see that she gets scrubbed up."

"You're going to buy her clothes?"

"Well, you can go buy the clothes if you'd like, and I'll see that she washes up."

"Never mind, Stoner. You buy the clothes. Meanwhile, I'll let her borrow something of mine, but I think I'm a little smaller in the . . ."

"In the what?"

"In the shoulders, you jerk! How long will it take you to sell the gun and go shopping?"

"A lot quicker than it'll take to get her clean."

◆ ◆ ◆

Brady was wrong. By the time he returned to the Last Chance Gulch Motel, Cynthia LaCoste had been sitting in front of the mirror wrapped in Lynda's bathrobe for over half an hour. She had combed and recombed her newly washed hair ten different ways as Lynda looked on and counseled. They had talked a lot about men, jobs, books, horses, trusting the Lord, and mostly about Brady Stoner.

Lynda met Brady at the door, but she didn't let him come in.

"Did you buy everything?"

"I think so. I just handed your list to the clerk at Penney's and came back and picked it up. So I'm not sure what's in there."

"Good."

"Give Cindy this money."

"Two hundred dollars?"

"When I explained the situation, my friend tossed in a little extra. He said the custom checkering on the wood made it more valuable."

"You bought all these clothes and had this much left?"

"I'm a thrifty buyer."

"Are you sure some rodeo cowboy didn't toss in a few bucks himself?"

Brady grinned but refused to answer the question. "I'll be in my room. I think we ought to try to get out to Lower Holter before it gets too late and see if we can spot Mendoza or that boat."

"Brady, wait out here a minute. Let me take these to Cindy."

Austin gave the clothes and money to a delighted Cindy LaCoste. Then she went back out to the hall where Brady was visiting with a slender housekeeper with very long, dark brown hair and a name tag that said "Carmen."

The girl giggled at Brady's last line. Then he stepped over to Lynda.

"You have a great ability to make friends quickly," she teased.

"It's a gift." He grinned.

"I don't think we should leave Cindy alone. She's still pretty much mad at God and you, and really down on herself. I'm afraid she might do something dumb."

"You want me to go out to the lake and check it out by myself? That way you could stay with Cindy."

"No, I need to be there, too. I was thinking we should take Cindy with us."

"The whole afternoon?"

Lynda took a deep breath before she continued. "Actually I can't believe I'm saying this, but why don't we take her with us for a few days until we figure out where she can go?"

"I can't believe you're saying this either."

"Brady, I don't think that lady has had one peaceful day in five years. For some reason, she's not afraid of you or of me. I think it would be a special retreat for her to be with people who care about her and treat her normal."

"Are you two getting along?"

"We have a truce."

"What do you mean?"

"She promised she wouldn't drink or smoke in the pickup or in the motel room, or blaspheme."

"What did you promise?"

"I'd let her use any of my perfumes, and I wouldn't try to convert her."

"And you both agreed to that?"

"Yes. What do you think?"

"I think it will last about thirty minutes."

"No. What do you think about taking her with us for a few days?"

"As long as we drive the truck, not that old Cad."

"Good." Lynda touched his right arm. "We'll be ready in twenty minutes."

"I'll be at the truck. I want to check out that metal detector Hampton left us."

"Brady, what happened back at that cowboy bar? Did you learn anything?"

"Sort of."

"What do you mean, sort of?"

"Well, I didn't learn anything about Jesse James's buried gold."

"What did you learn?"

"That the Double Diamond has five thousand acres in a patent deed and some government leases. And because of the lousy cattle prices, a person could buy it cheap. It has some out-of-state owners who are lookin' to dump it."

"Why on earth did you want to find that out? Brady, no you don't. You are not going to buy that awful place!"

"Don't worry. I don't have enough money to even think about it."

"I can't believe you'd even consider it."

"Darlin', you just saw it on a bad day. It could be a nice spread, really. Trust me on this. In the spring when there's calves frolickin' on the green hillsides and—"

"I don't intend to ever see it again. I don't want to hear about it. That's the most depressing excuse for a home I've ever seen."

"No, that old green Cadillac is the most depressing home you've ever seen. See you in twenty minutes." He turned and strolled down the hall. Lynda could tell by the length of his stride and by his swagger that he was less than happy.

◆ ◆ ◆

Cindy climbed into the narrow backseat of the extended cab pickup. "I can't believe you two are doing this."

Brady rode shotgun, with Capt. Patch, as always, in the middle. Lynda climbed into the driver's seat.

"I can't believe I'm starting to enjoy driving this truck. You should have seen me last year. I thought I'd grind the transmission in two before I got used to it."

"Well, me and the Captain can't believe we get to travel with two such nice-lookin' gals. Most of the time it's just him and me batchin' on the rodeo road."

Lynda drove back out to I-15 and headed north. Brady fumbled with some tapes, trying to find his latest Ian Tyson cassette. She glanced in the rearview mirror at Cindy, who stared out at the Montana countryside. Her sandy blonde hair hung straight to her shoulders, revealing a few gray strands. Her face was fresh-scrubbed, but the skin looked rough. Tight lines cracked around her large brown eyes. Her eyebrows were thin and seemed lighter than her hair. Her face showed no emotion at all. She had borrowed some of Lynda's Autumn Rose Blush lipstick. It made her mouth look softer than the rest of her face. Her nose, a little too wide but still teasingly upturned, was the only indication of her real age.

"Cindy, did you ever wear your hair short?"

"Uh, no. Why do you ask?"

"I just think a cute short cut with a little wave would look good on you. What do you think, Brady?"

"Me? Oh, it doesn't matter. 'Course, you know that I like hair that hangs down a girl's back."

"Listen, Stoner," Lynda lit into him, "not every woman enjoys having her hair look like a horse's tail! I think Cindy might like having short hair." She turned back to Cindy. "Of course, that's just my opinion."

The sun glared through the front windshield as they swung to the west around Rattlesnake Mountain.

"I don't figure you two," Cindy began again. "I've been following you for days. I trashed your truck. I kidnapped Lynda. I shot at Brady. And what do you do? You clean me up, buy me some clothes, and take me with you on some wild goose chase. How come you guys are doing this?"

Brady pushed back his black beaver felt cowboy hat. "Cindy, you don't belong up here in Montana living in a car. I just want to help get you back into some warmer country, settled in a little, so you can go on with your life. That's what friends are for."

"You saying we're still friends after all I've done?"

"If you'll have me for a friend."

"It feels a lot better having you for a friend than hating you. Although when I'm depressed, at least hate keeps me going. It gave me a reason to get up in the morning."

"Now you'll have to find something else to focus on every day," Lynda suggested.

"You know, you're harder to figure than Brady. He operates a lot out of guilt and honor. So I can sort of understand why he does what he does. But you—I don't even know you. This morning I dragged you off at gunpoint, threatened you, and cursed at your faith. Now we're sharing perfume and hairdo ideas. This is more bizarre than an afternoon TV talk show. I just don't get it."

"I don't either." Lynda glanced in the rearview mirror and shook her head. "Cindy, don't get mad. I'm not going to preach at you, really. But back on the mountain . . . well, I really felt that God told me that getting to know you was a part of the reason I'm out here in Montana. That's important to me."

"I haven't been able to hold a job in five years. I don't have any family that will speak to me anymore, the way I've lied and stolen from them. I've been in and out of recovery homes and hospitals. I'll probably always have that limp in my right leg. But this afternoon feels like a vacation from misery, the first break in anxiety I've had since that New Year's Eve."

Brady lifted his painful left arm to give Cindy a reassuring pat on the knee. From the image in the rearview mirror, Lynda saw Cindy wince and pull back, then take a big breath, and reach out and take Brady's hand in hers.

"I've been hiding out too long," she murmured. She continued to clutch Brady's hand. "Brady, are you going to marry Lynda?"

He pulled his hand back into the front seat as if bitten by a wasp. "Oh . . . well . . . yeah, someday. Providin' she'll have me, and I don't have to live in New York City."

Someday? Well, that's as good an answer as I've had so far.

"Someday? Just what does someday mean?" LaCoste demanded.

"When I get my ranch bought and a house built—things like that."

"The old 'I'll-marry-ya-darlin'-as-soon-as-I-buy-a-ranch' line. Lynda, that's the dumbest line a cowboy ever used. That's like saying, 'Honey, I'll marry you as soon as I win the lottery.' I spent five years barrel racing, and I've heard every line. Usually it goes this way: 'Darlin', you're the most beautiful barrel racer I've ever seen in my life. You're different from all the other girls. Yes, I'll respect you in the mornin'. In fact, as soon as I buy that ranch, I'll send for you. Now how about a toss in the hay?'"

Lynda glanced over at Brady and faked a scowl. "Well, rodeo man, what do you have to say for yourself?"

"Traveling with two pretty ladies isn't all I had hoped it would be. Why do I get this feelin' I'm goin' to be out-voted two to one on everything?" Brady animated his conversation by waving his arms and in the process banged Capt. Patch, who woke up with a bark.

"Three to one." Lynda laughed. "The Captain is on our side."

◆ ◆ ◆

For the next thirty minutes Lynda tried to explain to Cindy why they were headed to Lower Holter Lake. At Wolf Creek they took the frontage road that paralleled Pear Creek until they reached the Missouri River.

"The main place to launch a boat is on the east side of the lake. Let's head down that road first," Brady suggested.

"Now tell me again—just what exactly are you going to do if you find this Mendoza woman?" Cindy asked.

"Recover that final chapter," Brady explained.

Lynda caught a whiff of Cindy's Wilderness Radiance perfume and wanted to reach in her purse and splash some more on herself. Pride held her back.

"What I'd like to do is tie her with duct tape, hit her in the head with a rifle barrel, and toss her in the back of that boat of hers!" Lynda carped.

"Really?" Cindy pressed.

"Yes, but I'm just too nice of a person to do that . . . I think."

"I'm glad to see that other people are driven by revenge."

"Really, Cindy, I don't know what we're going to do. But if

she has that final chapter, it belongs to Atlantic-Hampton. I want it back—at least the two pages still missing."

The road ended five miles up the river along the east side of Lower Holter Lake. Mostly treeless mountains rolled down to the water's edge where the Big Belt Mountains seemed to part for the flow of the upper Missouri River. The buckskin-colored dead grass harmonized with the light blue sky. The water on the lake was choppy as the wind blew upstream.

They pulled into the parking lot near the small marina and boat launch.

"Do you see the van that was pulling Mendoza's boat?" Lynda queried.

"No boat. No van. No Mendoza."

"Are you sure that was her we saw earlier?" Lynda asked.

"I'm sure that was the boat I examined out at the Double Diamond. And I know a van was towing it, but I don't know if Mendoza was driving."

"There are only six rigs here."

"Park here and let me ask around," Brady ordered.

Brady and Capt. Patch bolted out of the truck and across the gravel and dirt parking lot toward several men fishing near the boat launch. Lynda reached into her purse and pulled out a small blue glass bottle of Beyond Temptation. While seeming to watch Brady, she dabbed a little on her wrists and neck.

"You really have a hang-up with perfumes, don't you?" Cindy commented.

"Oh, I don't know if it's a hang-up. I guess it's something I do when I'm nervous."

"What are you nervous about now?"

"Trying to find that final chapter and all."

"Oh, good." Cindy laughed. "I thought you were going to tell me you were nervous about me being around Brady."

I certainly wouldn't admit it if I was. Which I'm not.

"You're right. I need to get my hair cut," Cindy continued.

"I'm glad you're not jealous of me. Of course, I'm jealous of you, but that's to be expected. Have you ever taken antidepressant drugs? Probably not, huh? Well, don't get started. I need a cigarette. Brady doesn't have any cigarettes in the truck, does he? I'm sure he doesn't. He hates it when people smoke in his truck. Brady doesn't even chew. Did you ever meet a rodeo bum who didn't keep a can of Copenhagen in his back pocket? Of course not. But here's good, ole Brady the straight-shooter. He's the permanent designated driver of the Wilderness Circuit. Am I talking too much? You can't believe how long it's been since I had anyone to talk to. Or anyone I wanted to talk to. I need a drink. Did I really promise you I'd quit drinking?"

"You said if you took a nip, I could start preaching at you."

"It might be worth it."

"Cindy, drinking has stolen the last five years from you."

"No, drinking has kept me from blowing my brains out. I figure it's the only reason I'm alive."

"It's not the only way you could have survived. There might have been better ways that would have been healthier and a lot happier."

"Are you preaching at me?" Cindy's face flashed a harsh, bitter reflection.

"Did I really promise not to talk to you about the Lord?"

Brady yanked open the door. "Whoa! You two havin' a contest over who can smell the sweetest?"

"Is it a little strong?" Lynda queried.

"It took me forty rodeos to wear last year's smell out of the truck when you spilt that case of perfume."

Lynda felt a blush rising. "What did you find out?"

"None of them saw a van or boat like I described. But they said if we head up that dirt road about two miles, we'd hit Cottonwood Creek. If we follow that back down a few miles, we'll come to the upper reaches of the lake. Someone could launch a boat there and pretty much have the place to them-

selves. Fishermen usually don't go back there this time of the
year, but once in a while hunters will camp back there."

"Brady, I don't see any road beyond this parking lot."

"Right up that hillside, darlin'. You see those tracks, don't
you? Someone's driven up there today."

"Cindy, do you see a road up that mountain?"

"No, but if Brady says there's a road, then there's a road."

*If Brady says! If Brady said cows could fly, would you believe
him? This recovery is coming along much too rapidly. If you ever got
your life really together, I'll bet you could turn out to be a real bother.*

"You want to go up the mountain? Well, hang on, bucka-
roos!" Lynda drove the pickup to the end of the dirt road. Then
she stopped the rig and jammed it into compound low and
turned left.

"Lynda-darlin', you don't have to—"

"Be quiet, Stoner. I said I'm driving us up this mountain!"

"But—"

"You don't think I can do it? Hang onto your hat!"

The pickup ground and bounced its way up the steep
incline. Even though traveling under five miles an hour, Lynda
found herself ricocheting off the ceiling of the cab.

"Is she always this stubborn?" Cindy shouted.

"Just like a bulldog," Brady offered.

About three-quarters of the way up the mountain, she
slammed the truck into a hole between two half-buried boulders. The canoe that was tied down to the back of the pickup
bounced free and slipped over the tailgate. One piece of nylon
rope held tight to the rope hook and the boat.

"You lost the canoe," Cindy reported.

Lynda didn't slow down. "Nonsense. It's right back there.
We'll just drag it the rest of the way up."

"This lady stops for no one or no thing," Brady laughed as
he jammed his hand against the dash to steady himself.

Lynda reached the crest of the mountain, turned the rig

slightly to the right, then slipped it out of gear, and pulled the emergency brake.

"So there, Mr. Bareback Rider, I did it. Aren't you impressed?"

"I surely am. Shoot, I'd have been impressed if you'd stuck to the trail."

"What trail?"

"Down there at the end of the dirt road. When I said to follow those tracks, I meant the ones that swung around the mountain on a gentle incline. I had no idea you'd just drive straight up the mountain."

"It was rather exciting," Cindy piped up. "I thought we might roll backwards there for a while."

"A couple of wimps!" Lynda chided. "Now where do we go, cowboy?"

"Let me load the canoe back into the truck. Then unless you can make this thing fly, I'd suggest you head down the crest to that little roadway over there by those scrubby cedars." Brady pointed to the north. The two women watched him as he reloaded the canoe.

"It's a nice view from up here," Cindy remarked. "You can almost see all the lake."

"I would suppose no one's ever driven a rig up here before," Brady offered.

"You mean I drove where no woman has ever driven before?"

"No woman, no man—not even a space alien."

"Reminds me of some neighborhoods in the Bronx."

"Are you really from New York City?" Cindy questioned as Lynda urged the truck slowly off the crest of the hill.

"Oh, yeah," Brady injected, "she lives in a condo building about the size of Billings."

The road was no more than two parallel bare paths following the contour of the mountain and dropping down to a small stream. The tracks widened out after they turned back to the west. When the pickup reached the lake, they found a stand of cottonwoods and an alluvial dirt bank big enough to hold a couple dozen cars.

But only one was there. It was an old orange Ford van with a boat trailer parked against the base of the mountain. At this point Lower Holter Lake was not much wider than a slow-moving river.

"That's it. That's the rig I saw on the highway."

"She must have taken the boat out on the lake," Lynda surmised. "What do you want me to do?"

"Park over behind those cottonwoods." Brady motioned.

Lynda brought the rig to a stop and turned off the engine.

"The Captain and I will go over to that van and investigate."

"What do you want us to do?"

"Stay by the rig and come bail me out if I get into trouble."

"How will we do that?"

"Between the two of you, you'll think of something."

"Be careful, Brady. If that's her, she's the one who gave you that gruesome lump on your head."

Lynda and Cindy climbed out of the truck and stretched their legs as Brady and Capt. Patch nonchalantly wandered over to the van.

"What are you two going to do when you retrieve that final chapter?" Cindy asked.

"Celebrate."

"I'll be in your way, won't I?"

"Oh, no, I didn't mean . . . well, actually I did sort of figure that we would . . ."

"I was wonderin' if I could just stay one night at the motel? You know, just tonight? Then I'll leave in the morning."

Lynda walked around to Cindy, and both of them leaned

against the tailgate of the pickup as they watched Brady in the distance.

"Cindy, what are you talking about? Even if we did find that chapter today, that doesn't mean we want you to leave."

"You said you wanted to celebrate. See, I figured I could just stay in your room, and you two could—"

"What do you think we're going to do—run off and get married?"

"No, but . . . . well, Brady did mention marrying you. I know I teased him about it, but I think he meant it."

"And I'll think he means it when I see an engagement ring on my finger. Cindy, he might not need to own a ranch, but we've sure got to figure out the dueling careers before we make any plans."

"So I can stick around tonight?"

"Definitely. Besides, where would you go?"

"South. Maybe I'd go back to the Arizona Strip. At least it's warmer down there. It was a lot easier to hate Brady from a distance—you know what I mean?" Cindy shaded her eyes from the descending sun. "What's he doing anyway?"

Lynda looked over to see Brady crawling up on the luggage rack on top of the van. When he climbed down, he walked back toward them.

"What did you find out?"

"Nothin'. The van's locked. It's got New Jersey plates. I can't see anything suspicious inside—just normal-looking camping gear."

"What were you doing on the roof?"

"Seeing if I could pull open the vent and look down in the back. With those shaded windows you can't see anything in there. I thought maybe I saw a rifle."

"Then it was Mendoza!"

"Not necessarily. There's no law against packing a rifle. I

don't know if it's the same one that caught me. Come to think of it, I don't have any idea what kind it was she was toting."

"Are we going to wait here for her to come back?"

"Them."

"What do you mean, them?"

"There are two sets of tracks coming away from the van. If one person stayed with the boat after it was launched, that would make at least three people."

"But she was alone out at the Double Diamond."

"She must have joined up with some others."

"Maybe it's Drew!"

"The guy in your office?"

"Yeah. Mendoza said she knew Drew. Perhaps this is what she meant."

"I hope they know more about diving in lakes than your friend McCall."

Brady pulled himself up on the tailgate of the truck and looked down at Lynda and Cindy. "Maybe this isn't Mendoza at all."

"So what do we do?" Lynda asked. "Wait for them to return or go out on the lake and try to find them in a canoe?"

"Why not both?" Brady suggested. "A couple of us can go out on the lake, and the other one could stay here."

"How are you going to find anyone on a lake with a canoe?" Lynda asked.

"With a motor and a can of gas."

"We have that?"

"You didn't think we were going to paddle, did you?"

"I surely hoped not." She glanced at Cindy and back at Brady. "Maybe we should all go out on the boat."

"It won't hold three. Besides, someone has to stay here. If you ladies would like, you go out on the lake, and Capt. Patch and me will wait here."

"Do you know anything about outboard motors, Cindy?"

"No."

"Maybe you and Cindy should—" Lynda caught herself.

"I'll wait here," Cindy volunteered. "What am I supposed to do?"

"If someone comes in with a boat, they have to belong to that rig. It's the only one back here. So go over and visit with them—about fishing or something. But try to get a description of what they look like, and maybe you can hear something about what they're doing."

"What shall I say I'm doing here?"

"Tell them you and some friends are going to camp, and the others are out fishing, but they should be back any moment."

"How long will you be gone?"

"We have to be back by dark. It looks choppy out on the lake."

◆ ◆ ◆

Half an hour later Brady had the canoe in the water and Lynda Dawn Austin in the canoe. He yanked on the small engine. It caught right on.

"Hey, I'm impressed." She smiled.

"This ain't no dumb cowboy you're dealin' with, ma'am."

"Are we going right or left?"

"Back toward the main part of the lake. Upstream it's getting too shallow for an underwater cave. I figure we'll just putt along fairly close to this shore like a fisherman would, and we'll use those binoculars to scope the lake. If we make it all the way to the big boat ramp without finding Mendoza, we'll return to Cindy."

"Do you think it's all right to leave her there?"

"Sure. Capt. Patch is with her."

"He's not exactly a lap dog."

"Well, I couldn't think of any other combination that made sense."

"It's colder out here than I thought." Lynda pulled her coat collar up. "I should have brought my New York earmuffs. I don't think Cindy will stay with us long. She said she wanted to leave tomorrow."

"Leave to where? She's not leaving."

"Brady, we can't make her stay with us. She's an adult. She can go wherever she wants."

The dark green aluminum canoe slammed into a couple of small whitecaps and continued to slice through the lake near the east shore. Lynda sat in the front facing Brady, who kept one hand on the outboard. She tried to scan the western side of the lake with the binoculars but found the waters too rough for that.

"Do you see any boats?" she hollered.

He cut the engine back and let the canoe coast. "No, and I don't like the looks of this lake."

"What do you mean?"

"See how it slopes down on the sides with the mountains gently rolling into the water?"

"Yeah. What's that mean?"

"Well, if there was a cave, you would think it would be near a granite cliff where the rock drops straight off, the kind of place miners might have poked around in for gold and then left. That's where you would bury treasure. But a cave cut back in the dirt here would just collapse. This just doesn't seem like the right kind of country in which to bury tons of gold."

"Yes, but don't forget—we aren't trying to find the cave; we're just trying to find the people who are trying to find the cave."

"Good point. Whoever had the boat on that boat trailer is out here somewhere." He revved the motor back up, and they traveled in silence. Several times they shut the engine down and scanned the horizon with the binoculars. But they spied only a few small boats filled with fishermen.

What are we really going to say? "Excuse me, I wonder if you have the final chapter of Chance McCall?" Or "Trained police snipers are standing by waiting for your immediate release of a stolen book chapter. Please deliver the document, and don't make any quick moves."

"Brady, I'm really getting cold. Maybe it would be better to just wait at the van."

"I was thinkin' the same thing, darlin'. Let's swing straight across the lake and go up the other side. The shoreline looks flatter over there, so I don't think there'll be a cave, but maybe Ms. Mendoza hasn't figured that out yet." He guided the canoe to the west and straight into the setting sun.

I should have brought a blanket or something.

With her hands interlaced, she held her arms close to her body. The black satin jacket with the quilted lining felt as thin as gauze. While the wind off the water wasn't frigid, it was cold and humid, and the farther out into the middle of the lake they got, the harder it became to keep her lips from quivering. Finally when she could no longer keep her hands and arms from shaking, she yelled at Brady, "Could we stop?"

"What?"

"Slow down a minute."

Brady flipped a switch and killed the engine. The canoe continued to glide across the lake.

"You didn't have to turn it off. I was just getting cold going into the wind."

"It will probably get nippy after the sun goes all the way down."

"Brady, it's more than nippy right now. I think we should go back to the east and forget about the other side. It's just too cold out here going into the wind."

"You're the boss. 'Course, I could just scoot up there with you in the bow and hug you real tight and warm you up."

"You could? But wouldn't the boat tip over?"

"Probably. What do you say?"

"I dare you to make that same offer when we get back to the truck."

Brady laughed and yanked on the starting rope. The motor puttered and died. She watched him flip a switch several times, pump on a little rubber ball, adjust a small lever, and then yank on the rope again. The engine failed to start.

Even though the boat no longer glided into the wind, Lynda felt a cold chill that started at her neck and seemed to slowly creep down to her tailbone as she watched Brady repeat the previous steps. Once again he jerked on the starting rope—to no avail.

"Well, isn't this excitin', Lynda Dawn? Here I am, marooned in the middle of the ocean with a beautiful woman." Several more tugs on the rope left him shaking his head and wiping his forehead.

"Come on, Brady, start the motor. I want to get off the lake." Again he yanked on the rope.

"What's wrong? It was running fine when you turned it off."

Brady turned back around to face her and slumped back on the side of the canoe. He closed his eyes as the boat drifted aimlessly.

"Stoner, you've got to do something," Austin commanded.

"Here's what I figure—you swim ashore and go for help. I'll stay with the canoe."

"What?"

"I've got to stay with the ship. I'll hold your coat and boots."

"Brady, sit up and do something right now! This is not funny."

"Well, sweet darlin', what I'd really like to do is scream and yell and hit that motor with a lead pipe. But since I'm such a nice fellow, there's nothing left to do but laugh."

"Are you telling me you can't start the motor?"

"I'll tellin' you I can't start the motor."

"What are we going to do?"

"You want the good news or the bad news?"

"The good."

He rummaged under the canoe seat and pulled out a paddle. "Ta-dah! We will paddle home! If it was good enough for Lewis and Clark, it's good enough for me."

"They were on this lake?"

"They were on the Missouri River, right here."

"Where's the other paddle? I'll help you."

"That's the bad news. Only one paddle."

"It will take us forever to get back to Cindy."

"Not forever. But it will not be a speedy journey."

"I'm freezing."

"I know that, darlin'. I'm going to sneak up there on that middle bench. I paddle better from there. You keep the boat from tippin' over."

As he carefully stood up, the canoe shifted to Lynda's right.

"Brady," she screamed and threw her weight to the left. Stoner lost his balance and stumbled forward, barely able to keep from falling overboard. Hoping to help him, she shifted her weight back to the right. Brady's feet flew out from under him, and his chin crashed into the aluminum middle bench seat that also served as a cross-brace.

"Darlin', stop!" he yelled.

"I was just trying to—"

"Hold still. For Pete's sake, don't move!"

"I was afraid you would fall overboard."

"I should be so lucky." He raised himself carefully to his knees. Blood trickled down his chin.

"You're hurt!"

"Just busted my lip. You promise to hold still?"

"Yes." Her voice was quiet, her head held down and still.

Brady crawled up into the middle seat of the canoe, facing her.

"Now, if you promise not to dump either of us overboard, I want you to creep on back here with me."

"Is there room for both of us?"

"Sure, darlin'." He patted the canoe seat between his spread legs. "Come on. We'll huddle up a little and keep warmer. It's going to be a little slow gettin' back."

"Isn't there a danger?"

"Of falling into the lake? Or of sitting in my arms?" he teased.

"Stoner, I want to know right now, if I sit back there with you, are you going to try something funny?"

"What do you mean, somethin' funny?"

"You know, hugging and kissing and all that stuff?"

"Yep."

"You promise?"

"Yep. Trust me."

"Well, in that case, scoot over, cowboy!"

"Come on, darlin'."

"Just a minute. I'm not ready. Look the other way."

"Why? What on earth are you going to do?"

"Look back at the motor, Stoner!"

"Yes, ma'am." Brady turned around.

She stared at his dark brown, almost shaggy hair and slipped her hand into her jeans pocket and pulled out a small brass bottle about the size of a tube of lipstick. Still staring at the back of his head, she splashed some of it on her very cold wrists and extremely cold ears and neck.

"What's it called, darlin'?" he asked without looking around at her.

"You can smell it already?"

"Oh, yeah."

"It's called Tahoe Fascination. I thought it might be a good lake perfume. You can turn around now."

Scooting on her knees along the cold, damp canoe bottom, Lynda reached out for Brady's hand. *Hard. Callused. Strong. Tender. Lynda Dawn Austin, why does your heart always skip a beat when you lace your fingers in his?*

Carefully, she turned around and backed onto the little wedge of canoe bench available to her. Brady put his arms around her and pulled her gently back against his chest. Then she could feel his cold, chapped lips gently kiss her neck behind her right ear.

"Whewie, Lynda Dawn, I'm not sure that perfume is legal in Montana."

"Stoner, did you just pretend the motor wouldn't start?"

"So I could what?"

"You know, take advantage of me."

"With perfume like this stuff, you'd never get a jury to believe you," he chided. "I just can't help myself."

"You braggin' or complainin', cowboy?" she drawled. "You still didn't answer my question. Is that motor really conked out?"

"Does it matter?"

She leaned her head against his chest. "No."

"Good."

With his arms wrapped around her, he began to paddle on one side of the canoe, then on the other. Back and forth they went. Each stroke turned out to be a hug. Lynda was surprised that the canoe actually began to make progress as they retreated to the east side of the lake.

"Am I just imagining this, or have you been in this position before, Mr. Stoner?"

"Her name was Bunny," he confessed. "She taught me all I know about canoeing."

"Bunny? Someone is actually named Bunny?"

"Her real name was Little Rabbit. She was a member of the Southern Cheyenne Nation. But everyone called her Bunny. She and I worked about three weeks together one summer when I tore a ligament in my knee and couldn't rodeo. We were running a pack station up in the San Juans of southwest Colorado, near Durango, and when we got camp set up for the tenderfeet, we'd have some time to go out on the lake and . . . fish."

"Fish? In this position?"

"We had to row sometimes. I haven't seen her since that summer. I suppose she went back to Harvard."

"Harvard?"

"Yeah, she had a full scholarship. Majoring in Latin. I told you that, didn't I? That's where I learned some Latin phrases."

"You only said it was a long story, and I didn't want to hear it."

"Yep, every night she would teach me something new."

I'll bet she did, Paleface.

"I don't want to hear about it, Stoner."

"You'd really like Bunny. Had a long black braid just as pretty as a . . ."

"As a bronc tail. And a real sweetheart, no doubt. I said I don't want to talk about it."

"Don't worry, darlin'. There's just no comparison between the two of you."

"Oh?"

"The poor thing didn't have but one bottle of perfume, and she had to use the same old fragrance night after night."

"Night after night?"

"Fishin'."

"What did she use it for—bait?"

"You might say that."

"Stoner, I don't want to hear about any more of your 'sweethearts.'"

Does he do that on purpose? Does he just like to tease me?

He continued to row, and each hug seem to bring more warmth to her body. The breeze was at their back, and Brady blocked most of it. The sun was down, and the autumn sky was trading its blue luster for an evening gray. The only sounds were the slap of the paddle in the water and the easy breathing of Brady in her ear.

Lord, if I stick with this guy, I'll spend the next fifty years worrying about every pretty girl that walks his way.

"Did I ever tell you about that New York City book editor that I hung around with one time?" he blurted out.

"You mean that award-winning professional woman?"

"Yeah."

"The one with impeccable taste, a charming wit, and delightful repartee?"

"I was thinking of the one whose enthusiasm for everything she does is contagious. The one whose telephone voice gives me a tingly feeling that makes me feel good for about three days. Every time I see her, I have this strong urge to hug her tight and never let go. The one who's just bulldog enough to probably make a marriage work, no matter what kind of driftin' cowboy she decided to hitch up with. The one who spends her life wanting to do something important for the Lord. The one who has a perfume collection that would reduce the Prussian Army to blubbering fools. The only woman I've ever met that can cause me to forget all about rodeo. The one who's the cutest, sweetest woman I've ever met in my life."

"Oh, *that* New York City book editor. No, you've never told me about her. Whatever became of her anyway?"

"My dearly departed Lynda Dawn?"

"Dearly departed? You mean she died?"

"Nope. Just departed. You see, me and her and our eight kids were livin'—"

"Eight children? No wonder she departed."

"Well, we were livin' in a two-bedroom cabin out on the

Kaibab Plateau while I healed up after bein' bucked off a horse and drug through the desert for six miles. Just livin' hand to mouth on what she could make on her part-time job at the Dairy Queen."

"Dairy Queen? I thought she was a successful New York City book editor."

"Oh, she abandoned her career when she married me."

"She did?"

"Yep. Anyways, as I was sayin', the ten of us was livin' in this little cabin out on the Kaibab, and she was home-schoolin' the whole gang when a dozen rodeo pals of mine dropped in for a few days. 'Course, we had to put them up and feed 'em. Then they all came in with their duffels askin' her if she'd mind doin' their washin', ironin', and mendin'."

"All twelve of them?"

"Yeah, and most of 'em were bull riders. So naturally their clothes smelled like . . . bull. That's when she went runnin' and screamin' out the front door, jumped in our brand-new Dodge pickup, and tore off down the road."

"Did she ever come back?"

"Nope."

"She left the children?"

"Yep. Left me there with Larry, Loni, Lance, Laura, Linc, Lucy, Lester, and little Lilly Belle."

"What do you think happened to her?"

"I got word she moved to Key West and started an iguana farm."

"Stoner, that's the stupidest story I've ever heard."

"Well, what about you, Miss Lynda Dawn? Whatever happened to that good-lookin' rodeo cowboy you were chasin'?"

"Chasing? Good-looking? Oh, you mean old 'Darlin'-you're-a-real-sweetheart' Stoner."

"Yeah. Did he ever win that world championship buckle?"

"He did have his charms, of course. He was rustically handsome but bow-legged and always injured. If he didn't have a couple of broken bones, he'd consider the week a failure. But I'll say this for him, he was a smooth talker. He'd call me about three in the morning with that slow Western drawl. His 'Darlin', I surely do miss you' could melt a girl's heart faster than margarine on hotcakes. He was totally predictable once you were able to see things from his point of view. He had the roughest, callused hands and the most tender touch of any man I ever met."

"You've met quite a few, I imagine?"

"Oh, sure. I've been around. But none had his strength of character, intensity of emotion, and excitement for life."

"I heard all the ladies were crazy about him. He must have been really handsome."

"Nothing to brag about. Oh, he had strong arms and wide shoulders and all that. His eyes were his strength. He had a way of looking at a lady with sort of a boyish tease and twinkle. It made most girls just want to shout 'Yes!' no matter what the question was."

"You were probably too sophisticated for that."

"You're right. I just saw it as childish lack of self-control."

"So you dumped him?"

"Oh, no. I decided what he needed was a decisive woman of wisdom and talent to direct his energies."

"So you up and married him?"

"Yes. It was a lovely service. We held it during the first weekend in December."

"During the NFR?" Brady gasped.

"Yes. The darling said he was satisfied with just qualifying for the Finals in the number-one slot."

"Ranked number one, he walked away from the National Finals Rodeo?"

"Yes, wasn't that sweet of him? The columns reported it to

be one of the most glamorous weddings in mid-Manhattan that season."

"You got married in New York City?" he gasped.

"Why, yes. You should have seen him in his violet tux, tails, top hat, and black patent leather Gucci's."

"What?"

"He gave up rodeo completely and took a job with an advertising agency. He worked his way to being in charge of the very lucrative perfume account. We lived in a nice condo on the upper east side. The lease ran $4,500 a month, but Brady said it was well worth it. That's where we raised our adopted son."

"Adopted?"

"Well, I certainly wasn't going to interrupt my career with a pregnancy. So we decided to adopt little Sydney when he was already old enough to go to preschool."

"Sydney? You named him Sydney?"

"Yes, he's such a delicate little thing. But what an easy child to raise. When he's not practicing the oboe, he's rearranging his doll collection."

"His what?" Brady groaned. "When does this nightmare end?"

"You mean, whatever happened to my dearly departed?"

"He finally ran off?"

"No, he died."

"He did?"

"Oh, yes. You see, he was standing on the corner of 37th and Madison passing out 'Save the Coyote' flyers one day and—"

"No, no, no!" Brady groaned.

"Yes, he was passing out flyers when he made a mistake and tried crossing the street on a green light. He got run over by seven taxis and a Grey Line Tour bus."

"Died right there on the streets of New York City, did he?"

"Yes, and they say his last words were, 'It's okay, folks. I've been hurt worse than this before.'"

"Are you through?" Brady asked.

"I think so."

"That's the most horrible, disgusting, depressing picture of life I've ever heard."

"Thank you."

By now they had reached the eastern shore line. Brady paddled the canoe to the north, parallel to the water's edge. In the west one lone star shone in the late evening sky.

"Are you still cold, darlin'?"

"Yes. It seems to be getting colder."

Brady hugged her a little tighter as he rowed and kissed her softly behind one ear and then the other. "Does that help?"

"Yes, it does. But it probably needs to be done on a more regular basis—to sustain the warmth, of course."

"Oh, man, it sure is sad to see a woman your age having to beg for kisses."

"Begging!"

"It's pretty obvious you're getting desperate."

"Desperate? That's it, Stoner. You're out of here."

"What?"

"Go on, leave. Go home. Go back to your bunkhouse."

He just laughed and kept paddling.

For several minutes Lynda closed her eyes and rested her head on his chest. It was the most peaceful she had felt in a long time. *You know, Lord, if I had my way, I'd really like to spend a lot more evenings in this guy's arms. Like maybe for the next fifty years.*

◆ ◆ ◆

It was a kiss low on her neck and a soft whisper in her ear that caused her to blink her eyes open to the star-filled Montana night.

"Time to wake up, darlin'."

"I guess I dozed off."

"Yep."

"Are we almost there?"

"Yep."

"Did I miss anything?"

"Yep."

"Well, Mr. Yep, what did I miss?"

"I was talkin' to the Lord about you and me."

"You were? What about?"

"I promised Him that I wouldn't stick you in a cabin on the Kaibab with eight kids and a dozen rodeo friends if He promised not to put me in a New York condo with a kid named Sydney."

"What did the Lord say?"

"I think He said I'd better check with you first. So what do you say? How about an agreement? No Kaibab cabin with eight kids and no upper east side condo with Sydney."

"It's a deal."

"Good. 'Course, that doesn't get us one iota closer to fig-urin' out this relationship, does it?"

"No, but we've eliminated some possibilities. Is that where we launched the canoe?" She pointed to the shoreline.

"Yeah. It's kind of hard to see in the dark, but there's the van. It's still here, and there's no boat! We must have beat them back to shore. That's great. We'll just wait them out."

"Brady, I can't see your truck."

"It's back in the cottonwoods. I heard the Captain bark, did-n't you? He must be over there with Cindy. I'm going to slip back to the stern so we can raise the bow and ram this thing ashore."

They beached the canoe and exited without either getting too wet. Setting the outboard motor inside the flat-back canoe, Brady dragged the boat across the sandy dirt toward the dim silhouette of trees. Lynda walked ahead of him.

"Brady, where's the truck?"

"Cindy?" Brady called.

Capt. Patch answered with a bark.

"Where's the Captain?"

"Over here tied to a tree."

"Wait, wait, wait . . ." Brady stammered.

"And here's our camping gear all tossed in a pile."

"Cindy!" Brady screamed.

Both of them stared at the darkness.

"This is not good," Brady mumbled. "Cindy!" he yelled again.

"She's gone, Brady."

"Maybe someone came along and kidnapped her and stole my truck."

"Yeah, well, it was nice of them to tie your dog to a tree and leave us camping gear. Most vicious kidnappers aren't so considerate. Brady, she stole your truck."

"No, Cindy wouldn't do that."

"What are we going to do?"

"Maybe she—just went for a drive or something. She'll be back."

"Why should she come back?"

"I know Cindy. She wouldn't do something like this."

"She's a hurting, vengeful, and depressed woman."

"But she's changing."

"Come on, Brady, a woman can't change that much in just a few hours, not without the Lord's help, and it didn't seem that she was interested in asking Him for anything."

"She'll be back. I just know it," Brady insisted.

"And, dear trusting cowboy, what do you and I do in the meantime?"

"Build a fire and wait."

EIGHT

The clear Montana night sky flickered with stars that seemed to swarm only a few feet above their campfire. Folded olive-drab sleeping bags served as seat cushions and the canoe as their backrest. Side by side, the two faced northwest. The chilling breeze they had felt on the lake had died down, and the flames of the fire danced straight up.

The camping supplies dumped out of the truck included a small bag of hot teriyaki beef jerky and three cans of Dr. Pepper. They munched on supper as Capt. Patch slept across the fire from them.

From their vantage point, they could keep an eye on the van and boat trailer and the trail coming down parallel to Cottonwood Creek. Brady laid his head back against the canoe and pulled his hat down gently over his eyes.

"If I keep on runnin' into gun barrels with my head, I'm goin' to have to get a bigger hat."

"I still can't believe you built this fire without a match."

"Weren't you ever in the Boy Scouts?"

"Never."

"Neither was I, but I hear it's what you learn. All you need is a shoelace."

"Or a sleeping bag string," she added.

"Right. If you can make some dry shavings, you're in business."

"This stuff is hot." She waved a half-eaten piece of jerky.

"Yeah, the Captain refuses to eat it. I figure if you rub a couple of those together, you'll get spontaneous combustion."

Lynda scrunched down next to Brady and laid her head on his shoulder. She jammed her hands in her pockets to keep them warm. *Lord, I don't how I messed up Your message. I thought You were leading me to Cindy. I don't understand her. Maybe I just don't understand Your leading. I had so much more to say to her.*

"She's not coming back, Brady."

"Yes, she is, Lynda Dawn."

"I can't believe you could be so blind."

"I can't believe you won't give her more time."

"It's not my truck she stole. We can't go looking for that final chapter tonight anyway. While the motel room is warmer, and the mattress is softer, I don't mind being out here at all. As long as it doesn't rain or snow, I'll probably survive just fine. But what bothers me is that I got all emotionally caught up in this woman's struggles today and lost track of reality. I don't even know her. And you haven't seen her in almost five years."

"You know what I'm thinkin', darlin'? I'm wonderin' if you and Cindy concocted this whole thing."

"What?"

"You know, a romantic firelight supper—"

"You mean this stale jerky?"

"Quiet music . . ."

"What music?"

"The gentle sound of rushing water and the distant howl of a lone coyote. The next thing you'll tell me is that you can only find one sleeping bag!"

"If there's only one sleeping bag, you can sleep in the canoe with Capt. Patch."

"Oh, sure, I'd expect you to deny it. But when Cindy comes driving back here in the morning giving you the high sign, I'll know."

"Stoner, if I wanted to seduce you, it would be a lot easier than all this."

Brady propped up on his elbow and pushed his hat to the back of his head. "I can't believe you said that!"

"I didn't say it. It must have been the coyotes. Forget it," Lynda blustered. "What were we talking about before?" *Lord, I really, really, really wish we were married right now.*

Brady laid back and closed his eyes. "We were talking about when we thought Cindy would be back."

Lynda scooted away from Brady and sat up. "Here's what I figure. Cindy got to thinking about it and still wanted to get even with you. So she stole your truck and will probably run it over a cliff, knowing that you won't sic the sheriff on her. Then she'll spend the night at the motel. She told me she wanted to do that. After that she'll get in the Cadillac and drive back to Nevada, content that she really showed you a thing or two. What do you think?"

"I think you've been working in fiction too long."

"What's wrong with my story?"

"First, she dumped out all this camping gear. If she wanted to rip me off or make life really miserable, she would have left us with nothing. Maybe she forgot something at the motel."

"What? A bottle of wine?"

"If she comes driving up with a couple of pizzas, you're going to feel sorry."

"If she comes driving back in here with a couple of pizzas, I'll eat the boxes."

"Maybe something suspicious took place. Maybe another car pulled in and had somethin' to do with the van over there, and she decided to follow them and check it out. Wouldn't that be something if Cindy came toolin' back in here with that final chapter in her hand?"

"Brady, this is the most unbelievable conversation we've had since you told me about space aliens landing in Gallop."

"Roswell."

"There, too. What I want to know is why can't you just admit she ran off with your truck? Then we could hike out of here, notify the authorities, and try to figure out what to do next."

"So you're sayin' you don't want to spend the night out here?"

"Brady Stoner! How do I keep painting myself in a corner like this? Sure, I like being out here. And I want to be with you. You know that. I just wish you'd admit that we were both wrong about Cindy."

"But I'm not wrong about her."

"What does she have to do to change your mind about her?"

"I don't reckon there's anything she could do to change my mind. You see, the way I treat her depends on my choosing, not on her actions."

"That's absurd."

"Maybe. But it's a lot better in some ways. I don't have to know what she's doing at every moment. I don't have to determine her motives. And I don't have to try and determine which actions warrant my friendship and which alienate it. The lady's had a tough break, and she is going to spend every moment of her life living with the emotional and physical consequences. I've decided to cut her some slack."

"You think if you spend your lifetime treating her better than she deserves, it will make up for the pain she went through?"

"Nope, but I figure it might soothe the pain a little."

Lynda Dawn Austin sat staring into the flames and biting her lower lip for several minutes.

"Are you all right, darlin'?"

"Yeah."

"I didn't mean to offend you. I sure hope I didn't make you mad."

"Brady, would you just be quiet for a while?"

"Yes, ma'am." He got up and stirred up the fire. She watched him wander off toward the cottonwoods. He came back dragging a large tree limb. One by one he broke off small dead branches and placed them on the fire. When the blaze roared, he tugged one end of the stocky log onto the fire. Then he plopped down next to her and took her hand. Lacing his fingers in hers, he leaned back against the canoe and closed his eyes.

"Are we still on speakin' terms?" he finally asked.

Lynda refused to look over at him. "You shamed me something awful, Brady Stoner."

"Shamed you?"

"You and your noble attitude toward Cindy."

"I didn't aim to shame you. Shoot, I didn't even know I said anythin' noble."

"That's precisely why you shamed me. It was totally sincere."

"I don't think I'm followin' this."

"I told you this morning that I liked Cindy. I thought that maybe sharing my faith with her was a part of why I came out to Montana. But when she took off with the truck, I immediately assumed I was wrong. I figured that once again I had just been following my own whims and was not led by the Lord at all. So it was easy for me to quickly dismiss her as a wacko."

"Don't be too hard on yourself. You don't know her like I know her."

"Nor will I ever. That's the point. I judged her, accepted her, witnessed to her, rejected her—all from a distance. Then along comes old Brady who just loves them like they are and always expects the best from them. Just when I think nobody but God can treat people that way, you come along and remind me how shallow I can be. No wonder every woman in the West remembers your name. And all the time I thought it was that heart-stopping little-boy smile of yours."

"Darlin', I appreciate your confidence in me. But I'm not a saint. I don't do that good a job with lots of relationships. Before today I haven't talked to Cindy in almost five years. I've known where she was. I've driven by the place she was stayin' in Carson City three, maybe four times but never stopped. She's called and left word for me to get back to her a dozen times, and most times I never returned the call."

"Why?"

"Because I didn't know what to say to her. I just . . . I can hardly stand to admit that the reason I didn't give her a ride that night was just personal hurt and anger. So now the Lord's provided me with a chance to show a little extra kindness and patience. I figure it's about time to do something. There'll be plenty of opportunity to report her to the authorities tomorrow, if that's what I have to do. But just for the night, I'd like to give her the benefit of the doubt and pretend that she's doin' the right thing."

"I can accept that."

"I don't expect I can explain it too clearly. But the more you hang around me, the more times you'll probably not understand my actions. It's something you need to ponder. It's a real subjective thing. And I know it can be mighty aggravatin'."

"I said I can accept the way you are. Now don't go laying on sincerity like syrup. There's only so much nobility a girl can take."

"Yes, ma'am."

"Now that we've had this serious discussion, can we do something shallow and less profound?"

"What did you have in mind?"

With her hand still laced in his, she tugged him closer and closer until he was right by her side. Then she reached up with her free hand and pulled his head slowly toward hers until their lips touched and the brim of his hat was shoved upward by the impact with her forehead. She kissed his lips lightly.

"Oh," he said with a grin, "that shallow and less profound!"

Brady released his hand from hers and scooted his arm under her waist, drawing her even closer. His lips once again pressed hers, this time with purpose and enthusiasm.

Lynda quickly forgot about Cindy.

And the final chapter of Chance McCall.

And Lower Holter Lake.

And Montana.

And high and noble causes.

She thought about bridal showers and weddings and receptions and honeymoons. Mostly she thought about honeymoons.

His callused hand now gently held her cheek as he kissed her lips, her chin, and then low on her neck. Suddenly Brady got up and began kicking the fire apart. Within seconds the flame was gone, replaced by a dull glow of embers and the smell of thick smoke.

"You gettin' a little too warm, cowboy?"

His hand slid across her lips. "Shhh, darlin'," he whispered. "Someone's out on the lake."

"I don't hear anything," she countered in the same soft murmur.

"Just wait."

Without the fire and the kisses, the air felt cool on her perspiring forehead. Lynda took several deep breaths. *Lord, we've got to either get married or never come within three thousand miles of each other. I think I'm about to get very, very frustrated.*

Staring out into the darkness of the lake, she listened for a sound. *There better be something out there, Stoner—something significant . . . like the Spanish Armada.*

"There it is," he whispered. "Hear that hum?"

"Hum? You mean, like a motor?"

"Like an inboard. Look up north. There's a light. It's a boat all right. That's why we didn't spot them. They went right up the river to the north, not back to the lake," he whispered.

"How did you ever hear that a minute ago?"

"I'm a good listener."

She scooted up to where he sat and in the shadows found his face and kissed his ear. "That's not all you're good at. Do you think it's Mendoza?"

"More than likely. Let's just sit here and watch them come in."

"You think they can see us?"

"Nope, but they might be able to hear us. Let's just watch. One other thing . . ."

"What's that?"

He leaned over and kissed her ear. "There isn't any woman who can kiss as sweet as my Lynda Dawn."

"I presume you've had lots of experience?"

"Yes, ma'am, I have."

His hand lightly slid over her lips, muffling her reply.

The noise of the oncoming boat covered any conversation on board. Lynda and Brady sat in the dark side by side. Stoner held onto Capt. Patch's collar with one hand and muzzled him with the other.

Once the motor was cut, they heard voices. Most of the conversation centered on getting the boat trailer backed into the water and hand-cranking the boat up onto it. Lynda thought the voices belonged to two men and a woman.

"Three?" she whispered directly into his ear.

Brady nodded.

Once the headlights of the van were turned on, the watchers could see two men dressed in nylon jogging suits and dark knit caps pulled over their ears. From that distance, neither Brady nor Lynda could positively identify anyone. But the woman in the hooded sweatshirt did sound like Mendoza.

"I told you we had to go to the other lake," she announced.

"Will there be others up there looking for the gold?"

"Maybe. Someone has to have those missing pages."

"How about those two you left at the ranch?"

"One was tied up, and the other was out cold. Do you smell a fire? I smell a fire. Do you see any other cars out here?"

"Probably just a hunter's fire. Must be hunters out in these mountains."

One of the men drove the van out of the lake, the boat dripping a trail of water.

"Maybe those two at the ranch had the missing two pages and were searching for the rest of the chapter. Did you ever think of that? You should have searched their truck."

"They knew nothing and had nothing. She didn't even know what had been shipped to me. I told you, she was just a fluff from the city. He looked like a local cowboy."

Lynda jabbed Brady's ribs at the mention of the word *fluff*.

"Without the final chapter, it'll take them a month to find the right lake," Mendoza added.

"It might take us a month without those last two pages."

"I paid for a copy of the entire chapter," Mendoza fumed. "Somebody ripped me off, and somebody's going to pay dearly."

"You talking about this guy Hessler?"

"Yeah, but he doesn't have the brains to know which pages to rip off. I need those pages. There was a map and I believe some pictographs on them. I might need to send Tony to visit Hessler."

Brady leaned over, kissed Lynda's cheek, and whispered, "What pictographs? Who's Tony?"

She responded by kissing his ear and whispering, "Later."

"Later what?" he teased.

She jabbed him in the side with her elbow.

"Are you sure there's no one around? I do smell a fire," Mendoza again cautioned.

"Go look around if you want to. But that smoke could drift for miles in any direction. You aren't used to clean air."

"We're not going to drive out of here tonight, are we?" the other man questioned.

"Of course we are. I haven't spent the past six months setting this up to see it slip away in the last few days. Get in the van. I've got to get to Helena and make a phone call. I'm going to make sure I didn't get stiffed on this deal."

"I'm not driving out that goat trail in the dark," the man objected.

"I'll drive," Mendoza offered.

At the slamming of the door, Lynda leaned over and whispered, "Should we try and stop them?"

"They don't have the pages you want. It would be better to follow them and see if they can come up with the pages."

"Follow them?"

"When Cindy gets back with the truck. It should be easy to spot a van with a boat trailer."

The headlights from the van flashed their way. Both of them ducked down. Then the one left taillight of the boat trailer receded as the van rumbled up the dirt road next to Cottonwood Creek.

Brady released Capt. Patch, who scampered off toward where the van had been parked. Brady took out his pocketknife and sliced cottonwood shavings onto what was left of the embers. In a matter of minutes, flames warmed the air and their faces.

"They don't have the two most important pages either," Lynda mused, "but I wonder if they have the original chapter or just a copy?"

"If they have the original, then someone took those two

pages before Hampton copied it and before Drew Hessler stole it," Brady said pondering.

"This is getting more complicated. There's Junior and Spunky, this Mendoza gang and Drew, you and me—plus someone who actually has pages 451 and 452."

Lynda watched Brady continue to stoke up the fire. Then he picked up the sleeping bag he had been sitting on, unzipped it, and tucked it around her shoulders like a blanket.

"Come on, cowboy, there's room for another under here," she offered.

Brady sat down next to her and pulled the sleeping bag around his shoulders as they huddled near the fire. Capt. Patch rejoined them. The dog spun a few circles on the edge of the sleeping bag before he lay down.

Lynda brought her knees up to her chest and wrapped her arms around them. She laid her chin on her knees and stared into the flames.

I like being with him, Lord. More than anyone I've ever known in my life, I just like being with him. It doesn't matter if we're driving down the road or sitting in some little cafe or searching the desert for a lost manuscript or standing on the observation deck of the Empire State Building at midnight or sitting in the crowded stands of a rodeo or snuggled up under a blanket by a campfire. Actually I like the snuggled-up part best. Cindy's not coming back, and we can't hike out of here until daylight, at least. Worse things could have happened.

It's a long time until morning. Maybe we'll . . . Stoner, are you just going to sit there?

She glanced over at him.

"Well, darlin'," he asked, "what are you thinkin' about now? Have you got this thing figured out?"

"What thing?"

"The missing pages. What did you think I was talking about?"

"Oh, sure, the pages. No, it still confuses me."

Brady used a stick to poke the fire. "I've been thinkin' about it. And I've been wonderin' if you ever had those pages in the first place. What if old Chance forgot to send them? Do authors ever do that?"

"Oh, it happens. But do you mean to tell me you were sitting here thinking about that final chapter?"

"Yeah, and I, well . . ." He let out a deep sigh. "I wasn't really thinkin' about that book too much."

"And just what were you thinking about?"

"I was thinkin' about a rodeo in Vernal, Utah. I drawed up on a horse called X14, and when he came out, he would spin like a bull. Well, I marked him fine and then—"

"I'm certainly glad you had something important on your mind, Stoner."

"To tell you the truth, I, eh . . . it's just . . ."

"Just what?"

"I'm sure Cindy will come back in the morning. That road's too—"

"Stoner!"

"I was really thinkin' about how doin' this relationship with Lynda Dawn Austin right is just about the toughest thing I've ever attempted in my life. I'm no saint, and I've done my share of wrong things. I never wanted to do anything right as much as this. But sometimes I've got more hunger than willpower. You know how it is if you've been out in the desert a couple of days without water? And you make it back to camp, and your first inclination is to gulp down a few gallons of water? But you know you can't because it could make you seriously sick? Well, sometimes I just want a big gulp."

"You do?"

"Yep. Lynda Dawn, it doesn't help me one bit to have you nuzzled up next to me."

"You want me to move?"

"It would break my heart. I'm sure glad you're strong about this. It's one of the things that draws me to you. You've got high standards, and you never back away from them. Just knowin' that you'll keep me in line gives me some hope that we'll do this right."

"Me?" *I'm the strong one? Lord, help us! I thought Brady was the strong one.*

"Yeah, there you are trying to solve this mystery, and all I can think about is your sweet smell, your soft lips, and your warm body next to mine."

"We're in real trouble here, cowboy," she murmured.

"You too, huh?"

"Yeah. I lied. My thoughts weren't all that noble either. So what are we going to do?"

"Let's talk about Cindy," he suggested.

"Well, that ought to settle things down in a hurry."

"She needs to get a life. There's got to be something somewhere for her."

"She needs the Lord," Lynda suggested.

"Yeah, but what do we do with her if she refuses to consider a spiritual solution?"

"I don't know. Before all of this happened, what kind of work did Cindy do?"

"Besides barrel racing?"

"She must have done something else."

"She waitressed at a truck stop up near Cedar City, Utah."

"Not good. I don't think she would be able to spend her days around truckers—at least, not yet."

"She was a mighty good barrel racer in her prime."

"In her prime? Brady, she's not even thirty!"

"Yeah, kind of sad, isn't it?"

"She's got to have other talents."

"I'll tell you one thing she's mighty good at. At least, she used to be."

"Am I going to want to know this?"

"Relax, Lynda Dawn. Cindy can train horses. She can talk a horse out of meanness, and a glance from her eyes takes the fright right out of them."

"Can you make a living doing something like that?"

"Not really. In the spring a person could top out the remuda, but that's about it."

"Of course, if we never see her again, we won't have to worry, will we?"

"She'll be back, Lynda Dawn. Probably have a pretty good explanation, too."

"Well, if she comes back, we've got to find something for her. There's no way we can just wave and say, 'Hope everything works out for you,' and then ride off."

Brady stirred the fire with the stick.

Laying her head on her arms, Lynda closed her eyes.

The flames warmed her forehead, but her ears remained cold. The acrid smoke drifted toward her just enough to filter out the perfume on her wrists. Though her knees already felt stiff from the position, she was too comfortable to move. In the far distance, several coyotes howled in their customary half-panicked, half-lonely falsetto. The lake contributed no sound, and the fire offered only an occasional muffled pop and crackle. Above, she knew, was a sold-out audience of stars with their season tickets and silent witness.

You're a long way from New York City, Ms. Lynda Austin. You've been needing a break like this for a long time. A long, long time.

Brady lay against the canoe, his hat dropped over his eyes. His right hand rubbed Lynda's back through the padding of the draped sleeping bag. He began to hum a gentle, moody rhythm. In a few minutes, she could hear him softly sing:

*"'We're alone, Doney Gal, in the rain and hail,
Drivin' them dogies down the trail.*

> *Rain or shine, sleet or snow,*
> *Me and my Doney Gal are bound to go.*
> *We ride the range from sun to sun,*
> *For a cowboy's work is never done;*
> *He's up and gone by the break of day*
> *Drivin' the dogies on their weary way.*
> *We're alone, Doney Gal, in the rain and hail,*
> *Drivin' them dogies down the trail.*
> *Rain or shine, sleet or snow,*
> *Me and my Doney Gal are bound to go.'"*

He would sing a verse in his low, soft, mostly-in-tune baritone, hum the chorus, sing them both, or whistle softly. Lynda wasn't sure how many verses there were, but neither the fire nor the slow, steady rubbing of her back nor the song seemed to ever end.

The cold air of daylight stung her awake. She found herself zipped up tight in the green canvas sleeping bag, fully clothed, still wearing her boots. A very small fire popped and snapped. Her head and her toes were freezing. Although the sun had not yet risen, it was light enough to see across the dirt parking area.

She propped herself up on one elbow and stared at Brady as he walked slowly over the grounds with earphones on his head and the metal detector in his hands. She crawled out of the sleeping bag and warmed her hands and face at the little fire. Then she wrapped the sleeping bag around her shoulders and, dragging it like a train, hiked over to where he was searching. Seeing her approach, Brady turned off the machine, slung it over his right shoulder, and tugged down the earphones.

"Mornin', Lynda Dawn."

"Don't look at me. I know I look horrible."

"Well, darlin', if this is your absolute worst, you've got nothin' to worry about."

"That's what I like about cowboys. They spend so much time looking at cows, they aren't too discriminating. What are you doing?"

"Looking for buried treasure."

"Here?"

"I was just tryin' out the metal detector Mr. Hampton left with us."

"Did you find anything?"

"Oh, yeah. This is quite a sophisticated unit."

"What did you find?"

"Half of a rusted nail, a small lead fishing weight, and a gold mine."

"A what?"

"Well, the thing started squeaking like mad over there by the rocks, so I dug down with my pocketknife, and there's nothing but the bedrock. At one time the river must have channeled over here and washed out that cliff. So I figure there's a gold mine there."

"You're kidding me, right?"

"I think so. I really don't know much about these machines, except that I borrowed one once down in El Paso to find my ring."

"You lost a ring?"

"Sort of."

Brady walked back over toward the fire with Lynda trailing behind. "What do you mean, sort of?"

"This gal got mad at me and threw the ring I gave her out the truck window at a road construction zone. So after I took her home, I went back to search for it. I hiked up and down that highway for two hours but couldn't locate it, so I borrowed a metal detector."

"Did you finally find it?"

"Yep."

"I'll probably regret asking this, but what was this girl's name, and why did you give her a ring?"

"Oh, it's nothin', darlin'."

"Stoner!"

"Her name was Ashley Ann, and her daddy owned a horse I wanted to buy. All the rest of it gets kind of complicated."

"A real sweetheart, no doubt?"

"She was spoiled, selfish, bigoted, and bossy."

"Why on earth did you give her a ring?"

"All I can remember is that it sure was a purdy horse. It wasn't an engagement ring or anything like that. The rest is kind of fuzzy in my mind."

"I'll bet it is."

"I don't have any idea why Hampton rented this metal detector, but the next time we're at a rodeo, I'll bet we could use this in the parking lot and pick up some loose change."

"I'll remember that." She looked around at their scattered camping gear. "Sort of looks like a homeless camp under a bridge, doesn't it? Now what's the plan?"

"Wait for Cindy to come pick us up."

"How long are we going to wait? I think we could hike up to that other boat dock in a couple of hours. Even if she's coming in, we would meet her. We can save a little time that way."

"I think we ought to wait here for a while. I wouldn't want Cindy to think we don't trust her."

"Brady, we don't trust her. She stole your truck and deserted us, didn't she?"

"Well, if you're going to be technical about it."

"You just won't give up on her, will you?"

"Nope. Is that okay?"

Lynda slipped her arm into Brady's and stared off at the sunrise.

"Yeah, it's okay for a while. There's something inside of me that keeps hoping you're right, but I know with my mind that you're wrong." They trekked over to the yellow-leafed cottonwoods. "But we can't stay out here all day. If we don't see Cindy by noon, we'll have to start hiking."

"Or we could paddle the boat up to the marina."

"Would it be faster than hiking?"

"Nope. And we'd miss Cindy if she were drivin' in. But it sure is a lot more fun than walking." He leaned over and kissed her on the neck. Then he patted her on the backside. "Now go rustle us up some grub, and I'll scrounge up some more firewood."

"Grub? We don't have anything to eat."

"Well, I suppose that limits the choices. It doesn't have to be anything fancy."

"Good. Do you want me to cook your boots or mine?"

"Come to think of it," Brady said with a laugh, "I'm not very hungry."

"It's a good thing." She grabbed her purse and began to walk toward the lake.

"Where you headed?"

"To wash up. The ladies' room is this way, isn't it?"

"Darlin', that's one of the joys of Montana. The ladies' room is in any direction you want it to be."

Lynda lost her breath when the frigid water splashed on her face. She tried to dry off on the sleeves of her jacket, then dug Tahoe Fascination out of her purse, and rubbed it liberally over her neck and wrists. Her feet were cold in the black cowboy boots, and her jeans felt a little grimy. The green plaid flannel shirt stayed hidden under the black satin jacket. She tried combing her hair, then gave up. The dark brown shoulder-length locks displayed curls in places where there had never been curls before.

This is not wearing the same fragrance two days in a row! I haven't had a shower, so I couldn't switch perfume if I wanted to.

Brady had a good-sized fire blazing when she returned.

"Hey, isn't my hair beautiful? Did she dump out my hat, too?"

"Yep. I gathered things up in the canoe. It'll be easier to load when Cindy gets here."

"Well," she announced, "I've got breakfast ready. Look!" She held out a small foil package. "An entire package of sugar-free cinnamon breath mints."

"Isn't that nice, Capt. Patch? She fixed gourmet food. You might as well sit a spell, darlin'. We don't have a fishin' pole or a huntin' rifle or a mini-mart. Any minute I expect to see Cindy toolin' down that draw."

With their backs against the canoe, feet toward the fire, and dog scrunched in between them, Brady and Lynda jammed their hands into their coat pockets and stared into the morning flames.

"What are you thinking about?" she asked.

"Besides Cindy, Mendoza, final chapters, lost gold, missing pickups, and all that?"

"Yeah." She grinned.

"Skitzo Skoal. Did I ever tell you about that 89 I scored at Colorado Springs?"

"Yeah, but it was three in the morning, and I was sort of dozing off. Tell me again."

"Here's the thing. Clint had an 86, and Marvin and Mark both got bucked off, so I'm figurin' I've got a chance for good money in the go-round and . . . Are you sure you want to hear this again?"

"I've got plenty of time. Give me every last detail, cowboy."

He did.

After the description of the Pike's Peak or Bust Rodeo, they talked about Lynda's legal hassle to prove that she, her sister, and her brother were heirs of Martin Taylor Harrison. Then the discussion turned to plans for Thanksgiving, Christmas, and when to resume Brady's rodeo career. Sprinkled in between were conversations about Texas perfumes, packer boots, dresses with lace, Black Angus cattle, and cold Montana winters.

They hiked to the lake where Brady tried to teach her the fine skill of skipping rocks. Next he spent an hour teaching her how to operate the metal detector, but all she managed to dig up was a flattened Campbell's Soup can. They returned to the fire and settled in next to the canoe. Brady was describing the perfect way to roast rattlesnake meat when Capt. Patch let out a bark and leaped to his feet. They heard the rumble of a vehicle and spun around to stare up Cottonwood Creek.

"Is it Cindy?" Lynda asked, straining her neck.

"No, it looks like a white minivan."

"Maybe we can get a ride out with them."

"Oh, Cindy will be along shortly," Brady began.

"Stoner, it's after 11:00 A.M."

"You said we'll wait until noon."

"Look, if we can get a ride, we'll take a ride, right?"

"If they don't pull out until 12:00, that will be fine. But we made a commitment to wait, so we have to wait."

"A commitment to whom? To each other? We can change our minds, can't we?"

"I can't."

"Even if you're wrong?" Lynda pressed.

"I'm not wrong . . . yet. Wave to the nice folks, darlin'."

"That sort of looks like . . . What was the license plate on that van?" Lynda asked as the white and dirt-colored minivan circled the parking area, slowing down slightly near the lake.

"Wyomin'. Did you know those folks?"

"No, I guess not. Did anyone ever tell you there's a *g* in Wyoming?" she needled.

"Nope."

Suddenly the vehicle sped up and swung over by them.

"We got company, darlin'. Don't beg for food."

The windows were tinted, and the sun reflected off them in such a way that Brady and Lynda couldn't see who or how many were inside. Brady stood up as the van slammed to a stop. A roll of thin dust swept across them. Slowly the electric window lowered, revealing a woman reading a road map.

"Is this the road to Upper Holter Lake?"

Then the woman's eyes met Lynda's. "Ms. Austin?"

"Mrs. Gossman!" Lynda jumped to her feet.

L. George Gossman scrambled out from the driver's seat and around the front of the rig. He wore a new straw cowboy hat with a wide feather hatband. The hat slipped almost over his ears, held in place by his black plastic-framed glasses.

"What in the world are you doing here?" he demanded.

"I thought you went to Yellowstone for your vacation," she countered.

Gossman removed his hat and held it in his hand. "I thought you were in New York!"

"Sure is considerate of you to come callin' on us." Brady grinned. He tipped his hat to Mrs. Gossman. "Ma'am, I'm Brady Stoner—just an unemployed rodeo cowboy. I first met 'Georgie' down in the desert last fall, but I don't believe I had the privilege of makin' your acquaintance."

"Oh, my," she said, scrunching the map in her lap, "you're Ms. Austin's cowboy."

"I certainly hope so, ma'am."

"Ms. Austin," L. George Gossman continued, "I demand to know why you aren't in the office taking care of duties?"

"Because I'm in Montana taking care of duties."

"It certainly didn't look like you two were busy editing," he barked.

Brady scooted over to Gossman and wrapped his right

arm around the shorter man's shoulder. "Georgie, didn't we discuss all of this last year? I believe I expressed myself plainly concerning how I felt about you harassin' Miss Lynda Dawn, didn't I?"

"Yes, but—"

"And now that she has her own imprint, doesn't she set her own schedule?"

"Technically, but I'm still the editorial director, and I insist . . ."

Brady's grip on the man's shoulder made Gossman stop in midsentence. Stoner stepped back over to the van with the editorial director in tow.

"Mrs. Gossman, ma'am," Brady drawled, "has Georgie always been an insensitive pighead, or did this just happen during his advancin' years?"

The woman's stern and apprehensive expression melted in the light of Brady's teasing grin.

"You know, he's always been that way."

Brady liberated L. George as Mrs. Gossman opened the door. Brady held it for her and offered his hand, and she stepped down out of the van. She wore black stretch stirrup pants and a bulky dark green turtleneck sweater. Sunglasses hung on a gold chain around her neck, and she sported flat black shoes.

Brady released her arm and found she hadn't released his.

"Do you live out here, Mr. Stoner?"

"No, ma'am. I spend most of my time ridin' in rodeos. But please call me Brady."

"And you call me Carolyn."

Lynda scooted over next to Brady. *Call me Carolyn? I've known the Gossmans for years, and she never told me her name was Carolyn.*

"Well, Carolyn, while Lynda Dawn and Georgie are discussing company policy, why don't you and me take a little hike down to the lake? Did you know Lewis and Clark paddled their way right up this part of the Missouri on bull boats?"

"Bull boats?"

"Yep, let me explain. It's quite fascinating the way those were made."

She nodded at Lynda. "Nice perfume, dear. You must tell me what you're wearing today. Of course, one probably needs a place the size of Montana to wear something that pungent."

"Now look, Ms. Austin," L. George began, "I would like to know why you are out here."

"I'm looking for the final chapter of McCall's book. You haven't seen it, have you?"

"What? Me? Don't be ridiculous. The last time I saw it, it was in the Fed. Ex. pak on your desk."

"Oh? You have nothing to do with this project, so how did you know what's on my desk?"

"Don't be absurd. Are you accusing me of—"

"I'm accusing you of not answering my question."

"I believe Ms. Princeton reported that you received it. I must have walked by your desk and assumed it was in the shipping package."

"You know what's really strange?" Lynda stared off at the lake where Brady and Carolyn Gossman walked arm in arm. They were laughing about something. "Yesterday morning about this time, we ran into none other than T. H. Hampton and his new bride."

"Out here?" Gossman choked.

"Just down the road. It seems he had photocopied McCall's last chapter and was looking for the buried Confederate gold."

"He was?"

"Isn't that appalling? A man of Mr. Hampton's stature pirating a copy of that final chapter!"

"It's shocking!"

"Now tell me again, Mr. Gossman, what are you doing out here?"

"We . . . were at Yellowstone, and—"

"I thought you were going to the Caribbean again."

"Carolyn and I decided to come west instead."

"Isn't that nice? Of course, as you can see, not many people vacation on Cottonwood Creek just south of Lower Holter Lake. Especially in October."

"Oh, no . . . we aren't going to stay here. My word, there's nothing here. We were on our way up to, eh, Glacier National Park and thought we'd just poke around a little. Actually, Ms. Austin, I was lost and trying to find a place to turn around and get back to the Interstate."

"Oh, good. Then it doesn't have anything to do with the maps and pictographs leading to Jesse James's gold."

"Of course not. Just a coincidence actually. Do you mean to tell me that gold is supposedly buried around here? I thought it was in Utah, or something."

"Mr. Gossman, that's the stupidest excuse I've ever heard. What's the matter—didn't your copy of that final chapter have pages 451 and 452 either?"

L. George Gossman peered out at her from under his dark, shaggy eyebrows. "Do you have the audacity to accuse me of stealing a manuscript? I would think a person in your predicament would rather let things pass."

"Just what predicament am I in?"

"I am curious about what exactly an outspoken Christian woman like yourself and Stoner were doing back in here. Alone. Obviously, you were not looking for a book chapter when we drove up."

"What are you implying?"

"Only that before you begin accusing others of unethical behavior, you better consider your own."

Lynda's heart raced, and she could feel her face flush. She

hardly noticed Brady and Mrs. Gossman return. Waving her hand at L. George, she raged, "Are you questioning my faith or my virtue?"

"What I am saying," Gossman shouted, "is that—"

"Excuse me, Georgie," Brady interrupted. "Say, Carrie, can you drive this van?"

Carrie? He calls her Carrie?

Mrs. Gossman nodded her head. "Oh, I think so. Why?"

"Because if your husband has challenged Lynda Dawn's virtue, I'll be forced to break his arm or leg. I think it's a law in Montana whenever someone insults your girl's honor, you have to bust him up pretty bad, or else she'll dump you. So I figure you'll have to drive him to the hospital."

"Don't try to bluff me, Stoner!"

"I'm not. I mean every word of it. So just answer her question. Did you intend that to be an insult to her honor or her faith?"

"I, eh, I . . . you don't . . ."

"While he's trying to figure that out, Carrie, why don't you grab me that copy of McCall's final chapter you mentioned."

Mrs. Gossman opened the door of the van.

"Carolyn, what are you doing?" Gossman shouted.

"George, I'm really tired of treasure hunting. Brady says they have a lovely lodge in East Glacier. He said we can get there before dark if we hurry."

She reached into the backseat and pulled out a thick yellow file folder. "Here—this is all we have." She handed it to Lynda.

"Carolyn! How could you?" Gossman moaned.

"Really, George, we should have gone to Barbados." Then she turned back to Stoner. "Brady, dear, what did you say is the name of the reservation clerk at the lodge?"

"Laura-Lea Madison. When you call, tell her Brady told you to ask for the Frontier Suite."

"The one with the heart-shaped spa?"

"You'll love it."

"Come on, George."

"I can't believe this," Gossman muttered as he hiked back around to the driver's side of the rental minivan.

Carolyn Gossman glanced at Lynda. "And it's so nice to see you again, dear." She patted Austin's arm, then turned to Brady. "And what a special honor to finally meet Lynda's cowboy! Remember what I said. Next time you're in New York, you really must come up to our place on Long Island, and we'll throw a little party. Our friends would love to meet you." She stood on her tiptoes, clutched Brady's arm, and kissed him on the cheek. "Oh, and if you get to come up, by all means bring Ms. Austin along if you like."

She held out her hand as Brady helped her into the minivan. An act, Lynda thought, he was too eager to perform. He closed the door, but the van window was still rolled down.

"Say, do you two need a lift?" Mrs. Gossman queried.

Brady looked over at Lynda. She shook her head.

"We'll just wait and take a taxi." Brady winked at Mrs. Gossman.

"I don't suppose there's any better way out of here than that horrid cow trail around the mountain?"

"That's it."

"Well, you two get on back to whatever it was you were doing when we drove up." Carolyn batted her heavily mascaraed eyelashes at Lynda.

L. George Gossman spun his wheels in the loose dirt and rock of the parking area and bounced the van up the road leading along Cottonwood Creek.

"You didn't want to ride out with them?" Brady asked.

"No. You were certainly chummy with Mrs. Gossman."

"Nice lady. Did you know she used to jump horses?"

"Jump horses?"

"You know, in steeplechase races. She sure is a friendly gal. A little pushy though. Did you ever notice?"

"The thought did cross my mind. You didn't seem to protest too much, Brady, *dear!*"

"I got the final chapter, didn't I?"

"Yes, and I don't know if I want to know how you did it."

"Just a few 'yes, ma'ams.' *'Fortiter in re, suaviter in modo.'*"

"What?"

"'Resolutely in action, gently in manner.' That's my personal motto. At least, that's what Bunny always told me that meant."

"Your nature-girl, Native American Harvard buddy?"

"Yeah. Some ladies still enjoy being treated as if just being female is a position of honor and respect. Which, of course, it is."

"Yes, well, I wonder how you'd get along at a N.O.W. convention."

"A what?"

"On second thought, knowing you, you'd probably get along just fine."

"I'm surprised you didn't insist on riding out with the Gossmans."

"I wasn't about to ride out with L. George, and I wasn't about to let you ride out with Mrs. Gossman. I can't believe you called her Carrie!"

"Doesn't everyone?"

"I never called her anything but Mrs. Gossman in my whole life, and I have never, ever been invited to their place on Long Island."

"Maybe it's my gift."

"A gift of getting women to do and say strange things?"

"Oh? Does Lynda Dawn have an urge to do and say strange things?"

"No. I've been around you so much I've built up an immunity." She laughed a hollow kind of laugh. Then she hiked back over to the campfire and sat down with the yellow file folder in her lap.

"Look at this!" She pointed to the file folder label. "'Operation Goldstrike!' Can you believe that? Mr. Gossman really thought he would come out here and find the gold."

"Did they expect it to be lying along the edge of the road or what? Didn't they read the book and figure out it was hidden under water, if it exists at all?"

"Apparently not."

"Is it the original?"

"No, it's a copy, too. But it's clearer than Mr. Hampton's."

"Maybe you should have just duplicated that chapter and sent one to everyone in the publishing house. Sort of a Christmas bonus or something."

Lynda thumbed through the pages in the file folder. "It's incredible. The wildest thing Mr. Gossman ever did in his life was to jump over the turnstile when he didn't have a subway token. Now he's going to Montana to look for gold? Wait until I tell Kelly and Nina. This is getting really weird."

"And the wildest thing Junior ever did was marry Spunky. Come to think of it, that is pretty wild. I don't know why they can't be sensible like you and me."

"Bingo! Hey, look at this. Here's page 451."

"That's how Georgie found this lake. He had the map page. How about 452?"

"No, it's missing. But this map page is the original; the rest is a copy. Chance put this page on a blue paper that won't copy."

"Coverin' his bases." Brady nodded.

"So George just took the original. What did he think—that we wouldn't check?"

"It almost worked. Now you have ever'thing but the pictographs. How do they fit in anyway?"

"They showed the location of the cave. Look! This map shows a place on the northeast side of the lake called Gates of the Rocky Mountains."

"I've read about those."

"You have? Where?"

"In the journals of Lewis and Clark. They paddled right past some granite cliffs that seemed to open up and allow the Missouri to burst through."

"Would that be a good place for a cave?"

"An excellent place."

"Could the James boys have brought a boat up this far?"

"Not without having to portage from Fort Benton to Great Falls. After that they could have rowed upstream, I suppose. But there's lots of rocks in that canyon."

"We'll look for the one with pictographs."

"That whole canyon is probably filled with pictographs. Every tribe that wanted to cross the mountains probably came through that canyon. It's sort of like an Indian post office with messages left everywhere."

"Native American graffiti?"

"Yep."

Lynda flipped through the folder again. "Well, we have it narrowed down to one page."

"What if Gossman had had the entire manuscript?" Brady asked. "Would you just pack up and go back to New York?"

"It's a long walk," she kidded. "Besides, I think Ms. Mendoza needs to be challenged. I want to be there when you confront her."

"Me?"

"I'm sure you want to take a look at the lady who bashed in your head."

"In other words, Miss Lynda Dawn Austin isn't about to let that lady think she can get away with this."

"I guess that's it."

"Maybe if we sit here long enough, the rest of the manuscript will show up."

"If we sit here long enough, we'll starve. When are we leaving?"

"When Cindy gets here."

"Brady, I agreed to wait until noon. It's 11:55. We can at least start to straighten up things. Even if we're hiking out, let's load everything that we can't carry back into the canoe. Providing no one steals it, it will be easier to load up later on."

"Why don't we just wait until 1:00?" he suggested.

"Brady, you said if I waited until 12:00, we'd hike out of here."

"Babe, she's drivin' in here to get us."

"You are so stubborn! She isn't coming back, Brady. A woman who is otherwise a real sweetheart stole your $22,000 truck and isn't coming back. I wish you were right. I wish she'd drive in here right now. I wish I had another chance to tell her how the Lord could help her get her life together!" Austin was shouting now. "But we don't get another chance, Brady. Just admit you were wrong about Cindy. I was wrong about Cindy. We were both wrong about . . ."

A distant rumble and a horn honk caused Brady to glance up the dirt trail along Cottonwood Creek. Capt. Patch barked twice and took off up the creek on a wild sprint. Lynda didn't bother looking around but read the sparkle in Brady's eyes.

"It's her, isn't it?" She sighed. "Oh, man . . . I just know it's her."

"Yep. Well, at least it's my truck."

The silver-and-black Dodge extended cab truck roared up to the grove of cottonwoods. The engine died, and the window rolled down at about the same moment. Cynthia LaCoste stuck her face out. She wore a dark green turtleneck under a green-and-black plaid flannel shirt. Her hair was combed straight down. Small black earrings, Autumn Rose Blush lipstick, and a liberal amount of Lynda's perfume completed the picture. The expression on her face was someplace between worry and fear.

"I can explain. Really!" she appealed to them.

"Explain what, darlin'?" Brady drawled as he and Lynda ambled over to the pickup. Capt. Patch had jumped into the back of the rig and pushed the sliding back window open. He curled up beside Cindy.

"About takin' your truck and all."

"Lynda and me have been havin' a little argument about that."

Austin poked Stoner in the ribs. *Brady, please don't tell her I gave up on her.*

Cindy opened the door and slid down to the ground. "What were you arguing about? Or do I want to know?"

Brady slipped his arm around Lynda's shoulder. "I said you'd bring us back lunch, and Lynda Dawn insisted you'd be bringin' breakfast. So who won?"

"I brought hamburgers."

"What did I tell you, darlin'?"

Lynda looked over at Cindy and nodded. "Yeah. Brady was right."

"You two knew I'd come back?"

"I never doubted it for a minute, Cindy-girl. Our little stakeout worked great. We were over here when they came off the lake and even snagged a map of Upper Holter Lake from one of Lynda's New York friends who stopped by for a visit. Anyway, she can explain. I'll start loadin' up the gear. Darlin', how about you grabbin' those burgers, and let's eat as we get packed up."

Austin and LaCoste both stepped toward the cab of the truck at the same time. Cindy looked up at Lynda's eyes and then stepped back. "You're right," Cindy murmured. "You're his darlin' now."

Reaching over Capt. Patch, Lynda grabbed two white burger bags and noticed a large unopened bottle of Jack Daniels whiskey. With the bags in one hand and the bottle in the other, she walked to the back of the rig where Cindy and Brady loaded the canoe.

"Is this meant to be a part of lunch?" she asked Cindy.

"I can explain."

"Well, this is a mighty good time for it." Brady finished shoving the inverted green canoe over the top of the cab. He took a sack of burgers from Lynda's hand, fished one out, and then passed the sack back.

Cindy began, "This is all hard for me to do. Do you realize I haven't said more than two sentences at a time to anyone in years?"

Lynda set the whiskey bottle on the dirt at her feet. Then she climbed up and sat down on the pickup rail next to Brady. She bit into a cold, half-stale, cheap hamburger. It tasted wonderful.

"Yesterday I got nervous and edgy waiting for you. I didn't know when you were coming back, and I didn't have anything to do. I was feeling kind of sick. So I thought maybe I'd drive into Helena and get myself some medicine and maybe buy us a pizza or something."

"You mean, medicine like that Jack Daniels?" Lynda pointed at the bottle.

"Eh . . . yeah, that's about it. But when I got to town, I realized I couldn't just drive back out here and drink because I had promised Lynda I wouldn't."

"You want a burger, Cindy-girl?" Brady offered.

"Not 'til I spill all of this. Anyway, you two probably don't know this, but I don't drink in bars. I'm scared spitless to be around men when I'm drinking. So I go lock myself in my room and drink. Well, I figured I'd slip over to the motel room and down a bottle—that bottle right there on the ground.

"But here's the thing. When I got to the room, there were all of Lynda's things—her clothes, her laptop computer, her boots. I'm thinkin' this lady who hasn't known me for twenty-four hours and should hate my guts is my roommate and trusts me with her things. In that recovery house in Carson City, we had to keep all of our private belongings in a locked trunk that was nailed to the floor.

"I sat there on the bed and stared at Lynda's things, then at the bottle in my hand. It just felt wrong to drink in Lynda's room. It's weird. It was like you were right there in the room. I didn't drink. You can see that the bottle hasn't been opened."

"Why did you bring it out here?" Lynda asked.

"Because I figured if I told you that I bought a bottle but poured it out and didn't take a drink, you wouldn't believe me. So I wanted to prove to you I didn't open it.

"This is going to sound stupid, but it's the truth. I went into the bathroom and washed my face. Then I . . . I pulled off my clothes and crawled into bed between those clean white sheets."

Tears rolled down Cindy's cheeks. "I haven't slept in a bed in over three months. You can't imagine what it's like to have to sleep fully clothed in a sleeping bag in the back of a car with one hand on a rifle night after night. I crawled into that bed, and I stretched my arms and legs, sort of spread-eagle, and just cried because it felt so good. It was the first time in five years that I wasn't afraid to go to sleep."

LaCoste began to sob. Lynda slipped down off the truck and wrapped her arms around her, holding her tight and rocking her back and forth.

"I slept for sixteen straight hours. I wouldn't have woke up then, but the housekeeper banged on the door. I'm really sorry I deserted you two like that."

Cindy tried to stop crying. Lynda released her grip.

"It's all right, Cindy. We understand. You just needed the rest, girl. Actually we had a pretty good night, didn't we?"

"Sure did, babe," Brady answered.

"You aren't mad at me?"

"No," Lynda replied.

"I was so scared driving out here. I kept thinking that you probably hiked out and told the authorities that I stole your truck. I imagined the cops would pull me over, and I'd be thrown in jail. I don't think I could survive in jail."

"Cindy, I'll be real honest. I was worried about you," Lynda began. "I was afraid that you had gone off the deep end or something. But Brady, he just kept saying we're going to wait right here until Cindy comes back. I need to apologize for all those things I was thinking about you."

"You need to apologize to me?"

"I'd feel real guilty before the Lord if I weren't honest with you."

Cindy stared at Lynda without saying anything.

"Am I preaching at you?"

"Probably . . . but it's okay. I, eh, just haven't been around anyone like you for a long time." She glanced at Brady as he tied down the canoe. "For about five years, I suppose."

"Time to load up, ladies," Brady announced. "What about that?" He pointed at the whiskey bottle.

"Leave it," Cindy suggested.

"That's littering," Lynda worried aloud.

"Then I'll try to please you both." He tore the seal on the bottle, opened it, and dumped the contents in the dirt. Then he tossed the bottle into the back of the truck.

"Remind me to toss that out. Now which one of you is driving? My left arm is hurting something fierce."

"I'm in the backseat," Cindy called out and climbed into the truck.

Lynda drove the rig slowly up the creek and around the

trail at the base of the mountain. She explained about
Mendoza coming off the lake way after dark and how the
Gossmans just happened to show up with a copy of the final
chapter. Brady and Capt. Patch finished eating the hamburgers and fries.

◆ ◆ ◆

Twelve miles north of Helena, Montana, they came to the exit
that led to Upper Holter Lake. Lynda didn't slow down.

"Whoa, you missed your turnoff," Brady pointed out.
"Mendoza said they were headed for Upper Holter."

"And I'm aiming for the motel. I've been in these clothes
for over twenty-four hours and have had to use the same perfume two days in a row. We'll go freshen up. Then you and I
will come back out here."

"And me?" Cindy asked.

"You, girl, are going to go to bed. I figure you have five
years of sleep to catch up on. If you get hungry, call out for a
pizza or something, but mainly just sleep."

"Are you serious?"

"Yes."

"I think I will."

"Good."

"I won't drink. I promise."

"I trust you."

Cindy looked her straight in the eyes. "You're crazy, Lynda
Dawn."

◆ ◆ ◆

It was almost three o'clock when Lynda finished cleaning up
and pulled on her black boots. She dialed Brady's room number.

"You ready to go catch those chapter rustlers, cowboy?"

"Yes, ma'am, I reckon I am."

"Good, I'll call Kelly and then meet you at the truck."

"Is Cindy coming with us?"

"No, she's already conked out."

"That's one tired lady. I'll go get the rig gassed up. Meet you out front in ten minutes."

Lynda hung up the phone and sighed. Then she turned to look at Cindy and noticed that the sheet was pulled over LaCoste's head.

Lord, keep her safe and peaceful for a long, long rest.

Punching another number into the phone, she looked in the mirror above the motel dresser and brushed her hair back over her ears with her fingers. *You look ravishing, Ms. Austin. It must be your charming personality he's so crazy about.*

"Atlantic-Hampton Publishing Company. How may I direct your call?"

"Hi, this is Lynda. Put me through to Kelly, please."

"You'd like to speak with Ms. Princeton?"

"Yes. If she's left already, I'll talk to Nina."

"Ms. Princeton is in. Whom should I say is calling?"

"This is Lynda—Lynda Austin."

"Thank you, Ms. Austin. What is the nature of your call?"

"Who is this?"

"Atlantic-Hampton Publishing Company."

"No, who are you? The one on the phone."

"Fawn Lake."

"Are you new at the job?"

"I've worked for Mid-Manhattan Temps for over six years."

"Yes, well . . . look at your phone list by your right hand. Whose name is by #6?"

"Lynda Austin. Oh, it's you! You work here?"

"You've got it. How about ringing through to Kelly? She's #14."

"I know what number she is. Why didn't you use the inter-com? You've tied up a phone line this way."

"Because I'm in Montana. Now are you going to ring me through to Kelly, or do I call the president of Mid-Manhattan Temps and bring your brilliant six-year career to a screeching halt?"

"There is absolutely no reason to threaten or mistreat temporary help. Statistics show that temp help is doing 21 percent of the work in mid-Manhattan on any given day."

"You're right," Lynda sighed. "Sorry I got ticked. Now just tell me one thing, Fawn Lake. Am I going to get to talk to Kelly or not?"

"I'll ring and see if she's still here."

Where is Spunky when you really need her? On a honeymoon, of course.

"Kell?"

"Lynda-girl, where are you?"

"In a motel in Helena, Montana."

"At one in the afternoon?"

"It's 3:00. We're on Mountain Time."

"And just who happens to be in the room with you?"

"Her name's Cynthia LaCoste. She's an old girlfriend of Brady's."

"You're kidding me, right?"

"No, and I only have a minute. Brady and I recovered two copies of the final chapter of McCall's book. All we need is the pictographs on page 452."

"Where did you get the copies? From that Mendoza woman you told me about?"

"No, we got one copy yesterday from Junior and Spunky and the other from—"

"Wait, wait . . . wait. Our Junior and his darling new bride had a copy of that final chapter?"

"Yes."

"And they were looking for the buried gold."

"Junior was. Spunky has already found her gold."

"I don't believe this."

"It gets more bizarre."

"Oh?"

"Brady and I were stranded out in the mountains overnight, and while we were waiting for Cindy to come back with the truck . . . of course I didn't really think she would come back, but Brady—you know what a rock he is—he never doubted for a minute . . . anyway while we were sitting by the fire, who do you suppose drives down Cottonwood Crick?"

"Crick? You're starting to talk like him, girl. I don't have any idea what this conversation is about."

"L. George and Carolyn Gossman drove in."

"Carolyn? Mrs. Gossman's name is Carolyn?"

"Yeah. They drove up in a rental van with a copy of the chapter—"

"Looking for the gold?"

"Yeah."

"L. George? Mr. Don't-you-dare-get-any-dust-on-my-black-patent-leather-elevator-shoes Gossman?"

"None other."

"Was he with Junior?"

"Nope. Strictly free lance."

"Well, why don't you just have a staff meeting out there? This is crazy. Gossman thinks going to Jersey is 'out west.'"

"What's happened in the office in the past couple of days?"

"Besides a temp receptionist who dresses wilder than Spunky?"

"Fawn? Don't tell me she has crimped blonde hair hanging to her waist."

"Nope. It's red. Anyway, besides Nina and me feeling

totally left alone and neglected as always, the big news for you is that you lost an author."

"What do you mean, I lost an author? Who? How? What house did he go with?"

"It's more serious than that. We got a call yesterday afternoon from Chance McCall's sister in Florida. Chance died in a diving accident."

"W-when? Where? How?" Lynda stammered.

"Five days ago. In the Bahamas. I guess he hit his head on something, lost consciousness, and surfaced too fast."

"He drowned?"

"Decompression blew his lungs out, the authorities said."

"I can't believe something like that could happen to such a veteran diver."

"Neither could his sister."

NINE

"Kelly talked to the authorities in the Bahamas," Lynda reported to Brady. "They said there were still a few unanswered questions concerning McCall's death."

"Like it might not be an accident?"

"They wouldn't go that far, but they are still looking into it."

Brady drove the truck north of Helena, the Captain seated between them. "What do you do with a book when the author dies before publication?"

"There's no reason not to proceed with the project. But it will cut down on some publicity, and the royalties go to the heir and assigns."

"Pretty tough to have a sequel. I surmise it makes an autographed copy mighty rare," Brady added.

"That's rather tasteless humor, Stoner."

"I reckon it is. Did you know McCall very well?"

"Not really. I met him once in Florida, and he came up to New York last July. Other than that, it's just been a few phone calls and letters."

"I suppose dyin' on a dive is not a bad way for a diver to go. Bull riders are always afraid of dyin' in a car wreck on their way to a rodeo. They want to be in the arena when they take their chances. How old a man was he?"

"In his early seventies. This guy was a pro, Brady. He started diving as a kid. Told me back in those days they would cut the bottom off a five-gallon milk can, mount some goggles in the side, and pump air through a garden hose with hand billows from a rowboat in order to dive. He knew it all. We had a whole series planned."

"Were they close to finding some sunken treasure or something?"

"That's one of the questions the Bahamians want answered."

"How about Chance's diving partner? What's he got to say about all this?" Brady quizzed.

"He brought Chance ashore. When the ambulance left with his body, the guy disappeared. No one's seen him since."

"Now this is beginning to sound like a sequel."

"It might be, especially if this first book does well." Lynda pointed to a sign along the Interstate. "Is that our turnoff?"

"Yep. There's the Sleepin' Giant."

"The what?"

"That mountain is called the Sleepin' Giant. See his chest . . . and face?"

"Sort of. Did you get that boat motor fixed?"

"Yeah. It was just a spark plug wire. It runs good now."

"Are we goin' out on the lake this afternoon?"

"Maybe, but the wind is pickin' up. We might just poke around the shore today and see what we can turn up."

Lynda stared out the window at the brown hillsides.

Chance McCall. Cindy LaCoste. People. That's what this world is about, isn't it? It's not about manuscripts, cover art, or royalties. It's not even about 90-point bronc rides or big Montana ranches. Sometimes I forget, Lord. Brady seems to have figured that out better than I have. I don't even have the foggiest idea about Chance's spiritual condition. Lord, have mercy on his soul.

"This deal with Chance dying has kind of sobered things up, hasn't it?" Brady pulled onto the dirt road leading to the lake.

"I'm not quite as enthused about confronting Mendoza," Lynda admitted.

"You know what I was thinkin', darlin'? If we could snag page 452, we ought to just pack up and go back to Jackson Hole for a few days before you have to go home. Let's sit around with nothin' to do but look in each other's eyes and dream."

"How do you do it, Stoner?"

"What?"

"Entice women with a word and a smile."

"You think I'm tryin' to entice you?"

"Well, you just did it. I don't even want to think about what we will do if we find that missing page. Focused. I'm going to keep focused and not think about the warm fire in the circular fireplace at the lodge nor the huge leather love seat nor what it feels like to have your hand in mine or your arm around me for hours on end."

Brady rolled down his window. The brisk breeze chilled the entire cab.

"What are you doing?"

"I figure we need to lower the temperature in here a tad."

"You getting steamed up, cowboy?"

"About like a barbecued jalapeño."

"Sorry."

"You are not."

Lynda knew she was blushing. "No, I'm really not. What are we going to do, Mr. Brady Stoner? Every time we get together, we seem to have less and less self-control?"

"Well, I reckon one of these days, we'll just have to get married."

"Brady Stoner, are you proposing to me?"

"Do you think I ought to?"

"Wait a minute. Are you asking me whether I think you ought to propose to me?"

"Yeah. What do you think?"

"I think you better make up your own mind," she huffed.

"And I think that horse is about to make it to the highway!"

Brady whipped the truck to the left and slammed on the brakes, blocking the dirt road. Barbed wire fences paralleled the road on both sides, with about five feet of dead grass and weeds between the fence line and the road. Trotting straight toward them was a long-legged bay horse. Its saddle was slipped around to its right side; its reins dragged the dirt. About two hundred yards down the road, a cowboy waved his hands and shouted something.

"You and the Captain take the south side. Block off that grass between the fence and the truck. Just wave your hat at him and holler. Besides, he won't come that way. The Captain will see to that."

"What are you going to do?"

"Rope him, of course."

While Lynda and Capt. Patch jumped out and guarded the south, Brady pulled a worn nylon rope out from behind the seat and built himself a coil.

The horse, ears up and lathered, started toward Lynda, but Capt. Patch lunged at him. The horse broke around to Brady's side of the truck. With his loop lying partially on the ground behind his right hand, Brady left the lane clear and waited on the far side of the truck. When the horse got even with Brady, he effortlessly tossed the loop over the horse's neck. He dallied the other end of the rope around a large steel truck hook bolted onto the front chassis of the Dodge.

The horse almost flipped over when he hit the end of the rope. Both the rope and the Dodge held. After a couple of kicks, the horse quieted down. Soon it foraged in the dead grass by the roadside.

A tall, very thin cowboy hobbled up the road with a crumpled hat on his head and a coiled rope in his hand. "Man, oh, man, I surely am glad you come along, partner! Once X-it got to the highway, no tellin' what would've happened."

Lynda noticed that the man's shirt was ripped and his jeans and vest were covered with dirt and mud.

"Looks like X-it stepped in a prairie dog hole," Brady offered.

"Dog hole, nothin'! That son of a bucker ran three miles before throwin' me into the dirt. That's why we call him X-it. He has a tendency to make a fast exit anytime he can."

"You work for the Hilgers?"

"Hilgers sold out a few years ago, but I'm running this part of the range. You throw a smooth hoolihan, partner. You ain't lookin' for work, are ya?"

"I'm workin' for Miss Lynda Dawn right at the minute, but I might like a rain check on that offer."

"You have a spread around here?" he asked Lynda.

Lynda stared blankly at Brady.

"No, she doesn't have a ranch. I'm helpin' her with a little . . . research."

The man looked Lynda up one side and down the other. Then he turned to Brady and grinned. "Research? Do you get paid for it?"

"Eventually. Say, do you mind if I take a crack at settlin' down old X-it?"

"Be my guest. I'm not lookin' forward to bein' the next one on his back."

Brady began singing the song about Doney Gal that Lynda had heard the night before. As he softly sang, he walked up to the horse and began brushing the animal's neck with his hand. After a while he rubbed its rump and then its belly. Finally he reached under the animal and loosened the cinch. With the saddle pulled back up in place, he yanked the cinch down. The horse tried to kick him, and Brady slapped the animal across the nose.

"Don't you do that to me, X-it!" he scolded. The horse raised his foot to kick again, and Brady raised his hand as if to strike the horse's nose. X-it put his hoof back down.

"Now you're actin' smart!"

Holding the reins, Brady slipped the rope off the horse's neck and walked the animal slowly to the east past the pickup and the audience.

"You three keep him from breakin' to the road," he drawled as he tossed his rope upon the hood of the truck. "Does he spin right or left?"

"Bucks straight ahead," the man replied.

"He's goin' to spin today," Brady predicted.

"You better let me twitch him while you climb aboard."

"Well . . . let me give him a shot this way."

Again Brady tugged the cinch and rebuckled the Blevins. Then using the rein, Brady yanked the horse's head to the left. With his left hand on the saddle horn, he jammed his left foot in the stirrup and smoothly swung up into the tooled saddle with a Cheyenne roll on the cantle.

Immediately X-it began to protest. He tried to buck, but with his head held sharply to the left, he couldn't do much without falling forward. Instead, responding to Brady's heel kicks, the horse spun around and around to the left.

Quickly Brady pulled up on the reins, stopping the horse, then jerked the reins to the right, and spun the horse in the opposite direction for several minutes. Lynda and the tall cowboy leaned against the truck as they watched.

Pulling the horse's head away from the truck, Brady punched his boot heels into the horse's sides and hollered, "All right, X-it, show me your best stuff!"

The horse dropped his head and kicked his hind feet straight behind him. He jumped, bucked, and twisted several more times and then broke for a distant corral on a gallop. But Brady, sitting straight and relaxed, reined the horse and put him through the right and left turns all over again. This time when Brady stopped, the horse bucked one meager jump, then quit.

"Well, I'll be," the cowboy drawled. "That ol' boy knows horses."

"He rides barebacks in the rodeo," Lynda bragged.

"That don't mean two spits to me, lady. He ain't hanging onto no handle for eight seconds with X-it. What's his name anyway?"

"Stoner. Brady Stoner."

"He ever work over in Judith Basin?"

"I don't think so. He came out of Idaho and has cowboyed in Nevada, Utah, and Arizona."

"Well, he can work for me any day. I'll tell you that right now."

Brady rode X-it down toward the distant corrals, turning him left, then right, then backing him up to a gate, then bringing him back at a walk, a canter, and a trot. Reaching the truck, Brady rubbed the horse's neck.

"You did good, X-it! You mind your manners, and I'll bet there's some sweet oats in your feed bucket tonight."

Brady climbed down and handed the reins to the cowboy.

"The lady says your name is Stoner." He shook Brady's hand. "Well, mine's Thomaston—Red Thomaston."

"Nice horse, Red. I noticed some scars on those front legs. When did he hit barbed wire?"

Lynda looked at the reddish brown horse's legs and couldn't see any sign of injury. *How does he know that?*

"A couple years back. Someone pulled a wire gate open and left it stretched across the lane. He hit it running to the barn.

Almost had to put him down. But he's just too nice a horse to lose."

"Probably does good out in the open."

"Yep, he's got plenty of cow-smart in him. You sign on, and I can guarantee you'll get X-it in your string."

"You hirin' this time of the year?"

"Nope, but if you need to winter out, I'll make exceptions."

"Would you sell X-it?"

Red pushed his hat back and put his hands on his hips. "You serious?"

"Yep."

"You plan on haulin' him in the back of that truck?"

"No, I'll work somethin' out."

"Well, he's stubborn but not mean. Like you said, good horseflesh. You want to make an offer?"

I can't believe this. He's going to buy a horse? You don't just stop in the middle of the road and buy a horse! He already has two horses.

"Tell ya, Red, set me a fair price. I don't have any idea what you got in him, and I don't want to insult you."

"What's $1,800 sound like?"

Brady slipped his hand down the horse's front left leg. X-it raised his hoof and Brady inspected it. Then he rubbed X-it's fore cannon, and the horse flinched a little.

"Well, if he hadn't run into the wire, and if he didn't buck for breakfast . . . $1,800 would be in the ballpark. I'll give you $900, and you will never have to iron the humps out of him again."

Isn't $900 insulting when he wanted $1,800?

Red reached in his back pocket and pulled out a small, round tin of Skoal. He offered some to Brady, who declined. "Horses are kind of expensive right now. I couldn't replace him with anything but an old pack horse for that kind of money. But I do appreciate your help today, so I suppose I could cut you a deal and dip down to $1,500."

"Mighty decent of ya. 'Course, he is kind of weak in the rear end. Strictly a three-, four-hour horse, I reckon. Couldn't ride him all day without breaking him down. I'll give you $1,000 even."

"You've never seen X-it cut out a sick calf from its mama. He don't take no guff from any bovine. Make it $1,250."

Are they really doing this? Is this how they always buy and sell horses?

"Well, he's a fine animal, Red. Needs some work, of course. You're carrying the papers on him, I suppose. I'll give you 1,100."

"Papers? Ol' X-it here is a grade horse. But he sure has a lot of the conformation of a quarter horse."

"And the brains of a thoroughbred. Eleven is the best I can do, Red."

"Well," Red drawled, "just as a personal favor to ya, I'll go against my better judgment and say yes." He reached out his hand, and Brady shook it.

"Here's what I'd like to do. We got some business to take care of for a few days. Then I'll figure out how to ship him over to my folks' place in the Owyhees. I'll give you a hundred dollars now and the rest when I come back to pick him up. If I'm not back in seven days, you keep the hundred."

"Sounds fine to me."

"Good. Lynda Dawn, darlin', give Red that hundred dollars you owe me, will ya?"

"Oh . . . sure," she stammered. "Eh, will traveler's checks be all right?"

"I reckon the bank will take 'em just fine, ma'am."

Lynda dug into her purse and pulled out the traveler's checks and began to sign some of them.

"You two doin' a little fishin'?" He pointed to the canoe in the back of Brady's truck.

"No, we're lookin' for some folks who might be out on the lake."

"I'll tell you what. Normally at this time of the year, there aren't many people out there. But in the last couple of days folks have been swarmin' down the road—vans and boats and minivans. Must be havin' a calico ball back there in the Gates."

"We'll just have to go pay our dues," Brady commented. "Come on, darlin', we'd better hurry before the band starts playin'. Red, I'll be back for X-it within seven days."

"I reckon you will. That job's open, you know."

"Thanks. Give X-it some sweet oats tonight. I promised him some, and I never lie to a horse."

"You got it, partner. Say, if you two get caught in here tonight, you can stay at the bunkhouse." He pointed to some distant buildings beyond the corrals. "I don't have anyone wintering down here yet."

"Thanks for the offer. If it storms us, we might take you up on that." Brady tipped his hat and climbed back into the truck.

Half a mile down the road Lynda turned toward him and shook her head. "I don't believe you. You just parked in the road and bought a horse."

"Yeah. Ain't he a beaut?"

"What are you goin' to do with another horse?"

"I'll top him off in a couple weeks and sell him for $1,800."

"You enjoyed that game of haggling, didn't you?"

"I suppose. But I just couldn't pass up a deal like that. When a man gets an urge to buy a certain horse, well, there's just no holdin' him back."

"The horse or the man?"

"Both."

I wonder how often he gets the urge to buy a horse? I can just see it now—there goes the grocery money or the car payment or new clothes for the children. How many horses is enough? Do I really know what it means to marry a cowboy? That is, provided he ever gets around to asking me.

"I was thinkin' about what Red said. He said vans—"

"And minivans!" Lynda added. "Do you think L. George Gossman has the nerve to come back in here?"

"He's your buddy, not mine. It could just be that the fishing is good, and it's someone else. I don't know why we assume they're all looking for that Confederate gold."

The road around to Upper Holter Lake led them along the base of a nearly treeless, grass-covered mountain. The farther they went, the steeper and rockier it became. After a few miles they arrived at a large dirt and gravel parking lot next to the boat launch. It was little more than a flat dirt pad hastily pushed out by a rusting bulldozer, which stood on the north side of the lot like a monument to the landing's creator.

Boats of various sizes and conditions were stored haphazardly in the lot. Down near the shore was an old single-wide trailer house with a small front porch and a sign that read Frank's Boat Rental & Expresso.

Brady pointed. "There it is! There's Mendoza's van."

"Isn't that Mr. Gossman's rental minivan?" Lynda asked as she pointed out a white Chevy.

"Boy, I'm slippin' in my old age. I thought for sure I sweet-talked Carolyn into going to that lodge in East Glacier."

"What's the matter, cowboy? Hasn't that dimpled charm ever failed before?"

He grinned from ear to ear. "Not that I can recall."

You could work on humility a tad, Stoner.

"I don't understand why that van's here. This doesn't make sense. Maybe it's not the Gossmans."

"Well, that's Mendoza's rig. I know that," Brady asserted.

"Do we have time to find them before dark?"

"Let's take the camping gear in case we need to park it for the night."

"But Cindy's expecting us to come back."

"She'll probably sleep until morning. Besides, we might not stay out here. As soon as it starts getting dark, we'll turn around and come back. Then we'll hit it first thing in the morning. I've got a feeling some of the others might not be up to camping either."

"At least Junior and Spunky aren't out here. There's no way she'd settle for cold jerky and a damp sleeping bag on her honeymoon."

"You figure we'll be in damp bags tonight?" Brady asked.

"A girl never knows where she'll end up when she travels with Brady Stoner."

"Well, maybe I'll surprise you this time. Maybe we'll just stay in Red's bunkhouse tonight. You stay in bunkhouses often?" he teased.

"From time to time." Lynda tried to use her best spoiled-rotten-brat accent.

Brady packed the canoe with sleeping bags, matches, and some snacks they had brought along. Lynda grabbed a bottle of something called All Night Long and splashed it on her neck and wrists. She refused to look in the vanity mirror on the back side of the pickup sun visor.

"Is the Captain coming with us?" Lynda asked.

"Nope. He doesn't like boats. He said he wanted to stay and guard the truck."

"What will he eat?"

"The catch of the day."

"Which is?"

"Whatever he catches."

Lynda glanced through the gear already stowed in the canoe. "You sure the motor's going to work this time?"

"Yep," he assured her.

"That's too bad." She climbed to the front of the canoe.

The little outboard whined at the rear of the canoe. Within

minutes Lynda dragged out a sleeping bag and draped it over the back of her head and shoulders, careful to keep it out of the water.

"It's getting colder," she shouted.

"Maybe so, but I'm two days younger than you," he hollered back.

You're getting deaf, too, Stoner.

As they proceeded north on Holter Lake, Brady stayed close to the shoreline. The flat-backed canoe bounced on the waves, each one jarring Lynda and splashing a little water.

"Can we slow down?" she finally called out.

"Wait a minute, babe," he replied. "Let me slow down. I can't hear you." The canoe coasted for a while as the motor idled. "Now what did you say?"

"I said, slow down, Stoner. You're freezing me out."

"Oh, yeah. Sorry. I guess I was thinkin' about something else."

"It wouldn't be a horse named X-it, would it?"

The little-boy smile.

The excitement in his eyes.

The sudden blush in a tanned face.

The cowboy hat pushed back revealing a very white upper forehead gave the answer.

"It was more than that." Brady revved the engine up to a moderate speed. "X-it's about eight years old."

"How do you know that?"

"I saw it in his teeth."

"All I saw was that he needed to brush and floss."

"Well, he is about eight, just finishing his squirrely teenage years, as far as horses go. I figure about the time he's twelve or fourteen, he'll settle down and make Brady, Jr., a fine cuttin' horse, providing he really has any cow-sense at all."

"Providing who has cow-sense? X-it or Brady, Jr.?"

"X-it."

"So there's going to be a Brady, Jr., huh? You plan on getting married, do you, Stoner?"

"Dad gum it, Lynda Dawn, you and I both know we're goin' to get married someday."

"How many little Bradys did you plan on having?"

"Four."

Well, four's better than eight. At least he's working in the right direction. Does he think having children is like buying horses? You just stop and pick one up whenever you get the urge?

"You see, darlin'," he continued, "I figure four little bronc-ridin' Bradys for me and four little barrel-racin' Lynda Dawns for you."

"Just how many wives to you intend to have?"

"Just one, darlin'."

"Well, this one is too old for all of that. You better find you a healthy eighteen-year-old."

"Really?"

"We're not kids, Brady."

"But if we'd get started right away, you'd be all done by the time you were forty."

"I'd be all done a lot before then."

"Well, then, how about just four? Maybe I'd get lucky, and they'd all be boys. What do you say to that?"

"Is that what you call a proposal? We aren't going to get started on anything until I have a ring on my finger, cowboy."

"Did you ever notice how every conversation we've had in the past few days leads to marriage?"

"Yes."

"It's almost like it was on purpose."

"It is." She raised her eyebrows and smiled a closed-lip smile.

"Oh," Brady mumbled. Then he sped the motor. Soon Lynda was again bouncing along, being slightly splashed.

◆ ◆ ◆

Lynda had the sleeping bag pulled completely over her head by the time Brady shut the motor down and let the canoe coast. Peeking out, she saw Brady point to the east. She let the sleeping bag slip to her shoulders and stared at a boat anchored about a hundred yards from them near a sheer granite cliff that ran right into the water.

"Is that them?" she called.

"The big one tied up to the cliff is Mendoza's boat. I have no idea on the other one. Hand me the binoculars."

Lynda dug them out of the sack.

"The little one's called *The Latte*. My guess is it's a rental boat from Frank's. Do either of the Gossmans know how to scuba dive?"

"I don't think so. They go down to the islands every year, but I've never once heard them talk of diving. L. George thinks he's pushed the envelope of excitement if he orders something new from the deli menu. Why do you ask?"

"Because there doesn't seem to be anyone on that rental boat. Of course, Mendoza's has a little cabin, so I can't see anything over there. . . . Besides, it seems to be around on the back side of that rock cliff."

"Maybe they're all over on Mendoza's boat."

"Why? They don't know each other, do they? But then we don't know for sure the Gossmans are here."

"Don't we need to get a little closer? I can't see much," Lynda stated.

"Until we know what's going on, I figure we should keep a distance. We know Mendoza's got a gun somewhere."

"What are we waiting for? Can't we just go up there and demand the manuscript?"

"I don't reckon she'll want to give it up."

"Well, we aren't going to just wait here, are we?"

"Nope. Let's beach this canoe and hike up on that rocky bluff. We can scope it out from up there."

"Lead on, Pioneer Stoner."

Brady found a fairly flat stretch of shoreline and rammed the canoe into the dirt beach. Lynda hopped out and held the boat until Brady worked his way to the bow. Then she helped him pull it ashore.

"We could camp in this little landing if we have to," he suggested. "It's so isolated no one would know we're back here."

"That sounds dangerous."

"I don't think so," Brady drawled. "I'd be here to look after you, darlin'."

"That's what makes it dangerous."

He smiled. "Come on, you carry these."

He handed her the binoculars, which she hung from her neck. He dug his carbine out of the loosely rolled olive green sleeping bag.

"What are we going to need that for?" she asked.

"Snakes."

Lynda stared up at the mountain ahead of them. "You're kidding me, right?"

"Relax. Most of the snakes are hibernating already."

"Most?"

"I'm taking the gun as a precaution. The last time I saw Mendoza, she smacked me over the head with one of these."

Brady led the way. His blanket-lined denim jacket was buttoned up and his hat pulled down tight enough to barely flatten his ears. The mountain was steep, but by taking each step carefully, Lynda had little trouble making it to the top. Brady waited for her. Standing next to a lightning-scarred pine, he waved at her to hurry up.

"What do you see?" she asked as he stared in the opposite direction of the lake, looking down the metal sights of the carbine.

"Let me borrow the glasses."

She handed him the binoculars.

"Wow! That's what I thought!"

"What is it? What are they doing? Let me see," she urged.

He handed the binoculars back to her and pointed her toward a distant hill that stood lower than the peak they were on.

"Where are they? I don't see them. Are they over there by that deer? I can't find them, Brady."

"Look at that deer, darlin'. Have you ever seen a bigger rack on a muley? And me without a Montana license. Have you ever seen anything as pretty as that?"

"It sort of looks like all other deer."

"You've got to be kiddin', Lynda Dawn." He took the binoculars back and again raised them to his eyes. "Look at that animal. He's magnificent. That is the ultimate of what a mule deer is supposed to look like—from the black tip on his tail to those big, old ears. He could make 'Boone & Crockett.'"

"What?"

He glanced at her in obvious disgust. "You wouldn't just save the rack on that one. No, ma'am, I'd get the whole head stuffed—no, no, I say taxidermy the whole beautiful animal." He put the binoculars down and looked her in the eyes. "Wouldn't it be great to have him stuffed in that pose and put him right there in our den next to the big rock fireplace? Talk about dramatic."

Once again the sparkle in his eyes.

The little-boy grin.

The innocent expression.

Good grief, he's serious!

"Stoner, let's have it out right here. I do not want that animal stuffed in my house—ever!"

"Really?" His face reflected his total surprise. "Oh . . . well, maybe I could put him out in my shop. That would be all right, wouldn't it?"

"Are we hunting mule deer or a final chapter?"

"Oh, yeah . . . I got a little sidetracked. But you've got to admit he's one beautiful animal."

All I will admit, Stoner, is that I know absolutely nothing about what it means to marry a cowboy. Please, Lord, no caribou heads, no bear rugs, no Bambi's mother. It's just not me.

"Where's Ms. Mendoza's boat?"

"I take it we're changing the subject," Brady replied.

"I think we came up here to scout out those boats."

"Yeah, let's go take a look. Hey, did I ever tell you about that moose head I've got hanging in my bedroom back at my folks' house?"

No. No. Please, not a moose head!

"In your bedroom? How in the world do you have room in your bedroom?" She followed Brady across the granite mountaintop toward the lake.

"It's crowded, all right. Shoot, I can't stand on my bed anymore without hittin' my head on those horns."

He's thirty-one years old, and he stands on the bed? Lord, maybe there are some things better left unknown until way after marriage.

"I wanted to put the moose head in the den, but Mom wouldn't allow it. She said the thing looks hideous. Especially after I lost one of its eyeballs."

We haven't met yet, Mrs. Stoner, but I think I'm going to really like you.

"I don't want to hear about it, Brady."

They reached the edge of the granite cliff several hundred feet above the lake. From the top they could look straight down on *The Latte*. There was one lone pine tree about fifteen feet high to their right and a rotting log parallel to the cliff. Brady dropped down on his knees and peered over the log at the water below. Lynda joined him.

"Can you see anything?"

"Still no people. But if there were, I could read their lips from here. I can't see Mendoza's boat. It must be straight below this overhang."

"What do you think is going on?"

"I have no idea."

"Someone's got to be down there."

Brady stepped over the log and out to the edge of the rock overhang. He got down on his knees and peered over the edge.

"Be careful, Stoner. It's steep."

"It's 2,500 feet less steep than the ledge in the Grand Canyon last year."

"Don't remind me."

Finally he lay down with his head and shoulders over the edge.

"Hey, here they are!" Brady whispered and pointed. "There's a little sandy beach right straight below this cliff. We couldn't see it from the lake."

Lynda leaned out from the log, but she couldn't see anything. "Where?"

"Come on out here, darlin'."

"No way."

"Crawl on your belly, honey. It looks like we found all of them."

"Who's down there?"

"Georgie and Junior . . . Mendoza and a couple others."

"Junior's down there, too? I can't believe this. Do you see Spunky and Mrs. Gossman?"

"Nope." He continued to speak softly.

"I've got to see this."

"Come on, darlin', crawl on your belly."

"Brady, I'm not crawling on my belly. Not for you. Not for any man." She stood up and climbed over the log. As soon as she faced Brady and saw him lying out over the cliff with the water far below him, she felt the blood race from her face.

Immediately, she dropped to the rock bedside him. He reached back and took her hand as she crawled toward him.

"Nice view, huh, babe?"

Getting alongside him, she frantically clutched his arm with both hands.

"Why, darlin'," he teased, "you get romantic in the strangest places."

"You make a move on me here, Stoner, and I swear I'll bite your nose off," she growled between clenched teeth.

"I thought you liked high rises."

"I don't like leaning over the edge of them. Now where are they?"

"Here, take the glasses. They're right down there on that little white sandy beach."

"Hold them to my eyes."

"What?"

"I am not turning loose of you, Stoner. Hold the flippin' binoculars to my eyes!"

Brady reached around, holding the field glasses to her eyes.

"Boy, you can get real bossy when you're scared spitless."

"I can get violent, too. Why is that one guy pointing a gun at Mr. Hampton? I don't see Spunky or Carolyn either. Maybe this is just a man's thing."

"Not completely. Mendoza's down there, and she's waving her hands like she's the one giving orders. I think it's time we go break up their party."

"How?"

"We'll have to hike back to the canoe and paddle real quietly around that granite point."

"Then what?"

"I don't have any idea in the world, but I'm sure you'll think of something."

"Me?" Lynda gasped.

"Sure. This is exactly why you flew out here, isn't it?"

Brady rocked up on his haunches, then stood, and walked back to the fallen log. Lynda crawled on her stomach all the way back to his feet.

"You're getting a kick out of seeing me crawl, aren't you?" she snapped.

"No, ma'am."

"You're grinning."

"Well, I don't rightly think I've ever seen a woman crawl before. It's sort of comical. I surely wish I had a camera."

Lynda struggled to her feet and brushed off the front of her coat and jeans. "I wish I had some perfume," she mumbled.

It was tougher going down the mountainside than it had been climbing up. Lynda held on to the back of Brady's shoulder most of the way. The wind continued to whip off the lake. She was chilled to the bone. She kept digging the heel of her boots into the dirt, but several times Brady had to grab her to keep her from falling.

At least, that was his excuse.

They reached the canoe, and Brady shoved it back toward the lake.

"What's the plan, cowboy?" she asked as he crawled into the boat.

"You divert 'em, and I'll disarm them."

"Shouldn't we go get the police or something?"

"Yeah, I figure if there's a phone at Frank's Boat Rental, we could get there in an hour. If they hurry, we could get the sheriff across the lake here in another hour and a half. What do you think would happen to Atlantic-Hampton's finest in two and a half hours?"

"Yeah, right. Well, what's this diversion thing?"

"We'll paddle down there and not use the motor. I'll get out this side of the sandy beach, and then you paddle right up there by Mendoza's boat."

"What if they shoot me?"

"They won't—at least, not until they find out what you're after."

"Just where are you going to get out? There's no shoreline leading up to that little beach. It's sheer granite cliff right into the water."

"I'll get into the lake and swim around the bend after you've diverted their attention. I'll take the carbine with me and sneak in behind them."

"Brady, you can't get in this water. You'll freeze."

"You'll just have to think of some way to warm me up later."

"I'll build a fire," she replied.

"That sounds like fun." He winked.

"A campfire, Stoner!" Lynda sat in the middle seat in front of Brady, his arms wrapped around her while he paddled.

"I'm kind of glad Bunny taught you how to row like this. Do you think this plan is going to work?"

"I don't know, but we've got to try something. Hampton and Gossman look like they need some help. They'd help us if we were in trouble, right?"

"Not if it involved bodily harm, frigid water, and 30-caliber bullets."

"It's bound to be an adventure." Brady gave her a tight squeeze.

Lynda's arms began to quiver. She held them tight against her body and rubbed them.

"You nervous, darlin'?"

"Yes, and I'm freezing to death. I think it's going to be a lot colder than last night."

"You're right about that. If that bank of black clouds drifts over, we'll get snow."

"What clouds?"

"Look over there—perched on top of the Big Belts. That's snow, darlin'."

"You can't get in that water, Brady. It's just too cold."

"It'll work, darlin'."

"Brady, I'm scared. I'm just a New York City editorial wimp. You cowboys do this sort of thing all the time, but I don't know if I can pull it off."

"Lynda Dawn, don't sell yourself short. I saw you bluff down Joe Trent and thugs in Shotgun Canyon. You can do it."

"But that was spontaneous. I just did it without thinking. It's all this thinking that frightens me."

"Baby, we're a team—you and me. We can do it. But we can't talk anymore. We're gettin' too close. Remember what I told you."

"Be careful, Brady. Let's get this over with before I panic and faint or something."

Brady stopped the canoe near the granite cliff and tugged at his boots. He signaled for Lynda to help. She yanked and yanked, trying not to fall out of the boat. *Well, this is the first time, but I don't suppose it will be the last time I have to help him pull off his boots.*

He emptied his pants pockets and shoved his wallet into one boot and crammed his belt with the big silver "1988 Cheyenne Frontier Days Bareback Champion" buckle into the other boot. He pulled off his denim jacket and folded it down among the camping gear.

Hanging the coiled rope over his shoulder, he pulled out the carbine and shoved in a couple more bullets. He quietly cocked the lever of the '94 Winchester and released the hammer down to a locked position. He handed her the carbine and then slipped over the side into the water.

She could see by his expression that the frigid water took his breath away. Still wearing his black beaver felt cowboy hat, he reached out and took the gun from her. Brady pushed away from the canoe and held the carbine in his right hand above the water. He signaled her to paddle on around the corner.

This is not happening to me. I am not here. I'm in my bed at home and having a very, very vivid dream. I'm going to wake up in front of the television watching an old movie. Lord, have mercy on us. What in the world am I going to say to this Mendoza woman?

She heard the sounds of a heated argument, and suddenly the beach came into view. L. George Gossman was sitting down, his hands tied behind his back. The top was smashed out of his new straw cowboy hat, and Lynda noticed blood on the side of his face. She didn't know if he had a cut lip or a bloody nose. Two men and a woman surrounded a panic-stricken T. H. Hampton, Jr. One of the men held a rifle.

When Lynda slid into view, the conversation stopped. Everyone on shore stared at her. "One of you come down here and help me bring this boat ashore!" Lynda demanded.

The bullet from the man's gun sailed over the bow of the boat, and a plume of water shot up behind her.

"You!" she shouted at the gunman. "Put that gun down right now, or I'll have every lawman in the state of Montana on your trail before sundown! I said, get down here and help me pull this boat ashore."

"Ms. Austin," Junior blubbered, "you've got to talk to them!"

The two men glanced at Mendoza. She motioned for them to help Lynda come ashore.

Brady, it's time. Do your thing. Now! What if he drowned? Oh, man, I don't want to be here!

"Well, if it isn't Miss Prissy from mid-Manhattan. Bring her over here, Harper . . . and bring that oar. Maybe we can beat a little information out of these three."

With the canoe securely beached, one man carried the rifle, and the other yanked Lynda's arm with one hand and carried the canoe paddle with the other.

"Mendoza, you really don't want to spend the rest of your

life rotting in Montana prisons," Lynda barked. "Now release these men and return our manuscript before the charges become more serious than felony theft."

Glancing over at the canoe, Mendoza stepped up to her. "I see that cowboy was smart enough to dump you."

Now, Brady . . . now! Come on, Brady! Maybe I paddled too fast. Did he want me to wait?

"Claudia, I'm sure I can get her to talk!" The man released his tight grip on her arm and slid his hand down across her derriere.

Lynda swung around so quickly that the crack of her clinched fist into his chin caused him to stagger back. He immediately raised the canoe oar over her head. The report from Brady's carbine resounded off the granite cliff, sounding like a cannon. The oar shattered in the man's hands as the bullet slammed into it. Everyone, including Lynda, jumped when Brady shouted, "Face down in the sand! Right now!"

Hampton and Gossman fell onto the sand, but Lynda and the others remained standing. Mendoza nodded to the man with the rifle.

"'This bullet is aimed at your head, buddy," Stoner yelled, his voice booming off the granite like a tent revival preacher. "You so much as turn that rifle toward me, and I'll shoot you and claim self-defense. No jury in Montana would convict me. It's your choice. Either lay on top the sand or be buried in it!"

"Mister, this ain't my deal. I just got hired to dive. I don't aim to die for no treasure map." He tossed the gun to the sand and flopped down on the beach as did the other man, still clutching his splinter-pricked hand. Ms. Mendoza defiantly held her position.

"Get the rifle, darlin'!" Brady hollered. "Mendoza! In the sand!"

"Shoot me if you have the guts, cowboy," she hissed. "I don't do subservience."

Lynda retrieved the rifle and stepped up to Claudia Mendoza. "What's the matter? You too prim and proper to lie in the dirt?" Lynda raised the rifle as if to strike Mendoza with the barrel. Trying to protect herself, the woman threw her arms up in the air and staggered back. Austin bluffed the blow, and Mendoza tripped over T. H. Hampton, Jr., and fell to the sand.

"On your stomachs!" Brady shouted. "Not you, Georgie and Junior."

Brady, nobody calls him Junior to his face. Please, don't call him that again.

"Darlin', stick that gun right in the back of Mendoza's head. If she tries to grab at it, just pull the trigger. Junior, go over there and untie Georgie. He looks a little tuckered. You two, put your hands behind your backs, or I'll have to shoot your legs."

Even in the shadows of dusk, Lynda saw that Brady's lips were almost blue, the water still dripping from his soaked clothes. But his hat was dry, and his eyes blazed.

Lord, keep him from getting really sick. Keep him safe. Keep us all safe.

"Brady, you're freezing!"

"I'll warm up as soon as we get these tied up. Junior, come over here."

T. H. Hampton, Jr., scooted over to Brady, leaving the untied L. George Gossman nursing his bleeding lip.

"Junior, hold the carbine on this one." He handed the gun to Hampton.

"Actually," T. H. muttered, "I'm not very good at this sort of thing."

"Just jam it in his back. If he even tries to look around, pull the trigger."

"Don't shoot me," the man yelled. "I'm not gettin' paid enough for this."

Brady squished and sloshed over to tie the other man.

Suddenly, the prone man reached around to grab Brady's legs. Stoner dropped with his knees square in the man's back and shoved the man's face into the sand.

"Dumb move, mister! Real dumb." Brady slipped a loop of his rope around the man's neck, pulled the rope tight, and then yanked the man to his feet.

"Are you the one who busted Georgie's lip?"

"It was her idea."

"Pull off your jeans, mister!"

"I can barely breathe." The man tried to loosen the noose with his hands.

"I can cure that," Brady growled. "Pull off the pants. I don't intend to stand here all day dripping wet."

With the rope still pulled tight and the other two pinned down to the sand, the man took off his jeans.

"On your belly!"

The man dropped to the sand, and Brady removed the loop from his neck and tied his hands behind his back.

Within a few minutes a screaming, cursing Claudia Mendoza and the other two were tied hand and foot, prostrate in the sand. Brady had slipped out of the wet jeans and pulled on the diver's dry ones. Then he removed his wet shirt, put on his blanket-lined jacket, and shoved bare feet into his boots.

"You still look like an ice cube," Lynda cautioned.

"I'll get a fire going when we get back to the rig. There's nothing to burn out here. You did it, Lynda Dawn. You got 'em lookin' your way while I snuck up behind."

"I thought you'd never show up."

"It's this funny little cove. It's a sheer drop-off into the lake. It's like the cliff sloughed off just in this one spot. It was tough to climb out of the water, like gettin' out of a swimmin' pool without gettin' your gun and hat wet."

"You want me to get you a sleeping bag to wrap up in?"

"I'm doin' better with some dry clothes. Georgie, how's your lip?"

"It's feeling much better since you two showed up. Frankly, I was afraid we wouldn't pull through this ordeal."

"What were they lookin' for? That pictograph page?"

"Yes, and as you know, we don't have it."

"Stoner," Hampton spoke up, "I feel like a dumb fool running around out of my element. I can't imagine what I was thinking."

"You were thinking about tons of Confederate gold. Sort of like *Treasure of Sierra Madre*, isn't it? How did you two team up? I thought you and Spunky were headed to Red Lodge and Georgie and Carolyn to Glacier."

"Well," Hampton began, "we stopped in Helena for lunch yesterday, and Spunky decided to go on the Victorian home tour. After that she insisted that's what she wants to buy. So we stayed over to look at some properties. We just happened to be at a restaurant when the Gossmans came in today."

"We decided to drive over to Missoula and up the Bitterroot Valley to Glacier," George explained.

"Spunky insisted on showing Carolyn some of the homes we'd looked at, so George and I . . ."

"You two decided to have one last peek at where the gold was buried?"

"Exactly. We were just going to drive out and look from the shore. But when we found a marina where you can rent a boat, we decided it wouldn't hurt."

"Well, it did hurt!" Gossman held his lip and looked over at the three on the sand. "I intend to see that they spend the rest of their lives behind bars," he gruffed.

"That isn't going to happen. Assault and battery, attempted manslaughter, receiving stolen property—that will be about all they face. But that ought to keep them busy for a few months."

"A few months!" Gossman exploded.

"George," T. H. Hampton cautioned, "for Pete's sake, relax. This isn't the city. It's a different world out here. And I certainly don't want my friends in the East to read about this. It must be the stupidest thing I've ever done."

Not counting divorcing your wife to marry Spunky?

Hampton turned to Austin and Stoner. "Frankly, whatever charges we can make without causing a big brouhaha would be best. I would just as soon see that none of this makes the papers."

"It doesn't matter to me." Brady shrugged. "All we're after is that missing page, and it's a cinch it isn't here."

"Well, I'm not about to let them go free. Look what they did to my lip!" Gossman protested. "And I have no idea what happened to my toupee."

"It makes you look a lot more rugged." Brady grinned.

"It does?"

"Without your toupee and with that scar, you look more like a short Sean Connery than an old Dudley Moore," Lynda suggested.

"You think so? But I've always worn—"

"Wear a cowboy hat to the office. That will keep your head warm," Brady suggested. "But if you really want to keep this quiet, I've got a plan." As Mendoza and the men lay in the sand, Brady huddled with Lynda, Junior, and George and described their course of action.

Within minutes, Hampton and Gossman were in Mendoza's boat driving it back out to where their rental boat was anchored.

"You can't steal my boat," Mendoza shouted.

"No problem. We're just going to anchor it out there about fifty yards."

"What are you going to do to us?"

"Nothing."

"You're going to shoot us in the back, aren't you?"

"You're not worth a bullet."

Brady waited until Gossman and Hampton had transferred over into their rental boat. As soon as they were on their way back across the lake, Brady began to release the ropes on the three.

"Don't even think of getting up. We've got two guns on you, and we'd love to have an excuse for pulling the trigger."

"What are you going to do to us?"

"Leave you right here and go call the sheriff. Of course, if you get in your boat and haul out of here, you might not even be at the lake when he arrives."

"But we can't get to our boat."

"Sure you can. One of you can swim out there and bring it over for the other two. You're the diver. Maybe you ought to swim."

"But my dry suit is in the boat."

"Oh, the water's really quite nice once you turn numb. But if I were any of you, I think I'd swim out there whether the other two do or not. I mean, what guarantee do the ones waiting have that the swimmer will really bring the boat back over for them? Yes, sir, that would certainly worry me somethin' fierce."

"That gun belongs to me!" Mendoza shouted.

"This gun right here? The one you beat me over the head with?" Brady tossed the gun halfway out to the boat. "Whoops! I dropped it. But that shouldn't be a problem. You've got professional divers on your team. But don't spend too much time. You won't want to be out here when the sheriff arrives." He turned to Lynda. "You ready to go, darlin'?"

"Can we stop by their boat and pick up my original manuscript?"

"Sounds good to me. Well, it surely was nice meetin' you three. Sorry we can't stay for supper!"

With Austin loaded up and pointing the carbine at the three on the beach, Stoner shoved the canoe back into the water and started the motor. He boarded Mendoza's boat and found the original missing chapter, minus pages 451 and 452.

This time both Lynda and Brady wrapped themselves in the sleeping bags and headed back across the water.

He always works best under pressure. Must come from all those years of riding broncs. Stoner, you done good, babe. You done real good!

It was dark by the time they reached the boat dock. Gossman and Hampton were already gone. Frank's Boat Rental was all closed up, and the only two rigs in the parking lot were Brady's and Mendoza's. They spoke little until they had the canoe loaded back into the pickup and the heater on high warming the cab.

"I still can't believe you jumped into that water!" she said. "I don't know if you're mostly brave—or mostly crazy."

"All cowboy, I reckon."

"Cowboy or not, you're going to get pneumonia."

"Wouldn't be the first time." He shivered. "'Course, I'd need you to stay out here and nurse me back to health. Have you got an extra six weeks?"

"Hardly. I've got to catch a plane on Monday."

"I don't think Hampton or Gossman would get on your case, would they?"

"You know, Stoner, things will never be the same around the office. This treasure hunt thing humbled them pretty good."

"Don't go makin' it a big deal around the office. A man has a tough enough time livin' with his shame, without others shovin' his face in it."

Lynda picked up Capt. Patch. He let out a quick yelp of protest and then settled down on the backseat where she tossed him. She scooted over next to Brady and laced her hand in his.

"Your hands are freezing!" She put his hand to her lips and kissed his fingers.

"My ear is cold, too."

She leaned over and kissed his ear several times.

"Boy, are my cheeks cold!" She could tell he was trying to hold back a smile. She kissed his cheek.

"You know what's really, really cold?" He flashed the little-boy smile.

"What, Mr. Indiana Jones?" She grinned.

"My lips!"

"Oh, well, let me see what I can do."

Several minutes later she finally pulled back.

"I'm not sure if you're warmed up, cowboy, but I'm about to boil."

"Look at this." Brady pointed to the windshield. "I haven't steamed up a truck like this since—"

"I don't want to hear this, Stoner!"

"I gave a ride to—"

"Stoner, I really don't want to hear this!" she shouted.

"Those nineteen-year-old triplets!"

"I don't want . . ." She pushed away from him and looked him in the eyes. "What triplets?"

He pushed his hat to the back of his head. "I lied."

"What triplets?" she demanded.

"No, really, I made it all up just to hear you whine."

"I didn't whine."

"Well, you did squirm and squeal."

"I didn't squirm and squeal."

"Oh?"

"What triplets, Stoner?"

"Hold that thought for a minute. I've got a little business to do."

Brady jumped out of the rig and pulled his carbine out from behind the pickup seat.

"What are you going to do?"

"Settle a score." He began to walk over to where Mendoza's van was parked.

"You'll get even colder out there. Get back in here. 'Vengeance is mine, saith the Lord,'" Lynda cautioned.

"An eye for an eye, and a tire for a tire. That's justice, not vengeance."

In the dark the flash of gunfire blazed out of the barrel with each explosive sound. Brady paid his last respects to four fairly worn Goodyears. He slipped the gun into the scabbard behind the seat and climbed back into the driver's side.

"Brady, that was just out of spite."

"Darlin', I believe a person has got to reap what they sow."

"But that's for the Lord to settle, isn't it?"

"I don't figure I ought to bother Him with little matters like this. Especially if I can take care of it myself."

"I don't think that would hold up to the Scriptures, Stoner."

"Are you preachin' at me?"

"Yes."

"Do you intend to do that often?"

"Only when it's needed."

Brady was silent as they drove out of the dirt and gravel parking lot. She moved back over to the right side of the bench seat and rolled the window down just a little. The heater roared, and the cab was extremely stuffy. Capt. Patch reclaimed his territory between them.

Lord, he's like that wild horse. Just when I think he's settled into a predictable routine, he leaps fences.

Halfway out from the lake to the Interstate, Brady suddenly pulled the rig over to the side of the gravel road and quickly opened his door.

"What's the matter?" she asked.

"Darlin', I'm not feelin' too good." He got out, stood next to the truck, and stretched his arms. "I think I'm gettin' real dizzy."

He had barely finished the sentence when he collapsed, his body slamming into the dirt roadway.

"Brady!" she screamed.

He didn't move.

Capt. Patch reached him before Lynda, but neither could bring him around. He lay crumpled in the dark dirt roadway. The wind blew colder, and the clouds, only a few moments before on the western horizon, now covered half the stars.

"We've got to do something," she said to the dog, who seemed content to sit on his haunches and stare at his master.

"Brady!" She got down on her knees and cradled his head. "Brady . . . come on, sweetheart . . . oh, man. Come on, please, Brady."

I've got to get him to a doctor . . . to a hospital. I've got to get him into the pickup. Brady, you're the one who has to take care of me. I can't take care of you!

She frantically glanced up and down the road looking for help. Other than the headlights from the pickup, there were no lights in any direction.

Junior and Georgie should have stuck around. Brady bailed them out. They should have helped him.

"Brady, honey . . . come on, baby . . . come on." She slapped his face lightly and rocked his head in her lap.

Mendoza and the others will come in the van. Even with flat tires, they can drive this far. If they find us here . . . Lord, help us. Please help us!

"You've got to be all right, Brady. If something happens to you . . ." The tears streamed down her face.

From the dim glow of the truck's interior light radiating out the open door, she could see his blue lips and silent, lifeless-looking face. She bent over and began kissing his cheeks, his forehead, his lips. Her tears smeared across his face. She sat up and wiped them with her hand.

Then suddenly his eyes were open. He blinked twice and turned his head toward her.

"Brady!"

"I think I passed out."

Lynda had planned to say, "Brady, we need to get you into the truck and take you to a hospital. Let me help you to your feet. Just lean on me, and I'll walk you around to the other side. Then I'll drive you straight to town. You had me worried for a minute, Brady Stoner, but everything's going to be all right now. Don't you worry. I'll take care of you."

That's what she meant to say. Instead, when he struggled to sit up, she threw her arms around him and cried. *He's so cold. Oh, Lord, he's so very, very cold!*

His words were the first. "Darlin', I'm freezin' out here. Let's get in the truck."

Lynda helped him to his feet, and he climbed into the driver's seat.

"Scoot over, cowboy. I'm not about to let you drive," she managed to say, wiping her face on her sleeve.

"I'm freezin', baby," he mumbled. "I've got to get warm."

"I know, honey. I'll take care of you. Really. Don't go passing out on me again. I'll take you to the hospital."

"I don't want to drive to Helena. I think this is gettin' real dangerous. Once my adrenalin let down, I guess I turned out colder than I thought. Let me wrap up in those sleepin' bags. I need some sleep. I just want to lay down."

Oh, man, I've got to keep him awake . . .

Lynda flipped the light on high beam and could see the corrals on both sides of the roadway.

There's a bunkhouse up here. He said we could stay. They must have a phone or something. I could wrap him up. Build a fire. Something!

"Brady, let's get you in that bunkhouse. Where is it?"

She drove through a tall log archway and to the rear of the

corrals found several unpainted buildings. She pulled up to the only one with windows.

"Come on, cowboy, let's get you inside."

Brady walked to the front door by the light of the head-lights without talking, Capt. Patch by his side. Lynda pulled the two sleeping bags out of the back of the truck and scurried up to the door.

"It's locked, Brady. How did he expect us to get in?"

"Must be a key hanging around here," Brady mumbled, as he stood rubbing his arms and rocking back and forth on the heels of his boots.

"Don't you go fainting on me again, Brady Stoner!" Lynda explored the doorjamb with her hands and searched the front step with her eyes.

"I can't find it, Brady."

He pointed over toward the side of where she stood.

"Under the cow pie."

"You're kidding."

"We used to do that. No one but a cowboy would ever look under there."

"Do I have to pick it up?"

"Turn it over with your boot."

Lynda flipped the dried pile of cow manure aside and spot-ted a brass key laying in the dirt. She quickly opened the door and ushered him into the room. The only light came from the headlights shining through the open door.

"Where's the switch? Don't they have electricity?"

"Probably not." Brady stepped over to a wooden table and fumbled with a box of stick matches and a kerosene lantern. "I can't seem to get one to light. I'm going to lie down, darlin'."

"Wait . . . wait." Lynda hurried over and lit the lantern.

A round woodstove squatted in the middle of the square, bare wood-floored room. Three sets of bunks were scattered around. Each had a mattress, but there was no bedding in sight.

Other than the beds, stove, table, chairs, and a long counter along one wall, the room was empty.

"You better turn off the rig. Maybe you should park it behind the bunkhouse in case Mendoza and gang come creeping out along this road."

"I'll be right back," she called.

By the time she parked the truck and brought in some belongings, Brady had tossed a sleeping bag on the lower bunk, pulled off his boots, and crawled in.

Lynda locked the door behind her and set a bag of snacks, her purse, and the carbine on the table next to the lantern. There was wood in a box next to the woodstove, and she was surprised when she opened the cast-iron door to find newspaper and kindling stacked inside.

They must always have this ready to light.

She lit the paper and left the door cracked open a little to give the fire draft. Lynda pulled a chair over by Brady's bed.

"How are you doing, cowboy?"

"I want to sleep."

She put her hand on his forehead. "Your head is burning up. You have a bad fever."

"No, I'm cold."

"Let me get you the other sleeping bag."

"You'll need it," he mumbled.

"I need you well—that's all I need."

She unzipped the bag and pulled it over him, tucking it at his sides. Then she pulled off her coat and rolled it up for him to use as a pillow.

It sure seems funny for me to be taking care of you, Brady Stoner.

She walked over and inspected the room, finding no telephone, no blankets, no dishes, nothing. She jammed a couple of big pieces of firewood into the woodstove and closed the iron door. Then she picked up the lantern and set it on the chair by Brady. He looked like he was asleep.

Should I leave him here and go get a doctor? Am I supposed to keep him awake? Don't people go to sleep right before they freeze to death? Lord, I'm not good at this. Do I just sit by the bed all night? Down in Shotgun Canyon he sat by my bed. I just don't know what to do!

She bent over him and whispered in his ear, "Are you getting warmer, honey?"

He pulled the sleeping bag up around his sweating forehead. "No. Did you light the fire? This room is like an icebox."

"The fire's burning good." Sitting on the edge of the bed, she tugged off her boots.

"Scoot over, cowboy, I have no intention of letting you freeze to death." She turned down the wick, and the lantern slowly flickered and died. Then she scrunched her way down inside the sleeping bag next to him.

His jacket and jeans felt chilled, his feet painfully frigid. With the sides of the sleeping bag pushing them together, she cradled him in her arms. He opened his eyes, nodded his approval, and then closed them. Then within a moment, he was asleep.

TEN

Lynda woke up sitting in a chair with a sleeping bag pulled over her head and faint memories of a mostly restless night. Feeling warm in the cocoon-like wrap, she recalled hearing the grinding sound of steel wheels on a gravel road as she pulled herself out of the bunk sometime during the night and went to the smudged window to stare as Mendoza's van ground its way to the highway.

I think I built up the fire, hung Brady's wet clothes around the room to dry, and settled down in this chair.

Brady!

Tugging the sleeping bag off her head, she stared through the dim morning light in the bunkhouse at an empty bunk and a tightly rolled bedroll.

"Brady?" she called, staggering to her semi-cramped legs and looking around the room. "Stoner, where are you?"

She pulled open the door to the bunkhouse and was hit by a blast of crystal-clean, icy-cold Montana air. Retreating to the warmth of the woodstove, she pulled on her black satin NFR jacket and thought for a moment about dragging a sleeping bag around her shoulders.

All right, Austin, it's only October in the Rockies. You can take it.

She stepped outside, shoved her hands into the coat pockets, and searched the horizon. To the west were the Gates of the Rockies Mountains and Upper Holter Lake. Just beyond the corrals to the west were several outbuildings. She hiked past the truck toward the smallest of the structures setting by itself twenty yards out into the pasture. The four-foot-square building had an old faded sign on the door that read, "Punchers." Beneath it someone had carved "& Punchettes."

"Brady?" She tapped on the door lightly. "Are you in there, Brady?" Getting no response, she banged on the door and hollered, "Are you sick?"

She had just made up her mind to peek inside when the sound of hoofbeats on now-frozen mud caused her to spin around.

"Who you talkin' to, darlin'?"

"Brady Stoner, what are you doing on that horse?"

Capt. Patch bounded to her feet, jumped up and licked her hand, and then scampered off.

"Oh, me and X-it decided to go for a spin. He sure has a smooth gait, darlin'. He might make you a good horse once he gets the humps smoothed out."

"But you can't be riding a horse. You're supposed to . . ."

"Well, I didn't have a saddle with me, so I have to ride him bareback. 'Course, I didn't have a bridle either. I just made this little halter out of bailin' string. Would you like to ride him? You can sit in front of me and we can—"

"Stoner, I do not want to talk about that horse. You are supposed to be sick in bed. I've been nursing you all night, and then I go to sleep for ten minutes, and you run out here to ride that horse. You're a sick man. Now get back in there where it's warm."

He grinned a little and patted the bay horse's neck. "Well, X-it, it looks like we riled Mama. I guess it's back to the corral for you."

"Brady, I don't understand. You were sick. Real sick. It was like you were freezing to death. Now you just get up feeling fine?"

"I don't remember much, darlin'. Am I supposed to be sick in bed? That explains what you were doing sleeping in the chair beside me when I got up this morning. Let me put up X-it, and I'll come in. I don't want to work him for much over an hour anyway."

She retreated to the bunkhouse and the warmth of the woodstove. *He's been up for over an hour? This is confusing, Lord.*

Lynda dug a mirror out of her purse and spent ten minutes trying to do something with her hair. Finally she put on her lipstick, dabbed on a little Pretty Wild, and jammed her cowboy hat on the back of her head. She was digging through the brown paper sack of snacks to find something for breakfast when Brady walked in, boot heels hammering on the wooden floor.

"What do you want for breakfast? Tiny powdered-sugar doughnuts? Or potato chips?" she asked.

"I'll have the doughnuts. You can have the chips."

"I think I'll pass. Brady, I can't believe you feel good this morning. You were so sick."

"What happened, babe? I don't remember much."

"What do you remember?"

"We were drivin' out toward the highway, and I, eh, I stopped the rig because I didn't feel too good."

He paused.

"Then what?" she asked.

"I woke up over in that bunk with you asleep in the chair. I didn't want to bother you, so I built up the fire and slipped out to visit with X-it."

"That's it? That's all you remember?"

"I remember I was cold, real cold. What happened, babe?"

"You really don't remember anything?"

"You'll have to fill me in."

"Pull up a chair, cowboy, and eat your doughnuts. This might take a little time."

Brady straddled the chair backwards and dug into the package.

He looks the same all the time. Twenty-four hours a day, seven days a week. Jeans, boots, long-sleeved cotton shirts, big buckle, black hat pushed back. Hair always two weeks late for a trim, beard one day late for a shave. Powdered sugar on his chin. And a head crammed with horse dreams. Do they ever outgrow it, Lord?

"Go ahead, darlin'. You sure you don't want one of these?" His words fogged the air with powdered sugar.

"You pulled off the side of the road, stepped out of the truck, and passed out."

"I did?"

"Right in the road and . . ." Suddenly she found herself start to tear up. She took a deep breath. "I was really scared, Brady."

"It's okay, darlin'. I'm feelin' fine now."

"I don't understand that. How can you be so sick at night and feeling so good the next morning?"

"I've built up an immunity to feelin' bad." He laughed. "Go on, tell me how you got me to the bunkhouse."

"I couldn't budge you off the road, and I was worried about Mendoza and the others coming by. But you came around and . . . You don't remember any of this?"

"Nope."

"You came around, and I got you in the truck. I wanted to take you to a hospital in Helena, but you insisted you needed to warm up and get some sleep right away. So we found the bunkhouse, and I lit the fire and got you to bed in the bunk and then . . . Are you positive you don't remember anything else?"

"No. What happened next?"

"You were freezin' but had a fever at the same time.

Anyway, I didn't know what to do, so . . . I put the other sleeping bag over you, and then . . . well, I crawled in with you."

"You did what?"

"We were both fully dressed. I just wanted to warm you. I didn't know what else to do, Brady."

"What did I do?"

"You asked me to marry you."

"I did what? But . . . you're puttin' me on. I didn't . . . did I?"

A big smile broke across Lynda's face. "Had you worried, didn't I, Stoner?"

"Sort of . . . I mean, it's what I . . . You were just joshin', right? About the sleepin' bag and all."

"That part was true. I did climb into your bag to warm you up."

"Really? Lynda Dawn Austin actually did that?"

"Don't worry, Stoner, you didn't miss anything. It was about as romantic as lying in the snow with a 175-pound sack of frozen potatoes."

"You braggin' or complainin'?"

"Neither. After an hour or so, I heard a rig grinding steel rims on the gravel, so I went to the window. I couldn't see the road clearly, but I presume it was Mendoza. After that I stoked the fire, and it seemed like you were warming up. At least your lips weren't blue or your forehead hot. So I camped out in the chair. I don't remember pulling that sleeping bag over me though."

"I did that when I woke up. I got up and changed into my own clothes. I didn't want to bother you, so I thought I'd just go out and visit with X-it. Naturally, the conversation got around to early morning rides, and he said as long as I'd buck him out a little, a ride would be just fine."

"Stoner, you look like a little boy with a new toy. I'm really, really glad you're doing better. But don't you think you should go have a doctor check you out?"

"Look, darlin', I don't know if it was your prayers or your warmth, but I'm feelin' just fine."

"You don't plan on fainting again, do you?"

"Fainting? No, no, darlin', I didn't faint. Only women faint. I passed out."

"Is every cowboy as outspokenly sexist as you are?"

"Oh, no, most are worse."

"Do you feel like traveling? I think we still have motel rooms in Helena. And with any luck, Cindy will still be there."

Brady began to roll up the other sleeping bag. "Where do we go from here with the manuscript? We seem to have cleared the lake, and there's no trace of the pictograph page."

"That's a good question. We almost have the whole chapter. I guess I could have it printed without that page."

"Or you could just make it up. You know, scribble something that looks realistic."

"It wouldn't be Chance's original. Besides, I don't even know what Indian pictographs are supposed to look like."

"There's plenty out there on that granite cliff. That's the problem—they're all over the place. No one knows which ones mark the treasure cave. Why, when I was swimming around to the little cove, I even noticed some below the water line."

"What did they look like?"

"Like buffalo being chased over a jump."

"A what?"

"A place where the Indians chased buffalo over the edge of a cliff and then picked up the chops and roasts and robes at the bottom."

"They actually did that?"

"How else would they kill buffalo before they had horses?"

"Didn't the Indians always have horses?"

"You're kiddin' me, right? Everyone knows that horses were brought over by those culture-destroying Europeans."

"A facetious Brady Stoner's getting political?"

"You're right. I shouldn't let it bother me. Someday I'll just wake up on my ranch and realize that the revisionists have written me out of existence. That's when the Lord takes me home. At least I know there are horses in heaven."

"There are?"

"Sure. When the Lord returns, what does the book of Revelation say He'll be ridin'?"

"A big white horse?"

"Exactly. And I've already put in for stable duty."

"What do you mean, stable duty?"

"Heaven's going to be a great big old city, foursquare, right?"

"Yes."

"I don't exactly like city livin'. So while the rest of you are enjoying them heavenly high rises, I asked if I could live out by the stables and take care of those big white horses."

"The Bible according to Brady Stoner."

"Well, it's not a new translation—just a Western paraphrase."

"I'd like to hear more," Lynda added.

"I reckon it would take an entire lifetime to hear it all."

She glanced down at her watch. "I've got time."

He stared at her for a minute until she felt a little fidgety.

"Did you really crawl into my sleeping bag?" he asked.

"Yeah. Pretty reckless, wasn't I?"

"Pretty. Very pretty." Then a wide, dimpled grin broke across his face. "Whew! That woodstove is surely making it hot in here. You ready to hit the trail, darlin'?"

"Let's ride, cowboy."

Lynda gathered up their belongings while Brady wrote a note to Red Thomaston about using the bunkhouse. Both were startled by a knock at the door. Brady held his finger over his mouth and pointed for her to look out the window. She tiptoed over and glanced out, then scooted back to him.

"Is it Mendoza or one of that bunch?" he whispered.

"No."

"Red Thomaston?"

"No. I've never seen the guy. Maybe a fisherman. He's pulling a boat behind his rig."

"I'll go talk to him."

Lynda followed Brady to the door and looked over his shoulder.

"Good morning," the man said beaming. He stood several inches shorter than Brady. The lines around his eyes in his chiseled, tanned face revealed his age as about fifty-five to sixty. His salt-and-pepper hair was cut so short he almost looked bald.

"Mornin'." Brady nodded, tipping his hat. "Somethin' we can do for you?"

"I hate to bother you so early. I'm sure you've got chores to do."

"No bother, partner. The missus has already fed them sick heifers, milked the cow, and put up twelve quarts of preserves. We git up early around here."

"Yes, well, here's what I need. I'm Dr. Curtis Leonard from the University of Southwest Florida. I'm doing a historical paper on this area and was wanting to talk to some local people who are familiar with the geology around the Gates of the Rockies canyon walls. Perhaps you or your wife know of someone who could—"

"Brady's an expert on ever'thin'," Lynda drawled.

"Is that right?"

"Yep. *De omni re scibili et quibusdam aliis.*"

"Eh . . . what?" the man stammered.

"That there's Latin," Brady informed him.

"Well, yes, of course, but what I need is someone who speaks English and could show me on a map where to find the—"

"It means I know ever'thin' worth knowin'—and more!"

"As I was saying, I need someone who knows about the pictographs."

"Pictographs?" Brady glanced back at Lynda, who raised her eyebrows.

"Did I say something wrong?"

"Did you say pictographs or petroglyphs?"

"Eh, well, I, eh . . ."

"Well, Doc, as I'm sure you know better than me, pictographs are painted onto the rock; petroglyphs are chiseled into the rock. Them Indians did it both ways."

"Oh, yes. Certainly. I misunderstood your question." The man tried to glance over Lynda's shoulder into the bunkhouse. "I'm concerned with, eh, pictographs, I believe."

Brady stepped out onto the porch. Lynda followed, shutting the windowless door. "I've seen 'em all," he continued, "and they don't make no sense to me."

"I'd like to see them all, but I'm especially interested in those that might be on the lake."

"What do you aim to do with 'em?"

"Do with them? I just want to make sure they are preserved in the historical journals."

"No foolin'? You write books, do ya?"

"Yes."

"Darlin', ain't this our lucky day? A real, live writer! You're the first writer we ever met, although we did go and hear Baxter Black at the county fair last year. Do you know Baxter?"

"I'm afraid not. Say, I have some maps out in my pickup. Would you mind coming out and looking at them? Maybe you could tell me where the pictographs are."

"Let me git my jacket." Then he turned to Lynda. "You better git them biscuits out of the oven, darlin'."

"If you'll excuse us a moment," she said.

"I'll wait for you out by my truck."

Lynda and Brady ducked back into the bunkhouse, and

Brady retrieved his jacket near the woodstove. "Dr. Leonard! Who does this guy think he's kidding?"

"Brady, it's Leo."

"Who's Leo?"

"Chance McCall's diving buddy. His name was Leo."

"Whoa, now that makes sense. Have you seen him before?"

"Never. But why would anyone show up here looking for a special pictograph?"

"He obviously knows nothing about pictographs or petroglyphs."

"If it's Leo, he's wanted for questioning in connection with Chance McCall's death."

Brady grabbed up his carbine. "Babe, if that's true, maybe he has a copy of the pictographs. Chance must have kept a copy at home. Perhaps Leo found one."

"Or stole one."

"That's why you're carrying the carbine."

"Me," Lynda choked.

"Yeah, it won't seem like a threat in your hands."

"How are we going to find out if this is really Leo?"

"I'll think of something subtle."

"That's scary," she teased. "I think I will carry the carbine."

"Did you get the biscuits out of the oven, darlin'?"

"This ma and pa thing is gettin' pretty corny."

"Maybe we'll get a glimpse of that last missing page."

"If this guy's Chance's friend, and if Chance didn't die by accident, this could be a dangerous man," Lynda cautioned.

"Don't worry, darlin'. As long as he thinks we don't know anything, we're no threat. If you spot that missing page, give me a signal, and we'll figure some way to get it."

"Do you think we ought to call the authorities in the Bahamas and tell them that Leo might be up here in Montana?"

"Yeah, but we can't do that for a while. Let's find the missing page. Then we'll let them know Leo's here."

"You really want me to carry this?" She nodded at the carbine.

"Yep. Just act nonchalant."

Nonchalant? Since when do you nonchalantly tote a gun?

Draping the '94 Winchester over both shoulders, she hooked one arm over the stock and the other over the barrel. Then she found she had to walk sideways through the door.

It was a cloudy, overcast day but with very little wind. Leonard had papers and maps spread across the hood of the white pickup. Capt. Patch was perched on top of the boat. Leonard stared at the carbine on Lynda's shoulders.

"Now let's take a look at them maps of yours," Brady began.

"Your wife always carries a gun?" Leonard quizzed.

The man slowly moved his right hand behind his back as if hiding something.

"She and the dawg are going to hunt some rabbits fer dinner," Brady explained. "You're welcome to stay and eat, of course."

The man relaxed his arms and nodded his head. "Now if you could look at this topo map and mark where the pictographs are," Leonard began.

"Just tell me which one you're lookin' for," Brady requested, "and I'll tell you where it is."

"What do you mean, which one? Did I say anything about looking for only one?" the man responded curtly.

"I just assumed you were like the others."

"What others?"

"Those New York people who came out yesterday. Ain't that strange. Ever'body wants to study pictographs. But they only wanted to see a certain pictograph."

"Did you show it to them?"

"Yep."

"Which one did they want to see?"

"That there's privileged information, of course. I keep ever'thin' in the strictest confidence."

"Are they still out on the lake?"

"Nope. They said they had to go to Seattle for supplies. Now don't that beat all. Why would you go to Seattle for supplies?"

"Brady, them folks paid you for your services," Lynda interjected.

"She's right about that. Why, I should open a pictograph information office right here on the ranch."

"You aimin' to pay, mister?" Lynda asked.

"I suppose I could. What's the goin' rate?"

"Five dollars per pictograph site. I know where twelve of them are on the lake. That's sixty dollars for all of them, but I'll give you the whole bucketful for fifty dollars cash."

"Fifty dollars? You've got to be kidding!"

Lynda pulled the carbine off her shoulder and immediately cocked it, letting the barrel lap over her arm and point to the dirt in front of Leonard.

He spun around and faced her, his right hand again going to the back of his jeans.

"Relax, mister. I just thought I saw a rabbit over there." She nodded her head toward the north.

"Well, I could pay something, but I won't be extorted at the point of a gun. Not by you. Not by anyone."

"Is he insultin' me, Brady?"

"Now, darlin', just settle down. Don't go gettin' crazy on me again like you did with that encyclopedia salesman—rest his soul."

Stoner, you jerk. Don't paint me into some psycho corner!

"Which will it be, mister? You want one location or the whole package?"

Leonard looked up and down the empty dirt road and then around at them. "If you can show me where one pictograph is, I'll pay you twenty dollars."

"I'll be dad gum, woman. You can go to town this after-noon and buy yourself somethin' new!"

The barrel of the carbine jammed into Brady's ribs, and he jumped back. "Don't ever, ever call me 'woman,'" she snarled.

Brady backed away and leaned over to Leonard. "It's that time of the month," he explained. Then he stooped down in the driveway and drew an outline of the lake in the dirt. "I don't read maps real well, so here's the lake . . . and here are the Gates. Now which pictograph are you looking for?"

Leonard pulled a folded piece of paper out of his shirt pocket and opened it up.

That's it! It's page 452.

Brady didn't skip a beat. "You're lookin' for the buffalo jump? Yep, I know where that one is."

Squatting on his haunches, Leonard spread the map on the dirt, but he didn't take his hand off it. Brady leaned over and traced the images off the paper onto the dirt map.

"We ain't seen no money yet, Brady," Lynda cautioned.

"She's wanting that shopping trip." Brady nodded at the man.

Leonard pulled out his wallet and cautiously handed Brady a twenty-dollar bill. Brady immediately handed it to Lynda.

"Why, thank you, darlin'," she drawled. "I think I'll just go shoppin' this afternoon at K-Mart and buy myself somethin' frilly."

"Look," the man huffed, "where is the—what did you call it? The buffalo jump?"

"Take your boat straight east across the lake from the boat dock. It's a good five miles or more. You'll find a tiny little cove with a beach. It's not more than thirty feet wide and twenty feet deep. Kind of hard to spot until you come right up on it."

Don't tell him, Brady!

"Then you go about two hundred yards past the cove to the east. You'll find the buffalo jump about ten feet above the water line. It's kind of out of the way. Most folk don't even know it's up there. If you take your time, you'll find it. It's about right there!" Brady marked with his finger on the dirt map.

"Good, good!" the man rejoiced. "Two hundred yards past the cove. I can find that."

Leonard folded his manuscript page and put it back into his pocket. He reached over as if to erase Brady's pictograph copy in the dirt when Lynda shouted, "Well, I'll be! Here comes Cindy Lou!"

Brady and Leonard both stood up. Down the roadway to the east, Cindy LaCoste's old green Cadillac tooled toward them.

"Mister, are you married?" Brady asked him.

"No, why?"

"Then you don't want to be here when Lynda Dawn's sister Cindy Lou pulls in. She'll latch onto you like a Gila monster and never let go."

"I'm too old to get married again," he grumped and bent over to erase the dirt drawing.

"That's jist the type she likes," Lynda added. "They die off quicker, and then she can go find a new one."

"Oh?" He stood up again and gathered his papers and shoved them into the cab of the pickup. He was half a mile down the highway when Cindy pulled up. "Don't let her run over my pictograph sketch. I'll grab a pencil and paper out of the truck."

Brady, with Capt. Patch by his side, scooted around the bunkhouse to the Dodge truck. LaCoste climbed out of her car and walked toward Lynda.

"You look good, Cindy," Lynda greeted her.

"I kind of do, don't I? I smell good, too." She held her wrist up to Lynda.

"Northern Lights/Northern Nights?" Lynda asked.

"Yeah. It sure is strong. I thought the clerk at the motel was going to hit on me right there in the lobby."

"Are you okay?"

"Yeah. I didn't puke. Maybe I am getting better. What I can't figure is why you rent two rooms and never use either of them."

"Brady got sick last night, and we stayed at the bunkhouse."

"How's he doing now?"

"He seems to have had an incredible recovery."

Brady trotted back out to the driveway.

"Hi, Cindy-girl. You doin' better?"

A little spark lighted in Cindy's eyes when she heard Brady's voice. "Yeah. I slept for two days. What are you doing?"

Brady got down on his knees and began to transfer the pictograph images from the dirt to the paper in his hand.

"Writing a book." He laughed. "It's one of the missing pages of Lynda's book."

"Where did you get it?"

"From the guy driving that white truck, pulling a mighty big boat, and carrying a 9mm Ruger in his belt."

"Is that what he kept reaching for?" Lynda asked.

"Yeah. That's why I let him go. I think he might be the type to use it." Brady finished the drawing and stood up. Then he handed the paper to Lynda. "There you go, Ms. Austin. Page 452. Crudely drawn, yes, but the original pictographs are also crudely drawn. Your book is complete."

"Thank you, Mr. Stoner. Your mission has been accomplished."

"How about yours?"

"Not yet."

"What are you two talking about?" Cindy questioned.

"Well, for one thing, I think we've got to call the authorities and see if this really is the Leo they're looking for. And if so, do they want Montana authorities to apprehend him?"

Cindy looked puzzled.

Brady shook his head. "You aren't going to let him get away with it, even if you have your whole chapter, are you?"

"No. Are you?"

"Nope."

"What are we going to do? Go after him?"

"Think I'll stay away from the water for a while," Brady replied. "Let's call the authorities and wait at the parking lot. He has to come back there sooner or later."

"I'm lost. What's this all about? I thought there was some lady named Mendoza and your boss and—"

"That was yesterday," Lynda stated. "Come on, girl, I'll tell you today's episode."

"You are the only two people I ever met whose life is more interesting than the soaps."

Brady loaded their gear out of the bunkhouse and locked up. He and Capt. Patch drove the truck while Lynda rode with Cindy in a much cleaned-up Cadillac.

When they reached the boat ramp, Leonard had already launched his boat. Brady and Cindy parked their rigs over by Frank's Boat Rental and Expresso. All three walked around to the front where a single wooden bench comprised Frank's entire "patio area." With coffee in hand, Brady and Cindy sat down facing the lake while Lynda retreated inside to use the phone.

She had to wait for Frank's four-party line to free up and the temporary receptionist to figure out the phone button before she got through to Nina.

"Lynda? Where are you? I can hardly hear you."

"Nina, listen carefully. I want you and Kelly to call the Bahamian authorities where Chance died and tell them we believe we've spotted McCall's diving partner. He's going by the name Curtis Leonard. He's here at Upper Holter Lake, between Helena and Great Falls, in Lewis and Clark County, Montana. If they need to pick him up, they should contact the local sheriff's office. We'll wait here at a place called Frank's Boat Rental to hear what they want to do."

"What in the world's he doing up there? I thought he was in the Bahamas."

"He's up here looking for lost treasure like everyone else. But unlike everyone else, he had page 452."

"The infamous pictographs?"

"Right."

"Did you get the page back?"

"No, but we have a copy of the drawings. I'll fax it to you. First thing in the morning you scan it and the rest of the chapter into the computer and get a copy to production. I want this book to come out as quickly as possible so all the treasure-hunting nuts in the country can have an equal shot. These maps and pictographs will make this a hot product. And if Gossman or Hampton call in, don't mention that you heard they were out here looking for gold."

"Right. Hey, did you hear Drew Hessler quit?"

"No. When did that happen?"

"His roommate called in yesterday and said that Drew got mugged over on 43rd."

"Mugged?"

"Yeah. He was beat up pretty bad. Had to have some stitches and everything. He said Drew had had enough of the city and was moving back to Vermont."

"Tell the cops to look for a mugger named Tony."

"Really?"

"That's just a hunch," Lynda offered. "Listen, Kell, I've got to go."

"Are you and the cowboy married yet?"

"Of course not."

"Engaged?"

"No."

"Well, good grief, are you—"

"No, we're not!"

When Lynda rejoined Brady and Cindy, he was talking horses.

"Did you tell her about X-it?"

"No. I was telling Cindy that L. J. Minor down in Ely has a pen of wild mustangs she got from the B.L.M., and she needs someone to break 'em and train 'em. I figure Cindy could get room and board and a couple hundred a head. It would give her someplace to stay all winter and spring."

"Cindy could do that?"

"She's one of the best I've ever seen."

"I thought you said it's isolated out there."

"It is."

"Sounds good to me," Cindy commented.

"Let me go call L. J.," Brady insisted.

"Right now?" Cindy asked.

"Yep. I don't like puttin' things off."

Lynda sighed to herself. *Except for marriage.*

With Brady gone inside, Cindy looked over at Lynda and then down at her own boots. "I've got a confession to make."

"What's that?"

"I read some of the notes in your Bible."

"What?"

"I woke up last night and wasn't all that tired. I spotted your Bible. And when I saw you had written in it, I read your notes. I thought it would be like a diary or something. I know I shouldn't have done it, but I did. I'm sorry."

"You can read the notes in my Bible anytime you want. What did you read?"

"It was funny, sort of. When I first saw you the other day, I was really jealous of you and Brady. It's not that I wanted him for myself—I just wanted him to be as miserable as I was. But after reading your notes, I'm jealous of something else."

"What's that?"

"You and God. All those little conversations with Him you write in your Bible. It's like He's right there taking care of you all the time. I've never known anyone like that. I mean, for me it always seems like . . ."

"Like He's ignored you?"

"Yeah. Sort of."

"What if God wanted to be close to you, too, Cindy, but you never gave Him a chance? You know how in the past five years you've trained yourself to shove away from men?"

"Yeah?"

"Well, what if you've been spending your whole life shoving God away?"

"That could be."

"You might give Him a try."

"Give who a try?" Brady interrupted.

"The Lord," Cindy replied softly.

"Really?" Brady looked at Cindy and then at Lynda. "You two want to hear some other good news? I just talked to L. J. She said the job is yours if you want it."

"Really?" Cindy's eyes lit up.

"Yep. She said you could come down anytime. She'll give you a cabin and groceries and $225 a head. You can take all winter. She doesn't need 'em ridable until May 15."

"How many does she have?"

"Sixteen, but she might pick up five more."

"That's only $3,600 for six months' work," Lynda deduced.

"It sounds wonderfully peaceful to me." Cindy sighed. "It's a place to be, something to do . . . and Lynda's given me some good things to think about. I've just spent the past five years without any of that. You can't imagine what a terrible life that is."

Cindy began to cry.

"I don't know why I bawl like this. I didn't used to cry, Lynda. Really. Even when I got throwed right there in

Cheyenne, just around that third barrel with thousands of people watchin', I didn't cry. Did I, Brady?"

"No, darlin', you didn't shed a tear." Brady held out his arms, and Cindy laid her head on his chest.

Lord, I'm going to spend the rest of my life watching Brady comfort some hurting woman, aren't I? It's okay. Really. If You lead him, I won't complain.

Too much.

◆ ◆ ◆

Three more cups of coffee, two more phone calls, and an hour later, Cindy stood up and announced, "It's time for me to leave."

"You goin' to Ely?" Brady asked.

"Yes."

"You remember how to get to Shawna's in Idaho Falls?"

"I remember."

"She said she'd stay up late and have supper warm when you get there. You should make L. J.'s ranch by dark the next day. I'm goin' to call and make sure you arrived safely."

"I know."

Lynda stood up and hugged Cindy. "I want you to call me. You have my home number. You call me whenever you need to."

"If I can find a phone."

"Call me collect. You know I mean it."

"I know."

Brady took Cindy's hand, and he and Lynda walked her to her car.

"You have enough money to make it to Nevada, but don't go wastin' it."

"I won't buy any booze, Brady. I promised you that."

"And I plan on checkin' on those horses before Christmas. You find one that a little girl can turn barrels on, let me know. I'm putting together a small remuda of my own."

"Horses or kids?" she teased.

Brady glanced over at Lynda. "You and Cindy gone in cahoots, have you?"

"Don't look at me, Stoner," Lynda chided.

Cindy got in the car and rolled down her window. Lynda noticed a new vitality in her eyes and a freshness about her face. The lipstick was straight, the hair combed.

"You know what? I'm glad I didn't shoot either of you."

"We're mighty glad you didn't, too." Brady laughed.

"You gave me something that I thought I'd never have again."

"What's that?" Lynda asked.

"Hope. Brady made me believe that maybe I could survive this life with a little enjoyment. And, Lynda, you gave me hope that maybe there's something better coming. Not that I have an abundant supply of it . . . but I've got a stash now, and the cookie jar's been empty for a long, long time. I have no idea why in the world you did it."

Lynda slipped her arm into Brady's. "You do too."

"Oh, you mean the God thing?"

"That's right. If you get serious with Him, I guarantee He'll be serious with you. Pretty soon you'll be the one writing notes in the margin of your Bible."

"Are you preaching at me?" Cindy chided.

"No. Because you already know it's true."

"How does she do that, Brady?" Cindy looked over at him. "You don't even know she's gone fishing, and suddenly you're caught on her hook and can't get loose."

"They teach them that in the city," Brady explained.

"Don't laugh—she's got you hooked, too, Brady." Cindy began to roll up her window. Then she looked at Lynda. "Would you do all of us a favor and marry that grinning cowboy and simplify our lives?"

Cynthia LaCoste drove west out of Upper Holter Lake.

"Is she going to make it, Brady?"

"To Ely?"

"And to wholeness . . . and to the Lord?"

"It's my hope and prayer, darlin'. If she does, one of my biggest burdens will be lifted."

Even though Frank weighed close to three hundred pounds, he had a tenor voice and sounded almost melodic as he called to them, "Got a phone call for Lynda Austin. Is that you?"

Lynda left Brady outside and hurried up the wooden steps to the phone. She spoke into the receiver. "Yes?"

"Lynda, it's Nina. The authorities definitely want to talk to that Leo. He's a professional diver and adventurer named Leo Curtis. He's wanted for piracy and extortion, as well as being a suspect in McCall's death. They've contacted the Montana authorities and asked that you wait there until someone arrives."

"What if he leaves before anyone shows up?"

"Just make sure you have his license number. They said whatever you do, don't try to apprehend him on your own. He is believed to be armed and dangerous."

"We know he's armed, but he didn't seem very dangerous."

"Don't try anything stupid," Nina lectured. "We're all anxious for you to get back safe and sound. What's your schedule now?"

"I don't know. I guess we have to drive back to Great Falls and take this gear back. Then we'll drive down to Jackson Hole. I hope we have time for one night in the lodge before I fly home."

"Kelly just said, 'Don't even think about coming home without an engagement ring!'"

"Don't count on it. I think Brady's getting paranoid on the subject."

"Put him on the phone. Kelly wants to talk to him."

"No way! He has enough women nagging him."

"What do you mean by that?"

"I'll tell you when I get back to the office."

"Don't you forget one word, Lynda Dawn Austin!"

"Bye, Nina."

She walked back out to where Brady sat, his collar turned up and hat pushed back. "What's the news, darlin'?"

"We're supposed to get the license number of Leo Curtis's rig."

"Leo Curtis, huh?"

"Wanted in the Bahamas for piracy and extortion, among other things."

"You're kiddin'."

"Anyway, they've asked that we stay here until Montana authorities arrive. We are not to apprehend Curtis, but leave that to the police. He is considered armed and dangerous."

"Are we talkin' about the same guy?"

"I think so."

Lynda sat down next to Brady and leaned her head on his shoulder. "You know what I was thinking?"

"Probably." He grinned.

"You do not, Brady Stoner! It just dawned on me that we know where the sealed cave with the gold is. You said you found the pictographs when you were in the water."

"I found them."

"So we know exactly what everyone from Mendoza and this Curtis guy to Junior and George were looking for."

"I guess we do."

"Doesn't it make you want to try and find it?"

"Nope."

"Why not?"

"I figure if a team of professional divers spent over half a million dollars and couldn't find it, neither can I. Besides, just thinking about that water makes my bones cold."

"Are you still feeling all right?"

"Yeah, but we might as well wait in the truck. It's warmer than out here. You want to grab us two more coffees? I'll go take down the license number of that van. Then we'll wait for the authorities."

◆ ◆ ◆

Brady was right. The truck was warmer. A whole lot warmer. The cab of the pickup was pretty well steamed by the time he rolled down the window and gazed out at the lake.

"Looks like Leo's boat is coming back. I thought he'd be gone longer. The sheriff hasn't shown up yet."

"I imagine the Bahamian government had to contact the State Department, then the justice system, and on down the line," Lynda offered.

"That could take days."

"I figure ol' Leo will keep looking for this gold for quite a while, don't you?"

"So why is he coming in now?"

"You gave him the wrong instructions."

"Sure, but there's plenty of pictographs around. You'd think he'd check them out for himself."

Lynda dug through a sack for the binoculars. Then she opened her door, stood up and leaned against the cab, and scoped the boat.

"Mendoza's with him!" she shouted.

"I thought you said she went by last night."

"The rig went by. . . . Maybe the other two went off without her. She must have spent the night out in that sandy cove."

"If she signaled him for help and they began talking, then he knows who we are."

"What difference does that make? They're two of a kind. Why don't they partner up and dive for the gold?"

Brady sat back down in the pickup. "Sure, and maybe they're coming in for some expresso. He knows we can turn him in. He's plannin' on more than just visitin'."

"What should we do?"

"Hold them down until the cavalry arrives."

"No, really, Brady. What do we do now?"

"I wasn't jokin', sweetheart."

"You weren't?"

"See that old wreck of a boat on that tireless, rusted trailer? I'm going to pull it across the entrance so they can't get out."

"What do you want me to do?"

"Run in there and tell Frank to lock the building, put his money in the safest place, stay behind the counter, and hold onto his handgun."

"He has a gun?"

"Wouldn't you if you were way out here? Hurry, and meet me up at the gate!"

Lynda warned Frank, who was sleeping in front of a thirteen-inch television set. He locked the door behind her. She darted out of the building and up the hill to where Brady dragged a squealing trailer across the road above the boat dock. He dropped the trailer and parked the pickup behind several stored boats. Then he purposely locked Capt. Patch in the cab, much to the dog's vocal displeasure.

Brady had pulled his gun out of the truck and was shoving a couple of bullets into it as he walked toward Lynda.

"What now? It looks like they're about to dock," she warned.

"I don't think we can con them or ambush them this time."

"We're not really going to shoot at them, are we? I don't think I can go through that again, Brady. This isn't a game like down at Jackson."

"All we need to do is keep them occupied until the sheriff arrives."

"What do you mean, occupied?"

"I figure if they're chasing us, they can't be looking down the road at who's driving in. Let's go out there in front of the big boat and let them see us."

"Won't they shoot us?"

"Not with a handgun—not from that distance."

Rocks flew up next to Lynda's feet as they heard the report of a gun. Brady shoved Lynda to the ground behind some stored boats and then dove on top of her.

"I thought you said they couldn't hit us from there with a handgun," she cried out.

"They can't."

"But they came pretty close."

"That wasn't a handgun. He must have had a rifle on the boat, too."

"Oh, great." Lynda squirmed to keep her leg from cramping under the weight of Brady's body. "I think the boat will protect me now. You can get off me, Stoner."

"Yes, ma'am. They both have guns, and at least one is a rifle. That does change strategy."

"What do we do now?"

"Hop in the truck and run for it."

"You're kidding," Lynda gasped.

"Yeah, we can't do that," Brady muttered. "The boat's blocking the way."

Two shots scattered around them.

"I think we need to move."

"Where to?"

"How about inside the old boat?"

"Will it stop a bullet?"

"I think so."

"How do we get there?"

"Crawl on our bellies."

"Stoner, how come you keep making me crawl every time I'm near you?"

"*Forsan et haec olim meminisse iuvabit.*"

A couple more bullets hit the dirt near them as Lynda dragged herself behind Brady to a big, old rusted boat.

"What does that mean—we, who are about to die, salute you?"

"No," he growled as he crawled, "that's *morituri te salutamus*. What I said was, 'Perhaps this will be a pleasure to look back on one day.'"

"Crawling through the dirt on my stomach while some ding-a-ling shoots at me will never be a pleasure."

"Come on, climb up in the boat."

Brady climbed on the iron hull and pulled Lynda up after him.

"This boat looks like the kind they used to have on Lake Michigan . . . or even the Keys. What's it doing in Montana?"

"Rusting from lack of use."

She crouched down beside Brady as he peeked out through a rust hole and fired a shot in the general direction of Leo's boat.

"Why'd you do that?" she asked.

"To keep them worried."

"Brady, they'll shoot us if they get a chance. What are we going to do?"

"Not give them a chance. Don't worry, darlin', the sheriff will be here soon."

"Do you really believe that, or are you just trying to cheer me up?"

Two more bullets bounced off the boat, and Brady returned a shot.

"This isn't fun, Brady. I want to go home. I want to leave right now!"

He put his left arm around her and gave her a weak squeeze.

"Lynda Dawn, did you know I make some of my best decisions under pressure?"

"Like what?"

"Well, one time while riding a saddle bronc at a rodeo in Clovis, I got my foot caught in the stirrup and was drug around the arena six times by my right ankle. Right there as I'm bouncin' around on the dirt in and out of those thunderin' hooves, I made an important decision."

"What was that?"

"That I'd give up ridin' saddle broncs and stick with barebacks where there aren't any stirrups."

Another shot hit something in the front of the boat, and the trailer tipped forward. Brady fired a quick shot.

"What do you think they're doing?"

"Sneakin' up on us, I reckon. That's what I would do."

"I'm about to wet my pants, and you aren't frightened at all!"

"That's because I just made another important decision that's been heavy on my mind lately."

"Does it have to do with a long-term commitment."

"Yep."

"Does it have a ring attached to it?"

"Yes, ma'am, it does."

"Providing we live through this, just exactly what important decision did you make?" she quizzed.

"I'm going to call him Bullet instead of X-it. Doesn't that have a good ring to it?"

Two more shots blasted. One pierced the rust and ricocheted inside the boat.

"Brady, I want out of here!" Lynda cried. "The boat's moving. . . . It's rolling down the hill!"

"It can't," Brady insisted. "There aren't any tires on those wheels."

"We're rolling toward the lake, Brady!"

"Those shots must have jarred something."

The boat and trailer crept across the road and picked up speed as the mountain dropped off steeply behind Frank's Boat Rental and Expresso.

Brady grabbed her hand. "Come on, darlin', jump off."

"I'm not jumping," she cried.

"It isn't any worse than fallin' off a horse. I spend half my life doing that."

"I don't!"

Brady leaped off the boat with Lynda in tow. They crashed into the dirt and rocks of the mountainside as the boat banged, crashed, broke free of the trailer, and toppled off a ten-foot drop into the lake. It landed upside down in about five feet of water.

Lynda lay next to Brady trying to catch her breath and take stock of her limbs and bruises.

"Stay down," he whispered.

Peeking above the grass, she saw Leo Curtis and Claudia Mendoza run down to the water's edge. Mendoza pointed a rifle at the boat, and Curtis held a pistol.

Brady put his finger up to his mouth to keep Lynda silent. Then he helped her to her feet, and they crept down the hill, stopping about twenty yards from the water's edge.

"Toss the guns down," he shouted with the carbine at his shoulder.

Mendoza and Curtis spun around, but neither dropped a weapon.

"Drop the guns!" Brady called again.

Leo Curtis raised his handgun at Brady.

"Shoot him," Mendoza yelled. "He won't shoot. He hasn't got the—"

The blast from Brady's carbine made Lynda jump back and put her hands over her ears. Leo Curtis screamed as the bullet tore through his leg midway between his hip and his knee. Brady had instantly cocked the carbine and now pointed it at

Claudia Mendoza, who threw down her gun and hollered, "Don't shoot! Don't shoot!"

"Brady!" Lynda called out as she heard a chorus of distant sirens. She spun around. "It looks like the sheriff."

"I told you they'd be on their way."

◆ ◆ ◆

It took five hours of explaining in the sheriff's office, four phone calls to New York, and one to the Bahamas before Austin and Stoner were allowed to leave Helena. And it took twenty-four more hours before they got back to Jackson, Wyoming.

◆ ◆ ◆

Lynda left the beauty salon and scooted across the street. For the first time in a week she felt clean and fresh. The scent of Naughty-N-Nice followed her to the park where Brady waited on a worn wooden bench. His hat was pulled down, his collar turned up, his hands jammed in his pockets, his jeans-clad legs stretched out in front of him, and his boots were crossed.

There's my cowboy. Timeless. He could be sitting on a bench in old Tombstone or Deadwood or Abilene. He looks like them, talks like them, acts like them, and even thinks like them. Cowboys like Brady will live on and on. They'll always be around.

"Howdy, darlin'. Your hair looks beautiful."

"Well, at least it's clean and combed."

"Sit down, Lynda Dawn. Let's talk."

She sat beside him, and he swung his arm around her shoulder, holding her tight.

"Okay, I give in!" he began.

"What do you mean?"

"The perfume. I really like that. What's it called?"

"I'm not telling you, Stoner."

"They ought to call it Blunt."

"Why?"

"Because it doesn't beat around the bush!"

"It's a little cold out here." She shivered and leaned against him.

"I've been colder."

"You sure have, cowboy. A lot colder. What have you been doing this afternoon while I was tied up with all those 'girl' chores?"

"I walked around town some . . . did a little window-shoppin' . . . a lot of thinkin'."

"What were you thinking about?"

"Everything from horses to shootin' old Leo. Darlin', I don't ever want to have to shoot another man, but I was certain he was going to shoot us. I did a lot of thinking about you and me this afternoon."

"What did you decide this time, cowboy?"

"I was in an art gallery where there is this picture of a cowboy and a pretty girl who's—hey, guess who I ran across at the gallery?"

"Are you changing the subject, Stoner?"

"Yeah, but guess who I saw?"

"Joaquin Estaban?"

"No. Peggy Gregg."

Lynda pulled back. "Who?"

"Miss Peggy that runs the Bird Cage Theater and does the daily hanging drama."

"Oh, that real sweetheart," Lynda jibed.

"Listen, they have to do a hanging tonight. It's sort of an encore performance after the season is over. It's a last-minute deal, and she's scrambling for actors so . . ."

"She needs you to help out?"

"Will that be all right? Peggy was really worried about pulling this off."

"So a damsel is in distress, and Brady Stoner is riding to the rescue?"

"Well, I hadn't thought about it quite like that." He pushed his hat back and flashed his little-boy grin. "There is one other thing, darlin'."

"Oh?"

"Peggy asked if you'd be in the skit, too."

"Me? I don't do street drama."

"See, there's this big finale where the schoolmarm is held captive by the villain, and I come to the rescue."

"Brady, I don't want to do it."

"Hear me out, darlin'. As soon as I shoot the guy, the schoolmarm runs—"

"I don't want to do it, Brady!"

"—and she throws her arms around me and shouts, 'What can I ever do to repay you?' Then she lays this big kiss on my lips, and the audience claps, and it's over."

"I said I . . . She does what?"

"Course, if you don't want to do it, I guess Peggy will probably be able to find some other gal."

"Did you say the schoolmarm kisses you on the lips?"

"That's the way it's written in the script. It doesn't take more than ten minutes for the whole sketch. But if the part doesn't fit you, maybe you'd like to be Ma Snodgrass. Then Peggy could be the schoolmarm."

"I'll be the schoolmarm."

"In fact, you might like the role of Ma Snodgrass. There are a lot more lines and—"

"I said, I'm the schoolmarm, and that's that!" she barked.

"Yes, ma'am." He slipped his arm back around her and gave her a squeeze. "You'll do a great job, darlin'."

"It will be more frightening than facing Mendoza and Leo Curtis. How do I let you talk me into such things?"

Lynda sat straight up on the bench and stared at the traffic, remembering the time in the sixth grade when she played a tree in the school play but forgot her one line. *"Help keep Michigan green." How could I forget that?*

She sighed and shook her head. "Well, let's go tell Peggy that you sweet-talked me into it."

"It's okay. I already told her."

"You what?"

"I knew you'd do it, darlin', especially once you heard about the kissin' part."

"I'm not very good at this sort of thing."

"I think you're really good at kissin'."

"I meant, the acting part."

"Peggy said your extemporaneous part last week was really good."

"That's because I wasn't acting. Have you got a script for me to look at?"

"Yeah, I thought we could go over the details while we have supper. I made an early reservation at The Cattleman's Cafe."

"Is the food good there?"

"Fair. But the booths are really private."

"Sounds like my kind of place. Cowboy, lead me on."

"Yes, ma'am, I surely will."

◆ ◆ ◆

The room was wood-paneled and dark. The steaks were piled high with green peppers and hot spices. The conversation bounced from *Confederate Gold* to the Grand National Rodeo in San Francisco to Lynda's proposed Christmas trip to Idaho to celebrate the holiday with Brady and his family.

Lynda ran her fork across her empty pie plate. "Brady, there was one reason I didn't want to come out here."

"You mean, havin' to say goodbye?"

"I've done plenty of dumb things in my life, but saying goodbye to you always seems like the dumbest."

"We surely do have good times, don't we, Miss Lynda Dawn?"

"Yes, Mr. Stoner. We surely do."

"I'm glad you're comin' out for Christmas at the ranch."

"I do have to check it out at the office," she cautioned.

"You'll come. I just know it. My folks will adopt you in a flash. 'Course, Mom will want to teach you how to put up some preserves or something."

"I'm nervous just thinking about it. What if they think I'm some prissy thing from the city?"

"Just be yourself. Don't worry about it. 'Let today's own worries be sufficient for today.'"

"You're right. I've got to worry about this street play. I'm glad she let us use our own names. That will help."

"You ready to go over to the Bird Cage and get our costumes?"

"I suppose. Do we get any rehearsal?"

"We'll probably read through the lines at Peggy's. Relax, darlin'. You'll do great."

"That's easy for you to say. You've done this before."

"Not really," he mumbled. "Come on, schoolmarm."

◆ ◆ ◆

The air was cold.

The sky was almost dark.

A crowd of nearly five hundred gathered in the street and sidewalks on the southeast corner of the city park in downtown Jackson, Wyoming.

Lynda walked with Brady through the crowd. Her blue calico dress hung to the street. Her heavy lace shawl warmed her shoulders a little. Her bonnet covered most of her forty-dollar hairstyle. Brady wore a bib-front Western shirt with a big white silk bandanna around his neck. He had spurs on his boots and a six-gun strapped to his hip.

"Brady, if I forget my line, you're going to have to cover for me."

"Just relax, darlin'. Be yourself. Have fun."

"But what tone of voice am I supposed to use?"

"Just pretend it's happening in real life. Just talk and act the way you always do, especially the kissing part."

"I take it you're looking forward to the final scene."

"Yes, ma'am, I am."

The center of the intersection was roped off. A table, two benches, and a self-standing hat rack were scattered in the square. Right on cue a six-up stagecoach came around the corner and parked to one side of the open area. Lynda Dawn, Peggy Gregg, and two costumed men got into the coach. Brady mounted a buckskin gelding, and he and two others rode back into the crowd. A shotgun blast that made Lynda jump signaled the beginning of the skit.

All I've got to do is climb out of the stage when Mean Matt pulls off the robbery, looking "frightened, yet coy." Scream when Mean Matt grabs me and threatens to shoot me. Run to Brady after he rescues me, throw my arms around him, and say in a very loud voice, "What can I ever do to repay you?" Then kiss him on the lips. I ought to do fine on the last part.

The play went well, and she could tell the audience was having fun. Brady was a natural.

If one of those college cuties gloms onto him after the show, she's dead meat! . . . It's getting close, Lynda Austin . . . "What can I ever do to repay you?" . . . then smooch. Lord, help me not to faint! At least, not until after the kiss. I wonder if I'm coy enough? Should I be more coy? Can a person be overcoy?

She was still rehearsing her line in her mind when Mean Matt roughly grabbed her and pointed the pistol at her calico-covered head. She let out an honest scream and held it a little too long.

I blew it. They're laughing at me. They're not supposed to be laughing. I told Brady I didn't want to do this.

His arm around her waist, Mean Matt dragged her out into the middle of the street next to the table. "Deputy, you throw down that there six-shooter, or it's the last time you see this schoolmarm alive. You savvy?"

"Mean Matt, you let loose of Miss Lynda Dawn right now, and I just might let you live until your hangin'."

"And ifen I don't?"

"I'll shoot you dead right here in the street in front of all these fine folks."

"Jist try it, and the schoolmarm goes with me!"

"Mean Matt, you're the lowest snake I ever met. Hidin' behind a piece of calico," Brady screamed. "I don't think I ever knowed any man so degraded and cowardly as to use a woman for a shield!"

Brady's pretty good at this.

"Nobody calls Mean Matt a coward to his face—and lives," the villain shouted.

Matt pushed Lynda aside. She tripped on her long dress and fell to the pavement, tearing a slit in it up past her right knee. Two shots echoed in the street, and Mean Matt took three minutes to perform one of the most comical dying scenes Lynda had ever witnessed.

Then everything grew quiet.

Lying on the pavement pretending to be mortally wounded, Peggy Gregg whispered in Lynda's direction, "Deputy, what can I ever do to repay you?"

Oh . . . wow . . . that's my line.

Lynda jumped to her feet and ran over to Brady. She tilted her head sideways, held her clenched hands under her chin, and cried in a very loud voice, "Oh, Deputy, you saved my life. What can I ever do to repay you?"

Everyone laughed at her sugary-sweet delivery.

Brady pushed his hat to the back of his head, put his hands on her still-shawled shoulders, and looked her in the eyes. "Miss Lynda Dawn, will you marry me?"

He didn't stick to the script! Oh, man, what am I supposed to say? I knew this would happen. I'm not good without a script. You know that, Stoner—you jerk!

He took a gold ring with a big, bright diamond out of his vest pocket and slipped it on her finger. She stared at the ring as her mouth dropped open.

"Well, Miss Lynda Dawn," Brady prodded, "what do you say?"

"Eh . . . oh, Deputy Stoner," she drawled with her hands locked under her chin, "why, why . . . of course, I'll marry you. Why, it would break my heart if I didn't!"

"Stoner, I'm going to murder you for changing the script," she mumbled with her teeth clenched.

"Kiss me," he whispered back.

Lynda threw her arms around his neck and planted a very dramatic, very loud, very phony kiss on his lips.

The audience roared approval.

Brady's return kiss wasn't phony. And he didn't turn loose.

"Brady, the skit's over!" Lynda muttered. "They're all watching us." He finally pushed away as the cast all stood up for a bow.

Lynda and Brady were still standing side by side when Peggy and the other actors crowded around them.

"That was quite a finale, you two." Peggy grinned.

"Brady changed the script. It kind of threw me off," Lynda tried to explain.

"So I noticed. It was great, kids. You two made my week." Peggy turned to go.

"Wait, Peggy!" Lynda called. She pulled the ring off her finger. "Here. I don't want to forget to turn in my props." She held out the ring to Peggy Gregg.

"Props? Are you kidding? The Bird Cage can't afford a gold ring and a one-carat diamond. Girl, you said you'd marry him. We all heard you. That's your ring!"

Lynda stared at the sparkling jewel in her hand for a minute. Then she turned to Brady. "This is a real diamond?"

"Yep."

"Then that wasn't part of the skit?"

"Nope."

"You mean, you really want to . . ."

"Yep."

Lynda started breathing real hard. Her chest heaved, and she started gulping for air. Her head felt light. "Stoner, did you just ask me to marry you—for real?"

"Yep. Are you going to do it, Miss Lynda Dawn—for real?"

Slowly she slipped the diamond ring back on her finger.

"Yep." She grinned.

Then she threw her arms around his neck and kissed him on the lips. This time she wasn't playacting.

And this time she had no intention of stopping.